Keys to the Open Gate

Keys to the Open Gate

A Woman's Spirituality Sourcebook

Kimberley Snow, Ph.D.

Conari Press
Berkeley, CA

Conari Press books are distributed by Publishers Group West

Printed in the United States of America on recycled paper
Cover design and illustrations: Kathy Warriner
Red Tara Drawings: Phyllis Glanville

ISBN: 0-943233-63-1

Library of Congress Cataloging-in-Publication Data

Snow, Kimberley.
Keys to the open gate: a woman's spirituality sourcebook / Kimberley Snow.
p.   cm.
Includes bibliographical references and index.
ISBN 0-943233-63-1 (trade paper): $12.95
1. Women—Religious life. 2. Spirituality. I. Title
BL625.7.S64   1994
291.4'082—dc20   94-343
                               CIP

For

Rachel

Barb

and

Julie

Acknowledgments

My thanks to Mary Jane Ryan, whose editing combines clarity and compassion,
to my husband for his unstinting support,
and to those in Trinity County who have contributed so richly to my life and to this book:
the extraordinary men of Junction City who all in their own way have helped me find the lost colors:
Chagdud Tulku, Barry, David, Wyn, Choyki, Bob T., John DeW, Bob S., Mike, Fred, John S., James,
Jeff, Glenn, Andy, and Joe;
and to the women: Candy, Gay, Phyllis, Linda Rose, Marilyn, Mary, Lisa, Jan, Rambhali, Kim, Maile,
Pamela, Prema, Donna, Laeh, Jane, and Tsering,
who constantly redefine the concept of "the feminine" by example, action, and presence.

Thank you for the blessings of our heart connections; may all beings benefit.

Thanks also to the authors and publishers who gave me permission to quote from the following works:

(An exhaustive effort has been made to clear all reprint permissions for this book. This process has been complicated, and if any required acknowledgments have been omitted, it is unintentional. If notified, the publishers will be pleased to rectify any omission in future editions.)

Excerpt from GRANDMOTHERS OF THE LIGHT by Paula Gunn Allen. Copyright ©1991 by Paula Gunn Allen. Reprinted by permission of Beacon Press. "The Dakini Principle" from WOMEN OF WISDOM by Tsultrim Allione. Copyright ©1986 by Tsultrim Allione. Reprinted by permission of the author. "Fragments of a Broken Past" by Rachel Altman from DIFFERENT VOICES: WOMEN OF THE HOLOCAUST, edited by Carol Rittner and John Roth, Paragon Press, 1993. Reprinted by permission of the author. Excerpt from WOMAN AT THE EDGE OF TWO WORLDS by Lynn V. Andrews. Copyright ©1993 by Lynn V. Andrews. Reprinted by permission of HarperCollins Publishers, Inc. "The Presences" from BORDERLANDS/LA FRONTERA: THE NEW MESTIZA by Gloria Anzaldua. Copyright ©1987 by Gloria Anzaldua. Reprinted by permission of Aunt Lute Books, (415) 558-8116. Excerpt from HEART OF THE GODDESS by Hallie Iglehart Austen. Copyright ©1990 by Hallie Iglehart Austen.

(continued at back)

Contents

Introduction

We undertake a spiritual search when we are homesick for light, when there is a yearning for connectedness. This yearning may take the form of a vague restlessness, pervasive boredom, or bedrock dissatisfaction. Some of us may have spent years in therapy or recovery only to ask: "What now?" Others might think a sense of inner emptiness stems from workplace, husband or lover, or friends, and while these may contribute, the cause and the cure lie within our own hearts and minds, our own way of organizing our thoughts and reacting to the world. Still others may face a crisis—the death of a child, the end of a relationship, a serious illness—which provokes a search.

The aim of this sourcebook is to help us as contemporary women to redefine spirituality for ourselves while discovering, through felt experience, how we tap into it. Although its material is drawn from Judeo-Christian, Buddhist, Islamic, Native American, Sufi, Hindu, Shamanic, Goddess, and other traditions, the book isn't a female study of comparative religion, but rather a practical resource for any woman who wants to participate in spiritual awakening, deepen her sense of self, and connect more fully with the world. The material here, based on writings from those who have traveled the surprising, rewarding, and sometimes perilous terrain of women's spirituality, functions as a field guide to a territory as yet only partially explored.

An underlying assumption of the book is that every woman is capable of deep spiritual experiences, but she must claim them, must consciously choose to walk through the open gate. In the West, for the most part, neither men nor women are commonly taught how to invite, cultivate, or maintain a feeling of connection with something larger and more permanent than themselves. Not only do we often lack the tools and techniques for getting in touch with our deeper being, we tend to be hampered as well by a thick wall of obscurations making us doubt the very existence of our indwelling spirit. Little in our post-modern, consumer culture leads us toward our soul's health and growth.

"Somehow the old argument that in the end truth must be the same for all is not very convincing when ultimate truth reveals itself to men only, or when men only have defined it, taught it, propagated it, are its sole authorities, and historically have defended it with outright wars."
—Bernadette Roberts

As women particularly we are not encouraged to trust our own instincts, to open inward or to relax into intuitive spirituality. Most women have had a glimpse into the sacred—a fleeting contact with a deeper self or with the whole world, moments flooded with love for everyone or a flash of knowledge or stillness. These glimpses can be expanded to become stable and, finally, ongoing states.

But this process takes time and effort. As Americans, we are used to the idea of "working" toward goals: physical fitness, professional success, a good marriage. We even "work" on a tan. Rarely, however, are we told that we need to concentrate energy on our connection with the holy—that we need to cultivate the ground where the spiritual seeds we plant can grow and flourish. This is especially true if we intuitively realize that our spirit is already complete within us, immediately available. The paradox is resolved when we understand that spiritual "work" often takes the form of learning to open inward and of identifying and removing obscurations, particularly those unique to women.

All humans need to master ignorance and attachment, pacify anger and impatience, lessen self-clinging, and become aware of—and sympathetic toward—the suffering of others. But women have yet another set of obstacles to deal with, challenges which stem from the near absence of the feminine on every level of religious life, plus the destructive attitudes that arise in both men and women as a consequence of this primary exclusion. Resulting barriers must be overcome not simply by more argument and analysis--although we need to become conscious of the real issues--but by practicing non-dual meditation as well as developing love and concern for every-one, not just other women. Meditations in this book—drawn from Eastern and Western sources--are designed to implement such changes and to render the practitioner more open and compassion-ate.

Keys to the Open Gate introduces a wide variety of writers and thinkers who address the subject of women and spirituality with acumen and insight. Reading about other traditions helps to break down boundaries and stereotypes, making us more aware of our commonality than our differences. To become conscious of our lineage as women, to tap into the motherline which crosses all religious boundaries, is to create a web of peace, the possibility of a spirituality that unites and heals.

The techniques and meditations presented are designed for everyone—beginners or advanced practitioners—for use in cultivating a spiritual garden. Because each woman's spiritual needs are unique, I've gathered a variety of exercises and readings so that you can pick and choose among them. Be completely honest with yourself in the effect that a particular meditation has on you; if it works, or if it leaves you cold, you'll know it. If it makes you uncomfortable in ways you don't wish to be challenged, you'll know that as well.

Because each tradition has holes and gaps when it comes to consciousness about or rituals for female experience, we need to draw on many sources to find wholeness within ourselves. Don't be afraid to test out techniques and methods—using a Buddhist teaching or a Wicca ritual doesn't transform you into a Buddhist or a witch, but different parts of us may be integrated by aspects of varying religions. Many of the exercises offered here turn up in several different traditions, with some elaborated upon by New Age practitioners and/or psychologists as well.

In organizing this book, I've tried to get to the light behind the stained-glass window, to share an appreciation of how each color helps to compose the whole extraordinary design of spiritual life. Therefore I include interviews and writings that investigate the relationship between spirituality and a woman's body; reevaluations and questions concerning women's role in Christianity, Judaism, and Islam; visions of the natural world from Native American and shamanic sources; pertinent readings and exercises from Goddess religions; ideas on the interface between creativity and spirituality; meditation techniques from Buddhist, Taoist and other sources; ways to practice that include the here, the now, the everyday; and inspirations from a variety of mystical experiences. References and bibliographies throughout provide additional sources for further investigation and contemplation.

The readings can be used to expand a sense of the sacred and enlarge traditional ways of relating to others, to deepen levels of being and reveal spiritual essence. The meditations and exercises can take you to a more profound level if you work with them, respond with your heart as well as your head, and don't hold back

"The task of our age is to draw on our spiritual heritage and, through reestablishing our collective female consciousness, to develop a way of life which doesn't need hierarchy at its base and which returns us to our efforts to live out the knowledge that we are all one."
—Anne Kant Rush

"From Judaism, Christianity and Islam to Hinduism, Buddhism, Taoism and Native American and Goddess religions, each offers images of the sacred web into which we are woven. We are called children of one God and 'members of one body'; we are seen as drops in the ocean of Brahman; we are pictured as jewels in the Net of Indra. We interexist—like synapses in the mind of an all-encompassing being."
—Joanna Macy

3

from the experience. Use your intuition to guide you toward meditations you connect with emotionally; suspend your rational mind; give your indwelling spirit a chance to make contact.

The process of finding and selecting these readings left me with a sense of gratitude at being able to participate in an incredible movement in which yin is rebalanced, the feminine liberated, and our motherline reconnected. Within the womanspirit movement, friendship with other women becomes a source of wonder and delight, our bodies feel whole again, and we connect with strength and care to all of humanity. I felt heart lines reaching out to unknown writers, revelation and delight in unexpected subject matter, and new ways to think and to be. Most of all I felt reverence for the spirit that guided me through the whole process. I hope you will benefit from these huntings and gatherings and make them your own. No one else can cultivate your soul for you or take responsibility for clearing away the debris that may keep you from connecting with and living in an ongoing state of compassionate grace. It is up to you to walk through the open gate to spiritual awareness.

"The entire world is being driven insane by this single phrase: 'My religion alone is true.'"
—Ramakrishna

A Note on the Organization of This Book

These readings and meditations are structured to correspond roughly to the seven energy centers along the human spine known as *chakras* in Kundalini yoga: root, sexual, power, heart, throat, third eye, and crown. This in no way requires a knowledge of or belief in the chakras, but it provides a method of organizing subject matter and suggests a developmental sequence. Although a number of different chakra systems exist—for instance, the Tibetans often combine the root and sexual as well as the third eye and crown chakras, thus ending up with five rather than seven—multiple traditions agree that these centers work to integrate various human functions and form part of the subtle or light body. Some representations show an additional chakra about seven inches above the crown of the head which, like an upside-down root system, forms a web linking all sentient beings, creating an image for the interdependence of life on this planet.

The root chakra, located at the base of the spine, has to do with survival and is pre-conscious; thus *Keys* begins with the second— or sexual—chakra related to reproduction. In this area, men's and women's physical differences and the world view arising from them are gender specific. Menstruation, sexuality, childbirth, abortion, and other events that come with having a woman's body simply don't happen to men, which perhaps explains why such experiences fall outside of the traditional rituals and established prayers of most religions. Thus, in Section 1, we draw from Native American, Wicca (witchcraft), Goddess, and Buddhist sources in particular to create a context that joins rather than divides a woman's body and spirit.

The next center, found in the solar plexus, relates to digestion, the generation of energy, and, by extension, to power. So Section 2 of the book addresses some of the many issues involving female oppression in patriarchal religions. Whether Christian, Jewish, Buddhist, or Islamic, women are beginning to articulate their own unique religious experiences, to reclaim their rightful place in the major traditions, and to suggest new ways to respond to the patriarchy with compassion and clarity.

The next chakra is located in the center of the chest, and is related to love and community. A new dimension opens when we move into the heart chakra, for love expands just as fear contracts. Enter the Goddess, the central subject of Section 3. Here we examine the need women have had of this figure on a personal and cultural level and the variety of ways in which modern women envision her, ranging from playful nymph to basic space. Readings about and meditations on such goddesses as Kwan Yin, Tara, Oya, Isis, Kali, and Mary help to give us a consciousness of her many manifestations, and feel the compassionate power of her presence.

The throat chakra controls speech, language, and communication. Section 4 includes readings, meditations, and exercises that foster communication and creativity, examining the ways in which writing and the arts can be used to support spiritual development or can function as the path itself. In addition, there are exercises involving visualization and dreaming—highly creative activities avail-

"Truthfulness anywhere means a heightened complexity."
—Adrienne Rich

5

able to everyone—that serve as communicating links between the unconscious and the conscious, the mundane and the sacred, self and others.

From the throat chakra, we move to the third eye in the middle of the forehead, entering even deeper into the psyche/spirit through meditation. In Section 5 we draw most extensively from the three main branches of Buddhism—Theravaden (Vipassana), Zen, and Tibetan—for exercises that range from Zen sitting to Tibetan deity practice. These are designed to make a person more mindful, more focused, more compassionate. Because the Buddha taught eighty-four thousand methods to attain enlightenment, many of the techniques popular in the West today were either borrowed from or can be found in Buddhism's treasure trove of mind wisdom.

The third eye represents a quantum leap, for it functions as a gateway to the final or crown chakra, symbolized by a thousand-petaled lotus indicating this center's diversity, multiplicity, and variety. All religions have a name for arriving at the crown chakra: "living in the Tao," "achieving a state of grace," "being in balance with all my relations," and so on. Integration, application, deepening, and synthesizing of consciousness take place in this chakra, and this leads to presence, to living fully in the moment.

Because of the sheer number of the "thousand petals," I've divided the material that relates to the crown chakra into two sections. Section 6 applies meditation itself to a woman's everyday life, bringing spirituality back to such daily activities as gardening, cooking, mothering, relating to other people, and social action. Such focus provides ways to embody female spirituality that include the here, the now, the everyday.

The last section of the book concentrates on those "still moments" when one comes to know a loss of self and a merging with something greater. As we examine women's mystical experiences we find that sometimes these arise spontaneously, heralded by a quirk of the senses—a trick of the eye, a humming in the ear. Other times, a natural environment creates a landscape in which one can be free of the ego and feel a part of the whole. In most cases, we must cultivate a silent space for mystical experiences, whether they are large and dramatic or one of what D. T. Suzuki called "a million little moments that make one dance."

"All paths are good. It depends on conditioning and tendencies. Just as one can travel to the same place by plane, railway, car or cycle, so also different lines of approach suit different types of people."
—Anandamayi Ma

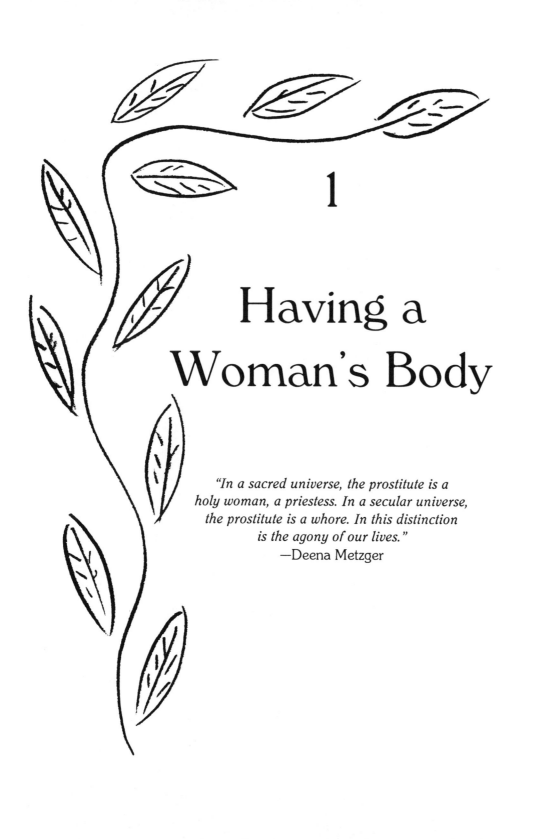

1

Having a Woman's Body

*"In a sacred universe, the prostitute is a
holy woman, a priestess. In a secular universe,
the prostitute is a whore. In this distinction
is the agony of our lives."*
—Deena Metzger

Many spiritual experiences have nothing to do with gender, but it is deceptive to think that religious experience will always be the same for men and women. Simply living inside of a female body produces a different life experience than existing as a male, yet until recently there has been little in our traditional religions encouraging us to place the physical aspects of a woman's body—menstruation, childbirth, rape, abortion, menopause--in a spiritual context. Much has been written on sexuality, of course, but largely from the male point of view. The Christian concept of a God up in the sky has resulted in negativity toward the body in general and female sexuality in particular. Little by little, this is beginning to change as women articulate their experiences and delve into nontraditional beliefs to draw together a collection of concepts, rituals, and meditations that fit a woman's felt bodily experience. Drawn from Native American, Goddess, Christian, Buddhist, and other sources, the readings and meditations presented here are designed to draw you into your body and to create heightened consciousness about what female embodiment entails for ourselves and others; to develop an appreciation of the lineage we share with all women, our motherline; and, finally, to suggest ways to heal the heart of the womb.

According to Angeles Arrien, human beings need to do only four things: show up, pay attention, tell the truth, and not be attached to the outcome. The first, showing up, is made difficult if we live in our heads rather than in our bodies.

Coming Home to the Body

Emotion is energy in motion in my body: embodied energy. This energy can become blocked or trapped in muscles gone tight from old-held patterns of unexpressed anger, fear, anxiety, rage, and deep grief. Our bodies manifest the energy patterns of our minds and hearts. When we begin to move through our bodies, giving physical expression to these held physical patterns, the blocks are broken apart and new energy is released. The old patterns are transformed into new ways of thinking, feeling, moving, and expressing.

When women begin the transformational process of conscious self-love and coming home to their bodies, fear often arises. Some fears come from the outside. In the past when women stepped outside patriarchy's boundaries, they were met with burnings, beatings, ridicule, and imprisonment in asylums. The revolutionary act of coming into our women's bodies is risky. Patriarchy hates women.

There are also fears that come from inside. There are voices inside our heads saying, "You're not good enough." "Don't be too beautiful, too powerful, too successful because they won't like you anymore." "Don't change your ways because you'll be left all alone." Other voices add, "You can't help the way you are; you're just a weak, helpless woman." "Don't rock the boat." They can sabotage our desire for growth. But because these voices are expressions of facets of our inner selves, we must not destroy or repress them, but rather find a way to transform their message.

In our bodies is our aliveness. Aliveness has to do with an area of consciousness called sentiment. We usually associate this word with feelings, sentimentality, nostalgia, the remembering of good times gone by. But sentiment is much more than things past. Real sentiment has to do with consciously connecting with the powerful, intense energy of the universe that flows through our bodies, minds, and spirits. It is about being fully present with this energy now. Sentiment comes from the Latin word *sentire*—which means "to sense." Where are our senses? In our bodies.

Sentiment as consciousness has different levels. The first level is the powerful, intense life force which is present in the universe. This force or energy is experienced as our basic aliveness. This level gives rise to what can be called our felt sense of reality. One woman, commenting on the abusive language of her spouse said, "It doesn't sound good in my body!" That was her way of expressing how the words she heard were connected to a felt sense of herself.

Where is this felt sense? It is in the muscles of our bodies, in the flow of our blood, in the beating of our hearts, and in the flow of our breath. This energy gives rise to feeling or emotion. Sentiment is an energy which bubbles up in us. It's been called 'enthusiasm' because it comes from the Latin words for "divine energy within." Calling sentiment an area of consciousness means that it is a way of knowing. Not only do our minds and hearts know reality, but our bodies also have a way of knowing that is vital to our experience of being fully human. When we are split off from our bodies we are disconnected from this way of knowing who we are, and our experience of full aliveness is severely diminished.

Many of us don't feel alive in our bodies. How can we connect with our basic aliveness? How can we transform energies of dullness, blockage, and deadness into the energies of new life? How can we experience the divine energies of our women's spirits, the energies many women refer to as the goddess?

I dance! I awaken my aliveness by free-form dancing to music of many different rhythms; I move without music as I give physical expression to my emotions; I sing and chant as I play my drum, rattles, or violin; I dance as I sing and sing as I dance. Then I feel myself coming alive, waking up, becoming consciously connected with the fullness and beauty of my own unique self. I become aware of how wonderful and mysterious it is to be the woman that I am. I become aware of how good it is to be a woman. I become aware of how good it is to be in my woman's body. I experience a new connectedness with all women, with all people, with the earth that grounds and supports my movements and with the air and sky that

*"Sweat your prayers, dance your pain,
and move on."*
—Gabrielle Roth

13

"There is a vitality, a life force, an energy, a quickening, that is translated through you into action, and because there is only one of you in all time, this expression is unique. And if you block it, it will never exist through any other medium and will be lost."
—Martha Graham

carry my singing and chanting. I become more conscious of the need to choose foods that will nurture and energize my body. As my body moves and stretches I experience new levels of my own consciousness revealing my connectedness with all life across all periods of time. Every day brings new movement and new experiences of the multidimensional person that I am.

Each time I begin to move into my transformational life-dance work I experience again my fear of the unknown, the unknown of who I am, the unknown of what may come forth in me. I experience my fear of being foolish, of not being enough, my fear that it does not really make any difference that I am here because it's all been done before perfectly by someone else. My inner voices can get very loud. Doing my life-dance is my commitment to physicalize my fear instead of letting it freeze my creativity and block my growth. It is a way of experiencing these fears as part of my aliveness.

Giving physical expression to my fears teaches me that that energy is connected to other emotions that are also waiting for me to reconnect them. I need to give physical expression to my emotional self, not just talk about my feelings. As I flow in movement from one piece of my story to another I begin to experience the contractions and expansions of my own birthing process. I remember the words of a poster that says, "I am a woman giving birth to myself." I experience through my body the sacredness of my own life. I find myself pushing through dark inner tunnels of shame, perfectionism, and insecurity. It is messy work giving birth to new life whether it is the life of another human person or new expressions of one's own life. As I move through those dark tunnels, I begin to discover light coming forth within me. At times it is experienced as deep forgiveness and nurturance that makes my body feel crystal clear.

At other times I have experienced myself as a beautiful eagle soaring high and grounded in her flight. With each breakthrough I encounter and recognize the mystery of the Goddess within my own being. The words of Arisika Razak echo through me, ". . . remember the beauty and sacredness of your womanbody. And remember that no matter how your personal body is shaped, whether it is abundant or slight, somewhere in the world a goddess is venerated who looks just like you."

The essence of the Divine is mystery. The encounter with

mystery is found for me in entering the movement of life. Since the movement is in my body, body-movement work is my spiritual path. On this path the mystery is hidden not in a golden tabernacle or behind a veiled cloth. It is hidden in my muscles, my blood, my breath. Body-movement work brings new meaning to the words "This is my body. This is my blood given for the life of all."

Walking this path involves choosing to love my woman's body, my woman's mind, my woman's spirit in all their parts. Walking this path involves being healing for myself, for others, and for our Mother Earth. Walking this path is transformative work. It involves experiencing that I am a Woman of the Universe being born anew each moment.

> Louise M. Paré
> "Self Image and Spirituality"
> in *The Spiral Path*

"Instead of vesting divinity in a transcendent other-worldly being, we recognize it as immanent in the process of life itself . . . we recognize that, like us, God is dynamic–a verb, not a noun."
—Joanna Macy

○ To experience a bit of what Paré is writing about, try this dance meditation: Go into your room by yourself, dim the lights, and close the door. Put on your favorite music and listen until you sink into it and can feel its beat in your body. Sway at first to the music, then begin to move in any way that your body seems to want to. Don't think; listen to the music, let your body talk. Let it jerk or sway or repeat a motion over and over. Allow your arms to flail about or to move in graceful arcs. Move your hips—do a dirty boogie or a sedate elephant sway. Pull your shoulders up and out of your body, roll them around to relax the muscles, then let the arms and shoulders shift as they will. Forget everything, listen to the music and move. Your body knows what to do. Your body knows where tension is knotted and where the blocks are obstructing your energy. Let your body dance out its kinks and knots. Keep your consciousness in your body as you twist, turn, dance.

When you feel totally in your body, let yourself be danced. Let energy flow through you, move you. Feel the dynamic energy of the world around you, the force of the music, the response of your muscles. Visualize the world dancing with you: the flowers swaying in the meadow, the leaves on the trees twisting and turning, the wind sweeping this way and that. See people the earth over in joyous movement: women rocking their babies, children hugging, men and women making love. Let all of that energy flow through you as you dance.

———————————

Rituals for women's rites of passage, although common in cultures that include goddess worship, have not been part of our Western religious heritage. Here, as often happens with those who open themselves to a dynamic spirit within—most recently called "the goddess" in this country—a ritual arises spontaneously to carry the emotion and meaning of an occasion.

Menarche Ritual

Some months after the daughters of two of us had their first menstrual periods, seven women plus the two adolescents spend a weekend at a hexagon-shaped house in the country with an open deck in the center. On Saturday afternoon the mothers prepare an altar in the womblike round enclosure, a cloth on which they set red candles and a pot of big red Gerber daisies, along with Goddess figurines, pine cones, an abalone shell filled with dried cypress needles, and other favorite objects that people had brought. The group silently drifts toward the circle from various doors and is seated on cushions. We listen as the order of the ceremony is explained. We begin by lighting the dried needles and passing the shell around the circle, breathing in the purifying smoke and fanning it gently to surround each body. We invoke the presence of the four directions and sing a melodic chant: *We all come from the Goddess and to Her we shall return like a drop of rain flowing to the ocean.* We tell the girls about some of the many, many cultural responses to menses as a visitation of transformative power, a sacred time set apart from the mundane. We tell them of the cultural

"The challenge is to persevere, for the sake of ourselves, our daughters, and all the daughters who follow, that we all might experience an equal, compassionate and more whole world."
—Jean Young

degradation of women's procreative power to potential danger and then shameful uncleanliness. We tell them of the invention of counting, the Paleolithic bone-calendars etched with twenty-eight marks, the cycle of women's blood and the moon. We read them a poetic myth of Hera, goddess of women and the powers of fecundity, who draws forth the lunar blood. We sing again: *She changes everything She touches, and everything She touches changes.* Then, one by one, the women tell the story of their menarche, that first visitation of Hera—the excitement, the embarrassment, the confusion, the family's response. After each story, the speaker receives a crescent moon painted with berry juice on her forehead. Some women also speak of their first sexual experiences, of how they hope the girls might think about their bodies and their womanhood. The girls tell their stories last, tales of red blood on white slacks during the middle of movies! The circle is filled with laughter and tears, blessings and hope. We sing a final song, *Listen, listen, listen to my heart's song.* . . . Then the women stand and form a birth canal, an archway with our upraised arms. The two mothers stand at the far end of the passageway, near the opening of the deck into the outer world. One at a time the girls pass through our arch of arms as we chant their names and kiss their cheeks. As they emerge as women, the mothers paint a crimson moon on their foreheads and hug them. Then come gifts and feasting. That was my daughter's menarche ritual.

> Charlene Spretnak
> *States of Grace: The Recovery of Meaning
> in the Postmodern Age*

○ Plan a menarche celebration with your daughter, sister, niece, or friend.

"As we see the Goddess mirrored in each other's eyes, we take that power in our hands as we take hands, as we touch. For the strength of that power is in the bond we make with each other. And our vision grows strong when we no longer dream alone."
—Starhawk

In some Native American traditions, menstruation is not "the curse," but a time for seclusion and visions.

Moon Lodge

> "The body is more than a sensual receptor, more than a physical vehicle, it is an instrument of superconscious awareness with a direct line to the soul."
> —Vicki Noble

The other practice concerns our use of the moon cycle, the cycle of our menses. We are presently reacting toward a whole new time on earth, a flowering of the tree of life. The dawn star has long since faded into the pale morning light, and golden day is close at hand—yet much still lies within the womb of mystery, in the womb of Buffalo Woman. We are being called to bring forth into reality what is waiting there for us, to awaken ourselves in the dream. And finding the dream is the function of the moon cycle, especially for the daughters of the earth, whose blood expresses itself with the tides of the moon's pull.

It is now that I speak to the feminine, the nurturing and renewing power within all, and especially I call to those who chose a female body, for we express Grandmother's pull most eloquently. Your moon cycle determines the thinness of the veil between you and the great mystery. As the new moon comes toward you, the veil thins, becomes gossamer and transparent. You feel the openness and sensitivity that begins to increase. You pay closer attention to where you allow yourself to be, the energy in which you are immersed, for you imprint very deeply in this receptive time. What you wish to receive, create, and magnify, you choose to surround yourself in now. You turn toward beauty, peacefulness, song, and thus call vision for a radiant, harmonious life for your children and the children of seven generations. You define what you give your attention to until the blood comes and then you retreat into the peaceful beauty and quiet of the moon lodge, leaving behind for a few days the everyday world: going within to center, paying attention to the womb, to Mother's mind within you, and on then into the great mystery waiting there. In the moon lodge you remember your vow to use this transparent veil in calling vision for your people, praying, "Not for myself alone, Great Spirit, do I ask this vision, but that all the peoples may live."

This information received as the menses begin is the clearest human picture from within the womb of the great mystery, from the unknown of our future. Among our dreaming peoples, the most prophetic dreams and visions (of the coming of the white peoples and other such almost incomprehensible changes) were brought to the people through the moon lodge. In other words, the most useful information comes from each of us women who use our moon time well. Conversely, for each of us who do not honor this time, much is lost, including the respect of others for our bleeding.

My call to you is to begin now to honor your moon time, to come together in small hoops (of perhaps eight women) and create a moon lodge, a communal women's retreat and meditation room for the beauty, for the quiet, for the transparent veil. Dedicate yourself to the quest for vision that will guide us and our families at the time. Within this lodge keep a large and lovely book for recording your visions, dreams, imaginings, and intuitive flashes. Make possible also a simple art expression for another kind of cord. These expressions will unify the information and make it available to all who come there; the dream will begin to unveil itself through strands woven from many women's dreams. The weaving created through the gatherings of shared vision on the new moon and the gathering to actualize those visions during the full moons will create a fuller tapestry, more easily understood and made real in the ordinary affairs of life. For this is the ultimate action—making the dream of peace real in the 'everydayness' of our lives.

> Brooke Medicine Eagle
> "Moon Lodge"
> in *The Spiral Path*

"We are so captivated by and entangled in our subjective consciousness that we have forgotten the age-old fact that God speaks chiefly through dreams and visions."
—C.G. Jung

○ The next time you have your period, set aside as much time as possible—an hour, a day—for quiet and meditation. Write in a "moon" journal or create some sort of art which will help to catch and express the intuitive insights that are available to you at this time.

To explore further the deeper spiritual meaning of menstruation, also see *Blood, Bread and Roses: How Menstruation Created the World*, by Judy Grahn, Beacon, 1993; *Red Flower: Rethinking Menstruation*, edited by Dena Taylor, The Crossing Press, 1988; and *The Wise Wound: Menstruation and Everywoman*, by Penelope Shuttle and Peter Redgrove, Paladin, 1986.

"I understood that our sensuality is grounded in Nature, in Compassion and in Grace. This enables us to receive gifts that lead to everlasting life. For I saw that in our sensuality God is. For God is never out of the soul."
—Julian of Norwich

Perhaps one of the most destructive aspects of Christian patriarchy is its view of female sexuality. Although one can understand its source—the church fathers who split the world into mind and matter, heaven and earth, spirit and body—the damage this duality continues to do is insidious. The musing below follows a dream in which "The world was a dance; God and ourselves dancing together. . . ."

Body as Temple of the Holy Spirit

All at once I thought that if I were allowed to see the world as God's body, this metaphor would also include a reappraisal of the dignity of our own bodies. Our bodies would then be more than 'brother Mule,' more than an instrument used by us Westerners and worn out by our active occupations. Then it would have its own intrinsic value and dignity. According to an old and meaningful saying in the Christian tradition, the body is the temple of the Holy Spirit. That means that we, in and through our bodies, are bearers of the Spirit, and that we must treat our bodies in such a way that this Spirit can shine through them.

It also means that the bodies of women and men have their own beauty, and that we may enjoy them with all our senses. Eroticism and sexuality also have their own value as belonging to God's good creation. We do not even have to use much fantasy here; there is a poetic story about it in the Bible, the Song of Songs. In it we hear the jubilation and delight of two lovers in total reciprocity, the characteristic of eroticism. Each of them is delighted in the other and makes the other a full participant. The garden in which they play is there in all its abundance of growth and prosperity, aromas and colors, and is the image of all sensual pleasure. There is reciprocal desire, and each one puts this into words, the man and the woman. The initiative for love comes sometime from the one, sometimes from the other, and neither is the other's object or is overpowered by the other.

It is this desire for one another, and the passion that seeks union, that makes the erotic such an exemplary image of the human desire for unity with God. It is precisely the spark of our spirit-bearing body which inflames us and drives us towards the beloved other and towards the Secret of our existence. Bernard of Clairvaux writes, "Jesus is the kiss of God which united God with humanity." We give this kiss when we kiss one another in love, tenderness and friendship.

From the very beginning there has been the relation, the unity. It is the basis of all our passion *and* all our *compassion* for one another. For over the sunlit garden in the Song of Songs, and stronger yet in the garden of Eden, there is also a shadow, a threat from outside, or from within one's own heart. "The bitter puzzle of the good creation" remains. . . .

If our body receives a sacramental meaning because it is included in the image of the world of God's body, then this is equally true of the woman's body as of the man's. So people with a female body must not be excluded from administering the sacraments, which are in a special way the signs and expressions of God's presence among people. This prohibition lies like a shadow over female corporeality, and all the arguments to justify it—tradition, Jesus' behavior, Christ's maleness—are rationalizations produced by fear of the female body.

> Catharina J. M. Halkes
> *New Creation: Christian Feminism*
> *and the Renewal of the Earth*

○ To become conscious of your body—that temple of the Holy Spirit—lie on your back and make yourself comfortable. Be aware of your toes, your arches, your heels. Soften and relax your muscles as you focus on them, dissolving tension and tightness. Slowly draw your consciousness into your ankles, up your calves, to your knees, thighs, pelvic area, then your waist. Slowly move up your trunk, chest, and into your shoulders. Concentrate on your fingers, palms, hands, wrists, forearms, elbows, upper arms, and shoulders. Bring your consciousness up through your neck, face, and forehead. Feel the back of your head. Imagine a central channel that extends through your body and the middle of your head and out the crown, and follow it with your consciousness. Reverse the process.

"For the erotic is not a question only of what we do; it is a question of how acutely and fully we can feel in the doing."
—Audre Lorde

"Sex has been called the original sin. It is neither original nor sin."
—Bhagwan Shree Rajneesh

The negativity of Christian attitudes toward the body and especially female sexuality prevents many women from staying within the church today. Although these attitudes stem more from the early church fathers than from Christ's teachings themselves, the damage goes deep in women's psyches. Most Jewish and Christian women see the forced choice between the body and the spirit as an area which must be radically reformed before women can fully participate—on inner and outer levels—in these existing traditions.

Sexuality and Spiritual Growth

Put bluntly, the point is not that it is possible, with effort, to put God in sex; it is that it is impossible to have authentic sex except in God. It is not only our understanding of sex that is at fault, but our assumptions about God. . . .

By the term "sex" is indicated the range of possible physical expressions of intimate relation in a life which has progressed through all its stages of development.

"Love" refers to the dynamic that moves anything towards its highest fulfillment. Love of any kind is continuous with the love of God (subjective: God's love for others, and objective: the love of others for God). To speak of differences of degree of love makes more sense than to speak of differences of kinds of love.

The relationship of love to sex in the various stages of development is neither simple identity (one cannot exist without the other) nor simple opposition (one replaces the other to exist). It is sacramental (through sex, human love is made visible and intelligible; through love, sex is brought to its own completion). Moreover, through the sacramentality of embodied love, divine love is made present and active.

The holiness of sexual life consists in the lovers' effort to co-work with the Spirit who moves them. That work is Christ's work of reconciliation, which includes and goes beyond personal development toward the improvement of the world.

Joan Timmerman
Sexuality and Spiritual Growth

For a good discussion of the evolution of the mind/body split and other such unfortunate ideas, see Elaine Pagels' book, *Adam, Eve, and the Serpent*, Vintage, 1988. Other books of interest include: Elizabeth Haich's *Sexual Energy & Yoga*, ASI Publications, 1975; Dion Fortune's *Esoteric Philosophy of Love and Marriage*, Samuel Weiser, 1974; and Omar Garrison's *Tantra: The Yoga of Sex*, Crown, 1983.

With the advent of AIDS and other sexually transmitted diseases, touch and intimacy are becoming increasingly important. Esoteric sexual practices consistently advocate withholding semen, a technique that many couples have spontaneously discovered for themselves. Here the author is speaking of a boy in her college dorm.

> *"Are all the trees, birds and animals heading for eternal punishment in hell? Can you call that sweet little songbird a pervert because he sings constantly to attract his mate?"*
> —Daniel (Shahid) Johnson

Making Love

We were, in fact, both virgins. I was on the health clinic's waiting list for birth control pills and was very afraid of pregnancy in this time of illegal abortions. Daniel did not trust condoms, having himself been born as a result of that more risky method. We both wanted the protection of the pill. This meant that for four months we would have to figure out how to make love without intercourse.

One day Daniel showed me an old Chinese Taoist pillow book he had found in Hawaii. It was an instruction manual usually given to newlyweds for practicing sexual arts. Illustrated with elegant watercolors and indecipherable Chinese characters, the book did have one English inscription in delicate penmanship: "Practice with careful tenderness. Breathe together."

We lay propped up over the exquisite picture book: Here were couples gazing tenderly into each other's dark eyes, their delicate limbs entwined in elegant postures of worship, abandon, and surrender as they stroked thighs, toes, bellies, gently sloped backs, or graceful buttocks. Their sensual play was artful. Our favorite picture was a couple in a garden, languid willow falling over their pallet as the woman lay back, contented and trusting, against the man's chest. Embracing her from behind, he held her breasts as if they were the most precious porcelain vases. At her feet a pink lotus burst open with their pleasure.

Another favorite was a bathing picture that Daniel and I decided to recreate every weekend. During the week I bought lavender soap, loofah sponges, and an East Indian bubble elixir that turned the bath an enchanting blue. He brought volcanic pumice stone for my feet, his mother's homemade tropical shampoo for my hair, and coconut massage oil for my sunburned skin. He made a life-size topographical map of my body, naming his favorite places after mountains and valleys he'd studied on maps of the ancient world. I wrote him primitive poetry, then recited it in our bath as we faced each other, encircled by candles. In our glowing water cave, we were two initiates, learning the luxurious language of touch and time.

Sometimes we'd play my Miriam Makeba album, with its African drumming, or listen to recordings of Tibetan chants. We didn't understand the words, just the rhythm. It flowed through our bodies—drum with our heartbeats, chants with our breath. The music moved our hands as we slowly caressed each other.

Sometimes we'd sit naked, back to back, like couples in the pillow book, and simply breathe together. I could feel his heartbeat through my backbone, and I trembled to hear his pulse in my body. Then, turning face to face, we let waves of energy wash over us. Each time Daniel felt himself on the edge of orgasm, we'd both keep still, our bodies against one another. Daniel discovered, quite by accident, that he could stop the urge to ejaculate by pressing on a sensitive point between his scrotum and his anus for several seconds. This pressure would only increase his pleasure, allowing him to build wave after arousing wave. Instinctively, I would place my hand on top of his head, the other on his buttocks. It was like holding the whole of him between my hands. After a moment, we'd both grow calm and tenderly draw away from the fire in our genitals.

"Breathe, breathe," we'd say, and inhale in sync. The energy moved to our heads and feet all at once like an ecstatic undertow, a sensual, slow flow that awakened arms, tingled in legs, and sung along our spines. "Bottom of the ocean" we called this joy, as our bodies tumbled together, sinking deep, settling at last on the seabed where the pulse of something greater like the sea rocked us. Our

> "Focusing one's mind on one's partner and nurturing the relationship are at the heart of conscious loving."
> —Caroline Muir

skin smelled salty, and our naked bodies gleamed like phosphorescent fishes. We gave off our own light, our own spinning gravity.

Daniel and I parted before I got the birth control pills, but in all our erotic explorations, we hardly missed "going all the way." Only years later did I recognize those months with Daniel as an intuitive blend of tantra, Taoist, and kundalini partner yoga. After Daniel left to study with a local guru, I finally got the pill—my own little compact wheel of life—and I lost my virginity with a young man who was kind but less inspired than Daniel. But I consider Daniel my first lover; even without intercourse or procreation, we made something alive and holy between us. We made love.

> Brenda Peterson
> *New Age Journal*, May/June 1993

O This exercise, designed to open the heart chakras, will help to deepen and spiritualize your relationship with your lover. Sit facing each other, with your right hand covering your partner's heart and vice versa, then each of you cover the other's right hand with your left. Look into each other's left eye, breathing slightly faster than usual. After every four or five breaths, sigh "Aahhh." Breathe together this way for forty to fifty breaths. Let the breathing relax; continue silently to look into each other's eyes until you feel your hearts connected and open. Deep emotions and reactions may arise that range from joy and laugher to sadness and tears. Don't try to control your reactions, just concentrate on your heart chakras and energy flowing between you.

"Centuries of cultural evolution and fear have polluted our ability to contact each other in truly vulnerable and expanding ways. As a result, and through no fault of sex itself, sex has become an obstacle to our spiritual development."
—Charles Bates

"Tantra is a yoga, a discipline that teaches each of its practitioners to come into union with their body and energy through awareness. It's a discipline that includes regular practice of energy meditations. These are called 'practices' because they are meant to be practiced, not only because they develop skill and mastery, but also because they keep practitioners immersed in the process."
—Robert Frey

In the West, Eastern esoteric practices have been interpreted in almost exclusively sexual terms, but this limits and distorts these practices. Hindu scriptures called Tantras describe—among many other things—ritual lovemaking, which combines sexual union, spiritual practice, right motivation, and the guidance of the heart. Ritual lovemaking, involving complex channeling of body energy, is central to both Taoist and Tantric traditions, where it is considered by many to be the most direct way to achieve liberation in a single lifetime. The emphasis is not on physical desire, but on using the sexual energies of the body to unblock channels and unleash a primal power called kundalini. To this end, mantra, prayer, visualization of the partner as god or goddess, retention of semen, and other techniques are used.

The authors of the following ritual—which they define as a simplified form of the secret rite of Tantric union—suggest that the lovers put aside plenty of time and enhance the environment with fruit, flowers, incense, candlelight, and soft music.

Tantric Sex: The Secret Rite

Sexual ritual—or *Maithuna Sadhana*, as it is known in Tantra— commences with both partners taking a bath or shower, preferably in cold water. This has the effect of vitalizing and toning up the psyche. Then the couple should lightly oil and massage each other. This should be followed by a brief period spent in stretching exercises, to relax the muscles and free the circulation of vital energies. Dance serves the same purpose and can be a most effective way of harmonizing mood and circulating energy between the couple.

In the next stage, the couple sit down, preferably with legs crossed in the lotus posture, and with the woman to the *right* of the man. They should practice simple meditation, clearing their minds of any worldly or habitual thoughts and regulating their breath by gentle alternate-nostril or *Solar-Lunar Breathing*. When both feel completely relaxed and harmonized, they are then ready to proceed with the Secret Rite itself. A simple aid to harmonization of breath and mood is shared singing, which can accompany a recording. The main point is that it should be devotional or transcendental in nature.

The first part of the Secret Rite is the honoring of the female principle, the *Shakti*, both externally and internally. The man performs external honoring by seating his partner on a pillow or cushion in front of him, lightly wrapping her body with a red or violet shawl of cotton, wool or silk. Imagining her as the most beautiful goddess in the whole universe, he should bring to mind her best qualities and gently massage her feet with perfumed oil. This massage should be concentrated on the region around and between her largest toes. Humming a Mantra gently to himself, the man should endow the moment with potency and expectation.

The couple should both perform inward honoring by remembering the purpose of the ritual, which is to become totally unified with one's origin. Evoking the Kundalini-power within each of them, they should visualize a molten-gold serpentine energy wave uncoiling at the base of their spines. The powers of fantasy and imagination should be drawn on to make the Kundalini excited. Conceived of as a primordial ecstatic female being, the Kundalini should be endowed with emotional energy. From this point on in the ritual, the partners must forget their personal, human identities and know themselves only as Shiva and Shakti, the Supreme Couple.

Nik Douglas and Penny Slinger
Sexual Secrets: The Alchemy of Ecstasy

"A sage once said that sex may be the lowest rung on the ladder of love, but that it's a ladder that can take you all the way to God. When sex is purified, it attunes you to prayer."
—William Ashoka Ross

The current "bible" on the subject of spirituality and sexuality is Margo Anand's *The Art of Sexual Ecstasy*, Jeremy P. Tarcher, 1990, but you might also want to look at the following books:

Jolan Chang, *The Tao of Love and Sex: The Ancient Chinese Way to Ecstacy*, Dutton, 1977.

Mantak Chia and Maneewan Chia, *Healing Love Through the Tao: Cultivating Sexual Energy*, Healing Tao Books, 1987.

Gedun Chopel, *Tibetan Arts of Love*, translated by Jeffrey Hopkins, Snow Lion, 1992.

Nik Douglas and Penny Slinger, *Sexual Secrets: The Alchemy of Ecstasy*, Destiny Books, 1979.

John Mumford, *Ecstacy Through Tantra*, Llewellyn, 1993.

Bhagwan Shree Rajneesh, *Tantra, Spirituality & Sex*, Rajneesh Foundation International, 1977.

Indra Sinha, ed., *The Great Book of Tantra*, Inner Traditions, 1992.
Douglas Wile, *The Art of the Bedchamber: The Chinese Sexual Yoga Classics Including Women's Solo Meditation*, SUNY, 1993.

There's even a magazine: *Tantra: The Magazine*, PO Box 79, Torreon, NM 87061-9900, which provides information on retreats, seminars, tapes, and books. A Tibetan Tantrika might be quite puzzled by some of their Westernized advertisements, including one for a "Tantric Bed & Breakfast."

"One of the greatest gifts of being in body is the potential of sexual energy to link up with the cosmos as you flood yourself and your beloved with delicious sensation and love. The consciousness expands beyond the sensual level, beyond the pleasure of the stimulus, because the motion of expansion allows mind—pure mind—to enter."
—Chris Griscom

Tantric and Taoist practitioners aren't the only ones who find that sexual union leads to the divine. Here a Western woman echoes that sentiment.

Sex and Soul

And what is the purpose of having an intimate partner? The purpose of intimacy is to massage the heart, to soften the muscles around our hardened places and keep pliant the places where we're already open. The circle of love is deep and strong. It can forgive mistakes and cast out error. It can foster greatness and bring forth new life. There is nothing it cannot do. Love is God.

It's no accident that millions of people say, "Oh, God," when they come. That's because he's there and they saw him. He *is* those moments when there is no argument, just pure connection. That *is* God. It's not *like* God, or *sort of* God, or to be thought about *in terms of* God. Love is God. To love another person—and I'm not saying that *every* time we come we love, but on the other hand it happens often enough to warrant the conversation—is to experience the divine.

Marianne Williamson
A Woman's Worth

○ Imagine reading this passage to your minister, priest, rabbi, guru, or teacher. How would your mother react to it? Your lover? How do their reactions affect you?

Candace Whitridge is a midwife and organic farmer in Trinity County, California. She speaks on the connection between midwifery and spirituality all over this country and in Europe, most recently in Denmark and Russia.

Childbirth as Spiritual Experience

Kimberley Snow: Why did you become a midwife?

Candace Whitridge: Quite simply, I was called to it. I was a fairly neurotic dramatic arts major when I saw a little invitation on a bulletin board from the nursing school for a tea. I liked the people, the serenity of the buildings, the way it all reminded me of the Nurse Cherry Ames books I read as a child. So I got into nursing. I loved it.

When I started working with women, with birthing, it felt really familiar. I said to myself, "I've done this before." I knew what to do spontaneously, knew how to sit beside a woman and care for her. This knowledge came from old memories.

As an obstetrical nurse I felt very limited, so in 1979 when a friend called and suggested that I enroll in the first midwifery school in California, I applied along with hundreds of other women, and was accepted. There I learned skillful means—how to suture, how to measure—which I see as the male principle. Then I moved up to Trinity country in Northern California and soon found that in the mountains, women had different attitudes about birth and natural processes. In one week I had two teenagers who taught me about the birth process. These women were not "experts" but they showed me how they wanted to be cared for by pulling from a deep sense of wisdom that was far older than they were. So my real teachers were the women I cared for, and the life process itself.

There are many parallels between the way a particular labor goes and how a child develops. Some women have what I call a torpedo birth—the first labor pain is a big one and the birth is very explosive and fast. These kids hit the ground running and this is their pattern all their lives. Other births sort of poke along and then speed up toward the end. These children are the ones who won't start on a term paper until the night before it's due. I've seen it happen over and over.

"The woman who brings a baby into the world is the quintessential shaman. She brings the soul from the 'other side' to this side. She incarnates it. She forms it within her body and brings it out into the world, through her own bodily process . . . . If we can take back our birthing, we can take back our Goddess."
—Vicki Noble

"No one can sufficiently capture in words the euphoria, the gratitude, and the total delight which can follow a natural birth. The 'high' of these moments is spiritual to the utmost, while remaining utterly physical."
—Qahira Qalbi

K: How does a home birth differ from a hospital birth?

C: As a midwife, what I do is to create an opportunity for women to birth spontaneously and joyfully. For this you need an atmosphere of trust. When women feel safe, they can let go and contact something that is bigger than they are. Otherwise they remain intellectual, trying to stay in control.

When you see a woman give birth, you watch her go somewhere else. She swells up in her power. You don't have this opportunity if you are in an alien environment of a sterile hospital, with strangers who have expectations, rules, routines to follow. This keeps women in their minds; their bodies don't get involved with the birth process so the mind/body dualism gets even deeper. They feel tyrannized by their biology and want a McDonald's baby—a quick take out.

It's hard for a woman to surrender to something that big in hospital conditions. Obstetrician means "to stand before" while midwife means "with woman." It's not the doctor's fault: he's trained in these large institutions and has been taught that women can't do it without them. Or without drugs. The first generation of babies born to drugged mothers was the first druggy generation of children. Maybe this is just a coincidence, maybe not.

Mountain women get into birth—they savor the experience. These women give birth as they live their lives. I was with one mountain woman who would weep and moan and carry on when she was having a contraction. When it was over, she'd sort of shake herself and say, "Mm. That was a good one." Then she'd take care of the family—telling this one to comb her hair or the other that there was tuna salad in the refrigerator. Another contraction would come and she'd howl and throw herself around.

Sometimes something really cuts loose in the birth process, even with women who live busy urban lives. In early labor, when they are still in their heads, the energy is very high: their voices are high-pitched, they raise their bodies up away from the pain. Midwives used to think that they could tell how much the woman had dilated by the pitch of her voice. Then you can see the power start to move in, and everything starts to drop—the voice gets deeper, the body gets heavy on the bed—like they are going down into the center of the earth.

As a culture we pull away from whatever we see as difficult or painful. We numb it. We see suffering as bad rather than as an opportunity to grow, change, transform ourselves. Women have always had this opportunity, but since childbirth has been taken over by hospitals, they've lost it. Lost the sense of the sacred as well.

Being a midwife is not just being at the birth, but in helping women understand the sacredness of the process. I tell women not to have any expectations going into labor; whatever it takes to get the baby born is appropriate, is perfect.

Care needs to go beyond measuring things. The mother does the pre-natal care, while I watch over her. You have to be careful what you say to a pregnant woman, what you feed her, just as you have to be careful about watering and fertilizing a growing plant. If you believe that you are growing a plant, then you will act one way, if you believe that the earth is growing the plant, you act another.

Our lives are so full of the mundane, a pre-natal visit to the midwife should be in the realm of the sacred. We speak of all sorts of things—the ways of women, the ways of life. Little odd thoughts and ideas often come in, or we share recipes, mythology. These moments are holy. And they help to build trust. They are just as important in preparing for the birth as measuring the height of her uterus. She begins to see herself and her experience in another way, one that goes beyond the ordinary.

These visits help to establish trust that builds up over the months. Then when she's giving birth she knows that I will be there watching over her. When she takes flight—and a woman can get way out there—if she looks at me and sees that I'm not upset, then she can let go into the process. She can go further than she ever thought possible. But in order to give in to something that big, there has to be trust. A woman has to trust herself and trust those around her.

I was with one woman who kind of drifted through the whole process. Her mother had told her that when she gave birth, she'd felt the power of God coming through her. She'd said that whatever you feel is a blessing. So what if there's pain—you end up with a baby, for god's sake.

After the birth, I asked this woman, "Did it hurt?"

"Yes, I guess it did," she said, as if she hadn't really noticed at the time. "But," she said, "I've always wanted a baby, and I was getting one."

"I think that the doctrine of the Virgin birth as something higher, sweeter, nobler than ordinary motherhood is a slur on all the natural motherhood of the world . . . . I place beside the false, monkish, unnatural claim of the Immaculate Conception my mother, who was as holy in her motherhood as was Mary herself."
—Elizabeth Cady Stanton

"Every single human being was drummed into this world by a woman, having listened to nine months of heart rhythms of their mother."
—Connie Sauer

31

"It follows that to be feminine is to be like a vessel: receiving, encompassing, enclosing, welcoming, sustaining, protecting, nourishing, embracing, containing, holding together—in other words, yin. However, this receptive and gestating function of vagina and womb is only half their story. The womb is also the organ that pushes forth mightily in birthing. Our understanding of the nature of femininity needs to be revised to take into account the birth—pushing yang function of the womb."
—Genia Pauli Haddon

I've also seen women in labor get up and do this sort of ancient dance—flinging their bodies this way and that. Or doing a heavy swaying movement. Some roar like a lion, other's make strange guttural sounds, or otherworldly noises. A birth song like that gives voice to pain, keeps women from being a victim of it.

I see the female species as a vehicle for continuing the magnificence that is life. With sexual reproduction, you take two things and a third emerges, so we have the potential for greater and greater magnificence. But we have to connect with the process. We've convinced women that they should fear childbirth, so there is all this pulling away from the experience. We've medicalized it, boiled it dry. We've taken birthing out of the realm of the sacred. And women have not only forgotten this, they don't even remember that there is something they've forgotten.

On a practical level concerning how to correct this situation, physicians should not be in charge of healthy, normal women who are pregnant. Midwives should take care of them. Physicians should be brought in only if there is something wrong, if there is a situation where their expertise and technology is needed. But otherwise, midwives in all countries should care for women in that culture, whether in urban centers or in the mountains.

Sometimes when I am examining a woman's body, I see it as the Trinity. There's this massive organ of the uterus, so powerful that it will expel life. I see that as the masculine principle. Then inside there's fluid, this flowing, changing, shifting liquid medium that I see as the feminine principle. Then there's the baby itself: all of this contained inside a woman's body. All of this just begins to explore the spiritual which culminates in a birth.

When I lecture at different places, people want to hear stories about the process of giving birth. It opens them up, gives them a sense of devotion, respect. I have an eight-minute-long slide show with music that I often present. It shows scenes of women in labor, of women giving birth, of families standing around the bed, of men holding their wives. It's designed to take the viewer beyond concepts about giving birth, and often tears will stream down people's faces as they watch the slides. It opens them up a little. They may close again, but still a tiny opening remains. People want to find God again, to feel reverence for something bigger than themselves. They can't do it by looking up in the sky, by looking out there. Women are empowered by seeing other women give birth in joy. They take that in and it changes them. If women can regain trust in ancient wisdom, they can begin to conduct their lives on a different level.

For information concerning the slide show, call 1-800-299-3366 and ask for the Childbirth Graphics Department.

For the fascinating tape, "Fate of the Earth, Fate of Birth," write: Sister Mary McGillis, Genesis Farm, 41-A Silver Lake Road, Blairstown, NJ 07825.

To read more about the spiritual possibilities in birthing, consult these books: *Why Not Me? The Story of Gladys Milton, Midwife*, by Wendy Bovard and Gladys Milton, Book Publishing Company, 1993; *Spiritual Midwifery*, by Ina May Gaskin, Book Publishing Company, 1980; *Hearts Open Wide: Stories of Midwives and Births*, by Pam Wellish and Susan Root, eds., Wingbow Press, 1993; *Woman to Mother; a Transformation*, by Vangie Bergum, Bergin & Garvey Publishers, 1989.

———————————————

In Japan, where abortion is common, shrines are dedicated to the Bodhisattva Jizo who guides the souls of unborn babies through the underworld. Parents often leave toys at the foot of these shrines. Here a woman describes a ceremony in which she participated in the U.S.

Jizo Ceremony for Aborted and Miscarried Children

We sat in a circle making small red bibs.

"Jizo Ceremony for Aborted and Miscarried Children," read the large hand-lettered sign behind the registration desk of the Celebration of Women in Buddhist Practice Conference.

"I'm not going," a woman beside me had said aloud, though no one had asked. Now she sat across from me, her head bent over scraps of red cloth.

The ceremony was led by Yvonne Rand from the Green Gulch

"If men had babies, there would be thousands of images of crowning."
—Judy Chicago

"While I do not believe abortion is something that should be legislated against, I do feel it is an option that should not be taken lightly. Even if it seems that the best choice is to terminate a pregnancy, we must acknowledge we are ending a potential life. This seems more honest that acting as if our 'pro-choice' stance does not involve taking life, even though we may assume that life is not fully realized, conscious or developed."
—Margot Wallach Milliken

Zen Center. She seemed stern, businesslike, almost severe. She'd begun the session by telling us that we'd make bibs for an aborted or miscarried child (or children), then, in a group ceremony at the end, offer the bibs to Jizo, the bodhisattva who guides unborn children through the underworld. A bodhisattva, she explained, is dedicated to helping others and has vowed not to pass into nirvana until everyone is enlightened.

Red cloth, scissors, thread, needles were laid out on work tables. Once we assembled our materials, we were to sit in a circle and talk as we made the bibs. The activity of cutting out the cloth, finding who had the spool of thread, an extra needle, helped to channel the nervous and sometimes fearful energy that kept building in the room. Sitting in a circle, sewing, this grounded us, sunk us into a tradition we felt in our bodies even if we'd never experienced it directly in our busy modern lives before.

In Japan, Yvonne Rand said, where abortion is very widespread, statues of Jizo are common. At many shrines, children's clothing—little coats, bibs, dresses—and toys are heaped high. Through the open door out on the grass, we could see a two-foot-high statue of this bodhisattva, Jizo, made of stone.

Yvonne, who didn't seem severe once she began talking, spoke for a while about abortion, then grew quiet. We sewed in silence. Then a woman near me spoke, in a flat voice.

"I've had three abortions."

"Two," another woman added.

"I'm still pro-choice," a woman said a little defensively. Several women—including me—nodded.

An academic woman who'd seemed stiff and guarded at a workshop earlier in the day began to speak. "I'm pro-choice, too." Her voice wavered and cracked. "I'll always be pro-choice. My abortion was the result of a rape."

Pain—shared, visceral pain—swept the room.

"I had two abortions in my early twenties." A slim, grey-haired woman spoke. "I didn't know that it would be the only time I'd ever be pregnant."

My oldest daughter, too, had had two abortions in her early twenties. I'd found out about them afterwards, and not from her. I cut out two more bibs, tiny ones to tuck inside the one I was making for myself. I'd been forty-seven at the time, my three girls finally raised and out of the house. I couldn't have gone through all that again. Nor did I want to. I'd just been thankful that abortions were legal. They hadn't been when I'd gotten pregnant at nineteen. I'd had to marry—so it seemed at the time. A one-option system. And what about those who didn't have marriage as an option?

A writer whose work had influenced and helped many of us started to speak, stopped, then started again. "We were in the Middle East when I miscarried. Twin girls. If I'd come back to the States they might have had a chance. But I didn't. They would have been thirty years old last week."

Again a wave of pain. I felt my heart squeeze, my throat tighten, eyes blur. Such ancient pain carried by the motherline.

I worked on the two little bibs. I'd never thought of my daughter's rather cavalier abortions as missing grandchildren before. Grandchildren I'd never hold. She'd been married—but angry at her husband—for the second one. She didn't tell him about it till after the divorce. Heartless.

My own abortion brought my partner and me closer together. We were in danger of splitting apart at the time. Separation had seemed inevitable, but we found each other again through the experience of the abortion. We've been together now for over fifteen years, stable, happy.

Name the fetus, Yvonne said. Name the fetus and talk to it before you say goodbye.

The name "Jizo" came to me, like the bodhisattva. A little boy. He would have loved me, I knew that. Loved me in a simple, direct way that my oldest daughter never had, never could.

Always tormenting me, herself. What is this karma between mothers and daughters? Why this rage of fury?

"I didn't want a baby, I didn't want to be like my mother," a woman in the room said as if following my private train of thought. Other women spoke up, saying more or less the same thing. I had a confused sense of women trying to abort their mothers, not their children.

"I am ashamed," a beautiful Asian woman in the circle said, "that I didn't ask permission from the fetus. Afterwards I went to a healer and he said to do that. If you're thinking of having an abortion, talk

> *"Every woman contains her daughter in herself, and every daughter her mother."*
> —Carl G. Jung

35

"Repentance doesn't mean guilt. It means just really seeing what we've done out of our separateness; and then begins the process of being at-one-ment."
—Charlotte Joko Beck

to the fetus, explain your situation. Ask the baby to come at another time. Now I counsel my patients to do this. Very often they report a spontaneous abortion."

Again a palpable wave of pain rose in the room. We were united in something timeless. I'd never felt such a sense of shared anguish, of a common physical experience that went too deep for words. Personal distress transmuted into group suffering. I no longer knew whose pain I was feeling.

"We wanted the baby so much." A woman with very short hair and a work shirt spoke. The woman beside her, her partner, placed a hand over the speaker's womb. "We'd planned it for years. We had to wait until we'd saved enough money, then we had to find a suitable donor. It took several tries for me to finally get pregnant. Then we were so happy." She started crying. Hr partner, also crying, began to speak.

"It seems a miracle that we'd be able to have a child at last, be parents. Only. . ." She couldn't talk anymore.

"The miscarriage hurt so much. It still hurts. Physically, I mean, as well as every other way. The pain never stops."

Late in the afternoon, Yvonne rose, led us outside to stand in a circ around the statue of Jizo. One by one we went up to the statue, bowed, placed a bib around his neck, and bowed again. The last time, the whole group bowed.

"Thank you Jizo," I said silently when it was my turn. "Thank you for getting us back together. Goodbye Jizo, take care of the little ones."

Some of us cried as we put our bibs around the statue's neck, others looked clear, cleansed. As we bowed in unison, we acknowledged each woman's act, each woman's loss, guilt, pain. Each child seemed to be our own as we said goodbye and gave it over to the care of the bodhisattva.

Joan Snider
Cold and Howling Hells

○ If you've had an abortion or miscarriage, perhaps you would like to create some sort of ceremony for the soul of the child. It doesn't have to involve making a bib, although it could. Take a moment now to think about what would be most meaningful to you—lighting a candle, planting a tree, writing a poem, whatever. As you perform the ceremony, contact the spirit of your unborn child, name it, explain the circumstances of your pregnancy and its termination, ask forgiveness if that seems appropriate, say goodbye, and let go.

According to Margaret Atwood, the Canadian poet and novelist, menopause is when we pause and think about men. This reconsideration of where our time and effort is spent forms only a part of a larger reevaluation, however, as we move from one phase of our feminine cycle into another—from mother to crone, as defined by the triple goddess of virgin-mother-crone.

Menopause

Women the world over are struggling to understand the true meaning, the essence, of their lives. I have experienced with my teachers that menopause is the gateway into the most sacred time of a woman's existence on earth, a time when she can at last discover the deeper meanings she has sought. And yet, this rite of passage is usually silent, an unspoken of and mysterious journey. We joke about our hot flashes in an attempt to make them less frightening. We have no idea that these symptoms of shifting hormones are also the kindling of a fire within that prepares woman for an incredibly powerful time of life. As we approach this new threshold, it has been shown to me that the alchemy of heat is present to clarify the body and spirit of negative debris. Hot flashes need to be welcomed instead of fought against. So when you take part in this experience, dance with the heat and ride it like a fractious horse, knowing that there is something going on that is far more important than the physical rebalancing of hormones and the transformations taking place in your body.

"Menopause invites our importune ghosts to come forward. It demands a more fundamental confrontation with our dark side. It is a period for coming to terms with the shadow."
—Elizabeth S. Strahan

The change of life is a time of release when a woman begins to reap the benefits of all that she has learned and done. It is the time when her spiritual life at last truly begins. Menopause is a process of rebirth from which a woman emerges with new responsibilities, new mirrors, and new power. At its nucleus is the discovery by each woman of her own personal mystery, an illumination of her private relationship to the totality of her own life process. As she develops, she begins to choreograph the new energies of the universe in a very new way.

Lynn V. Andrews
Woman at the Edge of Two Worlds:
The Spiritual Journey Through Menopause

During the past few years, menopause has gone from a taboo subject to one that everyone talks and writes about. Books that deal with menopause and consciousness and/or spirituality include: *Women of the 14th Moon*, by Dena Taylor, The Crossing Press, 1992; *The Pause*, by Lonnie Barbach, Viking, 1993; *The Change*, by Germaine Greer, Random House, 1991; *Is It Hot in Here or Is It Me? Facts, Fallacies, and Feelings about Menopause*, by Gayle Sand, HarperCollins, 1992; and *The Crone: Woman of Age, Wisdom, and Power*, by Barbara Weller, HarperSanFrancisco, 1985.

The Wise Woman Archetype: Menopause as Initiation, a sixty-minute audio-tape by Jean Shinoda Bolen (author of *Goddesses in Everywoman*), is available from Station Hill Press, Inc., Barrytown, NY 12507. (914) 758-5840. Order no. T0052. Other good books and tapes are available from them as well.

———————

Crones and grandmothers provide a source of wisdom and experience in many societies, but in Native American and mestizo culture, they create a special link to the past.

The Grandmother Songs

The grandmothers were my tribal gods.
They were there

when I was born. Their songs
rose out of wet labor
and the woman smell of birth.
From a floating sleep
they made a shape around me,
a grandmother's embrace,
the shawl of family blood
that was their song for kinship.

There was a divining song
for finding the lost,
and a raining song
for the furrow and its seed,
one for the hoe
and the house it leaned against.

In those days, through song,
a woman could fly
to the mother of water
and fill her ladle
with cool springs of earth.

She could fly to the deer
and sing him down to the ground.

Song was the pathway where people met
and animals crossed.

Once, flying out of the false death of surgery,
I heard a grandmother singing for help.
She came close
as if down a road of screaming.

It was a song I never knew
lived inside the muscle
of this common life.

"Grandmother conscious-
ness opens a woman to
images of the past, to the
face of the future, and to
the symbolic pattern of a
woman's life."
—Naomi Ruth Lowinsky

It was the terror grandmother.
I'd heard of her
And when our fingers and voices met,
the song
of an older history came through
my mouth.

At death, they say
everything inside us opens,
mouth, heart, even the ear opens
and breath passes
through the memories
of loves and faces.
The embrace opens
and grandmothers pass
wearing sunlight
and thin rain,
walking out of fire
as flame
and smoke
leaving the ashes.

That's when rain begins,
and when the mouth of the river sings,
water flows from it
back to the cellular sea
and along the way
earth sprouts and blooms, the grandmothers
keep following the creation
that opens before them
as they sing.

Linda Hogan
The Book of Medicines

For more on grandmothers, see Naomi Ruth Lowinsky's "Mother of Mothers:
The Power of the Grandmother in the Female Psyche," in *To Be A Woman: The
Birth of the Conscious Feminine*, edited by Connie Zweig, Jeremy P. Tarcher,

1990. This excellent anthology contains many other thought-provoking selections, including one on female yang energy.

The axiom "as above, so below" works in negative as well as positive terms. Here bodily sickness is linked to pollution, to being out of harmony with nature and natural law.

Interdependence

According to a large number of medicine traditions, the cause of the spiritual disharmony that has led to disease is a violation of some taboo. If, for instance, one abuses plants, a disharmony is created in the psychesphere which must be played out in some way until harmony is restored. Certain illnesses can be traced to mistreatment of a plant community, and treatment can be undertaken to restore harmony within the patient and within the plant community that has suffered.

It is the loss of harmony, an inner-world imbalance, that reveals itself in physical or psychological ailment. It also plays itself out in social ailments, war, dictatorship, elitism, classism, sexism, and homophobia. This chain of action-consequence ensues because balance and harmony are fundamental laws of the cosmos. Disorder brings about a series of adjustments whose purpose is to reestablish harmony.

While the person or community suffering the ailment is often guilty of violating a spiritual law (taboo), just as often the entire state of disharmony nation- or world-wide works its way out in psychesphere attempts to regain its equilibrium. When a community is out of balance for whatever nearest reason, its most sensitive members are most likely to suffer in their bodies and minds. Thus oftentimes the most advanced medicine people suffer a number of compensatory ailments, often having to do with immune system dysfunctions such as rheumatoid arthritis, diabetes, cancer, lupus, chronic immunodeficiency syndrome (CIDS or CFIDS), and acquired immunodeficiency syndrome (AIDS). Their very sensitivity on psychic and spiritual levels makes them lightning rods, drawing

"I believe AIDS is only one symptom of a planetary illness. Earth herself has been pushed to the edge of collapse."
—Keith Gann,
person with AIDS

*"Eternity is not the
hereafter. . . . This is it.
If you don't get it here,
you won't get it anywhere."*
—Joseph Campbell

the disharmony to themselves and grounding it, rendering it far less harmful to the larger community.

The notion of taboo violation as causative of illness may seem strange to modern minds, but it is no stranger than avoidance of radioactivity, toxic chemicals, or disease-bearing environments of all sorts. If one violates any of these strictures, disease is likely to ensue. In a similar fashion, traditionals know that it is unwise and unsafe to show disrespect to spirits, do violence to other life forms, engage in selfish behavior, or to abuse oneself or others. The exact forms of the disrespectful actions may vary, but by and large they are clear. Pretty Shield wasn't allowed to throw things at the chickadees because doing so was disrespectful of them. Her disrespect could have had grave consequences, so her grandmother hastened to clarify her situation with the birds and to admonish Pretty Shield strongly against repetition of her behavior.

This argument is not a case of "blaming the victim"—an accusation easy to make and difficult to dispute when the politics of our situation is so dreadfully confused and diseased. We native people are certain that disease is a symptom of spiritual disorder, but whether that disorder is the fault of the sufferers is another matter entirely. Indeed, there are powerful arguments advanced in the Indian community that many of us suffer from a variety of immune system disorders and other chronic debilitations because we are earth's children, and as she endures monstrous patriarchal abuse, we suffer as well, sharing in her pain and disease and in that way ameliorating its devastation and bringing some respite to her.

Native people are also convinced that disharmonious actions toward plant and animal communities turn them against human health and life. They become poisonous, where, before being mistreated, they were nutritious and safe for human use and consumption. Another consequence of disharmony is that they quietly disappear.

When Nau'ts'ity and Ic'sts'ity decide to have children before the time is right, Grandmother Spider comes to them and notes their decision. Saying that they have done this though they knew it was the wrong time (harmony is connected to what time it is, always), she advises them that she is going away. Clearly they do not care to follow her guidance, so she leaves them to follow their own devices, an action that is appropriate to the circumstances and thus restores at least some harmony in the cosmos. By and large, Indian people follow this track, seeing that the other intelligences around them act in that manner. Rather than confrontation or war, they engage in passive resistance, and if that fails they simply remove themselves physically or socially from the scene.

Right now, countless numbers of animals and plant species are following Grandmother's trail. They are leaving us to our own devices, rendering the planet more and more bleak and empty. Traditionals say that so long as modern people continue in their depredations of the planet, spewing negative thinking, disharmony, and disrespect for all that lives, famine, drought, and the loss of vast numbers of life-forms will continue to accelerate. Even the air is leaving. Violating taboos is very dangerous to all life, and while most Americans can blithely avoid the immediate consequences of disrespect, the human community over most of the world pays a very high price for our violations.

Paula Gunn Allen
Grandmothers of the Light:
A Medicine Woman's Sourcebook

○ With the aspiration to help our planet overcome poison, pollution, and negativity, buy a tree and plant it. As you dig the hole, pray for our planet, specifically keeping in mind the ways in which mankind attempts to live outside of nature. Pray that all will wake up to the damage that has been done and turn their incredible technology toward solving our eco-crisis, so that all our relations can live in harmony. Every time you pass this tree of peace, make it a habit to repeat the prayer.

"All of life is relationship."
—Swami Rama

43

After she was raped in a Chicago alley, the author dealt with the assault and its aftermath though her Buddhist practice, which stresses taking responsibility for everything that occurs in one's life.

"*Spiritual growth is not attaining a permanent perfected state that is rid of negative emotions or experiences. It is, instead, finding out who we are. Awareness and acceptance of all parts of ourselves grants us freedom and enables us to understand and have compassion for others.*"
—Carla Brennan

Rape

On a rainy, summer afternoon a few years ago, just two days after *sesshin*,[1] I was pushed into my car in a Chicago alley and raped. My husband and I spent an unbearable afternoon looking for the violator, to no avail. The police said that they would not investigate the case unless I agreed to prosecute the rapist, and I said, "Yes, I will prosecute."

Morally and socially, rape is an abomination. But there is no easy answer to the question of what to do about it or even how to come to grips with the facts of rape, war, and other atrocities of society. The questions and solution to the problems of violence in our global society are complicated. In some Middle Eastern societies in olden times, it was simple: castrate the rapist. Could it be so simple in modern times? Is jailing a rapist going to bring about a more peaceful world?

I now see rape as clearly a violent/power act, not a sexual one. My overriding fear is the moment of force at the beginning of the experience, more than the actual sexual act. It seems odd to me that the sexual aspect is what most people seem to respond to. If I had just been mugged, they would not have been so concerned. But for me, the fear is the moment of violence more than the sex. Still, being raped is the ultimate act of intrusion and disrespect.

I wrote the following as an expression of how I coped personally and spiritually with an act of violence against myself. In that sense, the writing is no more about Buddhist attitude than a social position about rape. The amazing thing, which I have tried to capture in this writing, is that my Buddhist practice clearly gave me the staff with which to walk through this experience. I actually was able to convert this catastrophe into an effective tool for my personal and spiritual growth.

RAPE: 1

I will not take this out on myself
I will not kill myself
after the invasion of this man
I refuse to turn against myself
and as I refuse
the anger goes outward.
I pound the sofa, pound and pound.
I kick my legs like a mad child,
no, no, no!
I will not do what He wants
devastate myself
("Have I hurt your pride?" he asks, that son-of-a-bitch)
I pound the shit out of him on the sofa.
My hands turn into knives.
I realize
I am stabbing *him.*

Yet all the insidious ways come out.
I overeat to punish myself.
I eat the feelings down instead of letting them ooze out
    of my pores
out my fiery, demonic eyes.
Why is a woman too pretty
for demonic eyes?
It's not ladylike to pound and pound
and yet I will not eat myself alive.
He is the culprit
He should eat *himself* alive, *he* self-destruct.

Thank God, I at least screamed for "Help!" in the
    beginning.
That I tried to defend myself, at least a little.
It hurts the most, this lack of defense,
this passivity and compliance of surrendering
thinking he would kill me.

"Rape is more than a physical and emotional shock; it is a brush with death and, in this sense, a profound spiritual experience for the victim."
—Carolyn R. Shaffer

45

Something so strong in me mourns,
wishes I could have protected myself
fought for my rights.

Hurl these spitballs of fire out!
I am not a compliant little girl
I am a screaming redhead with demonic eyes
and Knives coming out of my hands
and muscles bulging out my arms
who pounds and pounds him
until his death.

RAPE: 2

He pushed me into the car from behind,
I was screaming,
I sat in the middle of a man and boy, surrounded
they kept pushing my head down so my chin touched
    my chest
"Don't you look at me. Don't you look at me or I'll kill
    you"
over and over his mantra.
They pulled at my rings.

I took off my diamond wedding ring and gave it to
    them.
It was raining out and it was afternoon,
but instead I was under the full moon sitting zazen in
    the country
as I was just two nights before.
I thought in a flash of a second
this story:

THE MOON CANNOT BE STOLEN

Ryokan, a Zen master, lived the simplest kind of life in a little hut at the foot of a mountain. One evening a thief visited the hut only to discover there was nothing in it to steal.

Ryokan returned and caught him. "You may have come a long way to visit me," he told the prowler, "and you should not return empty-handed. Please take my clothes as a gift." The thief was bewildered. He took the clothes and slunk away.

Ryokan sat naked watching the moon. "Poor fellow," he mused. "I wish I could give him this beautiful moon."[2]

To go towards the enemy, no resistance
to go towards and merge with the object and therefore
　　　to lose the subject
These things I had contemplated fully the week before
　　　at sesshin
at Catching the Moon Mountain Monastery.
In the middle of this horrible commotion,
still calm from sesshin,
I tried to go towards my enemy, even in rape.
To the ordinary mind, this is heresy,
This is the guilt that I didn't defend myself.
But who is there to defend?
only to become fully the situation
a woman amidst a violent crime,
where passivity and compliance gets her out alive.
I tried to stay in the center now
to realize the impermanence of the horrific situation
one breath after the next breath
through the tunnel of this trap
until I was out.
So I couldn't see what direction he left in,
He made me kiss the front seat,
I knew it was over,
my heart pounding.
to go towards my victim
my oppressor as victim
I felt so deeply his suffering.
to go towards my oppressor's suffering
to become suffering
to be, simply in the action of the crime without
　　　judgment

I came out alive.
Who can be ungrateful or not respectful
Even to senseless things,
Not to speak of man?
Even though he may be a fool,
Be warm and compassionate toward him.
If by any chance he should turn against me
and become a sworn enemy
and abuse and persecute me,
I should sincerely bow down with humble language
In reverent belief that He is
The merciful avatar of Buddha,
who used devices to emancipate me
From sinful Karma
That has been produced and accumulated
Upon myself
By my own egoistic delusions and attachment
Through the countless cycles of Kalpa.[3]

Now two weeks later there are many
supposed-to's of hate.
I do not have the ordinary world's reaction
I think of and understand for the first time
this story:

NANSEN CUTS THE CAT IN TWO

Nansen saw the monks of the eastern and western halls fighting over a cat. He seized the cat and told the monks: "If any of you say a good word you can save the cat." No one answered. So Nansen boldly cut the cat in two pieces.

That evening Joshu returned and Nansen told him about this. Joshu removed his sandals and, placing them on his head, walked out. Nansen said: "If you had been there, you could have saved the cat."

Commentary:

Had Joshu been there,
He would have enforced the edict oppositely,

Joshu snatches the sword
and Nansen begs for his life.[4]

I did not know then that this
violator
would turn the world around
that the rapist would set my mind free.

    or

that My Anger would kill him
pounding and stabbing
my empty couch
at midnight.

Everything is in reverse.
I see in one of Frida Kahlo's paintings
that the roots of a tree are coming out of a skeleton
    buried in its soil
death fertilizing life
as this rape nourishes my understanding
and suffering teaches our souls.

But this is so upside-down to ordinary mind.
How dare I say, in ordinary mind,
the rape is a gift
and yet Zap! the hit of *kyosaku*
I understand
something.

I had been saying all winter
that the structure of my ego-building
had finally collapsed
and it was laying
in ruin and rubble
in the floor of my pelvis.
Head, shoulders, ribcage, spine, collapsed in a pile.
and now I say,

"If we can contain the conflict of the opposites—what our small egos want as opposed to what the Self or Destiny has ordained—if we can hold at the center, then we learn to think with the heart."
—Marion Woodman

Zap,
like a vacuum cleaner,
the rape sucking all the debris out
and spinning it with great force into the universe
clean and empty inside
Where is the person who got raped?

RAPE: 3

Seven weeks later. Today I didn't go to the studio to get the equipment. I realized that it was the repeat of the situation of the rape: parking the car in the alley, running up to get something and then the fear of that moment of getting pushed into the car. I decided to wait until someone could help me. I didn't like that I was still afraid. I don't talk about it much anymore but sometimes it peeps out of me. "Did you know that I still think about it every day, often many times a day?" I ask a friend. Sometimes when I'm alone, I'll just cry and then realize this sadness and vulnerability is the shock wave. I still constantly look around me in every direction when I'm on the city streets, especially at night. When I go to the zendo in the dark of the early morning, I look in every doorway and check the backseat of the car. I dream of fending off attackers, and everywhere I go for support, there is none. Sometimes when I'm talking to myself, this light blue, very soft voice will come up and tell me of her fears, weaknesses, and her needs for lots and lots of comfort. I know I've never learned to nurture myself enough. I have kept up my obligations and worldly duties, but, inside, I have been totally rearranged.

This rearrangement I've been calling a realization, which it is. Though I cannot pinpoint exactly what has changed in me, I know that I am different. I think the greatest realization of the whole experience was to see my spiritual practice in action. It succeeded in stabilizing me through this traumatic experience. "Spiritual Stability," my teacher calls it. I saw that the years of practice are built into my life; that I could not internally collapse, which would lead, perhaps, into an extended depression. Doing what I always do on a daily basis, I tried to maintain the most wholesome attitude of mind I could. There is nowhere to go. My friend writes me, "I wonder what the experience of your rapist was. It reminds me of when the Sixth Patriarch was pursued by his enemy, and he simply gave over the robe and bowl. The enemy is deeply moved by such resignation." But that state of mind has to exist before the attack, not intellectually, but *really*.

I felt for the first time a true sensibility of the Three Treasures: the Buddha, the Dharma, and the Sangha. Each in its own way made a web of support I could fall into like a net under a tightrope walker. I really felt that I took refuge in the Buddha, Dharma, Sangha, for I certainly could not walk through that experience alone. In many ways, my ordinary mind could not support the fact of rape. I was unwired. Only the Buddha realm as expressed by the Dharma could give me an attitude of mind that could embrace rape, and only through the love of the Sangha could I have the strength, will, love, and comfort to shed my ego and walk my path through this experience. To take refuge is "to retreat into a shelter that is safe from danger," and, because of a continuous practice, I did have access to the Triple Treasure. I surprised myself. I did act according to the belief that *every* experience is a powerful teacher, and I did transform, combust, move the energies of this negative experience.

Judith Ragir
The Path of Compassion

"There's often a big temptation for persons on the spiritual way to leave their ordinary life behind and seek a greater involvement in 'practice.' But they have to realize that our practice is always done right where we are."
—Joan Rieck, Joun Roshi

AUTHOR'S NOTES

1. *Sesshin*: a seven-day Zen meditation retreat.
2. Paul Reps, *Zen Flesh Zen Bones*, Charles E. Tuttle Co., 1957, p. 27.
3. Excerpted from the Bodhisattva's vow by Torei Zenji, from *Sutra Book for Dai Bosatsu Zendo Kongo-ji and the New York Zendo Shobo-ji*, Zen Studies Society, 1976.
4. *ibid.*, p. 128.

○ Say a prayer for everyone who has ever been raped, ask that their pain, humiliation, and suffering be lessened.

Say another prayer for their rapists.

_____

This exercise is particularly effective for those who have been sexually abused or assaulted. It is also healing for every women who has grown up in a patriarchal society in which women's sexuality is denigrated. It is to be read slowly to a friend or silently to oneself.

Opening the Heart of the Womb

In a safe, quiet space find a comfortable place to sit and settle in there as you let your awareness begin to come to the level of sensation in this body.

Just feel what sits here.

Feel the multiple sensations arising and dissolving in the body, tinglings here and there.

Feelings of warmth or coolness.

Feelings perhaps of the pressure of the buttocks on the cushion on which you sit.

Let awareness come to the multiple shimmerings and movements of the field of sensation we call the body.

And begin to direct the awareness toward the area where the legs meet.

Gradually awareness gently gathers there at the inner thigh, at the place where the upper leg meets the body.

Very gently now, awareness receiving sensation arising at this very tender, very powerful area of life, of birth, of being.

Just receiving very tenderly whatever sensations are generated there and noticing too whatever feelings, emotions arise in the approach toward this sacred area.

Allow this soft awareness to receive the sensations at the labia. Meet each moment of sensation with a mercy and care that pours from the heart into the body.

Feel the sacred place of power experienced as sensation floating in merciful awareness, in a tenderness, absorbing moment to moment each sensation arising.

Allow awareness to gather as it will without the least sense of urgency. Allow a merciful exploration of this area.

Feel the ruffled fringe of flesh that protects this tender area. Just allowing awareness to gather there gently with a healing mercy, receiving sensation moment to moment in a deepening softness and self-care.

Tenderly moving through the shadows and light into the area of the vulva.

Feel the muscles there as strength, their power, their wholeness.

Notice the multiple sensations that arise as awareness receives the vagina. Let them float in a healing mercy that receives the moment in loving kindness and a new strength.

Feel the light of awareness filling the holy body of the vagina.

Gently, gently allowing the light of your mercy to illuminate this moist, merciful cradle of life, of love, of healing.

Touching so tenderly the subtle wrinkles, as well as the powerful muscles of the vagina.

Let the vagina fill with your kind light, a soft glow brightening moment to moment with each sensation received there. The healing melting away whatever pain, whatever fear may reside there.

Allowing awareness to soften and receive life as it fills the body. Allowing mercy to merge with the sensations that arise in the vagina.

A merciful awareness moving so tenderly into the cervix and muscles. The tissues softening to receive this healing mercy, this light expanding into the great dome of the womb.

The womb filling with golden light, with infinite mercy and compassion for itself.

The light illuminating the cave of life, the sacred womb.

Feel its spaciousness, its openness, its homeness.

Let awareness receive the womb with mercy and loving kindness for yourself, for this tender heart.

Let your womb fill gradually with this golden light shining from your mercy, lighting and lightening this heart of life and being.

Let the heart of the womb open to receive its own great nature once again, to come home to itself, to make room for you in this great womb heart.

Let the soft light of that heart shine there, opening the womb of mercy, of forgiveness, of compassion for yourself.

Letting the womb soften, let its heart open.

Letting it just be at last in loving kindness, in a gentle healing

"We will not live as victims. We must dig deeply into the roots of our experience, extract all such feelings, and throw them into the face of the patriarchy, replacing them with our strength and power, thereby entering a new dimension of life—leaving all rapists behind with no victims to be found."
—Margo Adair

53

mercy.

And sense the fallopian tubes extending like branches from this sacred tree of life. The living trunk of the vagina extending through the cervix, spreading into the canopy of the womb, its branches like arms embracing itself.

Feel the loving kindness, slowly expanding in the womb, flow into the fallopian channels through which all life has passed.

Allow the light of the womb to move gradually into each of the great branches on the tree of life.

Allow the light of this great heart to bring mercy to itself, to heal itself in loving kindness, to allow itself its own embrace, its own fulfillment, its own completion.

Feel the warm golden light, flowing through the branches of the tree, entering as light into the ovaries. Shimmering in each seed within.

Feel the whole tree of light, of life, filled with its own healing power. Filled with tender mercy.

Feel the feathery ends of the fallopian tubes and the shining fruit at the end of each branch. The whole womb healing into a new mercy and self-kindness, filling with tender care.

Let the womb fill with love for itself and for all sentient beings everywhere.

As the heart gradually sinks into the womb, the upper heart and the lower heart merge to form the shared heart.

The upper heart and lower heart forming a single shimmering star, the shared heart of being, the heart of completion.

Let it be. Let the healing dissolve whatever pain remains in a new joy, in a new sense of our own great power to heal and to be at last.

Let the heart sink into the womb receiving itself in wholeness and mercy and joy.

As the light of healing suffuses the womb, receiving moment to moment each sensation and feeling in a profound gratitude for healing, sense all the other women who at this very moment also long to be free of the pains of the past. And let the light from the heart of the womb radiate out into the world, sharing this healing with all who now wish so to be free of these same pains and fears.

Let the light from the heart of your womb flood this world of pain and confusion, sharing this healing with all other beings.

As the light in your womb intensifies let it expand out to all the other wombs, all the other women everywhere who share this same path of healing, who too at this moment take birth anew.

Share the healing with all who reach out for completion.

Allow the light to be.

May we all be free of a past of pain and confusion.

May we let our wombs, our hearts, be filled with their own natural light.

May we be whole unto ourselves.

May we be at peace.

May all beings be free from suffering.

May all beings know the joy, the healing, of their true luminescent nature.

May we all meet in mercy, in non-injury, in compassion.

May we be healed.

May we be at peace.

May all beings be free.

May we all be free.

> Stephen Levine
> *Guided Meditations, Explorations and Healings*

"Our very selfish notion, to heal ourselves, to tend to our own wounds, may turn out to be the most radical notion of all, one that heals not only ourselves but eventually all, and thus transforms the social order absolutely."
—Susan Griffin

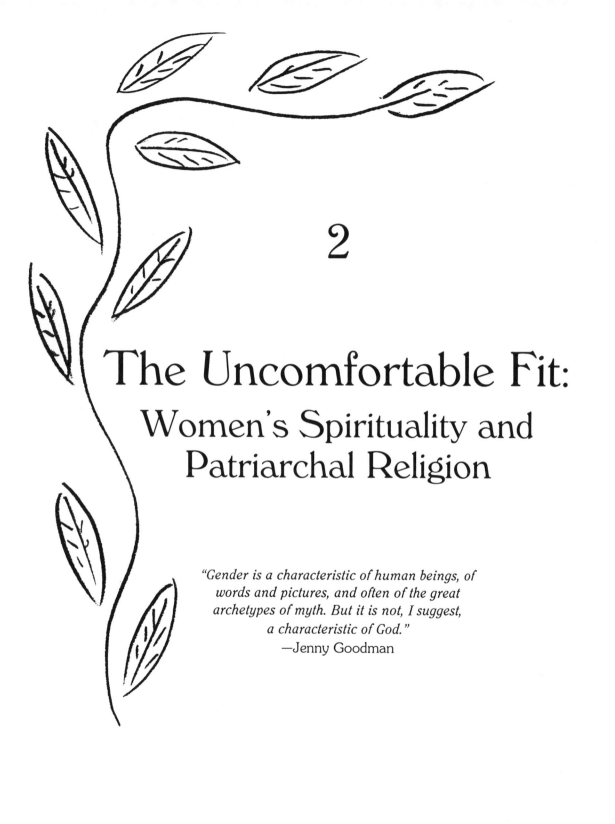

2

The Uncomfortable Fit:
Women's Spirituality and Patriarchal Religion

*"Gender is a characteristic of human beings, of
words and pictures, and often of the great
archetypes of myth. But it is not, I suggest,
a characteristic of God."*
—Jenny Goodman

As women, we are often led away from a feeling of spiritual connected-ness and into frustration, shame, or anger when we dwell on the issues that result from the patriarchal structure of our churches, temples, and medita-tion halls. The situation begins with a pervasive lack of representation of women and the feminine in almost every aspect of traditional religions, supported and reinforced by masculine God-language in the Judeo-Chris-tian scripture and liturgies, language which results in a host of ideas that patriarchy claims to be "natural." The Christian vision of a god "out there" rather than within produces negative attitudes toward embodiment in general and female sexuality in particular—attitudes that have far-reaching consequences both personally and culturally. A basic inequality of women and denigration of the feminine in established religions also leads to disputes concerning the ordination of women as priests, preachers, and rabbis; homophobia; sexual abuse in religious communities; and to the idea that as man serves his god, so woman should submit to her man. These issues—and this is just the short list—often create a conscious or unconscious barrier between women and the church or women and their indwelling spirit.

Upstream of all these issues—transcendence versus embodiment, male superiority versus female inferiority—lies the larger problem of dualism, so pervasive in our culture that it seems to disappear into unquestioned acceptance. In addition to the basic problem of dualism—the positing of everything in terms of polar opposites—we tend to choose one side against the other. For instance, male/female has become aligned in our culture with such other polarized concepts as mind/body, superior/inferior. This type of black-and-white thinking becomes automatic, leaving out the complexity of individuals and the reality of shifting, changing situations. Dualism can be transcended through meditation, not through argument or analysis. If we work with the fundamental duality of self and other in deep meditation and contemplation, if we can learn to unify the subject that perceives with the objectified world, then other polarities lose their potency. To become conscious of our tendency toward dualism forms the first step in overcoming it.

Good Question

Dear God, are boys betters than girls? I know you are one but try to be fair.

Children's Letters to God
Compiled by Eric Marshall and Stuart Hample

○ What other questions could we ask God concerning gender? Try to be fair.

_____

"She [Lilith] represents to us our innermost herstory. In reclaiming Her, we women throw off and pour away forever the poison about ourselves, our so-called inferiority, our evil inner selves, our guilt. On reclaiming Lilith we reclaim the breath of life that emerges as we give birth to our children, to our works of all kind; we reclaim our wisdom, our knowledge, our power, our autonomy."
—Astrophel P. Long

Long before the goddess became part of feminist conscious-ness, the women's movement celebrated Lilith, whose story is found in biblical Apocrypha. Lilith, the first wife of Adam and the original wild woman, rejected her second-class status sym-bolized by the "missionary position," and disappeared into the Void to be replaced by the submissive (but manipulative) Eve. Under patriarchal interpretation, Lilith became a demon who haunted children and pregnant women, thus inverting the "good mother" role. Unlike the Hindu goddess Kali, who incorporates both creation and destruction, Lilith became a dark destroyer in Judaism and "Queen of the Witches" in Christian tradition. Recent scholarship relates Lilith to goddess worship, to "wind" or "breath" or "spirit," thus connecting her to the African goddess Oya as well as to the "space" aspect of such Eastern goddesses as Kwan Yin and the Tibetan feminine spirits known as dakinis. Feminist psychological interpretation sees Lilith as "the breath of life," the symbol of women's wisdom and power which has become a source of evil under patriarchy: in short, a fitting patron saint for the women's movement.

LILITH

Lilith glared at God
"I'll not go back,"
She hissed at him—
"Adam is such a bore."

"That was my plan
You willful wench.
Lie down—
I'll tell you more."

Anon

Reclaim Lilith by becoming conscious of her energy in your life. Begin by reading *Women Who Run With the Wolves: Myths and Stories of the Wild Woman Archetype*, by Clarissa Pinkola Estes, Ballentine, 1992.

The idea of the Shekhinah, derived from the Hebrew word for "to dwell," is used to denote the presence of God in a particular place—the temple of Solomon at Jerusalem, for instance—or even a resting place or refuge for humans. Although the Hebrew word is feminine in gender, it is not used in mainstream Talmudic and rabbinical thought to denote a female essence or element within God, but has rather become synonymous with God's presence or glory. In the mystical tradition of Judaism known as Kabbalah, whose literature began in the first four centuries of our era and has ties with earlier goddess worship as well as affinities to Gnosis beliefs, Shekhinah became more and more personified as both divine and female. She appears on the Tree of Life, an important representation of Kabbalahistic thought, and as "the community of Israel." Although she is spoken of as "Queen, Daughter,

"On the one hand, women can choose to accept our absence from Sinai, in which case we allow the male text to define us and our relationship to the tradition. On the other hand, we can stand on the ground of our experience, on the certainty of our membership in our own people. To do this, however, is to be forced to remember and recreate its history. It is to move from anger at the tradition, through anger to empowerment. It is to begin the journey toward the creation of a feminist Judaism."
—Judith Plaskow

and Bride" of God, Jewish women themselves were not allowed to study the Kabbalah and were thus cut off from this rich heritage. The idea of Shekhinah remains full of contradictions, as well as a source of inspiration. Two different views of Shekhinah follow. The first uses the spontaneously arisen term Shekhinah and the dream it inspired as a basis for reclaiming woman's heritage within Judaism. The second is less taken with the term and the way Shekhinah has been traditionally represented.

"The task, therefore, involves not so much rediscovering new sources as rereading the available sources in a different key. The goal is an increase in 'historical imagination.'"
—Elisabeth Schussler Fiorenza

Shekhinah: I

The Question That Wouldn't Go Away

Shekhinah. Shekhinah. The word simply popped into my mind like an uninvited guest and wouldn't go away. At times it seemed to disappear, but then it would come again, quietly, this strange word—Shekhinah. It seemed to be waiting patiently for me to pay attention to it. After hearing it in my mind for three days I tried saying it out loud. "Shekhinah." It had an interesting sound. And when I said it, I felt a soft tug somewhere deep inside.

I began to ask my friends if they knew what it meant. It sounded as if it could be Hebrew, but although I knew some Hebrew, it was not familiar to me. When my husband and friends were unable to help, I tried the library in our small town but found no answer there either. Shekhinah. Shekhinah. It was becoming more insistent now, demanding my attention.

Still puzzling over what it could mean, I was sitting in my bedroom one morning when my friend Joan hurried through the door. She strode across the room and thrust a book into my hands.

"Let's try this," she said. I glanced down at the blue cover on which the word *Kabbalah* was written, and turned to the index. Running my finger quickly down the S column, I read: "Shekhinah: the feminine face of God."

The words sent shock waves rippling down my spine and goose flesh bristling on my bare arms because I realized at once that the Shekhinah was not an uninvited guest at all. She had been announced to me with great ceremony in a powerful dream a full month earlier.

In the dream, I happily soar high above the clouds on a great golden dragon until I wonder, "Is this all there is?" The dragon immediately descends to earth, alighting at the side of a jewel-like temple on a large body of water. I want to enter the temple, but I'm afraid to go in alone. I turn back to the dragon, hoping it will come and protect me. But this temple is human-sized and the dragon will not fit through the door.

I begin to climb the stairs to the entrance anyway, and now I see a ferocious temple guardian with bulging eyes looming menacingly in the doorway. Black dogs snarl on either side of him. With uncharacteristic bravery I continue walking, and as I stride through the door the guardian and his dogs evaporate as if made of fog.

Once I'm inside the doorway, an old man with long robes and a white beard emerges from an inner hallway to greet me. Without actually speaking, he lets me know that his name is Melchizedek. He is wearing a handsome dagger with a handle of turquoise and jade, and as soon as I notice this he presents me with a matching dagger, indicating that I am to wear it on my right side. Then he motions me ahead of him. It is clear that he expects me to lead the way.

I step into a long hallway with a high ceiling and red tiles on the floor. Walking slowly, we eventually come to a pair of polished wooden doors at the end of the corridor. I open them silently and lead the way into a large, empty room. A plain wooden stage is set against the far wall. At the back of the stage is a built-in cabinet. I approach the cabinet and pull open the doors.

I am dumbfounded by what I see. Rolled onto finely carved wooden poles is the most sacred object in Judaism, the Torah. I learned as a child that the Torah contains the five books of Moses written on parchment by an Orthodox scribe, and that if even one letter has been written incorrectly, the Torah cannot be used. I have never actually seen a Torah close up or held one, since these privileges were permitted only to men when I was growing up. But now I lift this Torah carefully out of its cabinet and cradle it to me tenderly as if it were a baby.

Then I notice something unusual. Instead of a mantle of velvet covering the scrolls, or a simple ribbon holding them closed, the

"Judaism can have no pretense to being a universal religion, Jewish culture cannot think of itself as a truly human culture, until they have opened themselves to, and faced the challenge of, the individual and communal self-understanding of women as women. Both Judaism and Jewish culture will, sooner or later, have to come to terms with the full weight and complexity presented by the lives of women—our particularity, our differences, the specificities of our experience with each other, with God, and with men. None of that can be articulated for us, understood for us, judged for us, defined for us, or explained to us, by men."
—Shelia Shulman

Torah has been sealed shut by a dark round blot of red wax. I look at Melchizedek. "This is a very special Torah," he says. Pulling out his dagger, he breaks the seal and rolls open the scrolls. They are absolutely blank. "The Torah is empty," he says, "because what you need to know now is not written in any book. You already contain that knowledge. It is to be unfolded from within you."

"What is this Torah for?" I ask.

My question seems to set in motion the next sequence of events. Without speaking Melchizedek lifts the Torah and lightly places it inside my body, from my shoulders to my knees. I accept this gratefully, feeling my body as a sacred vessel.

At once, a great commotion breaks out behind us. Spinning around, I see that the room is now filled with long-bearded patriarchs wearing black coats and trousers. They're holding hands, laughing, singing and dancing jubilantly around the room. They pull me into their celebration. As I dance I seem to see Moses, King David and King Solomon, and Abraham, Isaac, and Jacob. They, too, are dressed in black coats and trousers, dancing with such heartfelt abandonment that I catch their joy and am filled with it. Ecstatically we whirl round and round the room, laughing.

Finally the dancing stops and I ask, "What is this all about?" Melchizedek answers, "We are celebrating because you, a woman, have consented to accept full spiritual responsibility in your life. This is your initiation as one who will serve the planet."

As I wonder what this means, he continues, "And you are not the only one. Many, many women are coming forward now to lead the way."

"But who will be our teachers?" I protest.

"You will be teachers for each other. You will come together in circles and speak your truth to each other. The time has come for women to accept their spiritual responsibility for our planet."

"Will you help us?" I ask the assembled patriarchs.

"We are your brothers," they answer, and with that the entire room is flooded with an energy of indescribable kindness. I am absolutely confident in this moment that they are our brothers. I feel their love without any question. They say then, "We have initiated you and we give you our wholehearted blessings. But we no longer know the way. Our ways do not work anymore. You women must find a new way."

> Sherry Ruth Anderson and Patricia Hopkins
> *The Feminine Face of God:*

———————————————

Although Marcia Falk agrees below that "you women must find a new way," she does not see Shekhinah as being especially helpful in this process. Her article goes on to develop methods by which the feminine can be incorporated into the content and language of Jewish blessings.

"Perhaps Jewish women have been reluctant or ill-equipped to create a Jewish feminist theology, not out of insensitivity to personal experience or ignorance of Jewish tradition but out of their awareness of the potentially irreconcilable conflict between the two."
—Ellen M. Umansky

Shekhinah: II

The search for theological imagery is a journey whose destinations are rarely apparent at the outset. As many feminists have discovered, it is not merely a matter of changing male images to seemingly equivalent female ones: the relatively simple (though still courageous) act of "feminizing" the male God has proved, to many of us, to be inadequate and often absurd. For a feminized patriarchal image is still patriarchal, though now in transvestite masquerade. The process has been instructive, however, in clarifying our theological concerns: in translating the king into a queen, for example, we realize that images of domination are not what we wish to embrace. We find instead that our search for what is authoritative leads us to explore more deeply what is just, and that the results of these explorations are not well represented by images of a monarch, either female or male.

And so we find we must create new images to convey our visions, and to do so we must be patient (though not passive), for images will not be called into being by sheer acts of will alone. Rather we learn what artists know well: that authentic images arise from our unconscious as gifts; that out of our living, from our whole, engaged

65

"Alone, alone I remained,
and the Shekhinah,
even she
Her broken right wing on
my head, trembling.
My heart knew hers: she
feared for me
For her son, her only one."
—H. N. Bialik

selves, with the support of our communities, the images that serve us will emerge. We must trust the journey.

There are no shortcuts. The few female images already available in the tradition do not in themselves provide an adequate solution. The much-touted *Shekhinah*, used in recent times to placate uppity Jewish women (as in, "The tradition *has* a feminine image of God, what more do you want?"), will not suffice. The *Shekhinah* was not originally a female image; it did not become so until Kaballistic times. And when it became explicitly associated with the female, it did not empower women, especially not in Kabbalistic thought, where male and female were hierarchically polarized, nor has the *Shekhinah* fared much better in our century. I, for one, cannot think of the *Shekhinah* without recalling her burning tears as they fell on the young poet Hayyim Nahman Bialik's *Gemara* page. In Bialik's poem *L'vadi*, "Alone," the *Shekhinah* was a pitiful mama bird with a broken wing, invoked to portray the frailty of Jewish tradition in the poet's time. "Alone, alone," was the *Shekhinah*'s cry, for all had abandoned her.

Not that tears aren't valid. Not that I want my images of divinity to exclude solitude and suffering; these are important aspects of our experience that need expression in our theology. But should images of isolation and vulnerability alone be identified as the fundamental representation of God's "female side"? Do we wish to divide experience along these classically sexist lines? Sad as it is, I cannot help but feel that, far from redeeming women, the image of the *Shekhinah* has, until now, only supported the male-supported vision. In Jewish tradition, the *Shekhinah* has never been on equal footing with the mighty *Kadosh Barukh Hu*, the "Holy-One-Blessed-Be-He," her creator, her master, her groom, the ultimate reality of which she was only an emanation. And while I like the name itself—*Shekhinah*, from the Hebrew root meaning "to dwell"—I would like to see in-dwelling, or immanence, portrayed in ways that are not secondary to transcendence. So too, I would like to see autonomous female images, not ones that imply the essential otherness of women. *In the name of monotheism*, for the sake of an inclusive unity, I would like to see our God-talk articulate mutually supportive relationships between female and male, between immanence and transcendence, between our lives and the rest of life on the planet. In the end, it comes down to this: what I would like to see, I must help bring into being.

>Marcia Falk
>"Notes on Composing New Blessings"
>in *Weaving the Visions*

A good new book on the subject is *The Telling*, by E. M. Broner, HarperSanFrancisco, 1993. It's the story of how a group of Jewish feminists, Gloria Steinem and Bella Abzug among them, created a more inclusive Passover ceremony. Includes "The Women's Haggadah."

Although writer Rachel Altman's parents survived the Nazi death camps in Poland, many of her other relatives died in the Holocaust.

Procession of Women

In Jewish life women are the guardians of tradition—family, values, morality. In the old country, men sat for hours discoursing and arguing the Talmud, the book in which the law is encoded. But it fell to the women to insist that people behave as they should—as a *mensch*, a human being, should. The rituals of Jewish life and religious practice are not reserved for the synagogue; built into the liturgy are prayers to be spoken on awakening, prayers to be said when washing the hands, when seeing a rainbow, when eating a meal—prayers to be recited in the midst of life. In its purest form, Judaism brings us into an atmosphere of appreciation and aware-ness of every moment of life as sacred. At the center of Jewish life is the home, and at the center of the home is the woman.

At the same time, Judaism has discriminated against women: in Jewish mythology and tradition, women are given a clearly second-

"We open the pages of our sacred texts and we read mostly about the lives of men. The prophet is a woman who breaks the silence of history by speaking women's names into the void."
—Rabbi Lynn Gottlieb

"Thus in all of the women's descriptions, identity is defined in a context of relationship and judged by a standard of responsibility and care. Similarly, morality is seen by these women as arising from the experience of connection and conceived as a problem of inclusion rather than one of balancing claims."
—Carol Gilligan

rate status and until recently, we have been excluded from the study of Talmud and the rabbinate.

In thinking about the women in my family—in allowing myself to feel a longing to be part of their world—I recognize a certain irony. I bemoan the loss of my family [in the holocaust], of the Jewish world that existed in Eastern Europe before the war, with a grief that will never be assuaged. However, as a modern woman, I acknowledge that the Eastern European *shtetl* is not a world in which I would choose to live.

How different my grandmothers' lives were from mine! How can I—a woman who is educated and has explored options; a woman whose marriage was not arranged; a woman with rights, living in a time when a woman can choose to actively confront discrimination, can even become a rabbi—pretend to know them, these women who sat separate from men in the *shul*, who walked down narrow streets and bargained with shopkeepers, who raced home to complete the preparations for the Sabbath before the sun went down, who kept the children quiet so their husbands' studies would not be disturbed? How can I pretend to know my grandmother Miryam, who was pregnant for thirteen years of her life, who lived at the mercy of an illness that could not be named (though today it could probably easily be treated), whose life revolved around stretching a tiny piece of meat to provide food for fifteen people, while her husband sat at the kitchen table and prayed?

When I visited Israel in 1971, my aunt Chava invited me for Shabbat dinner. She made a point of telling me that she was not an observant Jew, that the dinner would be a secular celebration. At sundown, as is traditional, she lit the candles, her head covered with a shawl, her hands covering her face as she recited the prayer. Afterward, she turned to me sheepishly and said, "Since the war, I no longer believe in God. Every Friday night I light the candles and say the blessing over them, but I do not do it for God. I do it for the memory of my mother."

Like Chava, I am not an observant Jew, but I light candles on Friday night to usher in the Sabbath. I enjoy the peace that the ritual brings to my household, and I appreciate this weekly reminder to be grateful for the beauty of the creation. Also, it is a way of knowing them—the women of my family, the mothers and grandmothers and aunts and daughters who, in the midst of hunger, illness, war, persecution, brought light to the darkness. I visualize a procession of them, a line reaching back in time and forward from this moment. Covering my head with a scarf, circling my hands over the flames three times and reciting the blessing. I join this procession of women, welcoming their spirit into my life, into my daughter's life.

Rachel Altman
"Fragments of a Broken Past" in
Different Voices: Women of the Holocaust

Jewish women are actively trying to reclaim their religious roots, attempting to reshape Jewish memory and history so that the female and the feminine will be included in the liturgies, blessings, and *midrash* (storytelling). In addition, there are several different versions of a feminist Haggadah in circulation, and a large number of "moon groups": women who celebrate the new-moon holiday Rosh Hodesh, as a female ritual. Good resources are:

Pinina Adleman, *Miriam's Well: Rituals for Jewish Women Around the Year*, Biblio Press, 1986.

Karen Armstrong, *A History of God: The 4,000-Year Quest of Judaism, Christianity, and Islam*, Knopf, 1993.

Evelyn Torten Beck, ed., *Nice Jewish Girls: A Lesbian Anthology*, The Crossing Press, 1984.

Ellen Bernstein, *Let the Earth Teach You Torah: A Guide to Teaching Jewish Ecological Wisdom*, Shomrei Adamah, 1992.

Rachel Biale, *Women and Jewish Law: An Exploration of Women's Issues in Halakhic Sources*, Schocken Books, 1984.

Phyllis Bird, "Images of Women in the Old Testament," in *Religion and Sexism: Images of Woman in the Jewish and Christian Traditions*, edited by Rosemary Reuther, Simon and Schuster, 1974.

Esther Broner, "Honor and Ceremony in Women's Rituals," in *The Politics of Women's Spirituality: Essays on the Rise of Spiritual Power Within the Feminist Movement*, edited by Charlene Spretnak, Doubleday, Anchor Press, 1982.

Elly Bulkin, Minnie Bruce Pratt, and Barbara Smith, *Yours in Struggle*, Long Haul Press, 1984.

Marcia Falk, "Notes on Composing New Blessings," in Judith Plaskow and Carol P. Christ, *Weaving the Visions: New Patterns in Feminist Spirituality*, HarperSanFrancisco, 1989.

Elisabeth Schussler Fiorenza, *In Memory of Her: A Feminist Reconstruction of Christian Origins*, The Crossroad Publishing Company, 1983.

Rela M. Geffen, ed., *Celebration & Renewal: Rites of Passage in Judaism*, Jewish Publication Society, 1993.

Rabbi Lynn Gottlieb, "Prophecy and Spirituality: The Voice of Prophet Woman," in *The Spiral Path:* Explorations in Women's Spirituality, edited by Theresa King, Yes International Publishers, 1992.

Lesley Hazelton, *Israeli Women: The Reality Behind the Myths*, Simon and Schuster, 1977.

Susannah Heschel, ed., *On Being a Jewish Feminist*, Schocken Books, 1983.

Naomi Janowitz and Maggie Wenig, "Sabbath Prayers for Women," in *Womanspirit Rising*, edited by Carol P. Christ and Judith Plaskow, Harper & Row, 1979.

Melanie Kaye/Kantrowitz and Irena Klepfisz, eds., *The Tribe of Dina: A Jewish Women's Anthology*, Beacon Press, 1989.

Elizabeth Koltun, ed., *The Jewish Woman: New Perspectives*, Schocken Books, 1976.

Lilith (magazine), Lilith Publications, 250 West 57th Street, New York, NY 10019.

Raphael Patai, *The Hebrew Goddess*, New York, KTAV Publishing House, 1967.

Alix Pirani, *The Absent Mother: Restoring the Goddess to Judaism and Christianity*, Mandala, 1991.

Judith Plaskow, "Jewish Memory from a Feminist Perspective," in Judith Plaskow and Carol P. Christ, *Weaving the Visions: New Patterns in Feminist Spirituality*, HarperSan Francisco, 1989.

Judith Plaskow, *Standing Again at Sinai*, HarperSanFrancisco, 1991.

Susan Weidman Schneider, *Jewish and Female: Choices and Changes in Our Lives Today*, Simon and Schuster, 1984.

Tikkun (magazine), 5100 Leona Street, Oakland, CA 94619-3022.

Judith Romney Wegner, *Chattel or Person? The Status of Women in Mishnah*, Oxford University Press, 1988.

Ellen M. Umansky, "Creating a Jewish Feminist Theology: Possibilities and Problems," *Anima* 10, Spring, 1984.

This nineteenth-century feminist leader felt that the patri-archal church, the state that denied women the vote, the family that put the father at the head, and the economic system that did not pay the woman equally for her work must all be attacked simultaneously in order achieve female liberation. She was one of the first to see the ways in which society used religious beliefs about women to keep them subjugated. To the horror of many of her colleagues, in 1895 she wrote a feminist criticism of the scriptures, published as The Woman's Bible.

"Every time you don't follow your inner guidance, you feel a loss of energy, loss of power, a sense of spiritual deadness."
—Shakti Gawain

Personal Accountability to God

Let woman live as she should. Let her feel her accountability to her maker. Let her know that her spirit is fitted for as high a sphere as a man's, and that her soul requires food as pure and exalted as his. Let her live *first* for God, and she will not make imperfect man an object of reverence and awe. Teach her responsibility as a being of conscience and reason, that all earthly support is weak and unstable, that her only safe dependence is the arm of omnipotence, and that true happiness springs from duty accomplished. Thus will she learn the lesson of individual responsibility for time and eternity, that neither father, husband, brother, or son, however willing they may be, can discharge her high duties of life, or stand in her stead when called into the presence of the great Searcher of Hearts at the last day.

Elizabeth Cady Stanton
Declaration of Women's Rights
Seneca Falls, 1848

Almost a hundred years later, editors Carol A. Newsom and Sharon H. Ringe have completed *The Women's Bible Commentary*, John Knox Press, 1993, which covers the Old and New Testaments, plus the Apocrypha. For additional biblical scholarship from women see: Elisabeth Schussler Fiorenza's *Bread Not Stone: The Challenge of Feminist Biblical Interpretation*, Beacon, 1984; *In Memory of Her: A Feminist Theological Reconstruction*, The Crossroad Publishing Company, 1983; Rose Kraemer's *Her Share of the Blessings*, Oxford University Press, 1992; Carol Meyers's *Discovering Eve: Ancient*

Israelite Women in Context, Oxford University Press, 1991; and Phyllis Trible's *Texts of Terror: Literary Feminist Readings of Biblical Narratives*, Augsburg Fortress, 1984.

"Does belief in the Bible as God's revelation presume that it instructs women to reiterate in their current spiritual life the same socio-religious values that structured Semitic societies?"
—Justin O'Brien

The work of contemporary feminists who wish to remain connected to their religious roots is to separate the essence of their traditions from the patriarchal systems that have grown up around them—not an easy task. But just as it is the duty of traditional religions to overcome their patriarchal oppression of women, it is the current task of feminists to develop compassion.

Religion and Contemporary Feminist Consciousness

If religion centers in Mystery, and Mystery transcends sex (Paul's "in Christ there is neither male nor female" is a representative traditional line), then religious experience should transcend sex. In other words, the basal line in religion should be whether the person is open or closed, willing or unwilling to participate in Mystery. Nothing sexual draws this line. The radical honesty and love for which Mystery calls circumvent chromosomal differences. Yet it is also true that religious experience comes to persons who are sexed, and that sex colors its expressions. Naturally, experience and its expressions interweave. Further, most religious experience is mediated through one's tradition. That is, the cultural assumption into which one is born sets up the kinds of religious experience one is likely to have. So while no major religion would deny that Mystery can touch one directly, how one interprets such a touch is usually circumscribed by what one's tradition teaches. The glow of joy, the death of a child, the value of love, the role of sex, the way to peace, the place of self-denial—these manifold entries to Mystery normally are shaped or interpreted through a received tradition. What such traditions have said about the sexes, therefore, has shaped a great deal of what men and women have made of their best experiences—of their transforming insights, loves, and encounters with Mystery. One theme of this book, in fact, is that the religions have frustrated women's access to equality under Mystery by larding their experiences with perceptions of social inferiority.

Contemporary feminists are acutely sensitive to social inferiority. Those feminists who are also religious (open to Mystery) are therefore haunted by a dilemma: Must I choose between my feminism and my religion? Many feminists do in fact feel that the religions are irredeemably sexist. For them the religious traditions are that much more inauthenticity that liberation must raze. On the other hand, some feminists feel that to cut themselves off from Mystery would be truncating. It is no "liberation," they argue, to become dead-ended, dehumanized, separated from the beauty and power of a divinity that shows itself as love that can create and heal. So while they acknowledge much sexism within the religions, these feminists refuse to equate religion with oppression.

That is my position. Beyond doubt, the major religions of the world have a dubious record with regard to women. Beyond doubt, they have often been inauthentic mediators of religious experience. The very light and love within us that generate these judgments, however, are Mystery-borne—that is, religious. But because on occasion they have made possible this light and love, the religions have not been wholly corrupting. Part of our task, therefore, will be to winnow the wheat of authentic religion (genuinely liberating, viable yet) from the religions' sexist chaff.

Still, the chaff will be very prominent. For example, Buddhist women could not head the religious community. Hinduism usually held women ineligible for salvation. Islam made a woman's witness only half that of a man. Christianity called woman the weaker vessel, the more blurred image of the Image. Jewish men blessed God for not having made them women. Yet authentic religion, by each of these traditions' central confessions, holds most blessed honesty and love, which are hardly sex-specified. Each of these traditions, therefore, is a mixed bag. It has oppressed women socially while liberating many of them mystically.

Thus the religions, because they enroll human beings, are complex. Authenticity and inauthenticity vie constantly for their souls. Indeed the two are dialectically related, for authenticity is not

"We hold that the revelation of the divine to the feminine psyche may not be wholly understandable to the masculine consciousness, for which reason it has been largely ignored, not taken seriously, or simply brought into conformity with the masculine psyche."
—Bernadette Roberts

"If the first woman God ever made was strong enough to turn the world upside down all alone, these women together ought to be able to turn it back, and get it right side up again! And now they is asking to do it, the men better let them."
—Sojourner Truth

something one has or gets once and for all. Often it is just pulling away from inauthenticity. In fact, each time one pulls away, one sees the need for further withdrawal. So an authentic woman is one who keep plugging away at self-transcendence in knowing and loving, despite her inevitable setbacks of selfishness. So authentic religion is a tradition willing to pull itself out of the pits.

Denise Lardner Carmody
Women and World Religions

○ Positive, healthy anger provides energy to break through obstacles, find a solution, and move on. Anger that feeds on itself creates poison for oneself and for others. If you're filled with counterproductive anger, go into the woods, pick up a stone, and hold it to your forehead. Push every angry thought out of your mind and into the stone. Rest. Now force any residual anger into the stone as well. Bury the stone or throw it into a stream.

Early on, feminists recognized that female spirituality could not be divorced from politics and that social action would be needed to reintegrate the feminine into our culture and religion. This combination of feminist politics and spirituality is referred to here as the womanspirit movement.

The Womanspirit Movement

The womanspirit movement seeks to reclaim the spiritual-political powers neglected or suppressed throughout the patriarchal era, to develop a feminist force that attacks the patriarchy from all directions, and to create new ways of being and relating. . . .

The womanspirit movement is a necessity, not a luxury. Without it, we are operating with only half our potential tools and power. What we think we want is based on what we think is possible; one of womanspirit's most important functions is to create and implement a feminist vision. We need tools such as meditation, personal mythology, natural healing, dreamwork, study of matriarchal history and mythology, and ritual to reach beyond the possibility laid out for us by the patriarchy. We cannot wait until after the revolution for the new order to rise up, phoenix-like, out of the ashes of the old. We need to lay the groundwork now through lifetimes of hard work in researching, experimenting with, and practicing a new integration of "politics" and "spirituality." We need new ways of healing, self-knowledge, self-power, new ways of being and relating to ourselves, one another, the Earth, and the cosmos. If we neglect them, we will create only a new version of the overly competitive, dualistic, rational, technological patriarchy.

Ultimately the goals of spirituality and of revolutionary politics are the same: to create a world in which love, equality, freedom, and fulfillment of individual and collective potential is possible. If we unite the two approaches to these common goals, we will experience this fulfillment.

> Hallie Iglehart Austen
> "The Unnatural Divorce of Spirituality and Politics"
> in *The Politics of Women's Spirituality*

"Love is not a doctrine. Peace is not an international agreement. Love and Peace are beings who live as possibilities in us."
—M.C. Richards

○ Just as creating peace includes more than opposing war, the womanspirit movement goes beyond attacking patriarchy to create new ways of being and relating which include love and healing. But how do we get there from here? How do we avoid "good girl" role playing to develop compassion that springs from the heart? How do we recognize when we are adjusting to the human needs of others and when we are simply in deep denial? Start by praying for wisdom, equanimity, and compassion for ourselves and others.

> *"For too many people spirituality means being a 'nicer' person and loving a nebulous creator while fearfully retaining all the rules of morality and ideas of God they were ever taught. The accumulation of their old religious concepts often fester into moral guilt or self-righteousness, while effectively sapping strength from any new spiritual inspiration."*
> —Theresa King

Some within the womanspirit movement turned to witchcraft as a way to heal the split that modern women feel between spirituality and effective power. Here a modern witch gives an entry from her "Book of Shadows," a traditional "recipe book" of teachings and rituals used in witchcraft (also called Wicca or The Craft) ceremonies.

The Confession

We confess that we have all been captive to the masculine mystique and the feminine mystique. We have believed, either openly or somewhere deep within our psyches, that maleness is the measure of full humanity and femaleness in some mysterious way is flawed. We confess that we have only begun to understand how much damage we have done to ourselves and to each other under the sway of this mystique. Allowing our gender to define and limit our possibilities, we have disowned those qualities and needs and feelings in ourselves which do not fit. Thus alienated from ourselves, we have invested others with power and responsibility which belong to us alone. We confess that we are afraid of otherness, in those of the opposite sex as well as in those of our own. And we are afraid of our own otherness, those parts in ourselves that we have split off and do not claim, experiencing them as acting upon us from without.

We confess that we stand in need of cleansing in order that we might experience healing and wholeness.

So Be it.

Patricia Eagle
Book of Shadows

○ These exercises will help to cleanse us, and to aid in finding healing and wholeness:

Summoning: Mentally summon the presence of someone who has recently hurt or angered you, or maybe only irritated you. "Be" with their presence for a while and repeat: "May we be free of suffering." Then let them go.

Shape-Shifting: Summon the presence of someone who has done you wrong, then become that person imaginatively. Feel your face and body as their face and body. Abide as that person for a time, seeing the world through their eyes, feel their emotions, including self-love. Return gently to embodying yourself.

The Christian Gnostics flourished during the early centuries after Christ's death as one of many different groups calling themselves Christian. They differ greatly from what has become present-day Christianity in terms of the way in which the feminine is included, and show once again that antifemale bias does not spring from Christ's teachings themselves, but from the way in which they have been interpreted.

The Gnostic Gospels

Elaine Pagels in her work *The Gnostic Gospels* points out that the early Gnostic Christians were branded heretical by the orthodox church, and became largely forgotten until the discovery of 1,500-year-old texts at Nag Hammadi (Upper Egypt) in 1945. Some of these texts, which appear to be copies of even earlier gospels, see the orthodox church itself as heretical, perverting the true message of Christ.

Among the striking differences between Gnostic Christianity and the church that prevailed (and wrote ecclesiastical history) is the way in which the feminine is included rather than excluded among the Gnostics. Pagels explains that the language referring to God as a masculine-feminine dyad is specifically Christian, related to Jewish heritage rather than revealing pagan goddess worship.

One Gnostic group, which claimed to have received secret teachings from Jesus through James and Mary Magdalene, prayed to both the divine Father and the divine Mother. This female deity

"These heretical women— how audacious they are! They have no modesty; they are bold enough to teach, to engage in argument, to enact exorcism, to undertake cures, and, it may be, even to baptize!"
—Tertullian, c. 200 C.E., on Gnostic Christian women

"A myth ascribed to the Gnostic school of Valentinus related that in the timeless time before creation, the Feminine appears as the 'thought' of God; hence she is given the title Sophia, from the Greek word for wisdom. Being thought, she has a certain autonomy; she is free to look below and contemplate what she sees. Her gaze takes in all the negative aspects of the lower places, and she is filled with compassion."
--June Singer

is characterized in a number of different ways, which Pagels groups into three main categories.

(1) Several Gnostic groups see the divine Mother as part of an original couple. The teacher Valentinus begins by saying that God is in essence ineffable, but that the divine can be imagined as a dyad: the Depth, the Primal Father, along with Silence, the Womb and "Mother of the All." He describes how Silence receives the seed of the Ineffable Source and from this brings forth all emanations of the divine, which are ranged in harmonious masculine and feminine pairs.

Another Gnostic teacher wrote that divine power exists in everyone in a latent condition: "This is one power divided above and below; generating itself, making itself grow, seeking itself, finding itself, being mother of itself, father of itself, sister of itself, spouse of itself, daughter of itself, son of itself—mother, father, unity, being a source of the entire circle of existence."

Although Gnostics differed in whether they understood the masculine-feminine dyad to be literal or metaphoric, they agreed that the divine incorporated a dynamic and harmonious interplay of opposites, a concept closer to the Taoist view of yin and yang than the traditional Christian representation of God the Father.

(2) The divine Mother is characterized as Holy Spirit. The *Apocryphon of John* relates how, after Jesus' death, He came to John in a vision, saying: "I am the one who [is with you] always. I [am the Father;] I am the Mother, I am the Son." In other places, Jesus speaks of "my Mother, the Spirit," thus adding the feminine as the third aspect of the trinity.

A work attributed to the Gnostic teacher Simon Magus goes so far as to see paradise as the womb, and Eden, the placenta. Sethian Gnostics state that heaven and earth have a shape similar to the womb, that anyone who examines the pregnant womb of any living creature will find there an image of the heavens and the earth.

(3) In addition to the mystical Silence and the Holy Spirit, a third characterization of the divine Mother, as Wisdom, existed among certain Gnostics. Wisdom (Greek *sophia*; Hebrew *hokhmah*) not only created mankind, but made them wise. In certain Gnostic sources, Wisdom teaches Adam and Eve self-awareness, guides them to find food, and assists in the conception of their third and

fourth children (Seth and Norea). Wisdom even intercedes with God when he sends the flood to wipe out an ungrateful human race.

Another text discovered at Nag Hammadi, *Trimorphic Protennoia* ("Triple-formed Primal Thought") celebrates "the Invisible One within the All," the feminine powers of Thought, Intelligence, and Foresight. Later the voice says: "I am androgynous. [I am both Mother and] Father, since [I copulate] with myself . . . [and with those who love] me. . . . I am the Womb [that gives shape] to the All."

In a Gnostic poem entitled *Thunder, Perfect Mind*, a feminine power speaks: "I am the first and the last. I am the honored one and the scorned one. I am the whore, and the holy one. I am the wife and the virgin. I am [the mother] and the daughter. I am she whose wedding is great, and I have not taken a husband. . . . I am knowledge, and ignorance. . . . I am shameless; I am ashamed. I am strength, and I am fear. . . . I am foolish, and I am wise. . . . I am godless, and I am one whose God is Great."

For more on the Gnostic Gospels, see: Elaine Pagels, *The Gnostic Gospels*, Vintage, 1989; *The Nag Hammadi Library*, edited by James M. Robinson, Harper & Row, 1977; and *The Gnostic Book of Hours*, by June Singer, HarperCollins, 1992.

"There are two problems associated with the use of 'He' for God; one is sexism and the other is anthropomophism. Changing to 'She' (or 'You') may improve the situation vis-a-vis sexism, but leaves the problem of anthropomorphism intact."
—Jenny Goodman

"Not the least devastating gesture of patriarchal power has been to cast the cosmos itself—the life–force, energy, matter, and miracle–into the form of a male god."
—Robin Morgan

The masculine pronoun for God was once taken for granted and used as a means of enforcing woman's subordinate place to her husband. Mary Daly's Beyond God the Father, 1973, started the movement away from this idea as "natural." The argument specific to language is continued by Jann Aldredge Clanton here.

Beyond God as Male and Female

While several Christian denominations continue to debate the ordination of women, others have moved on to shake the foundation of patriarchy in the doctrine of God. Realizing the connection between God-language and patriarchal institutions, inclusive language task forces in various denominations propose revisions of hymnals and lectionaries. For many years the National Council of Churches has been considering the authorization of an inclusive language translation of the Bible.

These proposed changes evoke varied, often intense responses. Some view inclusive language as a peripheral issue. One young man believes that those who advocate balancing masculine with feminine God-language "are making a whole lot out of nothing." He further states, "I can't see how we can even remotely grasp God as Creator of the Universe and then try to limit Him to a strict male or female role." This man was totally unaware that he was limiting God to a male role by referring to God as "Him." A middle-aged man reacted more strongly: "Anyone trying to categorize God as male or female has such a small mind, they must have a rather limited picture of a limitless being. God's sex is no more important than his height, weight, or skin color. He, in fact, has none of the above. Concern over God's sex is petty and inane."

In reacting against feminine language for God, these people present powerful arguments against masculine language for God as well. If they believe that categorizing God by gender limits God, then surely they would not call God "he." If the gender of God is so unimportant, then they should have no more problem referring to God as "she" than as "he." In reacting so strongly against feminine references to God, they reveal the ancient bias that women are inseparable from their sexuality. Calling God "she" brings up the issue of God's sex in ways that calling God "he" never has. Since the church has explicitly and implicitly taught that men are more spiritual than women, it has allowed men to rise above their carnality to perform the sacred rituals, while keeping women tied to the flesh. Therefore, a "she" God might not be worthy of worship. A "she" God would be no God at all to some people. If God is She, God is not God.

Although the church has traditionally afforded masculinity more honor than femininity, a "he" God is likewise limited by human gender stereotypes. If God is He, God is not God. Exclusive masculine references to God restrict God to human understandings of gender. Although some argue that the pronoun "he" is generic, the predominant images and traits it evokes in the mind are masculine, since it also serves as a specific reference to a male. Furthermore, as generic terms pass out of standard English usage, the argument for masculine references to God will continue to lose credibility. The generic "he" derives from patriarchal society, which determines masculinity as the norm and even projects masculine gender onto God. However, a God confined to one human gender could never be the infinite, almighty God whose thoughts are not our thoughts and whose ways are not our ways (Isaiah 55:8).

As we have seen in this study, neither the Bible nor Christian history limits God to the masculine gender. The Bible presents a remarkable variety of divine metaphors, many of them feminine. Using language that creates only a masculine image of God is unbiblical and idolatrous. Leading theologians throughout the centuries have risen above the bias of their milieu to offer glimpses of a God larger than masculine gender. From St. Ambrose's "womb of God the Father" to Tillich's "ground of being," we discover the possibility of progressing beyond gender concepts of God by including male and female. Just as the early Christians' experience of God demanded the expansion of God-language to include three Persons, so we can describe more fully and enlarge our experience of God through language that includes both genders.

My study has revealed that inclusive God-language has profound implications for the Christian church. This language frees and empowers women and men to exercise their gifts within the church.

"The most basic reason, it appears, for uneasiness with female metaphors for God is that unlike the male metaphors, whose sexual character is cloaked, the female metaphors seem blatantly sexual and involve the sexuality most feared: female sexuality."
—Sallie MacFague

"To see the smug expression on Jerry Falwell's beefy face when he expounds on the 'moral depravity' of feminists is to witness male privilege incarnate."
—Charlene Spretnak

Women gain the self-confidence and autonomy to achieve, create, and lead. Men discover deeper capacities for spirituality, intimacy, and change. The church gains wholeness and redemptive power through the mutuality of men and women in leadership and ministry. As the church breaks down rigid hierarchies and roles, it gains the contributions of each unique member. When the church values women and men equally, it becomes a model of justice and peace.

Although some advocate a time of exclusive use of feminine references to God to balance the centuries of masculine God-language, my emphasis has been on expanding and enriching our doctrine of God through inclusive language. Changing the nature of the limitation upon God from masculine to feminine would be no permanent solution. However, including male and female in our metaphors for God offers fuller understanding of God and greater wholeness for humanity. Since human beings come in the form of one gender or the other, speaking of God as including both genders contributes to a doctrine of God beyond humanity. Calling God "she" focuses on the metaphoric nature of our language for God in ways that calling God "he" does not, because masculine references have become habitual. Feminine references jar us out of habits inconsistent with our theology. Balancing masculine and feminine references to God leads the imagination beyond anthropomorphism to a transcendent God. In addition, speaking of God as male and female provides a powerful affirmation of male and female human beings.

As we have seen, it is not sufficient to use masculine God-language and argue that it is generic, not specific; analogical, not literal. There is no way we can expound a doctrine of God as transcendent Spirit and use only masculine references to God. We simply cannot have it both ways. My study intentionally overemphasizes the gender of God. But we have to focus upon the gender of God in order to transcend it. The way to a God beyond male and female is through a God who includes male and female. The imagination can more easily leap from androgynous to transcendent concepts of God than from masculine to transcendent concepts of God.

Just as the day will come when female pastors are called simply "pastors," not "women pastors," the day will come when the gender of God ceases to be an issue. Through speaking of a God inclusive of male and female, we will progress to deeper understandings of God beyond male and female. We will then experience more fully the power of God and the glory of being female and male in the image of God.

Jann Aldredge Clanton
In Whose Image? God and Gender

○ In the past two decades, the interlaced roots of patriarchy have been extensively analyzed and documented, and the harmful results of feminine exclusion have been fully articulated. Scholars have shown over and over the ways in which women and the feminine have been ignored or distorted at every level of the church and how their exclusion is embedded in the very language itself. Now it is time to move on.

Here's how to start. Decide that today, whatever has been keeping you in an angry, upset state—the obsession that has interfered with your connection with spirit, blocking you from the light—this instant, you'll start to get over it. Give this problem a name, write it on a sheet of paper, and then burn it. Plant a flower or a tree, mixing the ashes from your paper with the soil. Water the plant well and watch it thrive.

Think about the ways in which living under patriarchy hurts men. Understand how being shut off emotionally creates inner as well as outer pain. Remember that the men you know did not invent patriarchy, but were raised to feel that it is "natural." Imagine yourself being born and brought up as a male. Comprehend fully that being compassionate toward men does not stop you from taking political action, but makes you ultimately more effective.

Think of ways you can help men. Start utilizing them today.

_____

"I can be angry. I can hate. I can rage. But the moment I have defined another being as my enemy, I lose part of myself, the complexity and subtlety of my vision. I begin to exist in a closed system."
—Susan Griffin

"Buddha started a tradition of leaving home to follow the spiritual path . . . . Homelessness is a state of mind, a questioning, a deep realization there is no place to rest or to hide. And a monk can be as attached to his robe, his bowl, and his poverty as a rich person to his countless possessions. We shouldn't confuse sincere practice with some particular lifestyle."
—Fran Tribe

Unlike Catholic nuns who are fed, clothed, and sheltered by their Church, Buddhist nuns are essentially on their own in both the East and the West. To discuss the many issues involving Buddhist nuns, Sakyadhita (Daughters of the Buddha) called a conference in Bodhgaya, India, in 1987, where the Dalai Lama— who continues his support of Buddhist nuns today—gave the opening address. Inspired by its success, Sakyadhita continues to sponsor conferences and to publish a newsletter. The following is from a talk given at the first conference in Bodhgaya.

Living as a Nun in the West

The subject of Western women embracing Buddhism and living as nuns in the West is a provocative one. It concerns being a woman in what is still a fairly male-oriented society and a spiritual person in a very materialistic, non-religious, even anti-religious society. Living in the West means living in a materially developed country with a high standard of living, but there is also a deep understanding of individual freedom, and appreciation for it. . . .

Being a Spiritual Woman. I have talked with Catholic nuns in Bavaria, a very conservative area, who say that nobody understands why they have become nuns. They are asked, "If you are beautiful and intelligent, why become a nun?" People in the West often feel that being a nun must mean that you are trying to escape something or that you have some deepseated problem. There is very little support for such a path, even for the Christian nuns. Therefore, there is very little encouragement or supportive understanding.

On the other hand, in recent years many people have been experiencing a crisis of meaning in their lives. They encounter irritations and a gnawing dissatisfaction that leads to religious questioning. In such an atmosphere where we meet people who are searching for meaning in their lives, to be a nun in the West can be something very beneficial.

I can never forget talking with a Catholic nun who said, "You are the first person who understands my reasons for being a nun." Even though I am a Buddhist nun, following an Asian religion, the Catholic nun and I felt ourselves acknowledged and supported by one another. Regardless of what denomination they follow, sincere practitioners have a deep appreciation for each other. As His Holiness [the Dalai Lama] often stresses, religious practitioners are all pulling the same rope; we have to pull together and support each other.

Being a Western Woman. Although Buddhist practitioners come from many different countries, such as Sri Lanka, Nepal, India, Taiwan, and Japan, we have many things in common. While acknowledging all the interests we share, I also recognize certain differences in our situations and experiences. It is important to be aware of the differences, too, to gain a deeper understanding of one another.

Some of these differences are superficial, but they reflect our varied conditions and orientation. For example, the behavior of the Western nuns may come as a surprise to our Asian sisters. We may often seem to lack discipline and respect for others. Our whole outlook on forms, rules, regulations, and conduct appears to be radically different. The root of this difference lies in the fact that we have undergone a long process of mental development centered around becoming more sensitive to our own needs, rather than just following an accepted set of rules. We have gained a deep appreciation of individuality. It is too simplistic to say that this process has resulted in a tremendous egotism that needs to be destroyed. Of course, there is the involvement of ego, which we must eliminate along with greed, hatred, and ignorance. There is a tremendous grasping at a solidly existing "self" or "I." Still there is something more subtle involved here than pure egotism, and it needs to be explored. I would describe this process as the first step of an intuitive awakening, of being able to listen to our inner wisdom and gain an understanding of our direction.

Finding Our Own Way. From the first day, ten years ago, that I came into contact with Buddhism, I felt very strongly that I must be careful not to simply superimpose new patterns on my existing experience. I did not want to adopt some sort of set structure, but rather to incorporate Buddhist values in dialogue with my background as a Western person. It was never my intention to live my whole life in India or Nepal. The time I spent there was always seen as a time of learning in preparation for returning to my country and

"Monks and scholars should accept my word not out of respect, but upon analyzing it as a goldsmith analyzes gold, through cutting, melting, scraping and rubbing it."
—Buddha

"Renunciation literally means 'to abandon.' What is it, on a spiritual path, that we are trying to abandon? According to Buddhist teachings, what we hope to abandon are suffering and the causes of suffering."
—Tenzin Dechen

trying to adapt the wisdom I found there to my cultural environment in the West. This type of dialogue requires great courage, since we have as yet no indigenous role models. . . .

It is not effective for Western students to follow set rules without really understanding how they operate and how they help us to grow. Lama Yeshe [her teacher] always stressed that if we do not understand something, the transformation it works is not as deep. Practice based on mere faith is useful, as it helps in creating less negative *karma*, but the transformation is much deeper if one's faith is based on reasoning and real understanding. It is wonderful to know the *sutras*, [scriptures] to learn them by heart, to be able to quote them—but it is more important to truly understand them.

Practice in East and West. Asian people love to memorize the texts, but Westerners feel a need for more silent, contemplative meditation. This is the experience of many Western *Sangha* [group of practitioners] members living in *Dharma* communities. When discussing the daily monastic or center schedule, we realize that the traditional way would be to have an hour of *puja* [devotions, often chanted] in the morning and an hour of *puja* in the evening, but it just does not feel right to us. If I have to chant a *puja* for an hour in the morning, I do not feel clear, open, and sensitive during the day— I just feel full. Many of the ordained and lay sisters and brothers in the West feel that an hour of silent meditation in the morning is a better preparation for the day, helping to set the motivation for the day's activities in a peaceful and positive mode. We feel that a silent practice is more effective in opening and centering our minds. If recitation works for others, that is beautiful; but, with all due respect, it is not for everybody. . . .

To sum up, although it is difficult to live as a nun in the West without the support of a monastic environment, I am happy to have been a pioneer, and I want to investigate with others how we can best implement the Buddha's teachings in the West. I am confident that in time we will find suitable and effective ways of life in which lay and ordained practitioners in the West will inspire and support each other in new ways.

Sylvia Wetzel
"Finding Our Way" in *Sakyadhita*

There's a wealth of material available today concerning women and Buddhism. The introduction to Tsultrim Allione's *Women of Wisdom*, Routledge & Kegan Paul, 1982, provides a brilliant, comprehensive analysis of the feminine in Buddhist practice which is followed by biographical sketches of female Tibetan practitioners. Sandy Boucher, *Turning the Wheel: American Women Creating the New Buddhism*, Harper & Row, 1988, gives a very personal account of many of the women—students as well as teachers—involved in Buddhism in the 1970s and 1980s. She also includes a responsible treatment on the fraught subject of male teachers' sexual involvement with their students. Other books well worth dipping into include:

Leonore Friedman, *Meetings with Remarkable Women*, Shambhala, 1987.

China Galland, *Longing for Darkness: Tara and the Black Madonna*, Viking, 1990.

Rita Gross, *Buddhism Beyond Patriarchy*, SUNY, 1992.

Deborah Hopkinson, Michele Hill, and Eileen Kiera, eds., *Not Mixing Up Buddhism: Essays on Women and Buddhist Practice*, White Pine Press, 1986.

Kahawai Journal of Women and Zen, Diamond Sangha, 2119 Kaloa Way, Honolulu, HI 96822.

Joanna Macy, *Despair and Personal Power in the Nuclear Age*, New Society Publishers, 1983.

NIBWA (Newsletter on International Buddhist Women's Activities), c/o Dr. Chatsumarn Kabilsingh, Faculty of Liberal Arts, Thamasat University, Bangkok 10200, Thailand.

Diana Y. Paul, *Women in Buddhism*, Asian Humanities Press, 1979.

Ellen Sidor, ed., *A Gathering of Spirit: Women Teaching in American Buddhism*, Primary Point Press, Kwan Um Zen School, 1987.

Sakyadhita Newsletter, 400 Hobron Lane, #2615, Honolulu, HI 96815.

Karma Lekshe Tsomo, *Sakyadhita: Daughters of the Buddha*, Snow Lion, 1988.

Janice Willis, ed., *Feminine Ground: Essays on Women and Tibet*, Snow Lion, 1989.

Women & Buddhism, a special issue of *Spring Wind—Buddhist Cultural Forum*, vol 6, nos. 1, 2, and 3. Zen Buddhist Temple—Toronto, 46 Gwynne Avenue, Toronto M6K 2C3, Ontario, Canada.

Snow Lion Newsletter & Catalogue, PO Box 6483, Ithaca, NY 14851, 1-800-950-0313, which includes a Women's Studies section, carries most of these books as well as announcements of retreats for women.

"The understanding that suffering is basic, the first noble truth of Buddhism, brings with it some relaxation from the constant struggle to avoid pain. As I understood this I became dissatisfied with feminism's more superficial discussion of suffering. Feminist theology has never distinguished between avoidable pain caused by patriarchal, sexist values and institutions and the basic pain of being human, nor has it ever considered the inevitability of suffering, no matter how perfect social arrangements may be. While eradicating patriarchy and the suffering it causes remains an important priority, it is clear such an agenda is naive if it is the only method for understanding and dealing with suffering."
—Rita Gross

"The tendency to split ourselves is so deep, to see ourselves as split, separate, apart from. Even the words 'women and Buddhism' in my thoughts imply a kind of separation, because I see myself then as somehow outside Buddhism, trying to get in."
—Donna Thomson

"To search for knowledge is a sacred duty imposed upon every Muslim."
—Hadith

Not everyone agrees that the Islamic tradition derives from a single source. The author here points out that the Qur'an *(Book of Revelation seen as the word of God by Muslims);* Sunnah *(the practical traditions of the Prophet Muhammad);* Hadith *(sayings attributed to the Prophet Muhammad);* Fiqh *(Jurisprudence) or* Madahib *(Schools of Law); and the* Shariah *(codes that regulate every aspect of Muslim life)—all contribute to what is cumulatively referred to as the Islamic tradition. Although most people speak of this tradition as if it were unitary, it actually contains inner inconsistencies and contradictions. The main sources—the Qur'an and the Hadith—have been interpreted mainly by men, rendering the practice of Islam rigidly patriarchal. Riffat Hassan feels that it is paramount that feminist theology be developed in the context of Islam in order to liberate not only Muslim women but also Muslim men. She is one of the few women who use primary sources in order to participate in a theological discussion on women-related issues in Islam today.*

Women and Islam

In view of what women in the major religious traditions of the world have suffered in the name or interest of patriarchal values or systems and structures of thought and conduct, it is hardly surprising that many feminist theologians consider the rejection of patriarchy a prerequisite for the liberation of women from various forms of injustice. However, when patriarchy is seen as indissolubly linked with the "core" of a religious tradition—for instance, with God in the context of Judaism, Christianity, and Islam—then the rejection of the one generally involves the rejection of the other. This is why a number of feminist theologians have in the post-patriarchal phase of their thinking gone beyond their religious traditions altogether. Rejecting God, who is identified by them with maleness, they have also, oftentimes, rejected men-women relationships and childbearing, seeing both heterosexual marriage and childbearing as patriarchal institutions used to enslave and exploit women.

However, to me, patriarchy is not integral to the Islam embodied in the Qur'an nor is God thought of as male by Muslims in general.

Rejection of patriarchy does not, therefore, have to lead to rejection of God in whom a Muslim's faith is grounded. Here it needs to be pointed out that being a Muslim is dependent essentially only upon one belief: belief in God, universal creator and sustainer who sends revelation for the guidance of humanity. As Wilfred Cantwell Smith (*Islam in Modern History*) has remarked insightfully, "A true Muslim . . . is not a man who believes in Islam—especially Islam in history; but one who believes in God and is committed to the revelation through His Prophet."

God, who speaks through the Qur'an, is characterized by justice, and it is stated with the utmost clarity in the Qur'an that God can never be guilty of *zulm* (unfairness, tyranny, oppression, or wrongdoing). Hence, the Qur'an, as God's Word, cannot be made the source of human injustice, and the injustice to which Muslim women have been subjected cannot be regarded as God-derived. Historically . . . some of the passages in the Qur'an have been interpreted in such a way that they appear to support what seems—from a twentieth-century Muslim feminist perspective—to be unjust ways of thinking and behaving. However, given the incredible richness of the Arabic language, in which virtually every word has multiple meanings and nuances, it is possible—and necessary—to reinterpret these passages differently so that their import or implication is not contrary to the justice of God.

To me, in the final analysis, post-patriarchal Islam is nothing other than Qur'anic Islam, which is profoundly concerned with freeing human beings—women as well as men—from the bondage of traditionalism, authoritarianism (religious, political, economic, or any other), tribalism, racism, sexism, slavery, or anything else that prohibits or inhibits human beings from actualizing the Qur'anic vision of human destiny embodied in the classical proclamation, "Towards God is thy limit" (Surah 53: *An-Najm*:42; trans. by Iqbal,57). The goal of Qur'anic Islam is to establish peace, which is the very meaning of *islam*. However, from the perspective of the Qur'an, peace is not to be understood to be a passive state of affairs, a mere absence of war. It is a positive state of safety or security in which one is free from anxiety or fear. It is this state that characterizes both *islam*, self-surrender to God, and *iman*, true faith in God, and reference is made to it, directly or indirectly, on every page of

"The misconception that Allah has, throughout history, sent his revelation, wahy, to men only is quite common. In a subtle way, over the centuries, as men came to monopolize the field of Qur'anic commentary, the belief was spread that lack of revelation to women is a sign of the superiority of men. Allah has, however, given no sanction to this kind of male-oriented thought. Nowhere in revelation are we given masculinity as a cause of Allah's communications. Allah chooses and ennobles on the basis of taqwa (consciousness and awareness of God), not on the basis of gender."
—Kaukab Siddique

89

"I don't see Islam as patriarchal at all. I see the practice of it as extremely patriarchal. In Islam men and women have equal value. There's no need to develop a feminist theology. There's a need to put into practice the theology that already exists."
—Karen English

the Qur'an through the many derivatives of the roots "s-l-m" and "a-m-n" from which *islam* and *iman* are derived respectively. According to Qur'anic teachings, peace can only exist within a just environment. In other words, justice is a prerequisite for peace. Without the elimination of the inequities, inequalities, and injustices that pervade the personal and collective lives of human beings, it is not possible to talk about peace in Qur'anic terms. Here it is of vital importance to note that there is more Qur'anic legislation pertaining to the establishment of justice in the context of family relationships than on any other subject. This points to the assumption implicit in much Qur'anic legislation, namely, that if human beings can learn to order their homes justly so that the rights of all within its jurisdiction—children, women, and men—are safeguarded, then they can also order their society and the world at large justly. In other words, the Qur'an regards the home as the microcosm of the *ummah* and the world community, and emphasizes the importance of making it "the abode of peace" through just living.

Despite everything that has gone wrong with the lives of countless Muslim women down the ages due to patriarchal Islam, I believe strongly that there is hope for the future. As an increasing number of Muslims—men and women—begin to reflect more and more deeply upon the teachings of the Qur'an, they begin to see more and more clearly that the supreme task entrusted to human beings by God, of being God's deputies on earth, can only be accomplished by going beyond patriarchal views and values. The message contained in Surah 4: *An-Nisa':*34, which ensures justice between men and women in the context of childbearing, can be extended and universalized to embrace all aspects of human interaction and relatedness. As this happens, the shackles of patriarchal traditions will fall away and the Qur'anic vision of what it means to be a Muslim will begin to be actualized in a world from which the women's inferiority and "crookedness" has finally been expelled.

Riffat Hassan
"Muslim Women and Post-Patriarchal Islam"
in *After Patriarchy*

For more on women and Islam, see:

Amutullah Armstrong, *And the Sky is Not the Limit*, Pir, 1993.

Azizah al-Hibri, ed., *Women and Islam*, Pergamon, 1982.

Marianne Alireza, *At the Drop of A Veil*, Houghton Mifflin, 1971.

Lois Beck and N. Kiddie, eds., *Women in the Muslim World*, Harvard University Press, 1978.

Nawal el-Saadawi, *The Hidden Face of Eve: Women in the Arab World*, Zed Press, 1980.

Elizabeth Fernea and Basima Qattan Bezirgan, eds., *Middle Eastern Muslim Women Speak*, University of Texas Press, 1977.

Yvonne Yazbek Haddad, *Women, Religion and Social Change*, SUNY, 1985.

Susan Haneef, *What Everyone Should Know About Islam and Muslim*, Kazi Publishing, 1978.

Maryam Jameelah, *Islam and Muslim Woman Today*, Muhammad Yusuf Khan, 1976.

Fedwa Malti-Douglas, *Woman's Body, Woman's Word*, Pir, 1993.

Fatima Mernissi, *Beyond the Veil*, John Wiley & Sons, 1975.

Mona Mikhail, *Images of Arab Women: Fact and Fiction*, Three Continents Press, 1979.

Naila Minai, *Women in Islam*, Seaview, 1981.

Sachiko Murata, *The Tao of Islam*, SUNY, 1992.

Kaukab Siddique, *The Struggle of Muslim Women*, American Society for Education & Religion, Inc., 1986.

_____. *Toward Understanding the Basics of Islam*, Thinker's Library, 1986.

Rafi ullah Shehab, *Rights of Women in Islamic Shariah*, Indus Publishing House, 1986.

Those who have gone beyond the boundaries of traditional Christian thinking assume that this will be as easy for others as it has been for them. Others advocate working lovingly and compassionately for change within our existing religions.

Changing of the Gods

Whatever we use to mirror our experience—be it dreams, visions or literature—sacred scriptures of the new age will be in continuous flux. Our texts will be unable to reflect the infinite diversity of experience possible in a culture that permits a variety of

"Depending on whether we feel in control of our changes or at the mercy of them, change may excite or frighten us."
—Dorothy Riddle

91

styles of life and thought. There will be many texts to read, mull over, discuss and dream about. And we will change those texts often, knowing that our unwillingness to hold on to any single description of spiritual experience is not proof that we are fickle—it is proof that we are alive.

Can we predict anything about the new gods of the new age, except to say that there will be many of them?

When we study the religious thought of those who have already outgrown the father-god—the witches, the radical feminists, the modern psychologists—we see a direction inward. All of these people tend to place their gods within themselves, to focus on spiritual processes whose values they experience internally. Judging from these harbingers of our new religious culture the psycho-religious age will be a mystical one. It seems highly likely that the West is on the brink of developing a new mysticism—post-Christian, post-Judaic. It will most probably be a type of mysticism which emphasizes the *continual observation of psychic imagery.*

Naomi Goldenberg
Changing of the Gods

○ What will our religions be like in the future? What sort of synthesis do you imagine will grow out of the present ferment of psychology, Eastern thought, goddess awareness, and feminist theology on the one side and a tendency toward fundamentalism on the other? Envision your own religious tradition in the future, both as it will be if it does not change and also the way you would like it to become. How can you help to implement this vision?

After examining the matricentric and patriarchal ages, the authors here discuss the ecological crisis which the patriarchal mode of thinking has produced as well as the response of eco-feminism to this crisis. They conclude as follows:

Articulating the Vision

If we are to respond creatively to the end of patriarchy, we must proceed in a way that is based on and acts out of the unity of the spiritual and the political. But one thing further is needed: this new way of being can only become a reality if we are able to articulate a vision. The articulation of this vision is the primary task before women—and men—who wish to join the Holy One in the new dance of Creation. Some would argue that the new ecological, or omnicentric, age can be brought about through reformation of the present system. Thus, for example, both liberalism and socialism assume that women will be liberated when they are allowed to function like men in the public realm. However, such thinking is based on the erroneous assumption that the patriarchal structure is both normative and functional. It is neither. For, as [Thomas] Berry points out, the old story no longer provides a context capable of endowing life with meaning.

For, in fact, the old story broke down in the fourteenth century in the West with the coming of the Black Death. The response to that devastating plague was twofold: a movement by the religious community towards an understanding of redemption that would take us out of this tragic world and the formation of a scientific community that would enable us to escape the tragedy of this world by gaining control over it. These two divergent communities, the religious and the scientific, have been on opposing sides in our society ever since. But, in our own time, a new story is emerging which unites these communities. For we have become aware, through the emergence of human consciousness, that the psychic-spiritual has been part of the universe from the beginning. It is the role of the human to represent the moment in which the universe becomes aware of itself. The new story, based on a numinous, sacred understanding of creation, brings together the psychic-

"We tell you this: We are doing the impossible. We are teaching ourselves to be human."
—Martha Courtot

93

"While the goals of feminism are often expressed in terms of women reclaiming power in society, it is also imperative that this process of refeminization of culture include a change in the actual perception of life on the Earth."
—Gina Foglia

spiritual world of the religious community with the material-physical world of the scientist. What is required of the religious community to make this story a reality is threefold: a sense that our primary revelation of the Divine is to be found in the sacred character of the earth itself; an understanding of ourselves as part of the process of Creation, with Creation itself being a psychic-spiritual, as well as a material-physical, reality; and a way of thinking and acting that honors the integrity of all of Creation.

What is required of the whole earth community is that it act in a unified way to establish a functional relationship with the whole earth process. This interaction between the human and the rest of Creation must move beyond the recognition of national boundaries.

But it is not only necessary that the human enter into the life process of the rest of Creation; it is also necessary that the larger life community participate in our processes. One place to begin in this interaction between all the members of the total life community is within the context of ritual. We can employ new rituals to enable us to hear the voices of the trees, the rivers, the earth, the animals. Or we can expand the context of our present rituals. Thus, for example, when we invite those who are not physically with us to join us in a particular place and time—to be "present"—we can extend this invitation beyond people to include the mountains, the tulips, the foxes, the beaches, the extinct species. We can welcome their presence, not only to our rituals, but to all our meetings—to be part of every decision-making process. For how can any decision be considered valid unless its consequences for the whole earth community are considered? People with special sensitivity to and knowledge of species other than the human could become their voices. It is not that the rest of creation is not speaking to us; it is just that most of us do not yet have the ability to understand their methods of communication. For the earth indeed speaks: through the polluted waters, the oil slicks, the eroded soils, the vanishing rain forests, the paved jungle. But the earth also speaks through the pounding of the waves, the hum of a bee, the individuality of a snowflake, the flight of a bird, the birth of a child.

It is not only to the voices of Creation that we must respond; we must also respond to the voice of the Creatrix. In order to hear Her voice, we must be willing to call Her by name. If we take that risk—

if we learn to say the names of the Goddess with the same total love and devotion with which we learned to say the names of God, we will find that we are not moving alone into a new world. Rather, we will awaken into a new community that has existed all along beside the old community. In this new community there will be many familiar forms and faces, but also many which will surprise us. But, most of all, She will be there as She has been with Creation since the beginning. Accept her invitation; She is our bliss if we will but respond.

> Eleanor Rae and Bernice Marie-Daly
> *Created in Her Image:*
> *Models of the Feminine Divine*

Ever since the publication of Mary Daly's *Beyond God the Father* in 1973, there has been an explosion of books involving women and Christianity. Just to read the subtitles provides an education:

K. Armstrong, *A History of God*, Knopf, 1993.

C. W. Atkinson, C. H. Buchanan, and M. R. Miles, eds., *Immaculate and Powerful: The Female in Sacred Image and Social Reality*, Beacon, 1987.

L. Boff, *The Maternal Face of God: The Feminine and its Religious Expressions*, Harper & Row, 1987.

S. Cady, M. Ronan, and H. Taussig, *Sophia: The Future of Feminist Spirituality*, Harper & Row, 1986.

D. L. Carmody, *Feminism and Christianity: A Two Way Reflection*, Abingdon, 1982.

_____. *Seizing the Apple: A Feminist Spirituality of Personal Growth*, The Crossroad Publishing Company, 1984.

A. E. Carr, *Transforming Grace: Christian Tradition and Women's Experience*, Harper & Row, 1988.

Carol P. Christ and Judith Plaskow, eds., *Womanspirit Rising: A Feminist Reader in Religion*, Harper & Row, 1979.

E. A. Clark and H. Richardson, eds., *Women and Religion: A Feminist Sourcebook of Christian Thought,* Harper & Row, 1977.

A. Y. Collins, *Feminist Perspectives on Biblical Scholarship*, Scholars, 1985.

J. W. Conn, *Women's Spirituality: Resources for Christian Development*, Paulist, 1986.

P. M. Cooey, Sharon Farmer, and M. Ross, eds., *Embodied Love: Sensuality and Relationship as Feminist Values*, Harper & Row, 1987.

"What ails Christianity today is that it is not a religion squarely based on a single myth; it is a complex of juridical decisions made under political pressure in an ancient law-suit about religious rights between adherents of the Mother-goddess who was once supreme in the West, and those of the usurping Father-god."
—Robert Graves

> *"The attempt to 'write women back into early Christian history' should not only restore early Christian history to women but also lead to a richer and more accurate perception of early Christian beginnings."*
> —Elisabeth Schussler Fiorenza

Mary Daly, *Beyond God the Father*, Beacon, 1973.

———, *Gyn/Ecology*, Beacon, 1978.

———, *Pure Lust*, Beacon, 1984.

———, *The Church and the Second Sex*, Beacon, 1985.

S. Dowell and L. Hurcombe, *Dispossessed Daughters of Eve: Faith and Feminism*, SPCK, 1987.

N. A. Falk, and Rita Gross, eds., *Unspoken Worlds: Women's Religious Lives*, Wadsworth, 1989.

Elisabeth S. Fiorenza, *In Memory of Her: A Feminist Theological Reconstruction of Christian Origins*, The Crossroad Publishing Company, 1984.

K. Fischer, *Women at the Well: Feminist Perspectives on Spiritual Direction*, Paulist, 1989.

C. Galland, *Longing for Darkness: Tara and the Black Madonna*, Viking, 1990.

M. E. Giles, ed., *The Feminist Mystic: And Other Essays on Women and Spirituality*, The Crossroad Publishing Company, 1987.

Rita Gross, ed., *Beyond Androcentrism: New Essays on Women and Religion*, Scholars, 1977.

T. Hopko, ed., *Women and the Priesthood*, St. Vladimir's Seminary Press, 1983.

L. Hurcombe, ed., *Sex and God: Some Varieties of Women's Religious Experience*, Routledge & Kegan Paul, 1987.

T. King, *The Spiral Path*, Yes International Publishers, 1992.

U. King, *Women and Spirituality: Voices of Protest and Promise*, Macmillan, 1989.

G. Lerner, *The Creation of Patriarchy*, Oxford University Press, 1986.

Ann Loades, ed., *Feminist Theology: A Reader*, SPCK, 1990.

S. McFague, *Models of God: Theology for an Ecological, Nuclear Age*, SCM, 1987.

S. Maitland, *A Map of the New Country: Women and Christianity*, Routledge & Kegan Paul, 1983.

V. R. Mollenkott, ed., *Women of Faith in Dialogue*, The Crossroad Publishing Company, 1988.

E. Moltmann-Wendel, *The Women Around Jesus*, The Crossroad Publishing Company, 1982.

Nelle Morton, *The Journey Is Home*, Beacon, 1985.

Cynthia Ochs, *Women and Spirituality*, Rowman & Allanheld, 1983.

C. Osiek, *Beyond Anger: On Being a Feminist in the Church*, Paulist Press, 1986.

Elaine Pagels, *Adam, Eve and the Serpent*, Random House, 1989.

Judith Plaskow and Carol P. Christ, eds., *Reweaving the Visions: New Patterns in Feminist Spirituality*, Harper & Row, 1989.

L. N. Rhodes, *Co-Creating: A Feminist Vision of Ministry*, Westminster, 1987.

C. S. Robb, ed., *Making the Connections: Essays in Feminist Social Ethics*,

Beacon, 1985.

R. R. Ruether, *Religion and Sexism: Images of Woman in the Jewish and Christian Tradition*, Simon and Schuster, 1974.

_____, *Sexism and God-Talk: Towards a Feminist Theology*, Beacon, 1984.

R. R. Ruether and R. S. Keller, eds., *Women and Religion in America*, 3 vols., Harper & Row, 1981.

L. M. Russell, *Household of Freedom: Authority in Feminist Theology*, Westminster, 1987.

C. Smith, *Weaving the Sermon: Preaching in a Feminist Perspective*, Westminster/John Knox Press, 1989.

M. J. Weaver, *New Catholic Women: A Contemporary Challenge to Traditional Religious Authority*, Harper & Row, 1986.

J. L. Weidman, *Women Ministers*, Harper & Row, 1985.

M. T. Winter, *The Gospel According to Mary*, The Crossroad Publishing Company, 1993.

No longer a Christian, this author, a feminist free-thinker, has explored a variety of sources from Kali worship to Wicca and found a "fantastic coherence" in her "eclectic crazy quilt of spiritual paradoxes."

Christianity as Compost

We were discussing the issue of connection to one's religious past. Knowing I no longer identified as Christian, one of the women asked, "But you do draw on it in some ways still, don't you? Would you speak of it as your roots?" I paused, searching for words. That phrase has never felt quite right to me. From the root springs the tree; they are a continuous growth. The ecology of my spiritual life is more complex than that, with moments of radical discontinuity and continuity. "Compost," I heard myself say. And again, with an increasing sense of satisfaction that at last I had found the apt metaphor, "Compost. My Christianity has become compost." It has decayed and died, becoming a mix of animate and inanimate, stinking rot and released nutrients. Humus. Fertilizer. The part of

"We are crying for a vision that all living things can share."
—Kate Wolf

organic life cycles with which everyone gets uncomfortable and skips over in the rush to rhapsodize growth and progress and blossoms and fruition and rebirth. But in between is the dark, rich mysterious stage, when life decomposes into soil. It is a sacred time--like the dark no-moon new-moon in my meditation, that liminal stage and dangerous essential passage between the last slender waning crescent and the first shred of a shining waxing new one. Compost. A pile of organic substance transforming into a ground, a matrix into which we must mix other elements for the next seeds to sprout. Other vital forces must wet and warm the matrix. And additional deaths, so inevitable in changing/living, will need to feed this ground. Humus. It is from this that we are named human, to acknowledge our connection to the earth, the place where we stand in the vast living universe. If our traditions and symbols are truly part of living, then they are organic and will have rhythms of living and dying.

Emily Culpepper
"The Spiritual Political Journey"
in *After Patriarchy*

○ Visualize all the dualities in your life in the black-and-white symbol of yin and yang: male and female, good and bad, self and other, subject and object. When they are neatly divided, add your dynamic energy to the symbol and set it spinning. As it moves, change it into a multicolored kaleidoscope of an ever-changing pattern.

———————————

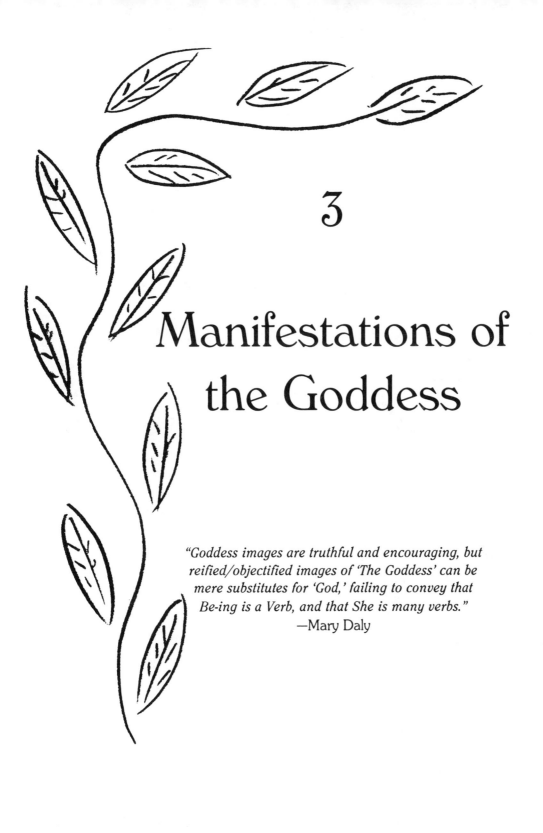

3

Manifestations of the Goddess

"Goddess images are truthful and encouraging, but reified/objectified images of 'The Goddess' can be mere substitutes for 'God,' failing to convey that Be-ing is a Verb, and that She is many verbs."
—Mary Daly

The goddess has many faces, many manifestations—none of which are mutually exclusive. Diversity, multiplicity, and shape-shifting are her most striking characteristics. Ways of approaching the goddess today fall into five basic albeit overlapping groups: a concern with the historical goddess as she exists in other cultures—Tara, Kali, Oya—or the prehistoric goddess of our own Western tradition—the so-called "fertility" goddesses such as the Venus of Wilendorf; the view that the goddesses depicted in mythology—mainly Greek, but increasingly from other sources such as Sumerian and Egyptian—are emblematic of certain psychological types or archetypes of modern women; Christian feminists who see Mary as a Goddess figure; those who see the Goddess as a vital spirit abroad in the land, a felt personal spirit which only has to be called to be present; and the goddess as nature, ground, or basic space. Within these broad outlines, as the following readings reveal, variations abound, as do interpretations and reactions.

I conducted an experiement recently and asked a wide variety of women how they envisioned the goddess. Here are the results.

The Goddess Envisioned

"To be fed only male images of the divine is to be badly malnourished."
—Christine Downing

Responses ranged from "I don't" to complex answers with layers of meaning. The most dismissive were those who had the least contact with current ideas about the goddess or were unsympathetic to the spiritual dimensions of the women's movement in general. Some saw the goddess as a spontaneously arising spiritual force evoked by an overabundance of yang energy in the culture, a source of renewal and sanity for women and men oppressed by centuries of patriarchy. To others the goddess simply meant God in drag, a means by which a "she" can be included in our descriptions of the Godhead. To many, the goddess is a vital source of nurturing energy available to anyone who has the courage and imagination to name Her. To the psychologically inclined, she becomes a constellation of feminine archetypes, partly but not completely defined by the Greek goddesses as interpreted by Jungian therapists. For the cynical, the whole goddess movement is a feminist ego trip taken advantage of by New Age bookstores to sell more cards.

For many women, the goddess isn't an idea, but a felt presence in their lives. Nelle Morton in *The Journey Home* gives a vivid sense of how the goddess "takes over" for her in crisis moments—like in a bumpy landing in a disabled plane. This experience of a presence "just under the skin" is repeated by women all over the country. A video producer from the San Francisco Bay Area reported: "My goddess group began spontaneously, I found myself building an altar and creating simple rituals because they seemed right in the moment. I talked to other women—one a complete stranger in a laundromat—who were doing the same thing. When we started meeting, this nonverbal spirit that we came to call the goddess seemed to invest what we did with meaning. Something alive and vibrant—some presence—started working through us. For the first time, I feel that I am having my own religious experience rather than something made for someone else that doesn't quite fit."

For some, using the term *goddess* creates a sense of the sacred in a way that the word *God*—with all of its patriarchal associations—does not. Contact with the idea of the goddess helps to break down the concept of God as male and leads to knowledge of how this informs our ideas about women. A nurse once told me, "I found it tremendously revealing the first time I heard someone use the term *goddess* instead of *god*. I couldn't take the deity seriously as a 'she.' Then I realized how denigrated the universal 'she' is in our culture. I see how it all connects now, why you feminists recognize Christianity with its male god as the linchpin for patriarchy. Still, I don't think that using the term *goddess* is much of a solution."

Carol Christ points out in "Why Women Need the Goddess" that using the term *goddess* is a way of empowering the female and feminine in our culture. Even among those who acknowledge their need for and the presence of the goddess in their lives, there are a wide varieties of ways in which she is envisioned. Catholics will refer you to Mary, Buddhists to Tara, Chinese to Kwan Yin, Africans to Oya, and so on, depending on what their religions include in the way of feminine deities. For others, *goddess* denotes such Greek figures as Hera or Aphrodite or—especially with Jungian therapists—psychological archetypes which correspond to these mythic females. To some it seems that these popular images are patriarchal versions of the female, whereas the *real* goddess is something completely different—something that doesn't blink at death but has a pitiless, primal power. Sylvia Perera discusses this concept of the goddess in *The Descent to the Goddess*.

For others, goddess worship—whatever form it takes—is a stage that one goes through. As a Yoga teacher put it: "I used to be 'into' the goddess, but now it seems dualistic. I have an altar that has gods and goddess. I think the emphasis on the goddess was something we needed to get out of the patriarchal mind set."

In some cases, the goddess is not personified, but perceived in more general terms. The early Christian gnostics and some modern feminist theologians see her as the Holy Spirit. "I see the Goddess everywhere," a witch recently remarked. "She is everything: rivers, trees, mountains, other people. Men have kept us from our true religion, our connections with ourselves. . . . During the women's

"If you want to be become a god/dess, you'll have to do it yourself."
—D. Rose Hartman

"Sometimes I wonder how I could ever have been so unaware, so unconscious not only of the central importance of the Feminine in how we construct our society and our world, but of what is now my most profound and indispensable sense of self as a woman and a person."
—Riane Eisler

holocaust, The Burning Times, thousands of women were burned as witches. Mainly because they had power—the power of the goddess." The goddess as mother nature has becomes increasingly important in eco-feminism, especially as it overlaps with the Native American vision of a world in which there is respect for the four-legged and winged as well as "all my relations."

In the wonderful Canadian movie *Goddess Remembered*, Jean Bolen remarks that she has a sense of the goddess as "life force, as affiliation, as that which links us all on a deep level to be one with each other and with nature." This reflects the concept in Tibetan Buddhism that the feminine is the ground, basic space; that whenever something comes into form, it is masculine.

Not everyone equates the feminine with the goddess, nor finds goddess worship desirable. "I thought god was bad enough," a student informed me, "why mess around with all this goddess business?" Thus, for some, the term *goddess* itself grates, and the women who use the word appear irritating and pretentious. A rebirther summed it up: "Hawaii is full of goddesses. Women 'honor' the goddess in each other. It's sort of a mutual ego-plumping activity. No one is named Cindy or Jane anymore, but Shekhinah or Isis. Instead of having regular jobs, they're 'Keepers of the Light' or 'Temple Virgins.' They're into goddess jewelry--lots of it and tons of filmy clothes. The goddess movement has become decidedly decadent. Certainly in Hawaii, and probably in places like Mt. Shasta as well."

Many people do have a problem with the self-importance or commercialization of the goddess movement, but retain a direct connection to the goddess herself. A writer: "I used to snub the goddess movement because I didn't like the women who were attracted to it. But in a women's creative group, I felt this wonderful sense of openness that I'd never experienced before. It's hard to put into words, but now I think the goddess is space. A sort of sympathetic openness in which I can define myself, become who I really am."

Kimberley Snow
The Sante Fe Sun, August, 1993

I wish I could include the covers of the goddess books available today as well as their names. A trip to a good women's bookstore is in order here. While you are there, be sure to check out the goddess statues, amulets, jewelry, cards, et cetera.

Margot Adler, *Drawing Down the Moon: Witches, Druids, Goddess Worshippers, and Other Pagans in America Today*, Beacon, 1986.

Hallie Iglehart Austen, *The Heart of the Goddess: Art, Myth and Meditations of the World's Sacred Feminine*, Wingbow, 1990.

Mariam Baker, *Woman as Divine: Tales of the Goddess*, Crescent Heart, 1982.

Anne Baring and Jules Cashford, *The Myth of the Goddess: Evolution of an Image*, Viking Arkana, 1991.

Pamela Berger, *The Goddess Obscured: Transformation of the Grain Protectress from Goddess to Saint*, Beacon, 1985.

Nancy Blair, *Amulets of the Goddess: Oracle of Ancient Wisdom* (book plus 27 amulets in pouch), Wingbow, 1993.

Jean Shinoda Bolen, *Goddesses in Everywoman: A New Psychology of Women*, Harper & Row, 1984.

Janine Canan, ed., *She Rises Like the Sun: Invocations of the Goddess by Contemporary American Women Poets*, The Crossing Press, 1989.

Anne Carson, *Feminist Spirituality and the Feminine Divine: An Annotated Bibliography*, The Crossing Press, 1986.

Carol P. Christ, *Laughter of Aphrodite: Reflections on a Journey to the Goddess*, Harper & Row, 1987.

Mary Condren, *The Serpent and the Goddess: Women, Religion, and Power in Celtic Ireland*, Harper & Row, 1989.

Menrad Craighead, *The Mother Songs: Images of God the Mother*, Mahwah, 1986.

Mary Daly, *Gyn/Ecology: The Metaethics of Radical Feminism*, Beacon, 1978.

Stephanie Demetrakopoulos, *Listening to our Bodies: The Rebirth of Feminine Wisdom*, Beacon, 1983.

Miriam Robbins Dexter, *Whence the Goddess: A Source Book*, Pergamon, 1990.

Irene Diamond and Gloria Orenstein, eds., *Reweaving the World: The Emergence of Ecofeminism*, Sierra Club Books, 1990.

Christine Downing, *The Goddess: Mythological Images of the Feminine*, The Crossroad Publishing Company, 1981.

Riane Eisler, *The Chalice and the Blade: Our History, Our Future*, Harper & Row, 1987.

Cynthia Eller, *Living in the Lap of the Goddess: The Feminist Spirituality Movement in America*, The Crossroad Publishing Company, 1993.

Nancy Falk and Rita Gross, *Unspoken Worlds: Women's Religious Lives in Non-Western Cultures*, Harper & Row, 1980.

"Most important, our discovery of Goddess attributes that may not have been previously defined as feminine leads us to the liberating realization that consciousness often includes the element of choice. Recognizing a characteristic that is generally designated as masculine today, but was an attribute of a Goddess several millennia ago, helps us to understand that this characteristic may not be gender specific at all."
—Merlin Stone

"The archetypal role of the new femininity is to stand as a priestess of the fullness of life as it is, with its unpredictable pitfalls and unfathomable depths, richness and deprivation, risks and errors, joys and pains. She insists on personal experiencing and personal response to the needs of the human situation."
—Edward C. Whitmont

Janet and Stewart Farrar, *The Witches' Goddess*, Phoenix, 1987.

Matthew Fox, *Original Blessings: A Primer in Creation Spirituality*, Bear & Co., 1983.

Elinor Gadon, *The Once and Future Goddess*, Harper & Row, 1989.

China Galland, *Longing for Darkness: Tara and the Black Madonna*, Viking, 1990.

Jo Garcia and Sara Maitland, *Walking on the Water: Women Talk about Spirituality*, Virago, 1983.

Demetra George, *Mysteries of the Dark Moon: The Healing Power of the Dark Goddess*, HarperCollins, 1992.

Marija Gimbutas, *The Civilization of the Goddess*, Harpers, 1991.

_____. *The Goddesses and Gods of Old Europe: Myths and Cult Images*, University of California Press, 1982.

_____. *The Language of the Goddess: Unearthing the Hidden Symbols of Western Civilization*, Alred van der Marck Editions, 1988.

Judith Gleason, *Oya: In Praise of the Goddess*, Shambhala, 1987.

Robert Graves, *The White Goddess*, Farrar, Straus and Giroux, 1987.

Elizabeth Dodson Gray, *Sacred Dimensions of Women's Experience*, Roundtable, 1988.

Nor Hall, *The Moon and the Virgin: Reflections on the Archetypal Feminine*, Harper & Row, 1980.

Hallie Iglehart, *Womanspirit: A Guide to Women's Wisdom*, Harper & Row, 1983.

Buffie Johnson, *Lady of the Beasts: Ancient Images of the Goddess and Her Sacred Animals*, Harper & Row, 1988.

Susan Lee and Susanah Libana, *You Said, What Is This For, This Interest in Goddess, Prehistoric Religions?* Plain View, 1985.

Helen Luke, Woman, *Earth and Spirit: The Feminine in Symbol and Myth*, The Crossroad Publishing Company, 1985.

Caitlin Matthews, *Sophia, Goddess of Wisdom: The Divine Feminine from Black Goddess to World-Soul*, HarperCollins, 1991.

Sheila Moon, *Changing Woman and Her Sisters,* Guild for Psychological Studies, 1985.

Shirley Nicholson, ed., *The Goddess Re-Awakening: The Feminine Principle Today*, Theosophical Publishing House, 1989.

Vicki Noble, *Motherpeace: A Way to the Goddess Through Myth, Art and Tarot*, Harper & Row, 1983.

_____. *Shakti Woman: Feeling Our Fire, Healing Our World: The New Female Shaman*, HarperCollins, 1991.

Carol Ochs, *Women and Spirituality*, Rowman & Allanheld, 1983.

Judith Ochshorn, *The Female Experience and the Nature of the Divine*, University of Indiana Press, 1981.

Mayumi Oda, *Goddesses*, Volcano, 1988.

Carl Olsen, ed., *The Book of Goddess Past and Present*, The Crossroad Publishing Company, 1985.

Gloria Orenstein, *The Reflowering of the Goddess*, Pergamon, 1990.

Carol Orlock, *The Goddess Letters: The Myth of Demeter and Persephone Retold*, St. Martin's Press, 1987.

Raphael Patai, *The Hebrew Goddess*, Ktav, 1967.

Judith Plant, ed., *Healing the Wounds: The Promise of Ecofeminism*, New Society Publishers, 1989.

Judith Plaskow and Carol P. Christ, eds., *Weaving the Visions: New Patterns in Feminist Spirituality*, Harper & Row, 1989.

Rosemary Radford Ruether, *Sexism and God-Talk: Towards a Feminist Theology*, Beacon, 1983.

_____. *Womanguides: Readings Towards a Feminist Theology*, Beacon, 1985.

Penelope Shuttle and Peter Redgrove, *The Wise Wound: Myths, Realities, and Meanings of Menstruation*, Bantam, 1990.

Monica Sjoo and Barbara Mor, *The Great Cosmic Mother: Rediscovering the Religion of the Earth*, Harper & Row, 1987.

Charlene Spretnak, *Lost Goddesses of Early Greece: A Collection of Pre-Hellenic Myths*, Beacon, 1981.

_____. *States of Grace: The Recovery of Meaning in the Postmodern Age*, HarperCollins, 1991.

Charlene Spretnak, ed., *The Politics of Women's Spirituality*, Anchor, 1982.

Starhawk, *Dreaming the Dark: Magic, Sex and Politics*, Beacon, 1982.

_____. *The Spiral Dance: A Rebirth of the Ancient Religion of the Great Goddess*, Harper & Row, 1989 (1979).

_____. *Truth or Dare: Encounters with Power, Authority, and Magic*, Harper & Row, 1987.

Diane Stein, *The Women's Spirituality Book*, Llewellyn, 1987.

Merlin Stone, *Ancient Mirrors of Womanhood*, Beacon, 1979.

_____. *When God Was A Woman*, Dial, 1976.

Barbara Walker, *The Woman's Dictionary of Symbols and Sacred Objects*, Harper & Row, 1988.

_____. *The Woman's Encyclopedia of Myths and Secrets*, Harper & Row, 1983.

Edward C. Whitmont, *Return of the Goddess*, The Crossroad Publishing Company, 1982.

Diane Wolkstein and Samuel Kramer, *Inanna, Queen of Heaven and Earth: Her Stories and Hymns from Sumer*, Harper & Row, 1983.

Marion Woodman, *Addiction to Perfection: The Still Unravaged Bride*, Inner City Books, 1985.

_____. *The Pregnant Virgin: A Process of Psychological Transformation*, Inner City Books, 1985.

Patrice Wynne, *The Womanspirit Sourcebook*, Harper & Row, 1988.

Connie Zweig, ed., *To Be A Woman: The Birth of the Conscious Feminine*, Jeremy P. Tarcher, 1990.

"The patriarchal ego of both men and women, to earn its instinct-disciplining, striving, progressive, and heroic stance, has fled from the full-scale awe of the Goddess. Or it has tried to slay her, or at least to dismember and thus depotentiate her. But it is toward her—and especially toward her culturally repressed aspects, those chaotic, ineluctable depths—that the new individuating balanced ego must return to find its matrix and the embodied, flexible strength to be active and vulnerable, to stand its own ground and still be empathetically related to others."
—Sylvia Perera

A number of nifty tapes, including Jean Shinoda Bolen's *Goddesses As Inner Images*, are available from New Dimensions Tapes, PO Box 410510, San Francisco, CA 94141-0510, (415) 563-8899. Then there's The Great Goddess Collection Gift Catalog, c/o Star River Productions, PO Box 7754, North Brunswick, NJ 08902.

"Our discontent and subtle suffering spring from the loss of the feminine values, and we face formidable obstacles in restoring this value."
—Robert A. Johnson

The interdependence between human and Creator may somehow be easier to imagine when the creative source is envisioned as "she."

Splendid Moments

Why do I imagine that the Creator
weeps for us (I won't call her
Goddess, God, It) when our
lives tremble at their roots—

when the rain won't come—
when the winter stays too long—
when love won't stay—
when soldiers do, war—

there was a time, I think,
when we knew how to plead
for rain, coax the spring,
love the bones of another,

when there were warriors
who hunted and prayed
to the wind and the animal
they longed to kill and eat.

Friends of mine have died of cancer,
bullets, no love, loss of faith,

their own hand, and as I write
of their lives, at times, I weep.

As author I spring them into being,
but then I must allow them their own
words and will if they are to live.
They teach me love.

* * *

And so we teach the Creator
love—does she weep for us
and laugh with us in those
splendid moments?

I would like to think so—
oh, yes—I would like to
think we are coaxing her into
being as we become.

Is this hubris—do we dare
to think she needs us—for her
becoming—that she could not
exist without us?

Does she smile at this—
does she marvel at her creation?
To dare to love is hubris,
she knows.

Alma Luz Villanueva
Planet: A Book of Poetry

○ Relate to God as female.

_____

In addition to the three manifestations of the goddess discussed below, I would add the idea of "basic space" which connects us all—a perception often mentioned in Eastern religious texts and one beginning to make its way into Western consciousness.

"If female history is different, if female biology is different, if female psychology is different, if all the hundreds of little responses to life's daily occurrences are different, how can the spirituality be the same?"
—Theresa King

Why Women Need the Goddess

If the simplest meaning of the Goddess symbol is an affirmation of the legitimacy and beneficence of female power writ large, then a question immediately arises, "Is the Goddess simply female power writ large, and if so, why bother with the symbol of Goddess at all? Or does the symbol refer to a Goddess `out there' who is not reducible to a human potential?" The many women who have rediscovered the power of the Goddess would give three answers to this question: (1) The Goddess is divine female, a personification who can be invoked in prayer and ritual; (2) the Goddess is symbol of the life, death, and rebirth energy in nature and culture, in personal and communal life; and (3) the Goddess is the symbol of the affirmation of the legitimacy and beauty of female power (made possible by the new becoming of women in the women's liberation movement). If one were to ask these women which answer is the "correct" one, different responses would be given. Some would assert that the Goddess definitely is *not* "out there," that the symbol of a divinity "out there" is part of the legacy of patriarchal oppression, which brings with it the authoritarianism, hierarchicalism, and dogmatic rigidity associated with biblical monotheistic religions. They might assert that the Goddess symbol reflects the sacred power within women and nature, suggesting the connectedness between women's cycles of menstruation, birth, and menopause, and the life and death cycles of the universe. Others seem quite comfortable with the notion of Goddess as divine female protector and creator and would find their experience of the Goddess limited by the assertion that she is not *also* out there as well as within themselves and in all natural processes.

Carol P. Christ
in *Womenspirit Rising*

○ Draw your own image of the goddess.

_____

Some women are unable to relate to Greek goddesses because their personalities—revealed by their pouts, competitions, and revenges—simply reflect the problems of women under patriarchy rather than a model for change. Others—for the same reasons—feel a deep connection to them.

Meditation on Six Greek Goddesses

There are many Greek goddesses understood as archetypes of the feminine, but according to Jennifer and Roger Woolger in *The Goddess Within,* the following six seem to resonate most strongly with today's women. Everyone has aspects of the different goddesses within their psyche, but one or two will usually dominate in a particular personality:

Athena: Goddess of wisdom and civilization. Today the Athena woman would be concerned with achievement, education, career, ideas, social causes, and politics.

Aphrodite: Goddess of Love. The Aphrodite woman's concerns center on relationships, sexuality, romance, beauty, art, and sometimes intrigue.

Persephone: Goddess of the Underworld. A Persephone woman is attracted to the spirit world, the occult, visions, mysticism, and matters connected with death and transformation.

Artemis: Goddess of the Hunt. An Artemis woman loves the wilds, athletics, adventure, and animals. She is likely to be involved in ecology, alternative life-styles, and women's communities.

Demeter: Goddess of Grain. The Demeter woman is likely to be maternal and nurturing, concerned with all aspects of childbirth and raising children.

Hera: Queen of the Heaven. The Hera woman focuses on marriage and partnership with men; she emanates in powerful female rulers and leaders.

"We have no adequate name for the true God/ess, the 'I am who I shall become.' Intimations of Her/His name will appear as we emerge from false naming of God/ess modeled on patriarchal alienation."
—Rosemary Radford Ruether

111

○ Go within and "feel" the different goddesses in your psyche. Which one dominates? With which are you out of touch?

"Faith is the centerpiece of a connected life. It allows us to live by the grace of invisible strands. It is a belief in a wisdom superior to our own. Faith becomes a teacher in the absence of fact."
—Terry Tempest Williams

In her study of the Virgin Mary, the author points out that Mary's virgin motherhood is the primary sign of her supernatural nature which—unlike the myth of the incarnate god—is often turned into moral exhortation. Thus Mary establishes a woman's destiny as motherhood, but does not herself get involved with the sexual intercourse required of mortal women. The myth establishes woman's purpose on the one hand and denigrates her sexuality on the other, pulling women first one way, then another. Throughout history, the cult of Mary has been interwoven with Christian ideas about the dangers of the flesh, especially in connection with the female of the species. Nonetheless, Mary provides tremendous solace, especially to those in trouble.

Comfort at the Hour of Our Death

For although the Virgin is a healer, a midwife, a peacemaker, the protectress of virgins, and the patroness of monks and nuns in this world; although her polymorphous myth has myriad uses and functions for the living, it is the jurisdiction over death accorded her in popular belief that gives her such widespread supremacy. When Catholics contemplate the darkness of death stretching before them, they cling to a light on the horizon that seems to them no will-o'-the-wisp but as constant as the moon, which is the Virgin's attribute. At the moment the finite plane of a mortal life reaches its term it intersects with the timeless, undifferentiated, immortal beauty and bliss epitomized by the Virgin and makes death meaningless. At the moment the believer fears that step across the gulf, as every man who knows himself a sinner must fear, the promise of the Virgin's ungrudging, ever-flowing clemency sustains him. That is why the best-loved prayer of the Catholic world—the Hail Mary—

ends with the pleas that the Virgin should "pray for us sinners, now and at the hour of our death."

Marina Warner
Alone of All Her Sex

For other good books on this subject, see: *Eunuchs for the Kingdom of Heaven,* by Uta Ranke-Heinemann, Viking Penguin, 1990; *Mary's Way,* by Peggy Tabor Millin, Celestial Arts, 1991; *The Black Madonna,* by Fred Gustafon, Sigo, 1990; *The Cult of the Virgin Mary,* by Michael Carroll, Princeton, 1986; and *Longing for Darkness: Tara and the Black Madonna,* by China Galland, Viking, 1990.

_____

Women are not the only ones who derive comfort from the goddess. Men need her as well.

The Holy Virgin

Adherents of alternative traditions may need to recognize that the figure of Mary has certain advantages over the resurrected (and at times concocted) Goddess images abounding today. Nearly two thousand years of continuous and fervent devotion makes Mary far more relevant, effective, and indeed alive than Inanna-Ishtar, Isis, Ceridwen, or other ancient Goddesses, who were worshipped long ago and far away. Moreover, one of Mary's signal characteristics is her willingness to respond to personal feeling more readily than to abstractions. The Holy Virgin seems different in essence from the various ancient Goddesses and also from abstractions such as the "goddess," "Gaia," and other forms promulgated by "politically correct" circles. Mary seems oriented to love rather than justice, to patient humility rather than assertiveness; she prefers faith to intellectuality, feelings to deeds.

Stephan A. Hoeller
The Divine Feminine in Recent World Events

"Mary is idealized in order to suppress the feminine shadow, and therefore ordinary women, confronted with Mary, can easily feel failures."
—Roger Horrocks

113

Here's a prayer to Mary written by Pope John Paul II

Mary, Queen of Peace,
> We entrust our lives to you.
>> Shelter us from war, hatred
>>> and oppression.

Teach us
> To live in peace,
>> to educate ourselves for peace.

Inspire us to act justly,
> to revere all God has made.

Root peace firmly in our hearts
> and in our world.

> Amen

> —Pope John Paul II

———————————

Jungian therapist Sylvia Perera, in her groundbreaking work, Descent to the Goddess, *presents a much grittier goddess than is found in the Greek pantheon or in popular culture. She works with the Sumerian goddess Inanna, to whom one must descend. The journey itself, as Perera describes it, entails unusual risks and profound changes.*

Descending to the Goddess

The motif of descent is commonplace in Jungian work. (It applies equally though differently to both women and men, although I am here dealing only with women's experience of the process.) We make descents or introversions in the service of life, to scoop up more of what has been held unconscious by the Self in the underworld, until we are strong enough for the journey and willing to sacrifice libido for its release. The hardest descents are those to the primitive, uroboric depths where we suffer what feels like total dismemberment. But there are many others imaged as descents into tunnels, the belly or womb, into mountains and through mirrors. Some of the easier ones we may need to have undergone, to loosen rigidities and raise energy, before we can risk the shattering descents to the depths of our primal wounds to work on the psychic-somatic level of the basic hurt.

These deepest descents lead to radical reorganization and transformation of the conscious personality. But, like the shaman's journey or Inanna's, they are fraught with real peril. Hopefully in therapy the therapist may "manage" and companion the descents with help from the unconscious, but some fall beyond the therapist's capacity or open into the unseen crevasses of psychotic episodes. All descents provide entry into different levels of consciousness and can enhance life creatively. All of them imply suffering. All of them can serve as initiations. Meditation and dreaming and active imagination are modes of descent. So too are depressions, anxiety attacks, and experiences with hallucinogenic drugs.

Descent as Controlled Therapeutic Regression

What I have seen and experienced in myself and other women who are successful daughters of the collective, often unmothered daughters of the animus and the patriarchy, is that we suffer a basic fault (Michael Balint's term). We do not have an adequate sense of our own ground nor connection to our own embodied strength and needs adequate to provide us with a resilient feminine, balanced yin-yang, processual ego. There is a fault in the basic levels of our personality—a deep split, maintained by loyalty to superego ideals that no longer function to enhance life, a loyalty that keeps the ego alienated from reality, in a regressed, inflated, Self-identified mode. Thus we need to undergo a "controlled regression" into the borderland-underworld levels of the dark goddess—back to ourselves before we had the form we know, back to the magic and archaic levels of consciousness and to the transpersonal passions and rages which both blast and nurture us there; back to the body-

"For each of us as women, there is a deep place within, where hidden and growing our true spirit rises. . . . Within these deep places, each one holds an incredible reserve of creativity and power, of unexamined and unrecorded emotion and feeling. The woman's place of power within each of us is neither white nor surface; it is dark, it is ancient, and it is deep."
—Audre Lord

115

"Thus I believe that the Goddess is unknown in at least three senses: 1) in the obvious sense, in which the Goddess herself, by virtue of Her Godhead, is necessarily ineffable; 2) in the sense that we do not know what the identifying quality of the feminine principle is; and 3)in the sense that we do not know what particular aspect of herself the feminine will manifest in the new era which we are entering."
—Beatrice Bruteau

mind, and the preverbal tomb-womb states, searching back to the deep feminine, the "dual mother" Jung writes about.

On the way down we shed the identifications with and the defenses against the animus, introverting to initially humiliating and devastating, but ultimately safer, primal levels. There we may learn to survive in a different way and to await the chance for rebirth. Sometimes we wait a long time, caught in coming to know our primal beginnings from a new perspective, feeling loosened from old meanings as if suspended out of life. In the depths of the underworld the opposing, chaotic energies of the Great Round battle in us while we feel ourselves to be without energy. They dismember the old animus ego complex and its faulty identifications.

Work on this level in therapy involves the deepest affects and is inevitably connected to preverbal, "infantile" processes. The therapist must be willing to participate where needed, often working on the body-mind level where there is as yet no image in the other's awareness and where instinct and affect and sensory perception begin to coalesce first in a body sensation, which can be intensified to bring forth memory or image. Silence, affirmative mirroring attention, touch, holding, sounding and singing, gesture, breathing, nonverbal actions like drawing, sandplay, building with clay or blocks, dancing—all have their time and place.

On this magic and matriarchal level the elements of ritual are potent and need to be respected, even encouraged. The gestures and enactments of psychodrama can be helpful to create or recreate a space, an emotion, a meaning, an archetypal pattern. But mainly the therapist must be guided by the powerful affective connections of the transference-countertransference, and by the images of dream and fantasy, to sense where and how the process wants to go. The therapeutic attitude is one of actively allowing each individual to be with him or herself in any way necessary. This may lead to all kinds of creative improvisations—actions and gestures and permissions, both symbolic and literal—to touch the regressed and hidden pre-ego, and to help it to learn to feel valid and to trust.

Such maternally nurturant and companioning behavior has profound effects, although these are often kept secret or left unspoken. Their impact may be revealed only in dream images, or years later reported as turning points in the work. Often part of the effect is due to the patient's or analysand's feeling that such acceptance and participation go beyond conventional parameters of verbal therapy and, therefore, suggest the therapist's willingness to "be unorthodox"—even defying some superego prohibitions. This seems to make the other feel deeply allied with and validated on the archaic-matriarchal level. An analyst—serving as the carrier of archetypal projections—must accept the other's deeply individual feelings and needs, caring more for them than for abstract and impersonal collective conventions.

* * *

Jung writes of the descent to the plant level as "the downward way, the yin way . . . to earth, the darkness of humanity." It is to this descent that the goddess Inanna and we modern women must submit, going into the deep, inchoate places where the extremes of beauty and ugliness swim or dissolve together in a paradoxical, seemingly meaningless state. Even the queen of beauty becomes raw, rotten meat. Life loses its savor. But it is a sacred process--even the rot--for it represents submission to Ereshkigal and the destructive-transformative mysteries that she symbolizes.

Sylvia Perera
Descent to the Goddess

○ Descend to your yang energy by concentrating on the "hara" or belly region about two inches below the navel. Let it go soft and focus your breathing through this belly-mind. Feel all of your masculine strength center there, notice how yang energy can be made gentle yet extremely strong and dynamic as you bring it into your woman's body.

○ Descend to your yin energy by nondual meditation: relax the mind, sit zazen, become one with nature, with another.

"Inanna's story confronts us with the great divide between Goddess and patriarchal consciousness . . . . From the vantage of the Goddess the underground is the primal womb, the matrix of all being, but to the patriarchy the underworld is an alien place of horror and dread."
—Elinor Gaden

Goddess statues or amulets often prove helpful for those of us who were raised without a goddess or female deity. We may not need these artifacts, but can simply go within, for no matter what our background, we can connect with our motherline, the lineage of female power and healing—ancient or modern—if we are able to overcome the smug little part of our mind that rejects that which is nonrational and out of the ordinary. Bypass this know-it-all brain by letting the imagination fully engage in the exercise. Every time you allow yourself to "dissolve," you help to lessen the power of the part of the mind that limits you to rational thought.

"Rituals created within a framework of women's spirituality differ in form and content from the empty, hierarchically imposed, patriarchal observances with which most of us grew up. They involve healing, strengthening, creative energy that expands with spontaneity from a meaningful core of values."
—Charlene Spretnak

Earth Goddess

Lie down, your arms folded left above the right. Close your eyes. Imagine yourself lying in a rich bed of earth. Take a few deep breaths, knowing that there is nothing you have to do, nowhere you have to go. . . . Imagine that your body begins to merge with the soil. Gradually your skin, flesh and bones dissolve into the earth, so that there is no separation. . . . As the earth breathes, you breathe. . . . Spend as long as you like in this deep silent repose. . . . Eventually, feel that you are being created anew. Beginning from the inside out, feel your organs, your bones, muscles and flesh reconstructed, your body and psyche refreshed. . . . When you are ready, stretch, open your eyes—and feel yourself reborn.

Hallie Iglehart Austen
The Heart of the Goddess

A wide variety of goddesses—and practices related to their worship—are made accessible through such books as *The Heart of the Goddess*, which includes images as well as meditations for goddesses around the world. Nancy Blair's *Amulets of the Goddess* includes a pouch full of amulets. Both are available from Wingbow Press, 7900 Edgewater Dr., Oakland, CA 94621. Women's bookstores often carry goddess statues and pictures. Also, Red Rose Collection Catalog, PO Box 280140, San Francisco, CA 94010, 1-800-374-5505, has a wide variety of goddess-related items as does The Great Goddess Gift Catalog, Star River Productions, PO Box 7754, North Brunswick, NJ 08902.

Earth-based religions incorporate the idea of a shaman or healer who is able to contact spirits through visions or by traveling to the underworld. This is done for the sake of the community—to heal a member of the tribe or to attain information needed for group survival or harmony. In the past few decades, a renewed interest in Native American religions has provided a model for living in balance with nature as well as a wealth of shamanic practices for women. Some think that the original shamans were women; certainly the tradition includes women and provides a powerful sphere for channeling female energy coupled with concern for the community. Joan Halifax rightly warns that the ego stands ready to insist on the credit when we take on the role of a shaman. "Psychic inflation" also results when an individual woman assumes goddess energy as her own personal property, not something that links her to the world at large. This linkage of ego to a personified goddess may account for the criticisms of pretention and unnecessary drama leveled against the goddess movement.

"The earth does not belong to us, we belong to it."
—Black Elk

Shaman Woman

There is a trap in the extraordinary. One begins to feel special and self-important, along with an absence of compassion. Maybe it is disappointing, this talk of simplicity in favor of the more dramatic aspects of being a shaman. What we all want at our core is to be free from suffering; we want to be in a situation of simplicity. We don't want to be driven by desire, or hate; nor do we wish to be caught in confusion. Moving past these three poisons means that we discover simplicity, harmony, relaxation, compassion, and wisdom. From this awakening arises the impulse to help others. . . .

An aspect that calls to be examined in our lives now has to do with the feminine and the earth. We need to look at our role as women in relation to helping people in our culture discover the extraordinary beauty of the earth. Part of this has come about for me because I have made a friend of my womanhood. I've discovered my woman shield to be deep and creative. I am not afraid of my woman. I have a strong sense of great joy in being her. By the same

119

"There is no form without the gift of the Mother and the Father. From Father Sky comes your consciousness and Mother Earth is your very bones. To sense the balance of the Mother/Father, Father/Mother within one's own being, one's own nature, is a way to renew the Earth, to renew our hearts, to renew the vision."
--Dhyani Ywahoo

token, I have a strong relationship with my man shield, the healer.

There has been a weaving together of sky consciousness with earth consciousness. I feel healed intellectually with the gift of Buddhism and from the experience of the shaman. The earth has healed my body.

Now I am bringing a sense of equanimity and harmony between these pairs of opposites to others. It is not so much as something to teach, but as something to be. Those who walk in the wilderness will sense that balance directly. One feels no need to build statues to the goddess. One can sit under a tree. One feels no need to create a throne for her to sit on. Her throne is everywhere on earth.

Joan Halifax
Contemporary Shaman Women

Shamanic wisdom relies on felt experience and oral teachings, but a great deal may be gleaned from the many books now available.

Sedonia Cahill & Joshua Halpern, *Ceremonial Circle: Practice, Ritual, and Renewal for Personal and Community Healing*, HarperCollins, 1992.

Gary Doore, *In Shaman's Path: Healing, Personal Growth and Empowerment*, Shambhala, 1988.

Stephen Foster with Meredith Little, *The Book of the Vision Quest*, Prentice-Hall, 1988.

Douchan Gersi, *Faces in the Smoke: An Eyewitness Experience of Voodoo, Shamanism, Psychic Healing, and Other Amazing Human Powers*, Jeremy P. Tarcher, 1991.

Joan Halifax, *Shaman: The Wounded Healer*, The Crossroad Publishing Company, 1982.

Joan Halifax, ed., *Shamanic Voices: A Survey of Visionary Narratives*, Dutton, 1979.

Michael Hart, *The Way of the Shaman*, Harper & Row, 1990.

Ruth-Inge Heinze, *Shamans of the 20th Century*, Irvington, 1990.

Shirley Nicholson, ed., *Shamanism*, Quest, 1987.

Vicki Noble, *Shakti Woman: Feeling Our Fire, Healing Our World: The New Female Shamanism*, HarperCollins, 1991.

Vicki Noble, ed., *Snake Power: A Journal of Contemporary Female Shamanism*, 5856 College Avenue #138, Oakland, CA 94618.

Gini Graham Scott, *Secrets of the Shaman Warrior*, New Falcon, 1991.

Roger Walsh, *Spirit of Shamanism*, Jeremy P. Tarcher, 1990.

Of related interest is a book by a student of Carlos Castaneda's *nagual,* Don Juan, describing her initiation: Taisha Abelar's *The Sorcerer's Crossing: A Woman's Journey,* Penguin Arkana, 1992.

Workshops & Foundations:

Dance of the Deer Foundation/Center for Shamanic Studies, PO Box 699, Soquel, CA 95073, (408) 475-9560.

Eagle Song Wilderness Camps, PO Box 121, Ovando, MT 59854. Brooke Medicine Eagle leads workshops here at Blacktail Ranch in Montana.

The Foundation for Shamanic Studies, Box 670, Belden Station, Norwalk, CT 06852; (203) 454-2825. Founded by Michael Harner.

Shaman's Drum, PO Box 430, Willits, CA 95490, (707) 459-0486. Contains calendar of workshops and events and resource directory for those involved in shamanism.

Snake Power: A Journal of Contemporary Female Shamanism, 5856 College Avenue #138, Oakland, CA 94618. Edited by Vicki Noble, creator of the Motherpeace Tarot Cards.

"Praised be my Lord for our mother the earth, that which doth sustain us and keep us, and bringeth forth divers fruit, and flowers of many colours, and grass."
—Saint Francis of Assisi

Native American religion provides a harmonious view of nature and the way in which "two-leggeds" can live respectfully within her. Exposure to this view can be extremely healing for anyone brought up with the idea that nature—like woman—is to be conquered. Many ecologists and eco-feminists are turning to a Native American world view as a model for a saner, more peaceful world. Many see the earth itself as a goddess—the mother of all goddesses, if you will.

Deepening Spirituality Through Nature

Mother, you gave us our very cells, you who are the deep, deep nest of all your children that ever have been, are now, and will be. You nurture and renew us. Our true mother, Mother Earth, we thank you for our life.

Father, you share with us the spark of aliveness, you who are the light that shines within us and all our relations from the beginning

"The purest acts of worship acknowledging her presence within us are the simple, significant gestures toward the natural objects outside us—touching a stone or a tree, drinking water and milk, being with fire or standing in the wind or listening to birds."
—Meinrad Craighead

to the end. Father Sky, we thank you for our life.

It is well that I have been asked to talk with you about woman and nature, and the potential for deepening our spirituality through nature. Spirit is father, sky, light, creation, the spark that ignites and lives within us all. Nature is mother, earth, womb of all possibility, nurturing and renewing place where we receive our bodies. These are our true parents.

When light reached into the dark ever-present womb and pulled forth two-leggeds, not just dust was made real, but starlight as well. We humans are earth and sky. We can be represented as a cross, a blending: Mother seen as looking across the horizon, Father as looking up. They cross at our heart.

Thus Spirit lives within Mother and within each of us. Father Spirit is not angry and vengeful as some of the old books would tell us, and certainly has not given up and left, as some modern thinkers propound. To stand quiet in Mother's beauty is to immediately recognize the aliveness that abounds. Spirit is incredibly alive, moving and dancing and singing in Mother's beauty.

Before we can say we have finished what is begun here, you must take yourself to a quiet place of Mother's beauty and see the life around you. Sit upon Mother. Balance and quiet yourself and consciously join yourself with the circle of all that is alive. If you find this difficult in the beginning, look at every tiny thing you see around you as you sit there, and picture it dead, as though its life is gone: no movement, no sound, no breeze. Every blade of grass, every tree lifeless, every four-legged, all the crawlers, the waters stagnant and putrid, the wingeds fallen and still. Then bring yourself into contrasting reality, and really see the life dancing around you. Breathe in the aliveness and find it in yourself. Feel and listen to your heart beat. Stop doing anything about breathing, and let yourself be breathed. Remember, then, the words "Father is alive within Mother Earth, within me and all things" and give thanks for life. When you have experienced this, then the remainder of what I say can be real within you rather than merely words.

Our present challenge is to awaken and embody Spirit within us, rather than to leave earth or our bodies to find Spirit. We are entering the time of the nine-pointed star, the star of making real upon earth the golden dream of peace that lives within us. We understand that finding heaven is not going somewhere else, but co-creating it here upon this beautiful earth. We are completing the cycle of the eight-pointed star, Venus, star of the heart, where the lesson has been about ourselves as the cross between sky and earth, and about letting the light and love of Father and Mother join at our hearts and shine forth unrestricted. Having understood and taken within us the knowing of Spirit, we can then use that light and love to manifest a peaceful, abundant, harmonious world around us.

In doing this we have a strong ally in our elder sister, White Buffalo Woman, mysterious holy woman who appeared long, long ago to the Lakota people bringing the sacred pipe and seven sacred rites. Her message, as was Creator's message in the beginning, is of oneness: Spirit lives within everything and thus we are related to all things through Spirit. Spirit is the vibration, the hum, the movement of everything from the tiny atom of a rock to the spiral growth of the tallest tree and the playful fun of children. Mother has her own special hum, as do all things. Her vibration, eight cycles per second, is healing and renewing to us when we experience it. In this modern world we have cut ourselves off from this song of Mother's body, alienating ourselves from her spirit, by producing noise and vibration to surround ourselves: electricity, motors, radio waves, interference of all kinds. Thus we feel the necessity to go into Mother's vastness to reconnect ourselves with the renewing and nurturing of her spirit.

> Brooke Medicine Eagle
> "Nature and Spirituality: Time of the New
> Dawning" in *The Spiral Path*

"Most of us are used only to awesome holiness of churches and lofty arches, cathedrals where, with stained glass and brooding silences, priests try to emulate the religious atmosphere that is to be found in the living earth in some of her secret places."
—Mabel Dodge Luhan

Books on Native American spirituality have surged into print as the ecology movement has grown. Recently many fine books by or about women in that tradition have begun to appear. These include:

Paula Gunn Allen, *The Sacred Hoop: Recovering the Feminine in American Indian Traditions,* Beacon, 1986.
_____ , *Grandmothers of the Light: A Medicine Woman's Sourcebook,* Beacon, 1991.
Lynn Andrews, *Medicine Woman,* Harper & Row, 1981. (Although Andrews states that her work is not connected with a specific Native American tradition,

> *"Nature is the signature of God. Understanding nature, you begin to see the metaphor, the microcosmic law, the macrocosmic law, that is within us every moment. We don't have to be incredibly wise. We just need to open our eyes and see what we live in."*
> —Coqosh Auh-Ho-Oh

she incorporates their basic view of nature into her writing.)

Beth Brant, ed., *A Gathering of Spirit,* Sinister Wisdom Books, 1984.

Ann Cameron, *Daughters of Copper Woman,* Press Gang, 1981.

Natalie Curtis, ed., *The Indian's Book: Songs and Legends of the American Indians,* Dover, 1950.

Mary Crow Dog and Richard Erdoes, *Lakota Woman,* Harper Perennial, 1991.

Brooke Medicine Eagle, *Buffalo Woman Comes Singing,* Ballentine, 1991. (Audio tapes available from New Dimension Tapes, PO Box 410510, San Francisco, CA 94141, (415) 563-8899.)

Nancy Falk and Rita Gross, eds., *Unspoken Worlds: Women's Religious Lives in Non-Western Cultures,* Harper & Row, 1980.

Sheila Moon, *Changing Woman and Her Sisters: Feminine Aspects of Selves and Deities,* Guild for Psychological Studies, 1984.

G. M. Mullet, *Spider Woman Stories: Legends of the Hopi Indians,* University of Arizona Press, 1979.

Twylah Nitsch, *Entering into the Silence,* Seneca Indian Historical Society, 1976

_____, *Language of the Trees,* Seneca Indian Historical Society, 1982.

_____, *Language of the Stones,* Seneca Indian Historical Society, 1983.

Steve Wall, *Wisdom's Daughter: Conversations with Women Elders of Native America,* HarperCollins, 1993.

Dhyani Ywahoo, *Voices of Our Ancestors,* Shambhala, 1987.

○ Here are three exercises adapted from various shamanic traditions. Notice how they all embody elements from the natural world—soil, trees, animals.

To Lose Your Troubles

Pick up a handful of earth and gaze into it; pour all of your problems and troubles into this handful of earth, outlining them in minute detail.

When you have finished, throw the handful of dirt behind you and walk away from it. Do not turn back.

Landscape

Cultivate a relationship with a particular landscape: a stretch of beach, a meadow or woodland, a rocky shore or mountainside, part of a canyon, desert, or valley. Go there and spend time. Draw pictures of it, write poems about it.

Really pay attention to "your" chosen spot, to each rock, tree, and plant. Watch the changing of the seasons, the interplay of light and shadow. Learn the names of the flowers and trees or the wildlife and birds. Recall this spot to quiet yourself.

Being an Animal

Don't just imagine yourself as an animal but try to become one. As a cat, or the mouse it chases, or a monkey—whatever creature you chose--begin to crawl, stalk, slither, pounce, crouch. Experience its realm as fully as possible, duplicating its movements and sounds. Go into the woods to forage, sinking as deeply as possible into the animal's being as it searches for food or shelter or tries to protect itself from predators.

When you read a story about an animal—a whale who swam up the Sacramento river, a laboratory monkey, a coyote hunted by ranchers—put yourself in the creature's place. Don't just imagine, but *feel* the animal's predicament.

Begin to watch animals; relate to them on a nonverbal level.

"No one with any sense would claim, or ever has claimed, that the witch rites of today are the unaltered rituals of our remotest ancestors. On the contrary, witchcraft today is the product of a long period of evolution, in the course of which there have been many changes and accretions."
—Doreen Valiente

Patricia Eagle, who lives in the San Francisco Bay Area, is a registered nurse, currently working on a graduate degree in Women's Studies. The word Wicca is an old term for "witchcraft" preferred by many modern witches.

Interview with a Witch

Kimberley Snow: How did you get involved with Wicca?
Patricia Eagle: I've had a personal urge to find some sort of spiritual truth ever since I was a very young child. I went to lots of different churches as I was growing up. Then, in my late teens, I met another woman who was interested in spiritual matters. We'd talk and dabble around in this or that and decided to meet once a month to work on our spiritual life. Since the full moon was a naturally occurring event and easy to keep track of, we'd get together then.

"The Goddess has at last stirred from sleep, and women are reawakening to our ancient power. The feminist movement, which began as a political, economic and social struggle, is opening to a spiritual dimension. In the process, many women are discovering the old religion, reclaiming the word witch *and, with it, some of our lost culture."*
—Starhawk

We'd both read a little in astrology, so we'd look at the stars and find the planets. We were living in Florida at the time and could see the whole sky quite beautifully. It gave us a real sense of where we were on the planet in terms of the other planets, the other constellations, learning where the zodiac was.

I began to realize things like that the moon was full in the opposite sign of the sun. That makes sense to me now, but then it was a revelation. I began to watch how the sun and the moon reacted to each other, how the moon reflected the sun, how the curve of the moon always pointed towards the sun whether she was waxing or waning, how she always came up two hours later, how she dragged her way through the zodiac rather than the other planets.

As we began to work in this practice, we started to walk around in a circle with incense or with water or something. Now where we got this information, I don't know. Some of it seemed to arise spontaneously; some of it crept in out of fairy tales we'd read, things we'd heard. As we walked around in a circle so that we'd have a place in which to do our work, we'd mark north, east, south, and west. Partly we did this to learn where the moon was going to rise. We had a rule of thumb to do our full-moon practice for three days on either side of the full moon. We eventually started putting things like candles to indicate the directions. Then we began making lovely little collections of magical objects—now I'd call them altars. We'd walk around in a circle three times. We somehow knew that less than three times wasn't enough, that the right number was from three to infinity.

After a couple of months, we met a few other women who were doing the same thing. The first time I met with them, I watched one woman cast a formal circle—a full nine-foot circle—complete with ritual. I was a little overwhelmed and intimidated, mainly because I'd heard so many negative things about witchcraft and about satanism. I'd always been frightened by the idea of black magic and didn't want to have anything to do with it. Yet I felt curious and was drawn to this woman, so I went into the circle and prayed that I'd be in the light and that only good, positive things would come of it.

K: Who were you praying to?

P: As a child, I'd had a mystical experience. I'd been in a field by myself and started to pray because I wanted to find some center. I didn't know who to pray to—I knew I wasn't a Christian—so I ended up praying to All Of Thou. By that I meant whoever was the appropriate person to pray to in order to find a positive spiritual path. Sort of a religious To Whom It May Concern. So I went out there with a pure heart and wept and prayed, wept and prayed, until I felt my crown chakra open. I still think that it's a futile task to try to construct a name for whatever power is out there, but for me, the use of All of Thou—the sacred familiar—worked. I didn't feel that the deity or the goddess or whatever was so cruel that I'd have to learn the right name in order to make contact.

So by the time I went inside the circle in Florida, I had a sense that pure motivation put me in touch with the sacred. I also had a sense that this was a different level than I'd been involved with before, and I was a little leery of it.

My friend and I started doing rituals with this group that included a man who'd been a ceremonial magician and had once been a Catholic priest, a woman named Wynona who has since become my teacher, and a few other people. Wynona very gently let my friend and I know that we'd been spontaneously casting a circle when we'd walk around three times, that putting things in the north, the east, south, and west was calling the directions. Later I worked with Native American as well as Tibetan Buddhist teachers who also circumambulate a space before they begin sacred work, and who work with the directions in much the same way. To find that many earth-centered indigenous religions have similar rituals has deepened my faith in the Craft.

At that point, the women's movement was very political and anti-spiritual, seeing religion as a trap and form of oppression. I didn't have any literature on witchcraft available to me at first. But Wynona very gently taught me that what I was doing did have a history and roots. I eventually learned that Wynona had been in a coven in the Carolinas years before that had come down through her family from England. The rituals and traditions arose from the old European religion.

When I realized that what I was doing was Wicca or witchcraft, I was a little taken aback because it had a lot of negative connotations for me. Bad spells and hexes didn't interest me. I think there are people who are attracted to the shocking nature of being a witch.

"It was always a political religion. It teaches the oppressed to stand up against the oppressors. On politics alone you burn out. You have to know the revels, you have to know the good deep belly laugh, you have to go out under the full moon and light a few candles."
—Z. Budapest

127

"To disbelieve in witchcraft is the greatest of all heresies."
—Malleus Maleficarum

I'm not. I'm very reticent about naming my practice.

Now that I know the history, of course, it all makes more sense. For example, *Malleus Maleficarum,* the Witch's Hammer, was used during the Inquisition as a "script" for the men of the church to follow when making witches confess. One of the things it says is that a woman who professes to heal is obviously a witch since only men can heal. Furthermore, a woman who claims she can heal and only hurts you should obviously be burned at the stake, but even more insidious—and even more in league with the devil—is a woman who claims she can heal and does so, because she then makes you believe in her and not in Christ's church. Thus if you are compassionately working as a midwife or a herbalist and your healing works, then that, in itself, meant that you were a witch and drawing your powers from the devil to confuse people. So the layers of confusion and oppression and misogyny that cover over witchcraft are pretty horrifying.

I've seen women who start to become quite powerful in their practice, then they begin to dream they are being burned at the stake or tortured. They become very frightened and go into Native American spirituality or some other form of practice rather than identify themselves as witches. That's because of this history. I think to use the term *witch* itself takes courage.

K: What's the connection between witchcraft and the goddess movement today?

P: I think Merlin Stone was the person who got the Goddess movement going. During our consciousness-raising groups in the sixties and seventies, we started asking, "Where are the feminine deities?" Merlin Stone, acting on intuition, began to do research and found all of these images of the goddess as an art historian. That's when she wrote *When God Was A Woman.*

Wicca has always worshipped the moon as the goddess—the fecund, earth-mother and the sun as the god—the spirit, the energizer. In our time, we've put far too much emphasis on the male part and not enough on the female. I think the emphasis on the goddess now is very healthy. We need to let the goddess reemerge and to pay attention to ideas about nurturing and caring, about being compassionate, about caring for the earth. If we take the analogy of the earth as our ultimate, primal mother and see how we have treated her, we see how much we need to rebalance.

K: Could you tell me more about your teacher. What did she teach you?

P: She always said that I was *her* teacher. She taught me that what I needed to do was to trust myself and know that what I was doing was appropriate, to learn to go into my center and listen to my own intuitive knowing. Years later she let me see her Book of Shadows.

A Book of Shadows is a book of rituals, prayers, and invocations from traditional witchcraft. In the old days, they would cast a circle and copy down the recipes of rituals from each others' Book of Shadows, and these would be passed down. Often this was done by moonlight since they couldn't meet during the day in the open. It's like a Bible.

Since Wicca is an earth-based religion, the holy days are the winter solstices, summer equinoxes, and the cross-quarter days halfway in between: Halloween, midsummer night, and Feast of Brigid or Candlemas, and May Day or Beltane. Those are halfway between the major holidays, what they call the wheel of the year. Since it is an agrarian-based religion, the festivals helped people know when to plant, when to sow, et cetera. The winter solstice is the rebirth of light, the rebirth of the god. The autumnal equinox was the death of the god. The holidays mark what they call the turn of the wheel of the year. They believed that they had to do the practices to keep the wheel turning. It's very shamanic in that sense.

K: What about community rituals?

P: The major feasts were about community building. Halloween, which is now the Catholic Feast of the Dead, is the witch's new year. It is said to be the time when the veils are the thinnest and you can contact the other side. A lot of praying for those who have passed: mourning them and celebrating those who had come in. The Spiral Dance which is done annually by Starhawk, Z. Budapest, and others reenacts this ceremony and is a very powerful ritual in which you call out the names of the dead and weep for them. Whether the dead is a person or a hope or an idea, you are able to feel the grief, especially since you are in a ceremony with hundreds of other people who are also weeping. It's very powerful. Then we move the energy around and name those who have been born that year, and call in the positive energy and the strengthening energy. We need that energy

"Belief in Wicca is on the rise. Because a basic tenet is that the earth is sacred and the female deity preeminent, Wicca holds strong appeal for those seeking a spiritual path that embraces both environmentalism and feminism."
—Catherine McEver

because this is the time of year when the weather starts to get dicey; it gets darker and colder. So you weep for the dead and call on your strength as a community to get through this time.

Beltane, which is the traditional May Day, is the celebration of fecundity, fertility, sexuality, Aphrodite. Weaving the May Pole is a delightfully festive way of saying, "Yahoo, we made it through the winter." There is a tradition of cauldron jumping where you light a fire under the cauldron and you jump over that to represent the power of spring. You call what you want to come to you, what you want to manifest. At the same time, you throw off what you don't want. Today, people will just write things they want out of their life on a slip of paper and throw it into a fire. I've heard that this custom originally came from the fact that people were sewn into their underwear in the fall, then when they cut themselves out of it in the spring, they'd throw it into the fire.

K: Your teacher taught you about these rituals and their history?

P: Actually, I was moving around the country, and she stayed in Florida. But once I realized that what I was doing had a history, I began to listen up. I went back to Canada where I'd lived and started a women's circle there. When I moved to the Bay Area, I haunted book stores, began working with political groups who also did ritual work. I took a course at the university from Starhawk and learned a lot from her. And from Z. Budapest. Once you open up to this sort of information, it just comes to you from all sorts of directions.

I do feel a deep connection to the woman I call my teacher, or high priestess, who has done an initiation for me with the traditional accoutrements of the olden times. I found that a very powerful experience. I had to own my own power to go through the initiation. I found it transformative as a woman to be put through a simple ceremony like that and to take possession of that part of myself. And yet I feel that a lot of women are priestesses, and you don't have to go through that ceremony to own your power. Yet the ceremony is a lovely thing to have in your life.

It becomes something of a paradox, for we don't want to set up a hierarchy. Partly that comes from a history of oppression. Witches didn't want to focus on someone who had a lot of information because they could be killed. Also, they needed to be able to know how to go into themselves because if others were killed, they didn't

"Witches are using religion and ritual as psychological tools to build individual strengths."
—Naomi Goldenberg

"Wheat and corn, wheat and corn
All that dies shall be reborn."
—Goddess song

have access to it anywhere else. They had to learn to go to their internal source where we are all connected to the divine. That's why the major training in Wicca is to teach you how to go to your own place inside and learn to pull it out. To learn to trust yourself and to know what is trustworthy within yourself.

K: How do they go about teaching that?

P: One way is by acknowledging it, knowing that trusting yourself, claiming your own power is how you go about doing it. Another is by example. But here we very quickly get into a problem about hierarchy. We in Wicca try to make each person a holder of the tradition—not just a few. Being careful of the earth, of each other, staying tuned into the intuitive part of ourselves that is connected with spirit—this needs to spring from each of us individually. Yet some individuals have more knowledge, more experience than others. Each of us has to decide if we are going to work individually as solitaries or if we want to be part of a coven or circle or if we want a teacher. If we decide we need a teacher, we need to check out the teacher. What exactly will they teach us? Are they in it for ego? What are the people around them like? We need to be careful.

I have been initiated and have initiated others, yet I've been in situations where no one knew that I was a high priestess, and I didn't make an issue of it. As a child, I always knew there was this priestess part of me, and I wanted to be the leader. I was rebuffed a bit, and embarrassed by it. Now I'm not really interested in that, but it's come to its own fruition as a reality in my life. Even so, I find its better to step back and let the people I work with find that intuitive place in themselves. Still, when I am in charge of a ritual, we cast a circle in the correct way and follow a certain script.

K: Tell me about casting the circle.

P: At first I didn't cast any way except the formal way. Whenever I felt that I needed to be clear about what was going on, I'd cast a circle and could work within it with a feeling of safety and protection. Then I started to cast mentally. I mean it's hard to cast a circle when you're driving down the freeway. I would visualize a silver or gold light around myself. I've found that I sort of roll my eyes around when I'm casting. I mentally go around three times, then I feel that I'm inside a circle of safety. I also made a nine-gored skirt which I sewed three ribbons around the bottom. I'd spin three times and be

"Anytime you use symbols to reenact something for a transformative purpose you are doing a magical act. The communion service is a magical ceremony. Praying is a magical ceremony. A lot of Christians wouldn't see it that way, but that's exactly what it is."
—Diana Paxson

"Everything the power of the world does is done in a circle."
—Black Elk

"When we sit in a circle it reminds us that the point of reference is the middle, and the middle is both empty and full of everything. . . . The circle is a cell. There are millions and millions of cells in the body of the Goddess."
—Anthea Francine

inside the circle. The important thing is to know when you want to be protected. You do this formally by walking around three times with water and salt and a candle, and calling the directions. Or you can do it mentally, placing it there by intent. I think it is easier to do mentally after you've done it physically according to tradition.

When I come out of the circle I need to do something to let me know that I've come to the other side of doing sacred work. Wynona taught me to put my hands flat on the ground when I was done and to literally put the energy back into the earth. To formally uncast a circle, you walk in the opposite direction from the casting with a candle and say three times, "Fire seal the circle round, let it fade beneath the ground."

This is especially necessary if you are doing trance work or some other very deep spiritual work. You just can't go from that to being able to deal with an angry clerk at Safeway. You need to recognize that you've crossed some boundary, and need to give yourself space and a period of transition.

K: Do you work with mixed-sex groups or with only women?

B: I've worked with both and the dynamic is very different. I don't know why but when women work without male energy, it is much easier to open ourselves, to let our intuitive places just flow among us and between us. This doesn't seem to happen in the same way when men are present. I don't know if this is the effect of years of patriarchy or a biological fact of female energy. I tend to believe the latter. I strongly support segregated worship, but also support men and women working together. I'm glad to see the men start to get into what has been traditionally women's spirituality.

K: Do you have a daily practice?

P: The cycles that I follow are more closely related to the cycles of the moon. The new moon is the time of planning and beginning and introspection, while the full moon is a time of celebration, more elaborate public ritual, and fruition. Once you start this, then everything you do to bring things to fruition is a part of the ritual. We in Wicca are an intensely freedom-loving lot, so I don't think if we were told to do a daily practice that it would work. We rely very heavily on intuition, so if we are led—from the inside—to place a flower on a spot where an animal was killed, then that's an appropriate ritual. To be aware of the fruitfulness of Mother Earth—

to see the beautiful faces of the children or the elders, to smell the wild lilac in our valley—that's our daily practice.

K: There is so much being published today on Wicca. Anyone can walk into a bookstore and buy one of these recipe books. Do you think this makes them into an effective, practicing witch?

P: I believe that witches are born, not made. They will discover the craft as their religion intuitively. So yes, if they are intuitively moved to walk into that bookstore and pick up that book, and do that ritual, then they can do it effectively if they are coming from the intent of wanting to practice. I think a lot of women intuitively create an altar, intuitively do practice without recognizing it. Sometimes, though, I think the terror of being labeled a witch and being accused of practicing witchcraft blocks them from their own spirituality.

K: If you can find your own spiritual center intuitively, then why use the word *witch?* Why not use the term *goddess,* which is more widely accepted?

P: I think some people claim to be a witch just because it is shocking. I think that the more I have learned about what I'm doing and the more I read the liturgies that have come down, I realize that that is my religion. Wicca, the old European tradition, seems something that I was born into. We believe in reincarnation, so I believe I've been a witch before. I'm saddened that Wicca, which is such a life-loving and gentle religion, has been so persecuted. I'm still frightened to say that I'm a witch, even to you. It's hard to own our own power. And very threatening to others. Yet it's a part of me that can't be denied.

Wicca is a religious tradition. It's a way of practicing so that you can connect with a spiritual center, a way of knowing who you are in the universe, where you are on earth, where you are in time, in the seasons, in the flow of generations. Of knowing what is appropriate for you to do whether you are maiden or mother or crone. It's a way of centering yourself in the universe, not of getting what you want. The purpose of Wicca as a sacred practice is to come to your sacred center. Then you have what you want. If you act from that center, then there's no difference from what you have and what you want, it's all one thing.

One of the women in our circle said, "I feel like I have my own tradition, finally. The songs that we sing together, the way that we

"From my point of view, the laws of physics are a subset of the laws of magic. The more you practice magic and understand the way it works, you can live in the world in such a way that you don't need it as much. The more I practice magic, the less I practice ritual. There's a sense of being one with the gods or being right with the Tao or the dharma or whatever. When you need money, it just shows up. When you need a job, a job happens."
—Don Frew

133

"A spell is sort of like programming a computer."
—Diana Paxson

are together, I feel like I've come home. I've always felt like I was singing someone else's song, but this is mine, this is ours."

Although information about witchcraft was once forced to be hidden, this is hardly the case today, for books abound. Many of the ones listed below contain bibliographies themselves. Starhawk's *The Spiral Dance,* republished and updated in a tenth-year anniversary edition, lists several pages of sources. Other books include:

Margot Adler, *Drawing Down the Moon,* Beacon, 1986.
Pamela Berger, *The Goddess Obscured: Transformation of the Grain Protectress from Goddess to Saint,* Beacon, 1985.
Marion Zimmer Bradley, *The Mists of Avalon,* Alfred A. Knopf, 1983.
Z. Budapest, *Grandmother Moon: Lunar Magic in Our Lives,* HarperCollins, 1991.
_____. *The Holy Book of Women's Mysteries,* 2 vols., Wingbow, 1986, rev. ed.
Mary Condren, *The Serpent and the Goddess: Women, Religion, and Power in Celtic Ireland,* Harper & Row, 1989.
Janet and Steward Farrar, *Eight Sabbats for Witches,* Robert Hale, 1981.
_____. *The Witches' Goddess,* Phoenix, 1987.
Anne Llewellyn, *Witchcraze: A New History of European Witch Hunts,* HarperCollins, 1994.
Diane Mariechild with Shuli Goodman, *The Inner Dance: A Guide to Spiritual and Psychological Unfolding,* The Crossing Press, 1987.
Ashlen O'Garea, *The Family Wicca Book,* Llewelyn, 1993.
Ellen Cannon Reed, *The Witches' Quabala: The Goddess and the Tree,* Llewellyn, 1986.
Starhawk, *Dreaming the Dark Magic, Sex and Politics,* Beacon, 1982.
_____. *The Spiral Dance: A Rebirth of the Ancient Religion of the Great Goddess,* tenth-anniversary edition, HarperCollins, 1989.
_____. *Truth or Dare: Encounters with Power, Authority and Magic,* Harper & Row, 1987.
Diane Stein, *The Women's Spirituality Book,* Llewellyn, 1987.
Luisah Teish, *Jambalaya: The Natural Woman's Book of Personal Charms and Practical Rituals,* Harper & Row, 1985.
Doreen Valiente, *Natural Magic,* Phoenix, 1978, 1986.
_____. *Witchcraft for Tomorrow,* Phoenix, 1978, 1987.
Barbara Walker, *Women's Rituals: A Sourcebook,* Harper & Row, 1990.
Marion Weinstein, *Positive Magic: Occult Self Help,* Phoenix, 1984.
_____. *Earth Magic: A Dianic Book of Shadows,* Phoenix, 1986.

COG, Covenant of the Goddess, may be contacted at PO Box 1226, Berkeley, CA, 94704.

Three excellent films on witchcraft are available through the National Film Board of Canada, 1045 Howe St., Suite 300, Vancouver, British Columbia, Canada B622B1, (604) 666-3838): *Goddess Remembered, The Burning Times, and Full Circle.* A good way to start an informal women's circle is to invite a few women friends over to watch one of these films.

Like witches, Pagans survived underground in Europe after Christianity became dominant. Also like witches, they are enjoying a revival today.

What in Heaven's Name Is Going On Over There?

"Some factual information about Neo-Pagan religion from the Center for Non-Traditional Religion"

It's a logical question heard spoken often between neighbors. In this country we are gifted with the freedom to do pretty much as we wish on our own property, whether it's having a family reunion, a barbeque in the yard, or a private religious gathering in our own homes. Sometimes we may not fully understand what our neighbors may be doing, and lack of understanding can easily bring unease and sometimes even fear. Things that we don't understand or are foreign or "different" to us can easily raise those sorts of unintentional feelings. Often we just don't understand someone or something, and that's unsettling. It is such fears that motivate us to unconscious, often prejudical behavior.

Since before the dawn of written history, people have instinctively gathered together in groups for the feelings of comfort and security that come with socialization and fellowship. One of our basic drives is that of spirituality--the need for the comfort and security of group worship of the Almighty. One of the oldest religious artifacts ever found on Earth was a small limestone carving, a figurine of a plump female, an object of veneration found near Willendorf, Austria, and named "the Venus of Willendorf" by

"In a day and age when excessive human population seriously threatens the viability of Earth's biosphere, I believe we must be especially wary of magical, ritual, or theological promotions of human fertility. I'm not suggesting that we ban Beltane or anything, simply that we seriously think through the implications of our thoughts and actions. On a practical level, it seems to me that public gatherings and festivals where Fertility is being celebrated should include distributions of condoms, for example, and the suggestions that Life, in all its forms, can be fruitful and fertile in a variety of ways, not just through the birth of physical children."
—Anne Newkirk Niven

"We are not a transcendental religion. We are not trying to transcend nature. Our religion is reality."
—Mark Roberts

archaeological scholars. This goddess statue has been dated to 28,000 B.C.! Throughout northern Europe there are many archaeological evidences of early people's veneration of an Earth Mother figure, a Mother Goddess from whom all things come, including the miracle of birth, death and rebirth. The forces of Nature were full of the dual polarity of male and female which produced all Life. No wonder that early people envisioned the Almighty as female, a Mother figure!

The basic neolithic concept of deity being represented by an immanent or internal dual polarity, a God and a Goddess force contained within every thing, was commonplace throughout northern Europe. Historically, this concept held firm throughout most of the world for thousands of years until the rise of the Judeo-Christian philosophy, which introduced the concept of a single, all-powerful and external or transcendent male God. In early Biblical translations, Genesis 1:26 first refers to deity as *Elohim,* which is a plural Hebrew word for god which includes *both* male and female genders. Later, in Genesis 2:7, the single male godform called *Yaweh* appears, to dominate the Old Testament and Judaism thenceforth. But in Genesis 1:26 we read that Elohim declaims the creation of *humanity—a population* of people, not just two. Later, in Genesis 2:7-9, Adam and Eve are created as a special, chosen people, special to Yaweh alone. Many people often overlook this small but telling detail. There were "other people," those who were not the "chosen people" of Yaweh in the Bible—the people of the land of Nod, east of Eden, from whence came Cain's wife, for example. These were the Pagans.

Prior to the rise of Judaism and Christianity, this nature-based form of worship we now call Paganism was almost universal throughout the world. Although each locale and people had their own names for their deities, they had no name for their religion because it was looked upon as universal and did not need differentiation from any other. Later, differentiation became necessary to distinguish the "old religion" from the newer religious movements. During the time of the spread of the Roman church throughout the urban population centers of early Europe, the Romans began calling the country people, who still practiced the old ways and worshipped the old gods, *pagani,* which meant "countrydweller." In the British

Isles, a stronghold of Paganism, the term *heathen* similarly meant the simple country folk who dwelt out on the heath or meadowlands and still honored the old gods. Neither term was originally intended as a denigration. When describing the religious movement known as Paganism, the word should always be capitalized, as with Baptist, Jew, or any other proper name.

Let's take a look at the Pagan religious philosophy. Since Paganism doesn't have a formal structure and hierarchy such as we are accustomed to in more traditional Western religions, there are many relatively small groups. There are a few national and international federations of these small groups, such as the Covenant of the Goddess (U.S.), the Pagan Anti-Defamation League (U.K.), the Fellowship of Isis (Ireland), and the National Alliance of Pantheists (U.S.). But these do not possess the familiar authoritarian church hierarchy. There are many other loosely organized regional federations which annually sponsor over one hundred open and semiopen gatherings throughout the US. Because of this small group autonomy, we can best define Pagan church groups by their similarities rather than by their differences. Remember, when Paganism was the *only* religion in Europe, everyone had their own ideas about the details of the religion, yet they were bonded together by the similarities. So it is even now.

Today, most people who define themselves as Pagans use the word as a general term for "native and natural religions, usually polytheistic, and their members." In simple terms, it is a positive, nature-based religion, preaching brotherly love and harmony with and respect for all life forms. It is very similar to Native American Indian spirituality. Its origins are found in the early human development of religion: animistic deities gradually becoming redefined to become a main God or Goddess of all Nature. This God or Goddess—bearing different names at different times and in different places—can be found in nearly all of the world's historic religious systems. Paganism does not oppose nor deny any other religion. It is simply a *pre*-Christian faith.

Most Pagans seem to agree on many of these commonly held beliefs:

✳ Divinity is immanent or internal, as well as transcendent or external. This is often expressed by the phrases "Thou Art God" and

"I came to Neo-Paganism out of a search for a celebratory, ecological nature religion that would appease my hunger for the beauty of ancient myths and visions without strangling my mind with dogmas or cutting off the continuing flow of many doubts."
—Margot Adler

"A Pagan world view is one that says the Earth is the Great Mother and has been raped, pillaged, and plundered and must once again be celebrated if we are to survive."
—Morgan McFarland

"Thou Art Goddess."

✳ Divinity is just as likely to manifest itself as female. This has resulted in a large number of women being attracted to the faith and joining the clergy.

✳ A multiplicity of gods and goddesses, whether as individual deities or as facets of one or a few archetypes. This leads to multivalued logic systems and increased tolerance towards other religions.

✳ Respect and love of Nature as divine in Her own right. This makes ecological awareness and activity a religious duty.

✳ Dissatisfaction with monolithic religious organizations and distrust of would-be messiahs and gurus. This makes Pagans hard to organize, even "for their own good," and leads to constant mutation and growth in the movement.

✳ The conviction that human beings were meant to live lives filled with joy, love, pleasure and humor. The traditional Western concepts of sin, guilt and divine retribution are seen as misunderstandings of natural growth experiences.

✳ A simple set of ethics and morality based on the avoidance of harm to other people. Some extend this to some or all living beings and the planet as a whole.

✳ The knowledge that with proper training and intent, human minds and hearts are fully capable of performing all of the magic and miracles they are ever likely to need, through the use of natural psychic powers which everyone possesses.

✳ The importance of acknowledging and celebrating the solar, lunar and other cycles of our lives. This has led to the investigation and revival of many ancient customs and the invention of some new ones.

✳ A minimum of dogma and a maximum of eclecticism. That is to say, Pagans are reluctant to accept any idea without personally investigating it, and are willing to adopt and use any concept they find useful, regardless of its origins.

✳ A strong faith in the ability of people to solve their own current problems on all levels, public and private. This leads to . . .

✳ A strong commitment to personal and universal growth, evolution and balance. Pagans are expected to be making continuous efforts in these directions.

 * A belief that one can progress far towards achieving such growth, evolution and balance through the carefully planned alteration of one's consciousness, using both ancient and modern methods of aiding concentration, meditation, reprogramming and ecstasy.

 * The knowledge that human interdependence implies community cooperation. Pagans are encouraged to use their talents to actively help each other as well as the community at large.

 * An awareness that if they are to achieve any of their goals, they must practice what they preach. This leads to a concern with making one's lifestyle consistent with one's proclaimed beliefs.

The group of people who may on occasion gather outdoors near your home, perhaps at a neighbor's place, and the people who have given you this pamphlet are followers of this pre-Christian religious faith. There is no need to fear them or their religion. They don't recruit or proselytize. They gather, often in robes, in serene, natural outdoor surroundings to be in contact with Nature during their services; otherwise you'd never know they were there. Their own children are encouraged to examine many other religions and make an informed personal choice of which to follow as they grow older. These people may call themselves Neo-Pagans, Wiccans, or simply Pagans. They are neither evil nor weird. They are not performing animal sacrifices or black magic. They don't kill anything as a religious practice. In fact, they hold Life in all its forms as sacred, and many are vegetarians. Few, if any, hunt wild animals for sport. They are simple, gentle people, people just like you and your friends, only different in that they hold to another view of spirituality than Christian, Moslem or Jew—one you just aren't very familiar with yet.

What does all of this mean? It should be quite obvious that Pagans are nothing to be feared, ridiculed or even singled out. Pagans are simply a little different in their approach to and acceptance of personal spirituality. Their religion is based on humanity's first stirrings to spirituality, of reverence towards the Earth as a living, breathing entity. They honor all living things, practice ecology, and are tolerant of those who follow a different

"I doubt it is possible/ probable to survive on Mother Earth without manipulating Her. Manipulation She doesn't seem to mind. She is, in fact, responding favorably to my manipulation of our back yard into an organic garden. Hurting Her is something else again."
—Carolyn Clark

path from their own. These are things everyone could benefit from studying.

Center for Non-Traditional Religions
Seattle, Washington

> *"I conjure the holy fire, the sacred* chandali *into which one throws one's past and all conceptions: god, mother-country, lover, Tomahawk cruise missiles, depth/strike bombs. Give up grasping, give up hope, then wake to the dangers of our fleshly bodies and body-planet."*
> —Anne Waldman

To receive a one-time mailing with more information and a library reading list about modern Paganism, please write to the Center for Non-Traditional Religions, Dept. XP, PO Box 85507, Seattle, WA 98145. This pamphlet may be reproduced freely provided nothing whatsoever is changed. © 1989 CNTR.

Oya, worshipped first by the Yoruba people of Africa, can manifest in natural forms, such as wind, fire, and buffalo, play a part at traditional funerals, and protect women in the marketplace. In more abstract terms, "Oya is the goddess of edges, of the dynamic interplay between surfaces, of transformation from one state of being to another." Like the dakini of Tibet, she is not the sort of goddess that can safely be put on a pedestal and expected to stay there—she is in motion, activity, wind. Also like the femine ground in Tibet, her patterns "suggest something like unified field theory of a certain type of energy that our culture does not think of as feminine." In writing about this living, shifting goddess, the author set out to combine two ways of thinking: African and European. Her inventive language and style cause small swirls and eddies to rise from the page, letting one feel the presence of Oya.

"Moon, sun, stars, volcanos, rivers, lakes, trees, corn, birds, Queen of Heaven and Mother of Earth, lawgivers, compassionate one, wrathful one, holy ones, wise ones, symbols of liberty, justice, victory, warrior women, hunters, ancestors, mothers, guardians, scribes . . . all of these have been symbols, roles and images of goddesses, of women."
—Gloria Orenstein

African Goddess Oya

Oya at her most awesome, untrammeled Oya, is a weather goddess. This is how she appeared before there was "world" as we know it and how she continues to manifest herself beyond the reach of meddlesome technological devices sent up to stimulate, alter, and pluck the heart out of the mystery of her storms. Caught in her updrafts, the religious imagination without apparatus seeks, though threatened with annihilation, to meet the weather goddess halfway, where sensuous experience remains possible. By reconnecting ourselves to the elements through which her urgent temperament expresses itself in patterns recognizable in our own swirls, inundations, and disjunctive ardors, we come upon a common language with which to invoke and reflect her power.

The sacramental language of the elements is not superseded by scientific formulae accounting for the smaller and smaller units to which the world's substances have been noetically reduced, nor does it suffer from translation. Vedic fire consumed shea butter in Bambara lamp basins of wrought iron. "Water" will always be the miracle flowing into Helen Keller's sightless hands as Annie Sullivan names it. For millennia wind, fire, and water have been chanted as

"When sleeping women wake, mountains move."
—Chinese proverb

primary constituents of an inhabited cosmos. Everywhere on earth they have been symbolically oriented about the magical circle drawn to encompass that space within which we seek to find ourselves. Therefore, by inheritance we cling to them still. As middle terms between energy systems of obscure purpose and our human desire to shape experience, the elements present themselves as matter already expressively organized, matter whose modes are reflected in and by our own moods—basal axes of our poetries. It is a language that the poet Sappho was the first, so far as we know, to make personal. Her elemental seizures were so deftly intimate as to exclude commentary. They happened as spoken. Soul-wind shook Sappho, and she became an oak in a gale. The catalyst she called Aphrodite. In another time and place she would have sacrificed to Oya.

All elemental discourse thereafter will seem clumsy, over-complicated. But silence is no remedy. That which has been muted, misunderstood, banished from consideration, or as yet undiscovered cries for articulation. To seek adequate words with which to trace her elemental patterns is an act of homage to the goddess of tropical weathers in hopes that her compassion may reciprocally illuminate inner equivalents with which we have struggled in private darkness. It has been a struggle intensified by patriarchal discountenance of powerful emotion—its problematic relegated to women "in need of help." In being coached by compliant mothers to stifle rather than outride our storms, to dam and conceal our floods, to bank our fires and give tinder over to future husbands, the Oya in ourselves froze in its tracks. Yet such ice particles, negatively charged, at the heart of the mounting storm are the mysterious, generative sources of Oya's lightning. Thus, in other ways obstructed, Oya strikes us—quirking here, cramping there. Done with our brains, the indefatigable goddess goes jaggedly to work upon our bodies, cutting off circulation, opening sluices, instilling victims who could be votaries with a variety of "female complaints," catching them up in mindless swirls of activity, throwing them down into incapacitating vortices, playing havoc with appetite. Stop, Oya, we beg you! We will sound your praises along all rivers from Hudson to Niger. We will hang prayer flags to flutter like laundry stretching from fire escape to fire escape, continent to continent. We will strive to know your winds the better to reclaim our part of fire.

>   Judith Gleason
>   *Oya: In Praise of an African Goddess*

See also Joseph Murphy's *Working the Spirit: Ceremonies of the African Diaspora*, Beacon, 1994.

————————————

Worship of the goddess Isis began in pre-dawn Egypt and spread throughout the Graeco-Roman world, lasting until roughly the fifth century C.E., when the Christians destroyed her shrines and built churches over their ruins. There is some evidence that Isis worship, especially in the goddess's role as healer, continued disguised as devotion to the Virgin Mary. Isis, in addition to being known as the great mother and healer, was revered as the Lady of the Words of Power. She is often depicted holding the ankh, *the sacred symbol of life. Isis, like many other female deities, inspired a personal relationship in her followers.*

Isis Healing Meditation

Go to a quiet place where you can be by yourself and not be interrupted. Sit in a chair, set your feet flat on the floor, rest your hands on your thighs, let your back be straight, and close your eyes. Center and relax yourself by taking deep slow breaths. Visualize yourself surrounded with radiant white light.

When you have finished these preparations, start imagining yourself journeying to a Healing Temple to receive healing for yourself. When you arrive, stand before the Temple's main doorway, and examine its shape, size, color, and design. Now, reflect on the healing you need and seek. When you feel ready, go through the doorway and enter the Temple.

"The Goddess shattered the image of myself as a dependent person and cleared my brain so I could come into the power that was mine, that was me all along, but that could never have been appropriated until the old limiting image was exorcised or shattered."
—Nelle Morton

"One vision I see clear as life before me, that the ancient Mother has awakened once more, sitting on her throne rejuvenated, more glorious than ever. Proclaim her to all the world with the voice of peace and benediction."
—Vivekananda

In the center of the Temple is the Great Goddess Isis. She stands facing you. Her winged arms are outstretched. She is radiant. Healing Love energy emanates from Her body and fills the Temple. She welcomes you and asks you to speak about the Healing you are seeking. You tell Her what you want to receive the Healing for. Then she tells you to come forward and receive Healing in Her embrace. You step forward, and she holds you to Her heart, gently enfolding you in Her winged arms and in Her Love and Healing Power.

Now experience Her energy flowing throughout your whole being as you chant "Isis, Isis, Isis" over and over. Let your consciousness merge with Hers. Absorb as much Healing energy as you sense you need, then imagine Her again. Picture yourself standing before Her with your own arms outstretched and give thanks to Her. As you visualize this, rise up from the chair in which you have been sitting during this meditation and stretch your arms out. Open your eyes and feel Isis Healing energy radiating from you as you look around the room. Then, hold your hands to your heart and affirm to yourself that you will allow the power of this Healing meditation to flow through your daily life.

Selena Fox, Circle Sanctuary,
in *The Goddess Re-Awakening:*
The Feminine Principle Today

Turning to Hinduism, we find reverence—and a great deal of respect—for female energy.

Shakti

Within Hinduism, the entire universe is a manifestation of Shakti, the creative primal feminine principle underlying the cosmos which energizes all divinity, every being, every thing. Shakti, the goddess, is known by the name *devi*, from the Sanskrit root *div*, to shine. The Shining One is known by different names and through different appearances, but remains the symbol of the life-giving powers of the universe. This cosmology reflects the biological fact that, in the womb, all life begins as female and only the addition of a new substance, the male hormone, turns the fetus into a male.

In India, the feminine principle has been worshipped since prehistoric times, often in womb-like caves and megalithic domes where an entrance is marked by carvings of the female yoni or genitals and stained with red ocher. On these caves and in Mother-goddess figurines, wear and discoloration show that worshippers touch the yonic parts, the source of all life and focus of the feminine cosmic energy. Throughout India, one may find shrines for the worship of the yoni and the lingam (male genital), symbolically represented in shallow bowl-shapes with erect pestle-like counterparts, often sculpted in stone.

Evidence from the ancient sites of Harappa and Mohenjo-daro show that the pre-Vedic, non-Aryan religion was peaceful and female-oriented. After the Aryan invasion, some of these goddesses were absorbed into the Vedic pantheon.

During the early period of Hinduism, called Vedic after the scriptures, the feminine earth goddess was worshipped despite the patriarchy of the Aryan invaders. The *Rig Veda* named Aditi the great womb, the progenetrix of cosmic creation. Agni, god of fire and creator-god, is held in her womb, the Mother-Womb, from which she gave birth to the important gods of the Vedic pantheon. Aditi, a benevolent and nurturing deity, is identified with the cow, giver of milk and nourishment. Other Vedic goddesses include Usas, the goddess of dawn, Ratri, the goddess of starlit night, Lakshmi, goddess of wealth, Sarasvati, goddess of speech or learning.

In post-Vedic Hinduism, through the period that corresponds to the scriptures of the Upanishads and Tantras, goddess worship continued in elaborate and complex forms. In the Trika School of Kashmir, for instance, Shakti is spontaneous vibration; when she expands or opens herself, the universe comes into being. When she contracts or closes herself, the universe disappears as manifestation. Thus the goddess alternates eternally between a cycle of manifestation and dissolution, between relative space and time and Absolute Space and Time.

"For as long as collective and individual consciousness feel nourished, contained, and inseparable from the womb of the Great Mother, they imagine her as an essentially benevolent, omnipotent, and all embracing being."
—Sukie Colegrave

"Great Goddess, who art Thou?
I am the entire world.
I am the Veda as well as what is different from it.
I am unknown.
Below and above and around am I."
—Devi Upanishad

In tantric cosmology, the whole universe is created and sustained by the dual forces of Shakti and Shiva, the feminine and masculine principles, although as Devi says in the *Devibhagavata:* "At the time of final dissolution I am neither male, nor female, nor neuter." "She" is formless, unborn, unceasing ultimate reality.

In some sects, it is felt that the masculine Shakti worshipper becomes "ideal" only by following ritual techniques which develop his own feminine qualities. In Vaishnavism, ritual transvestism for men is still practiced: men dress in women's clothes and ornaments, even retire for a few days each month. According to this doctrine, "all souls are feminine to the Supreme Reality."

As in Native American tradition, women during menstruation are seen as channeling special energies. In some ceremonies, menstrual fluid becomes holy, to be used in certain rituals. Tantric sacred art often depicts sexual congress, pregnancy and childbirth in high relief. This bold display of sexual union has been taken up by the West, and become a strange hybrid of sexual promiscuity and spiritual pretension which often leaves out the elements of pregnancy and childbirth.

Kali—or a particular version of her—has also become popular in the West. She originated in India, emerging from the forehead of the great goddess Durga during a mighty battle around the fifth century, A.D. Ajit Mookerjee, in *Kali: The Feminine Force,* describes her creation:

> Kali manifested herself for the annihilation of demonic male power in order to restore peace and equilibrium. For a long time brutal asuric (demonic) forces had been dominating and oppressing the world. Even the powerful gods were helpless and suffered defeat at their hands. They fled pell-mell in utter humiliation, a state hardly fit for the divine. Finally they prayed in desperation to the Daughter of Himalayas to save gods and men alike. The gods sent forth their energies as streams of fire, and from these energies emerged the Great Goddess Durga.
>
> In the great battle to destroy the most arrogant and truculent man-beasts, the goddess Kali sprang forth from the brow of Durga to join in the fierce fighting. As the 'forceful' aspect of Durga, Kali has been dubbed 'horrific' or 'terrible' in masculine-biased commentaries, without understanding of the episode's

inner meaning. The challenge of sakti (feminine force) with its vast Sakta literature has not been properly presented to the world from the feminine viewpoint to bring out its truth.

The author goes on to quote Leonie Caldecott in "The Dance of the Woman Warrior" (*Walking on the Water, Women Talk About Spirituality*, Jo Garcia and Sara Maitland, eds.) who points out that since the gods could not change their situation themselves, they created a goddess—the only moving element in the myth—to do it for them. Furthermore, the deadlock sprang from dualistic, opposed forces of god/antigod, good/evil, reflected most recently in the military forces of the cold war and more recent conflicts.

It is worth noting that these polarized concepts also provide the rationalization for patriarchy when they align "female" with matter/ evil/chaotic and place "male" on the side of mind/good/rational. Truly, a goddess as powerful as Kali is needed today to overcome our habitual tendency toward duality. As Mookerjee puts it:

> We have suffered the consequences of unbalanced power for long enough. Our world cannot any longer tolerate the disruption and destruction brought about by demonic force. In the present Kali Age, Kali is the answer, and she will have to annihilate again in order to reveal the truth of things, which is her mission, and to restore to our natures that divine feminine spirituality which we have lost.

Ramakrishna (1836-1886), after seeking and experiencing a vision of Kali, devoted his life to her worship. To him, and to his disciple Swami Vivekananda, Kali worship, which meant surrendering to the Great Mother, led to bliss and unity. Vivekananda predicted "the resurgence of the Mother into the consciousness of the world's population, after patriarchal religions had forced her into concealment in the unconscious." These ideas spread to England and later the United States under the name of Vedanta.

Ramakrishna saw everything as a manifestation of Kali, even Brahman. Like the fire and its power to burn, like the sun and its shining rays, he stated, Brahman and Kali are inseparable:

> Thus one cannot think of Brahman without Sakti, or of Sakti

"It is an exciting time—a time of crisis and opportunity, a time that systems theorists call a period of disequilibrium and hence of potential systems transformation. But the possibilities of a fundamental breakthrough rather than breakdown in our cultural evolution are not just of theoretical interest; they are of intense personal and planetary interest in a time when the Blade—the ancient symbol of a system based on force of the threat of force—is the nuclear bomb, and when 'man's conquest of nature' threatens the very ecology on which all life on this planet depends."
—Riane Eisler

without Brahman. One cannot think of the Absolute without the Relative, or of the Relative without the Absolute.

The Primordial Power is ever at play. She is creating, preserving, and destroying in play, as it were. This Power is called Kali. Kali is verily Brahman, and Brahman is verily Kali. It is the one and same Reality. When we think of It as inactive, that is to say, not engaged in the acts of creation, preservation and destruction, then we call It Brahman. But when It engages in these activities, then we call It Kali or Sakti. The Reality is one and the same; the difference is in name and form.

For more on the goddess in Hinduism, see:

Arthur Avalon, *Hymns to the Goddess,* Lotus Light, 1963.
_____, *Shakti and Shakta*, Dover, 1978.
_____, *Hymns to Kali,* Lotus Light, 1965.
C. Mackenzie Brown, *God as Mother: A Feminine Theology in India,* Inner Traditions, 1974.
David Kinsley, *Hindu Goddesses: Visions of the Divine Feminine in the Hindu Religious Tradition,* University of California Press, 1985.
_____, *The Sword and the Flute—Kali and Krishna: Dark Visions of the Terrible and the Sublime in Hindu Mythology,* University of California Press, 1975.
Shyam Kishore Lal, *Female Divinities in Hindu Mythology and Ritual,* Puna Press, 1980.
Leonard and Clinton Seely, *Grace and Mercy in Her Wild Hair,* Shambhala, 1982.
Erich Neumann, *The Great Mother,* Princeton University Press, 1961.
Sister Nivedita, *Notes on Some Wonderings,* Vedanta Press, 1993.
Margaret Noble, *Kali the Mother,* Vedanta Press, 1985.
D. R. Rajeshwari, *Sakti Iconography,* South Asia Books, 1988.
Barbara Walker, *The Woman's Encyclopedia of Myths and Secrets*, Harper San Francisco, 1983.

"Recovering information about Goddess reverence provides us with evidence that people in other times viewed the sacred as existing within all life. This concept is known as immanence. *It offers us a very different view of existence and reality than the concept of* transcendence, *the belief that a deity is above us—i.e., up in heaven. Yet, most mainstream religions today still regard divinity as transcendent."*
—Merlin Stone

The depiction of Kali in the West sometimes takes on the simplistic dimension of a black goddess of destruction. In India, Kali is much more complex and multidimensional. Springing from the goddess Durga's forehead during a battle of the gods, Kali began as a force for swiftness, for immediate and effective action which cuts through and destroys evil.

Kali

The name Kali has been used generically from antiquity. It has been the practice in India to attribute the achievements of one goddess to another. The idea is that the different manifestations are for a certain definite purpose, and in reality there is one Devi who assumes various forms to fulfil various purposes. Sometimes she assumes a frightening form and sometimes a benevolent form.

Kali's fierce appearances have been the subject of extensive descriptions in several earlier and later tantric works. She is most commonly worshipped nowadays as Dakshinakali—the south-facing, black Kali. Though her fierce form is filled with awe-inspiring symbols, their real meaning is not what at first appears—they have equivocal significance.

The image of Kali is generally represented as black: "just as all colours disappear in black, so all names and forms disappear in her" (Mahanirvana Tantra). In tantric rituals she is described as garbed in space, sky-clad (digambari). In her absolute, primordial nakedness she is free from all covering of illusion. She is Nature (Prakriti), stripped of "clothes." She is full-breasted: her motherhood is a ceaseless creation. She gives birth to the cosmos parthenogenetically, as she contains the male principle within herself. Her dishevelled hair (elokeshi) forms a curtain of illusion, the fabric of space-time which organizes matter out of the chaotic sea of quantum-foam. Her garland of fifty human heads, each representing one of the fifty letters of the Sanskrit alphabet, symbolizes the repository of knowledge and wisdom, and also represents the fifty fundamental vibrations in the universe. She wears a girdle of human hands—hands are the principal instruments of work and so signify the action of karma or accumulated deeds, constantly reminding us that

"The reemerging Goddess, metaphor, symbol, divine force, is larger than the Westernized idealized model of maternal being. When Hindus cry to Kali in their devotions "Ma! Ma!" they are not calling out to her as they would to their biological mother but to the mother of the universe, the life force that brought all into being and that sustains all that lives."
—Elinor Gaden

"The Mother is only terrible to those who are living in the illusion of separateness; who have not yet realized their unity with her, and known that all her forms are for enlightenment."
—Ajit Mookerjee

ultimate freedom is to be attained as the fruit of karmic action. Her three eyes indicate the past, present and future. Her white teeth, symbolic of *sattva,* the translucent intelligence stuff, hold back her lolling tongue which is red, representing *rajas,* the activating quality of nature leading downward to *tamas,* inertia. Kali has four hands (or, occasionally, two, six, or eight). One left hand holds a severed head, indicating the annihilation of ego-bound evil force, and the other carries the sword of physical extermination with which she cuts the thread of bondage. One right hand gestures to dispel fear and the other exhorts to spiritual strength. In this form she is changeless, limitless primordial power, acting in the great drama, awakening the unmanifest Siva beneath her feet.

Black Kali is worshipped in cremation grounds as Smashanakali. She makes her abode there to receive those who come to take rest in her.

As Virgin-creator, Kali is depicted as *sattva-guna,* white; as sustaining Mother, *rajas,* red; as the Absorber of all, *tamas,* black. In the equilibrium of the potential state there will always be disturbance arising from the desire for creation—a cycle of Kali's "opening" and "closing." Her world is an eternal living flux in which all things arise and disappear again. She is the archetypal image of birth-and-death, giver of life and its destroyer, "the vital principles of the visible universe which has many faces—gracious, cruel, creative, destructive, loving, indifferent--the endless possibility of the active energy at the heart of the world."[1] . . .

The Supreme Goddess is the source of all "energies," and the feminine divinities are principally her emanations, or her partial archetypal images. The immense array of the goddess-transformations of Kali are classified in descending order. Certain goddesses are complete manifestations of the supreme feminine; some are her partial emanations; some are fractions of her power; mortal women are included as "parts of parts of fractions" of the Supreme Goddess. . . .

Kali's three manifestations for the creation, preservation and destruction of the universe are represented graphically in the *Kamakala-chidvalli:* "The goddess of renowned form assumes, in time of protection, the form of a straight line; in time of destruction she takes the form of a circle, and for creation she takes on the brilliant appearance of a triangle.". . .

Kali is worshipped as Adya-Sakti, the Beginning of All. "I am Kali, the Primal Creative Force," as the *Saktisangama Tantra* states. After the Great Dissolution, Kali alone remains, as Avyakta Prakriti (Unmanifest Nature) in a state of potential power, the Supreme Sakti, the Eternal Feminine.

Ajit Mookerjee
Kali: The Feminine Force

AUTHOR'S NOTES
1. Leonard Nathan and Clinton Seely, *Grace and Mercy in Her Wild Hair*, Shambhala, 1982.

Ramakrishna (1836-1886), a Hindu saint and reformer, advocated nonsectarian worship and felt that ecstacy lay in worshipping God in the form of the Divine Mother, Kali. Here he gives a very simple formula for connecting with Kali energy.

Hymn to Kali

Kali, why should we make
the arduous journey
to distant sites of pilgrimage?
Simply permit this child, O Mother,
to breath Your Name with every breath
as though each breath were the last.
What need will then exist
for external rites
or study of scriptures?

Blissfully repeating KALI KALI KALI
at dawn, noon, sunset, and midnight
will be entirely sufficient.
The conventional forms of religion
may chase after this ecstatic lover,
but they will never apprehend him.
Conventional giving in charity
and conventional ascetic vows
no longer appeal to my heart,
since the delicate Lotus Feet
of Your Presence, O Mother,
have become my only study,
only prayer, only delight.

Ramakrishna
in *Great Swan: Meetings with
Ramakrishna* by Lex Hixon

When the bodhisattva of compassion, Avalokiteshvara, migrated to China and Japan from India and Tibet, he was often depicted as a woman. Technically sexless (or combining both sexes) and formless, the bodhisattva can assume any form, any gender. Since about the twelfth century, Kuan Yin has appeared in China (and in Japan as Kannon) as the goddess of mercy. As with the Virgin Mary and the Tibetan Tara, one's relationship with this goddess is personal and immediate.

Kuan Yin

When John Blofeld journeyed through China, he sought out the shrines of Kuan Yin. At one such shrine, he spoke to a monk about his feelings of affinity for Kuan Yin, his doubts about some of the claims he'd read about her influence, and the problems he encountered when trying to discern her true nature.

"You think too much," the monk told him. Then he held up a freshly picked lotus flower and exclaimed, "Kuan Yin is here in front of your nose. Smell."

Later, he encountered an old nun who had been worshipping Kuan Yin for many years. At first, the nun said, "I just recited Her name. It wasn't enough. I wanted to *see* Her."

So the nun had learned "a fine method" from an old monk: Sit on a hilltop or wherever is high enough to see nothing but the sky in front of you. A blank wall will do. Then with your mind you make everything empty. You say there's nothing there—only emptiness. Then you say, there *is* something. There's the sea and the moon— full and round. Then you see that—the sea, silver in the moonlight topped with little white waves. You stare at the soft brightness of the moon for a long, long time, feeling calm and happy. The moon starts to get smaller and smaller, but brighter and brighter. Finally the moon is this small seed of light that you can barely look at. This pearl starts to grow and before you know it, it is Kuan Yin Herself standing up in the sky, dressed in gleaming white robes. Her robes are shining and there's a halo around Her head. When She sees you, She smiles a lovely smile. She's so happy to see you that tears sparkle in Her eyes. If you keep your mind tranquil by repeating Her name and by not trying too hard, She will stay a long, long time. Then She will start to get smaller and smaller until there is only the sky. The sky and the sea vanish as well so there is only space left—lovely, lovely space going on for ever. "That space stays as long as you can do without you. Not you *and* space, you see, just space, no you."

> From John Blofeld
> *Bodhisattva of Compassion:*
> *The Mystical Tradition of Kuan Yin*

"The true nature of mind:
a cloudless sky."
—Rebecca Radner

O Follow the old nun's advice and see Kuan Yin. Pick a cloudless day and lie on your back, gazing away from the sun. Let your consciousness expand outward until it fills the whole sky, with no center, no circumference. Stay in this state as long as you can "do without you." Return to it as often as possible.

"Dakini: a very special type of female being who is capable of flying through space in her efforts to be of assistance, especially to tantric yogis. More subtly the dakini is the practitioner's link to a reality which is spacious and full of dharmic potentialities. The femininity of the dakini is linked with the symbolism of space or sky, the ability to give birth or to actualize the full range of expansive potentialities."
—Jeffrey Hopkins

Tsultrim Allione, an American, traveled to India and Nepal in the late sixties and was ordained as a Buddhist nun by His Holiness the Karmapa, head of the Kagyu school of Tibetan Buddhism. For more than three years, she studied the Tibetan language and religion, and did extensive solitary retreats. Deciding that she wanted to follow the Buddhist path without being a monastic, she returned to the United States where she married and had a family. She has researched the lives of a number of Tibetan saints and mystics, studied the role of the feminine in Tibetan Buddhist theology, and given workshops and teachings on the dakini principle. Even though she writes very clearly on the subject here, you may want to read this selection more than once.

The Dakini Principle

Dakini in Tibetan is "Khadro," which literally means "skygoer," or one who moves in the sky. The dakini is probably the most important manifestation of the feminine in Tibetan Buddhism, and appears many times in these stories. So we must try to understand her significance and her many forms.

In general the dakini represents the everchanging flow of energy with which the yogic practitioner must work in order to become realized. She may appear as a human being, as a goddess—either peaceful or wrathful—or she may be perceived as the general play of energy in the phenomenal world.

In order to connect to this dynamic energizing feminine principle the practitioner of Tantra (Tantrika) does specific practices. These practices take place at three levels. At the primary level the dakini is invoked and visualized as deity in the form of a dakini. For example, the dakini may be visualized first in front of the practitioner, and then this external figure is united with the Tantrika, and the mantra of the dakini is recited. This is a very general description of the "outer" practice of the dakini.

After one becomes accomplished at the level of the outer practice one begins the "inner" practice. At this stage the dakini is worked with through the activation of the subtle nerves (rtsa), the breath (rlung) and the essence (tig.le).

The third level of practice is called the "secret"; at this point there is a direct contact between the state of the practitioner and the energy of the dakini principle.

In Tantra one of the primary ways of looking at the manifestations of the dakini is as the wisdom energy of the five colors which are the subtle luminous form of the five elements. In Tantrism enlightened manifestation is divided into five aspects called the five families (Rigs.nga). These five "families" each represent the transformation of a gross passion or neurosis. The transformation of these five negativities into wisdom is the essence of the Tantric path.

In order to understand the five wisdom dakinis we have to go way back to the beginning, to the basic split. The split is between "I" and "others." This is the beginning of the "ego." The ego sees everything dualistically; there is a space which is "here" and which is "me" and "mine" and another space, "there," which is "them" and "theirs." This barrier between the internal space and the external space creates a constant struggle. The conventional search for happiness is the ego's attempt to redress this split by making it all "mine," but the ironic twist is that the more the ego tries to control the situation, the more the barrier is solidified. In the struggle the ego completely loses track of the basic split that is the source of suffering.

What happens after the dualistic barrier is initially created is that the ego forms a kind of governing headquarters which sends feelers out into the environment to determine what is safe and what will enhance itself and expand its territory, what is threatening and what is merely uninteresting or vaguely annoying. These feelers report back to central headquarters and the reactions to this information become the three fundamental poisons: passion (attraction toward what will increase its territory), aggression (toward what seems threatening) and "ignoring" or ignorance (toward that which seems to be of no use to the ego). From these fundamental poisons develop further elaborations, and we get into conceptual discrimination, further pigeonholing of perception and more complex forms of the three poisons. We end up with a whole fantasy world centered around the ego. A storyline develops based on these reactions and one thing leads to another. This is what Buddhists call the karmic chain reaction. The whole thing gets

"In the precious tantric tradition, 'desireless, blissful wisdom is the essence of all desirable qualities, unobstructedly going and coming in endless space.' This wisdom is called 'the Sky Dancer,' feminine wisdom, the Dakini."
—Thinley Norbu

155

"In fact, rather than define the Dakini as a human being, she is better understood as a moment's intuition of the emptiness and purity in passion when perfect insight and skilful means integrate."
—Keith Dowman

so complicated that the ego is kept constantly busy and entertained by the plots and subplots which develop from the basic dualistic split. This clinging to the fantasy that the ego needs to control its territory and protect itself from threats is the basis of all suffering and neurosis. However, since this process has been going on for lifetimes, the thickness of the plots and subplots sometimes becomes overwhelming. Meditation practice slows down the reaction patterns, and gradually things start to settle down and the whole process becomes a bit clearer.

Because the energy of individuals varies, their styles of relating to the basic split also vary. When the ego's frantic struggle is relaxed, the basic energy of the individual can shine through as wisdom. The way wisdom manifests will vary according to the nature of the individual, and thus we have the five Buddha families. Naturally not everyone fits neatly into a particular category and many people are mixtures of several families.

The five families are: Vajra (diamond), Buddha, Ratna (jewel), Padma (lotus), Karma (action). These are fundamental energy patterns which manifest in all phenomenal experience.

The Vajra family person in the unevolved state surveys and reflects the environment with sharp accuracy; there is a fear of not having the situation covered and, if there are any surprises, the reaction is anger, either hot or cold. The Vajra type is intellectual and conceptual, always trying to systematize everything. When this becomes neurotic, complex systems of how everything works are evolved which have little relationship to the situation at hand. When this angry, controlling intellect is transformed into its original state it becomes "Mirror Like Wisdom." It is associated with the element water, blue or white, the Buddha Akshobya and the dakini Dhatisvari.

The Buddha family person is associated with the element of space or ether. In its neurotic state it is dull and thick: the slang "spaced out" perfectly defines the Buddha family person whose intelligence is lulled to sleep. These people don't bother to wash the dishes or take care of themselves; everything seems to require too much effort. The Buddha family is associated with the "Wisdom of All-Encompassing Space," and when this dullness is purified it becomes open and spacious like the sky and the person is calm, open and warm. The name of the Buddha of this family is Vairocana and the dakini Locana.

The Ratna family is associated with the element of earth, the south, the color yellow and autumn. In its unevolved state this energy must fill up every corner because it never has enough. There is a tendency to be greedy and domineering, wanting always to be the center of things. The Ratna type needs to accumulate food and possessions. The negative quality of Ratna is pride; they want everyone to think they are very important. When this energy is purified into wisdom it becomes "All Enriching Wisdom." Without the attachment of the ego the expansiveness of Ratna seems to enrich every situation: wonderful things are created and the surroundings are enriched. The Buddha of this family is Ratnasambhava and the dakini Mamaki.

The Padma family person is involved with seduction rather than the acquisition of material things that concerns the Ratna type. The Padma person is interested in relationships and wants to accumulate desirable feelings. They want to draw others in and possess them. The mental pattern involves a dilettantish, scattered kind of activity. Projects are started and then dropped when the superficial glamor wears off. Pleasure is very important, and pain is rejection or abandonment. The wisdom which emerges when this energy is freed from the ego's hold is "Discriminating Awareness Wisdom" and this can be seen with Prajna, profound cognition. Aesthetics become enlightened and great art can be created with this energy which can see the relationships between everything. Padma is associated with the west and spring, the color red, fire, the Buddha Amitabha and the dakini Pandaravasini.

The Karma family person is very active and is always working at something. The Karma family dakini is often portrayed in profile because she is too busy to look at you straight on. This speed comes from the air element and can be very aggressive and impulsive. There is a tendency toward paranoia, a fear of losing track of all the plots that are going on, so they are usually frantically organizing everyone and everything, making sure things are under control. In its wisdom transformation this energy becomes "All-Accomplishing Wisdom," and enlightened activity begins to take place, which benefits many beings. The Karma family is associated with winter, the north, envy, the Buddha Amogasiddi and the dakini Samayatara.

Certain women are said to be emanations of these dakinis, and they have certain signs by which they can be recognized. Because wisdom is an inherent part of the energy, not a separate thing which follows on a linear pattern, the enlightened aspect might escape from the surveillance of the ego at any moment and therefore everyone has the possibility of

"Look into the mirror of your mind, the place of dreams, the mysterious home of the Dakini."
—Tilopa (988-1069)

"The gods and goddesses of Vajrayana are not arbitrary creations, but manifestations of the universal Void which occur spontaneously or are consciously produced during the meditation and the rituals. At times looked upon as external entities, in a deeper sense they are known to be patterns of redemption experienced inwardly on the path to enlightenment."
—Eleanor Olson

becoming a Buddha or dakini on the spot. We could have little gaps in the claustrophobic game of dualism, and clarity could shine through. Therefore even an ordinary "unenlightened" woman or situation could suddenly manifest as the dakini. The world is not as solid as we think it is, and the more we are open to the gaps, the more wisdom can shine through and the more the play of the dakini energy can be experienced. The primary way to relax the ego's grasp is to practice meditation. All Tantric visualizations and mantras are geared to freeing the energy of wisdom which is being suffocated under the solidified fantasies of dualistic fixation.

By consciously invoking the dakini through Tantric practices we begin to develop a sensitivity to energy itself. When looking at the iconography of the dakini we should bear in mind that through understanding her symbols and identifying with her, we are identifying with our own energy. Tantric divinities are used because we are in a dualistic state. Tantra takes advantage of that, or exaggerates it, by embodying an external figure with all the qualities the practitioner wishes to obtain. After glorifying and worshiping this external deity, the deity dissolves into the practitioner—then at the end of any Tantra there is a total dissolution of the deity into space; and finally after resting in that state the practitioner visualizes herself or himself as the deity again as they go about their normal activities.

Tsultrim Allione
Women of Wisdom

○ Visualize a rainbow in your heart. One at a time, "send" the colors out to all sentient beings, and feel these energies return to you bringing peace, compassion, and love.

Thinley Norbu is a Tibetan Lama who often teaches in this country. This poem, which is written to the dakinis—feminine spirits—of the five Buddha families, introduces the author's book on the subject. When I asked him for permission to use the poem, he wrote: "I appreciate your making a book on women's spirituality because in these degenerate times it is very important to do this due to the lack of positive, spiritual qualities and due to materializing which causes repulsive energy, separating male and female for material power and ordinary ego. Some excessively aggressive wrong points of view which are beyond compromise or mutual benefit between beings cause harm and seed hatred for future generations. So, if you can make this book, it will temporarily benefit beings, creating harmony particularly between men and women, and especially ultimately from blossoming spiritual, wisdom qualities to attain enlightenment for the benefit of all sentient beings. So for this reason, as you are requesting, I am giving you permission to quote my poem on the Five Wisdom Dakinis from Magic Dance *in your book."*

"Look upon a woman as a goddess whose special energy she is, and honor her in that state."
—Uttara Tantra

Five Wisdom Dakinis

Five Wisdom Sisters,

If we do not complement you,
You become five witches,
Making us ill and bringing us suffering.
Because we cannot banish you,
Always our fate depends on you.

Five Wisdom Sisters,

If we do complement you,
You become five angels,
Making us healthy and bringing us happiness.
Because we cannot separate from you,
Always our fate depends on you.

159

Five Wisdom Sisters,

Nothing can be done without depending on your mood.
Farmers cannot grow their crops,
Politicians cannot rule their countries,
Engineers cannot work their machines,
Doctors cannot heal their patients,
Scientists cannot do their research,
Philosophers cannot make their logic,
Artists cannot create their art
Without depending on your mood.

Five Wisdom Sisters,

Nothing can be known without depending on your grace.
Tibetan lamas cannot chant with cool highland habit,
Indian gurus cannot sing with warm lowland habit,
Japanese roshis cannot sit with dark cushion habit,
Muslin sheiks cannot dance with bright robed habit,
Christian priests cannot preach with loud-voiced habit,
Hebrew rabbis cannot pray with soft-voiced habit
Without depending on your grace.

Even the most mysterious miracles cannot occur without
complementing your purity.
Buddha Shakyamuni cannot rest with the tranquil gaze
of his lotus eyes underneath the Bodhi tree,
Guru Padmasambhava cannot play magically with
countless sky-walking dakinis,
Lord Jesus cannot walk weightlessly across the water,
Prophet Moses cannot see the radiantly burning bush,
Brahmin Sarahahpa cannot straighten arrows, singing
wisdom hymns with his arrowmaker girl,
Crazy saint Tilopa cannot eat fish and torture Naropa,
Greatest yogi Milarepa cannot remain in his cave,
singing and accepting hardships
Without complementing your purity.
You are so patient.

Whoever wants to stay,
If you don't exist,
Cannot stay.
Whoever wants to go,
If you don't exist,
Cannot go.
Whoever wants to taste or touch,
If you don't exist,
Cannot taste or touch.
Whatever our actions,
You are always supporting
Patiently without complaining.
But we ignorant beings
Are always ungrateful,
Stepping on you,
Calling you Earth.

You are so constant.
Whoever wants to be purified,
If you don't exist
Cannot be purified.
Whoever wants to quench their thirst,
If you don't exist,
Cannot quench their thirst.
Whoever wants to hear,
If you don't exist,
Cannot hear.
Whatever our actions,
You are always flowing
Ceaseless without complaining.
But we desiring beings
Are always ungrateful,
Splashing you,
Calling you Water.

You are so clear.
Whoever wants to fight,

If you don't exist,
Cannot fight.
Whoever wants to love,
If you don't exist,
Cannot love.
Whoever wants to see,
If you don't exist,
Cannot see.
Whatever our actions,
You are always glowing
Unobscuredly without complaining.
But we proud beings
Are always ungrateful,
Smothering you,
Calling you Fire.

You are so light,
Whoever wants to rise,
If you don't exist,
Cannot rise.
Whoever wants to move,
If you don't exist,
Cannot move.
Whoever wants to smell,
If you don't exist,
Cannot smell.
Whatever our actions,
You are always moving
Weightlessly without complaining.
But we envious beings
Are always ungrateful,
Fanning you,
Calling you Air.

You are so open,
Whoever wants to exist,
If you don't exist,

Cannot exist.
Whoever doesn't want to exist,
If you don't exist,
Cannot exist.
Whoever wants to know phenomena,
If you don't exist,
Cannot know phenomena.
Whatever our actions,
You are always welcoming
Spaciously without complaining.
But we ignorant beings
Are always ungrateful,
Emptying you,
Calling you Space.

You are our undemanding slave,
Tirelessly serving us,
From ordinary beings to sublime beings,
To fulfill our worldly wishes.

You are our powerful queen,
Seductively conquering us,
From ordinary beings to sublime beings,
Into desirable qualities.

You are our Wisdom Dakini,
Effortlessly guiding us with your magic dance,
From ordinary beings to sublime beings,
Into desireless qualities.

And so, I want to introduce you.

Thinley Norbu
Magic Dance: The Display of the
Self-Nature of the Five Wisdom Dakinis

○ Reread this poem five times to more fully realize the five wisdom
dakinis.

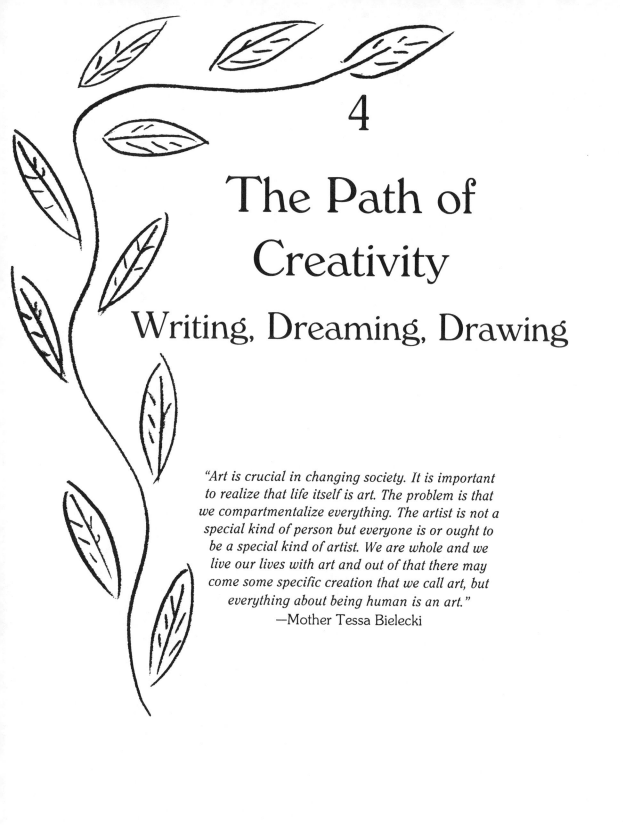

4

The Path of Creativity

Writing, Dreaming, Drawing

"Art is crucial in changing society. It is important to realize that life itself is art. The problem is that we compartmentalize everything. The artist is not a special kind of person but everyone is or ought to be a special kind of artist. We are whole and we live our lives with art and out of that there may come some specific creation that we call art, but everything about being human is an art."
—Mother Tessa Bielecki

Artists of all kinds—painters, sculptors, musicians—find and express spirituality in and through creativity, and many practitioners find their way to the heart of a spiritual tradition through its emotional and aesthetic expression in art or music rather than through theology.

In addition to relating to the art of others, the process of creativity can itself provide a sense of the sacred for women whether or not they think of themselves as artistic. Few things are as creative as dreams—those elaborate messages from the unconscious once believed to be sent by the gods. By working with dream symbols, keeping a prayer journal, or by creating artwork in a meaningful way, we are able engage deeper levels of our being, thus expressing and synthesizing elements in ways that often surprise our surface mind.

Over and over I have found that in writing, the sense of connection comes not at the point a book is published, but in the primary process of creation. When I'm writing hard, a sort of humming starts at the edge of my consciousness; earth slides away, the sky opens. I'm in, quite literally, another world. Something comes to me, through me, something sings me, hums me. When you are able to set aside your judgmental mind which limits you to what you think you can do well, you can participate in this primary creative act, can connect with this source.

Creativity—whether through writing, painting, or creative imagination—releases us into a timeless world where all things are possible. In this magical realm we can reclaim past events, retrieve former selves, live out what almost was, what could have been. Through creating, we are able to fill out the hollows and blank spaces in our lives, to make sense of and give reality to our experience. In this private arena where conscious and unconscious meet and interact, we are granted a unique opportunity to negotiate peace settlements between inner and outer, between self and other, between sacred and profane.

To think and to write about spiritual life is to engage actively in the process of integrating and shaping that life.

Writing as Meditation

Writing, like breathing, is a way of connecting the mind and the body, the conscious and the unconscious. Through writing, we can slip the moorings of our own personality to look at the world through another's eyes, to walk in their shoes. By imagining into their situation, we develop understanding and compassion, explore new ideas, new modes of being. Through writing and/or visualizing, we can overcome our fear of death by "experiencing" our own, thus leading us to live more lightly in the time we have left. Through keeping a dream journal, we can catch the hints and interpret the stories our unconscious sends us nightly. Through active imagination/visualization we can overcome psychological obscurations that block our spiritual path.

Over the years I found that it is easy to read coolly, superficially, only with the mind, but writing requires emotional involvement; it engages the whole self. By simply picking up a pen and writing for twenty minutes on a given subject, we often find out not only what we think about a topic, but also what we feel, what we fear, and what we hope. Writing about a subject will frequently reveal hidden truths and latent ideas in a way that nothing else can.

Writing in a journal or composing any kind of ongoing record of one's thoughts, activities, and events, creates a storehouse of information, even if incomplete and sporadically kept. Writing about your spiritual journey will help to deepen the experience as you write, and teach you to be more aware, more conscious of your ongoing process.

When writing, don't edit yourself as you go along. Don't worry about spelling, grammar, sentence structure, stylistic devices, or any of that. If you do, you engage the left side of the brain, and this inhibits the free flow of imagination and the ability to synthesize. Sometimes it helps to be less blocked if you write with your nondominant hand.

Putting emotions and buried experiences into words is the first step toward getting them into consciousness. After you've learned that writing can take you below a certain level of mind, then you're embarked on a profound journey that is perhaps best not talked about too much. There is something out there/in here, something conscious that holds the world together, something that is knowable, something that can be understood in silence, in loneliness, something that reveals itself gradually or swiftly, something that can be taken away sometimes for weeks or even years. What to call it? To name it might limit it, but let it work through you, trust it, trust yourself, trust the process that binds you both together. Trust and honor it. You have to be very quiet, very still to hear it, like catching a tune being played in the far distance. Learn to be still and let it work through you, heal you.

Kimberley Snow
Writing Yourself Home

○ A good method for beginning a writing meditation is to set the clock for twenty minutes and not let the pen stop moving until that time has elapsed. Don't worry about spelling, grammar, or style—just write. If you find that you are stuck, simply write the same sentence or word over again until the pen "takes off" on its own.

○ To visualize, or use what the Jungians call "active imagination" (see Robert Johnson's *Inner Work*, Harper San Francisco, 1986), simply relax the body, relax the mind, and open the inner eye to whatever images present themselves. Watch for a while and participate when your inner voice tells you to do so. Even though you may not be able to visualize clearly at first, by making the effort you create the means of a new way of perceiving.

For more on pursuing art as a path of self-knowledge and meditation, be sure to check out the following sources: Julia Cameron, *The Artist's Way: A Spiritual Path to Higher Creativity,* Tarcher/Perigree, 1992; Natalie Goldberg, *Writing Down the Bones,* Shambhala, 1986, and *Wild Mind,* Bantam, 1990; Joanna Field, *A Life Of One's Own,* [1936] Jeremy P. Tarcher, 1981; Frederick Franck, *Art as a Way: A Return to the Spiritual Roots,* The Crossroad Publishing Company, 1981; Shakti Gawain, *Creative Visualization,* Whatever Publishing, 1986; Judith Hooper and Dick Teresi, *Would the Buddha Wear a Walkman? A Catalogue of Revolutionary Tools for Higher Consciousness* (products and services to expand your mind), Simon and Schuster, 1990; Peter London, *No More Second Hand Art: Awakening the Artist Within,* Shambhala, 1989; Ronald S. Miller and the Editors of the *New Age Journal, As Above, So Below,*

"I suppose the reverse of Professor Higgins' question haunts me: 'Why can't a man be more like a woman?' Not that it is our job to save him–but all who are privileged and burdened to live just now do have some responsibility for creating a world that is safer and saner and more just than the one we have. What better way to do it than with words, holy words."
—Marilyn Sewell

Jeremy P. Tarcher, 1992; Sandra Shuman, *Source Imagery: Releasing the Power of Your Creativity*, Doubleday, 1979; Frances Vaughan, *Awakening Intuition*, Doubleday, 1979; and my *Writing Yourself Home*, Conari Press, 1990.

For more on painting and creativity, see Betty Edwards's *Drawing with the Right Side of the Brain*.

"Whenever you trying to pray, and man plop himself on the other end of it, tell him to git lost," say Shug. "Conjure up flowers, wind, water, a big rock."
—Alice Walker

This is from the play I, Mary MacLane, *about a writer born in Montana around the turn of the century. The author, Joan Melcher, a native of Montana, writes plays and screenplays in Southern California.*

Letter to God

Dear God:

I know you won't answer this letter. I'm not sure you will get it. But I have the feeling to write you a letter, though it should only blow down the whistling winds.

Now seems a fitting time for you to be personal with me—to give me a sign that you know I'm here. If you'd make me one far-off promise of a dawn to come after this tired darkness, I would walk toward the dawn in a straight road from which I should never turn aside. . . .

But I too want to tell you that I am thankful for the terrible beauty of this world. Only yesterday a light lingered on the hilltops back of town in tints of olive and copper and rose—so delicate, so radiant, so dumbly forlorn that I closed my eyes against it. Its flawless peace tortured and twisted within me.

And one summer day in Central Park in New York I saw a little yellow butterfly fluttering above a small plot of brilliant green grass. To you, God, used to the purpling splendor of untold worlds, that mightn't seem noteworthy.

But to me, the yellow of those little wings and the sweet bright green of the clipped grass entered in and beat hard on my imagination. It made me think wildly of you, God.

And two nights ago I went close to my glass and looked deep into my own dark grey eyes. They grew wide and deep and breathless-looking, realizing me human and alive. And presently I saw, back of their iris—my soul—like a naked girl, a willow in the wind, a drowning star at daybreak—an inherent, inexpressible grace—my soul of many ages.

Nobody knows how you do it, God. But it is all. I cherish it as a lonely one may who loves it with a passion and is never happy in it. And, for all of it, I thank you, God.

> Yours *very* sincerely,
>
> Mary MacLane

"What is a blessing? It is an event; a blessing is also that which turns a moment into an event."
—Marcia Falk

○ Reread Celie's letter to God in Alice Walker's *The Color Purple*. Write a letter to God.

○ Consider keeping a Blessings Journal.

Blessings Journal

Blessings—expressions of gratitude—are part of many religious traditions. Christians commonly give thanks before a meal, but in Judaism, blessings play a much larger role in daily life. Blessings, with their formulaic opening "blessed are you, Lord our God, king of the world," function as powerful tools with which to express spirituality and to forge a community. Many have come to rely on them in their daily lives to mark both extraordinary and ordinary occasions. However, the Jewish tradition, while it has great numbers of blessings—for seeing a rainbow, on meeting a wise person—has no blessings for the onset of menstruation or menopause or even for childbirth. Nor does it have a feminine variation for the formulaic opening.

A Blessings Journal is not necessarily Jewish nor does it always need a formulaic opening. A Blessings Journal is an ongoing record of

171

whatever makes you feel blessed. Write in it when you experience a spontaneous surge of gratitude—for a hummingbird that comes to your window, the way the light filters though a slatted blind, the smile of a passing child. Read it when you feel depressed.

For a comprehensive and innovative treatment of blessings, see Marcia Falk, "Notes on Composing New Blessings: Toward a Feminist-Jewish Reconstruction of Prayer," in *Weaving the Visions,* edited by Judith Plaskow and Carol P. Christ, HarperCollins, 1989. Falk illustrates how women can create their own blessings and how the feminine can be incorporated into the language in a variety of ways.

Prayer can be our intimate, private connection with the sacred or the way in which a community unites in public expression of its faith. Prayer takes many forms, from profound wordless meditation to attempted bargains made in crisis moments. The habit of prayer provides a center for spiritual life, a proven way of deepening the sacred. Praying for others develops compassion and weaves a living web of connectedness. This passage on prayer comes from my motherline: it's part of a Presbyterian Sunday School lesson my grandmother taught many years ago, sent to me for this book by my mother, who, at ninety-three, still teaches Sunday School in the same church.

Prayer

Next to the gift of God to mankind of His Son, our Savior, God's greatest gift to the world is prayer. The privilege of talking to our Heavenly Father, about anything, at any time, anywhere, with the assurance that He hears and answers is a heavenly gift, so loving, so gracious, a power available to His earthly children everywhere—and all He requires is to feel our need of Him.

Only through prayer can a soul have communion and keep in touch with the divine power of God and the spirit of Christ. We can conceive of a Christian without a Bible—though it is hard to do so—

"Prayer is relationship. In a relationship two persons are in a process of being present one to the other."
—Mary E. Giles

"At the heart of silence is prayer. At the heart of prayer is faith. At the heart of faith is life. At the heart of life is service."
—Mother Teresa

or a Christian who can love and obey God yet cannot see to read—but we cannot imagine a Christian *without prayer.* If Christ felt it necessary to pray, how infinitely more necessary is prayer for us. Prayer has been called the power which unlocks the doors of heaven; through it we have access to the heart of God. Without prayer there can be no communion with God, no fellowship with Jesus Christ.

There has never been a race or tribe, civilized or uncivilized, that has not reached out to a supreme being. In the Orient prayer is open. The Mohammedans pray on the streets and like to be heard above other noises. The Chinese write prayers on streamers and let them wave in the breeze. The public praying of Jews at their "Wailing Wall" in Jerusalem is one of the sights visitors do not like to miss. At certain sacred shrines pilgrims sometimes gather by the tens of thousands to pray, kneeling and prostrating. I have read that there are places where nuns in relays pray all day and all night.

But while prayer is a natural instinct, and God-given, in Jesus's time a great deal of praying had become meaningless and vain, so Christ initiated a new form of prayer. He made it a secret rite, a private act, a confidential communion with God, not a public exhibition. Jesus held a school of prayer for His disciples and taught them the true meaning of prayer, and He demonstrated it by His example. He retired to the solitude of the mountains or the quiet of the garden for communication with His Father, and warned His followers against professional religion, criticizing sharply the Pharisees—many of whom were snobbish and self-satisfied, in their desire to exploit their religion. Jesus told His disciples to take the opposite course by shutting out the world or anything which might divert their thoughts—to shut themselves in a private chamber to be alone with God. . . .

As we face problems, trials, conflicts, and fears without number, pity indeed the one who attempts to live a single day without the comfort and support which comes from a Higher Power through prayer. Jesus said, "All things whatsoever ye shall ask in prayer, believing, ye shall receive." But prayer is not begging. Too often God is thought of as a glorified Santa Claus, giving to people whatever they ask. The spirit of prayer, as Jesus defined it, is not to help us get what we, out of our human wisdom, want, but rather to help us accomplish what God would have us do. The secret lies not in pleading to change God's will, but in

"Prayer is not just spending time with God. It is partly that—but if it ends there, it is fruitless. No, prayer is dynamic. Authentic prayer changes us—unmasks us—strips us—indicates where growth is needed. Authentic prayer never leads to complacency, but needles us—makes us uneasy at times. It leads us to true self-knowledge, to true humility."
—Teresa of Avila

our trying to understand what God's will is for us. In every prayer we should include: *"Not my will, but thine, O Lord, be done."* We can then be sure that He will always give us something better than we ask for if we are submissive to His will.

M. Lily Hodges
Sunday School Teacher

○ Keep a journal in which you write your prayers and collect thoughts and feelings—yours and others—about prayer.

———————————

"Prayer in Benedictine spirituality is not an interruption of our busy lives nor is it a higher act. Prayer is the filter through which we learn, if we listen hard enough, to see our world aright and anew and without which we live life with souls that are deaf and dumb and blind."
—Joan Chittister OSB

The following guided meditation by a Jesuit from India provides a creative way to examine one's life.

A Testament

I ask for time to be alone and write down for my friends a sort of testament for which the points that follow could serve as chapter titles.

(1) These things I have loved in life:
Things I tasted,
looked at,
smelled,
heard,
touched.
(2) These experiences I have cherished:
(3) These ideas have brought me liberation:
(4) These beliefs I have outgrown:
(5) These convictions I have lived by:
(6) These are the things I have lived for:

(7) These insights I have gained in the school of life:
> Insights into God,
> the world,
> human nature,
> Jesus Christ,
> love,
> religion,
> prayer.

(8) These risks I took,
> these dangers I have courted:

(9) These sufferings have seasoned me:

(10) These lessons life has taught me:

(11) These influences have shaped my life
> (persons, occupations, books, events):

(12) These scripture texts have lit my path:

(13) These things I regret about my life:

(14) These are my life's achievements:

(15) These persons are enshrined within my heart:

(16) These are my unfulfilled desires:

> I choose an ending for this document:
> a poem—my own or someone else's;
> or a prayer;
> a sketch, or picture from a magazine;
> a scripture text;
> or anything that I judge would be
> an apt conclusion to my testament.

> Anthony de Mello SJ
> in *Hearts on Fire: Praying with Jesuits*

○ How can you use this for yourself?

_____

"Absolutely unmixed attention is prayer."
—Simone Weil

The following reveals the essence of developing compassion for another as separate from oneself, an esential element in using a journal for spiritual purposes. Thich Nhat Hanh is a Vietnamese monk who now teaches and works in the United States as a force for peace. Thomas Merton described him as "more my brother than many who are nearer to me in race and nationality, because he and I see things in exactly the same way."

"It is lack of love for ourselves that inhibits our compassion toward others. If we make friends with ourselves, then there is no obstacle to opening our hearts and minds to others."
—Pema Chödrön

The Unbearable Son

Suppose we have a son who becomes an unbearable young man. It may be hard for us to love him. That is natural. In order to be loved, a person should be lovable. If our son has become difficult to love, we will be very unhappy. We wish we could love him, but the only way we can is to understand him, to understand his situation. We have to take our son as the subject of our meditation. Instead of taking the concept of emptiness or some other subject, we can take our son as a concrete subject for our meditation.

First we need to stop the invasion of feelings and thoughts, which deplete our strength in meditation, and cultivate the capacity, the power of concentration. In Sanskrit this is called *samadhi*. For a child to do his homework he has to stop chewing gum and stop listening to the radio, so he can concentrate on the homework. If we want to understand our son, we have to learn to stop the things that divert our attention. Concentration, samadhi, is the first practice of meditation.

When we have a light bulb, for the light to concentrate on our book, we need a lamp shade to keep the light from dispersing, to concentrate the light so that we can read the book more easily. The practice of concentration is like acquiring a lamp shade to help us concentrate our mind on something. While doing sitting or walking meditation, cutting the future, cutting the past, dwelling in the present time, we develop our own power of concentration. With that power of concentration, we can look deeply into the problem. This is insight meditation. First we are aware of the problem, focusing all our attention on the problem, and then we look deeply into it in order to understand its real nature, in this case the nature of our son's unhappiness.

We don't blame our son. We just want to understand why he has become like that. Through this method of meditation, we find out all the causes, near and far, that have led to our son's present state of being. The more we see, the more we understand. The more we understand, the easier it is for us to have compassion and love. Understanding is the source of love. Understanding is love itself. Understanding is another name for love; love is another name for understanding. When we practice Buddhism, it is helpful to practice in this way.

When you grow a tree, if it does not grow well, you don't blame the tree. You look into the reasons it is not doing well. You may need fertilizer, or more water, or less sun. You never blame the tree, yet we blame our son. If we know how to take care of him, he will grow well, like a tree. Blaming has no effect at all. Never blame, never try to persuade using reasons and arguments. They never lead to any positive effect. That is my experience. No argument, no reasoning, no blame, just understanding. If you understand, and you show that you understand, you can love, and the situation will change.

Thich Nhat Hanh
Being Peace

"Spirituality is basically our relationship with reality."
—Chandra Patel

O One complaint against keeping a journal is that it makes a person too self-involved, but that doesn't need to be the case. You can develop compassion by coming to a true understanding of other people though writing about them. Start with a physical description of someone you know well, then tell their history. Where did they come from? What were their greatest challenges? Their biggest triumphs? Their turning points? Write about their personality. How are they different from other people? What makes them unique? What are their relationships like with other people? What makes them happy? Sad? Experience their suffering. What is their life like day by day? Imagine yourself as that person and write about your day. Write about yourself from their point of view. Become that person; walk in their shoes.

One of the best ways to deepen and integrate your spiritual experience through writing is to keep a special journal.

Spiritual Diary

Keep a journal describing the times and ways you connect to the spirit, your deeply felt connections to others or to the world, comments on the books you read or talks you hear, retreats or seminars you go to, or low points when you are not able to feel anything at all. Collect quotations that soothe or inspire you.

In *A Life Of One's Own,* Joanna Field writes that she started keeping what she called an "Opposites Journal" to try to maintain her life in balance. She noticed early on that for every strong opinion she had, she often held (or was capable of entertaining) its opposite. Also, periods of great happiness and deep despair punctuated her life, but when she was in one she couldn't remember the other until she read what she had written in her opposites journal.

This kind of journal is extremely valuable for breaking through dualistic or polarized thinking, especially if you mark some of the pages in columns so that you can list opposing thoughts side by side. In addition to personal entries, abstractions can pose a real challenge in an opposites journal. Such concepts as patriarchy, the visible world, romance, and the goddess yield many surprising insights.

———————————

Just as Jesus, brought up in the tradition of midrash, often taught in parables, the Sufis, who form the mystical branch of Islam, use stories to expand and ripen the minds of their pupils. Perhaps the best-known Sufi story is the one in which three blind men describe the nature of an elephant. The first man held its trunk and said an elephant is long and straight like a pipe; the second felt its ear, and claimed the animal to be broad and flat, like a rug; the last man groped around the elephant's leg, then declared it to be mighty and firm, like a pillar. They were all right, of course, about what they perceived, but wrong in trying to apply it to the whole.

The Tale of the Sands

A stream, from its source in far-off mountains, passing through every kind of description of countryside, at last reached the sands of the desert. Just as it had crossed every other barrier, the stream tried to cross this one, but it found that as fast as it ran into the sand, its waters disappeared.

It was convinced, however, that its destiny was to cross this desert, and yet there was no way. Now a hidden voice, coming from the desert itself, whispered: "The Wind crosses the desert, and so can the stream."

The stream objected that it was dashing itself against the sand, and only getting absorbed: that the wind could fly, and this was why it could cross a desert.

"By hurtling in your own accustomed way you cannot get across. You will either disappear or become a marsh. You must allow the wind to carry you over to your destination."

But how could this happen? "By allowing yourself to be absorbed in the wind."

This idea was not acceptable to the stream. After all, it had never been absorbed before. It did not want to lose its individuality. And, once having lost it, how was one to know that it could ever be regained?

"The wind," said the sand, "performs this function. It takes up water, carries it over the desert, and then lets it fall again. Falling as rain, the water again becomes a river."

"How can I know that this is true?"

"It is so, and if you do not believe it, you cannot become more than a quagmire, and even that could take many, many years; and it certainly is not the same as a stream."

"But can I not remain the same stream that I am today?"

"You cannot in either case remain so," the whisper said. "Your essential part is carried away and forms a stream again. You are called what you are even today because you do not know which part

*"Not only the thirsty seeks the water,
but the water seeks the thirsty as well."*
—Rumi

*"All creation teaches us
some way of prayer."*
—Thomas Merton

of you is the essential one."

When he heard this, certain echoes began to arise in the thoughts of the stream. Dimly, he remembered a state in which he— or some part of him, was it?—had been held in the arms of a wind. He also remembered—or did he?—that this was the real thing, not necessarily the obvious thing, to do.

And the stream raised his vapour into the welcoming arms of the wind, which gently and easily bore it upwards and along, letting it fall softly as soon as they reached the roof of a mountain, many, many miles away. And because he had had his doubts, the steam was able to remember and record more strongly in his mind the details of the experience. He reflected, "Yes, now I have learned my true identity."

The stream was learning. But the sands whispered: "We know, because we see it happen day after day: and because we, the sands, extend from the riverside all the way to the mountain."

And that is why it is said that the way in which the Stream of Life is to continue on its journey is written in the Sands.

> Idries Shah
> *Tales of the Dervishes:*
> *Teaching-Stories of the Sufi Masters*

○ Write a story using natural objects (rocks, flowers) or forces (wind, rain) as characters.

Two 1993 books concerning women and Sufism are available from Pir Publications: *Woman's Body, Woman's Word,* by Fedwa Malti-Douglas, and *And the Sky is Not the Limit,* by Amatullah Armstrong. There's also *The Tao of Islam,* by Sachiko Murata, State University of New York, 1992, which concentrates on gender relationships. The Winter 1994 issue of *Gnosis Magazine* is devoted to Sufism, and includes "Women and Sufism" by Camille Adams Helminski. For more general works on Sufism, consider the following books; to go to the very heart of Sufism, read the poet Rumi.

N. P. Archer, ed., *The Sufi Mystery,* Octagon, 1981.
O. M. Burke, *Among the Dervishes,* Dutton, 1975.
William C. Chittick, *Faith and Practice of Islam,* Pir, 1993.

_____, *The Sufi Path of Love: The Spiritual Teachings of Rumi,* State University of New York, 1983.

H. B. M. Dervish, *Journey with a Sufi Master,* Octagon, 1982.

Abu Bkr Siraj ad-Din, *The Book of Certainty: The Sufi Doctrine of Faith, Vision & Gnosis,* Islamic Texts, 1993.

Wali Allah al-Dihlawi, *Sufism and the Islamic Tradition,* Octagon, 1980.

Reshad Feild, *The Last Barrier,* Harper & Row, 1976.

_____, *Steps to Freedom,* Threshold, 1983.

Abu Hamid al-Ghazali, *Al-Ghazali: The Ninety-Nine Beautiful Names of God,* Islamic Texts, 1993.

Jean Houston, *The Search for the Beloved: Journey in Mythology and Sacred Psychology,* Jeremy P. Tarcher, 1987.

Sheik Nur al-Jerrabi (Lex Hixon), *Atom From the Sun of Knowledge,* Pir, 1993.

Kabir, *The Kabir Book: Forty-Four Ecstatic Poems of Kabir,* trans. by Robert Bly, Beacon, 1977.

Martin Lings, *Muhammed,* Pir, 1993.

_____, *What is Sufism?* Islamic Texts, 1975.

Seyyed Nasr, *Sufi Essays,* Schocken, 1977.

Annemarie Schimmel, *The Triumphal Sun: A Study of the Works of Jalaloddin Rumi,* East-West, 1980.

Idries Shah, *Thinkers of the East,* Penguin, 1972.

_____, *The Way of the Sufi,* Doubleday, 1969.

J. Marvin Spiegelman, ed., *Sufism, Islam and Jungian Psychology,* New Falcon, 1992.

L. F. Rushbrook Williams, *Sufi Studies: East and West,* Dutton, 1973.

For a free copy of the *Sufi Review* and to find out about *The Sufi Book Club,* write to Pir Publications, Inc., 256 Post Road East, Westport, CT 06880.

"Language uses us as much as we use language."
—Robin Lakoff

Many poets, including the one below, see the goddess as their muse. Here the goddess, the muse, and the anima combine into the Innerbird.

The Innerbird

There's this bird, this Innerbird—she means you well,
but she clenches in at times so very small
she's hard, tight, an acorn, a stomach-pain . . .

in other moods you feel her fluttering
like the purple wide-sleeved garment of a queen,
frantic within you—a wild queen's will

stirring your farthest reaches till you scheme
to set her free. That wish leads you to know
you're her idea: this bird invented you:

your purposes and due-dates are her trap,
her cage of concepts, arbitrary as a map
holding Montenegro, Montana, to one special place.

Go transparent. Disappear. And then the bird's released.
But never give that unbound bird your name,
or again she's small within you, seed within a cell.

Your absence lets her soar forth at her will—
at last she has no wrappings but the air,
and sweeps out hugely, and is everywhere.

Barry Spacks

○ Write a poem using an appropriate line or phrase from this book as the first line of the poem. For example: "The Wind crosses the desert, so can the stream"; "I am shameless; I am ashamed"; or

"Spirit is incredibly alive, moving and dancing and singing in Mother's beauty."

○ Write a poem about the goddess. For inspiration see *She Rises Like the Sun: Invocations of the Goddess by Contemporary Women Poets*, edited by Janine Canan, The Crossing Press, 1989, and *Cries of the Spirit: A Celebration of Women's Spirituality*, edited by Marilyn Sewell, Beacon, 1991.

○ Alternately, sing praises to the goddess, to the spirit within. Make up the lyrics and tune as you go along. Sing it while waiting in line, while driving; hum it to yourself in difficult situations.

"All God's angels come to us disguised."
—James Russell Lowell

———————————

Angels, called devas or spirits in other cultures, have always played an important part in the world's religions. The angel Gabriel announced Mary's impending pregnancy to her; six hundred years later, he dictated the Qur'an to the Prophet Mohammed. Angel, in fact, means messenger. The authors of Ask Your Angels *report that angels belong to a different species, one with a finer vibrational frequency than humans are used to. They are beyond gender, but can be seen as male or female, depending on the beholder. There are many different kinds of angels—some might appear as multidimensional spheres, as shafts, spirals or cones of light, ranging in size from a dot to a galaxy. The size bears some relationship to their function and nature: the larger they appear, the more collective is their function. In the following, Alma Daniel and her angel, LNO, discuss the relationship between human and angel.*

Contacting Angels

Even after LNO had become an established part of my life, I had my moments of doubt. All of what she was saying made sense, but I couldn't help but wonder whether it wasn't just a smarter part of myself that was talking. Finally, I asked, and this is what LNO replied.

183

"When we realize that it is our angel, our true self, the companion of our soul, who is the one who leads us to God, it's no longer relevant whether the angel is inside or outside—the paradox has been transcended And a new era of relationship between two species has begun."
—Alma Daniel

LNO: You can call these words your own thoughts, and they are, in the sense that you, Alma Daniel, selected the words and arrangement of those words. We do not communicate actually with words, but with vibrations, emanations. You pick up these emanations and put them into a coherence you call thoughts. This is why angelic transmissions translated into words will sound different from person to person.

It is a connecting and inspiring function that we perform when we communicate with you. Within each human is the divine spark, the God That Is. Through the soul's descent into physical matter, the spark becomes covered over, hidden, yet it remains within each human individual—and indeed within each living thing. Our function is to ignite the spark within, to fill you not with "our" thoughts, but to connect you with the knowingness that you already possess. You forget. Humans forget because the descent into matter lowers consciousness and brings about forgetfulness. Gravity pulls on you in more ways than one, not the least of which is that you sometimes forget levity. We come to inspire you with light, with lightness, and with laughter, and to remind you of what the God in you already knows.

Being a how-to person at heart, I asked her how she did this.

LNO: In a state of openness, when your normal limitations and earthly concerns have been suspended—through love, or a deep sense of peace—you open the channels, or circuits, to your own wisdom. Our function is to connect you with these knowings, some of which have been so deeply buried that when they come up you attribute them to some other. There is no other. You and God are It!

Frequencies, wave forms, vibrations, which are close to what humans experience as feelings, are the means through which we do this. Because we are not in physical form, we do not even have "thoughts." We are the messengers of God's will and you humans are the living examples of it. You are the manifestation of God's "thought" or will.

Alma Daniel, Timothy Wyllie,
and Andrew Ramer
Ask Your Angels

○ To get in touch with your angels, the authors recommend that you take out pen and paper, sit comfortably at your desk (or computer), and center on your breathing. Turn your attention inward and focus on your angel the way you sense the presence of a friend to whom you are writing a letter. Date your letter, write "Dear Angel," and simply let the words flow. You might want to ask for your angel's support and guidance and give thanks for its assistance in advance. Then sign the letter. Some people put their letters on their altar, others burn them, sending the message up with the rising smoke.

"Every blade of grass has its Angel that bends over it and whispers, 'Grow, grow.'"
—The Talmud

Angels are in, given the plethora of books on them as an indication:

Mortimer J. Adler, *The Angels and Us*, Macmillan, 1982.

William Bloom, *Devas, Fairies and Angels: A Modern Approach,* Gothic Image, 1986.

Sophy Burnham, *Angel Letters,* Ballentine, 1991.

_____ , *The Book of Angels,* Ballentine, 1989.

Ken Carey, *Return of the Bird Tribes,* Uni*Sun, 1988.

Henry Corbin, *Spiritual Body and Celestial Earth,* Princeton University, 1977.

Gustav Davidson, *A Dictionary of Angels,* Free Press, 1980.

Geddes MacGregor, *Angels: Ministers of Grace,* Paragon, 1988.

David Spangler, *Revelation: Birth of a New Age,* Rainbow Bridge, 1976.

Rudolf Steiner, *The Influence of Spiritual Beings upon Man,* Anthroposophical Press, 1982.

Terry Lynn Taylor, *Messengers of Light: The Angel's Guide to Spiritual Growth,* H. J. Kramer, 1990.

Theodora Ward, *Men and Angels,* Viking, 1969.

Also see the Red Rose Collection Catalog, PO Box 280140, San Francisco, CA 94128-0140, 1-800-374-5505, for other books and angel-related items.

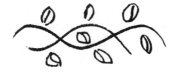

Here's a meditation using, of all things, a computer.

Computer Exercise

Turn off the computer and look at the screen or visualize a blank computer screen. A blank piece of paper will do. Tune into the blankness there, the lack of activity. Go into the screen and expand. Keep expanding. When you can no longer feel the edges of your consciousness, stop. Pause. Relax. Maintain this awareness as you leave your chair, take it into the home. But first, thank the computer for a good day's work and mentally wish that whatever useful you've accomplished during the day be shared by everyone.

Dreaming is probably one of the most creative acts that we perform. Like writing, it forms a connection between conscious and unconscious, visible and invisible, sacred and profane. Karen A. Signell's Wisdom of the Heart: Working with Women's Dreams, Bantam, 1990, *is a comprehensive guide for women who wish to understand dreams from a Jungian perspective. In the first chapter, which I summarize below, she describes how to capture a dream and work with it.*

Dreams

The techniques for remembering dreams are generally well known: stay still in bed without opening your eyes; try to recall an image. Catch that image "by the tail" to bring back the whole dream, bit by bit. Then let your thoughts and feeling gently relax. In that state, the meaning of the dream may come to you. Sometimes an idea may come without your remembering the dream at all. Check out the sensations of the body and see if any memories or feelings emerge.

"Messages from the gods, later translated as messages from the unconscious, have come through dreams in all cultures."
—Frances Vaughan

Then open your eyes and write down the dream, amplify the images, and let the dream speak.

In the Freudian method of dream analysis, one uses "free association," that is, consider the dream image and let another image spontaneously emerge from your unconscious. Then you take this second association and repeat the process until you have a string of associations that go back to childhood.

In the Jungian method of dream analysis, one "amplifies" the dream image by letting various associations appear without censoring or judging them. Unlike the Freudian method in which an increasing linkage of associations leads away from the dream like a string of beads, in the Jungian method one forms a set of associations from the dream image, then returns to the primary source of the dream to form another set, repeating this again and again like the petals of a lotus.

In order to amplify a dream, concentrate lightly on it, then note other images that float up from your unconscious. Return to the original image and see what thoughts, feelings, memories, or images now appear. Repeat this process until you feel you understand what the dream image means to you. Painting or drawing the image can also help in this process.

Since dreams share a common language with myth, art, folklore, and religious ritual, another form of amplification in Jungian dream analysis is to look for universal themes of myths and folklore that parallel images found in the dream. Because Western culture relies heavily on Greek myth with its heroes, power over death, subordination of women, and so forth, women may be disappointed in trying to understand their feminine nature through the use of these myths. In contrast, folk tales, fairy stories, songs, and rituals that spring from ordinary people (including women) trying to understand the nature of their lives and the unknown may prove more beneficial.

By getting in touch with a feeling in a dream, you can start a spontaneous process of amplification. Learn to listen closely to any tensions or other subtle feelings you notice in your body. For instance, a feeling of constriction in the throat might seem like a stifled cry and recall a memory of being alone in a dark room as a child, whimpering. Sometimes by concentrating on a feeling (ten-

"A dream uninterpreted is like a letter left unopened."
—Talmud

"Behind naming, beneath words, is something else. An existence named un- named and unnameable."
—Susan Griffin

sion in your elbow), you might release the energy there and be able to glimpse a host of hidden images and fears (such as raising your arm in anger). Try to find the image that goes with the feeling (and vice versa) for they are two sides of the same coin. Finding both adds depth and reality to your dream experience.

Your body sense can also indicate when you are hot on the trail of something, feeling mounting curiosity and excitement. When you say "Aha" or when there is a shift in mood, you know that your unconscious thoughts, emotions, or meanings have broken through into conscious- ness. You may feel a release of tension, surprise, or you may suddenly laugh or cry.

Sometimes a dream, like a stage play, has a plot, characters, conflict, and resolution. In this case, the setting (the family dining room, your first train ride) may indicate when and where an issue first occurred.

The unconscious also has an uncanny way of choosing characters that represent parts of the dreamer. A rule of thumb is if the character is someone you know well, the dream indicates some quality (recent sadness, for instance) in them that you've been overlooking. However, if the sad person in the dream is from your remote past or someone you don't know very well, then it is your own unacknowledged unhappiness that is being revealed to you. Ultimately, your dreams are all about you, calling your attention to certain qualities you are unaware of in yourself or in others.

A dream can be understood through what it says about your outer life and what is tells you about your inner life. Don't become discouraged in trying to make sense of your dreams, even though this is hard work whether you are a beginner or an old hand. Still, by proceeding with ease rather than with grim determination, you will go farther. Don't feel that you always have to labor at recalling and analyzing your dreams, for they do their work whether you remember them or not.

Taking a few minutes upon awakening to think about your dreams gives energy to your inner life and helps to connect the conscious and unconscious minds. Dreams are often messengers from the future, arriving weeks, or even years ahead of conscious understanding. By reviewing your dreams now and then, you can often see sequences and themes. By telling the dream to a friend or counselor, writing it down, or recording it on tape, you impress the dream on your psyche and make it come alive.

Because Jungian dreamwork takes place in the safety of a therapeutic setting, when working with dreams you might try to recreate a similar quiet setting that is imbued with a spirit of open receptivity which sets free the imagination.

A leaderless dream group of three people who meet for an hour and a half each week can be quite helpful. You might want to have each person tell a dream and have the other two members comment on it as if it were their own, saying what it means to each of them. In this way, others are not trying to explain your dreams to you, but leave you open to absorb whatever they say that rings true rather than having to resist interpretation. This gentle way of working with dreams is similar to the tradition that comes out of women's consciousness-raising groups.

Sometimes a dream may be too charged to share with others or even to work on oneself. Honor your resistance to tell anyone about the dream, but let it incubate—perhaps for years. If there is something your unconscious wants you to know immediately, it will repeat the message through dreams over and over until you hear it and deal with it.

You learn to understand dreams not by learning interpretation techniques, but by experiencing many dreams, developing confidence in your intuition, and cultivating your imagination. Knowledge is accumulated bit by bit in a nonconceptual way by examining many dreams—your own included—and keeping in touch with their feeling tone and the way it relates to the dreamer.

As you hear or read about other people's dreams, enter the experience of the dreamer and let yourself understand what the dream meant to her. Ask yourself what the dream would mean to you if your own, noting what reverberates with your inner landscape. You can treat any dream as though it were your own, for dreams draw upon layers of experience and the unconscious that are shared by all. It helps to stop now and then, to listen to the sounds from the depth, and discover meanings that resonate within.

○ Keep a journal exclusively for dreams and place it on your bedside table. Write in it as soon as you wake up. Writing down your dreams helps you to remember them as well as keep track of the motifs and messages they convey.

"Why had no one told me that the function of will might be to stand back, to wait, and not to push?"
—Marion Milner

See also *The Dream Workbook: Discover the Knowledge and Power Hidden in Your Dreams,* by J. Morris, Little, Brown, 1985; *A Little Course in Dreams: A Basic Handbook of Jungian Dreamwork,* by R. Bosnak, Shambhala, 1988; *Dreamtime and Dreamwork: Decoding the Language of the Night,* edited by Stanley Krippner, Jeremy P. Tarcher, 1990; *Dreams and Spiritual Growth: A Christian Approach to Dreamwork,* by L. M. Savary, P. H. Berne, and S. K. Williams, Paulist Press, 1984; and *Wisdom of the Heart: Working with Women's Dreams,* by Karen Signell, Bantam, 1990.

"We are close to waking up when we dream that we are dreaming."
—Novalis

The Buddha taught eighty-four thousand methods of spiritual practice. In the three main sects of Buddhism that have come to the West—Theravaden (Vipassana) from Southeast Asia, Zen from Japan, and Vajrayana from Tibet—the first two tend to stress sitting meditation for attaining enlightenment whereas the latter uses a wide variety of techniques. Some of the Tibetan methods, which may seem quite exotic to Westerners, require initiation into the practice by a lama or teacher, whereas others are available to everyone through books. Dream yoga falls in between.

Dream Yoga

Many of the methods of practicing Dharma that are learned during waking can, upon development of dream awareness, be applied in the dream condition. In fact, one may develop these practices more easily and speedily within the dream if one has the capacity to be lucid. There are even some books that say if a person applies a practice within a dream, the practice is nine times more effective than when it is applied during the waking hours.

The dream condition is unreal. When we discover this for ourselves within the dream, the immense power of this realization can eliminate obstacles related to conditioned vision. For this reason, the practice of the dream is very important for liberating us from habits. We particularly need this powerful assistance, because the emotional attachments, conditioning, and ego enhancement which compose our normal life have been strengthened over our many, many years.

In a real sense, all the visions that we see in our lifetime are like a big dream. If we examine them well, the big dream of life and the smaller dreams of one night are not very different. If we truly see the essential nature of both, we will see that there really is no difference between them. If we can finally liberate ourselves from the chains of emotions, attachments, and ego by this realization, we have the possibility of ultimately becoming enlightened.

> Namkhai Norbu
> *Dream Yoga and*
> *the Practice of Natural Light*

"The further limits of our being plunge, it seems to me, into an altogether other dimension of existence from the sensible and merely 'understandable' world. Name it the mystical region, or the supernatural region, whichever you choose. . . . We belong to it in a more intimate sense than that in which we belong to the visible world."
—William James

Several works are available about dream yoga and the lucid dreaming that spontaneously arises as a by-product of doing the "practice of the night," but to get the most out of this method, you need to talk to a lama or to attend a dream yoga retreat. Notice of Vajrayana retreats and books on Tibetan practice are listed in the Snow Lion Newsletter and Catalog, PO Box 6483, Ithaca, NY 14851, and in *Tricycle: The Buddhist Review,* Dept. TRI, Box 3000, Denville, NJ 07834. See also *Ancient Wisdom: Nyingma Teachings on Dream Yoga, Meditation and Transformation,* by Venerable Gyatrul Rinpoche, Snow Lion, 1993. For more on lucid dreaming, see *Creative Dreaming,* by Patricia Garfield, Simon & Schuster, 1975; and *Lucid Dreaming,* by Stephen LaBerge, Ballantine Books, 1986.

Creativity is often messy—look at childbirth—and cannot be neatly contained.

Messiness Is Next to Goddessness

If cleanliness is next to godliness, then messiness is next to goddessness. God creates order, gives us ten neat rules carved with no crossing outs in a stone tablet. The great Goddess, on the other hand, gives us life. Henry Adams said that order produces habit, but chaos produces life. Habit can be useful—do the dishes after dinner, brush your teeth, do not kill, know thyself—but *life* is chaotic—creative, unpredictable, uncodified.

The reality of the Goddess has been forgotten for many years and we have all been taught to believe that neatness counts. Once upon a time, though, before humans got organized and started hanging things up and putting things back, we knew about the Goddess who ruled over fertility, creativity, life, sexuality, and everything else dirty.

John Boe
"Messiness is Next to Goddessness"
in *Psychological Perspectives*
(Issue 27, 1992)

○ Whatever you had planned to clean up today, forget it. Create an artwork instead.

———————————————

Creating shamanic art—such as fetishes, dolls, or visual images known as yantras—is a way of coming in contact with unseen forces and enlisting their support and healing energy in our lives. Here Vicki Noble, the creator of the Motherpeace Tarot Cards, tells how to make a fetish. She says the less you know about "real" art—that is, the fewer preconceptions you have—the freer your mind and spirit will be in doing the work. Thus, the first thing that needs to be released is the belief that you aren't "artistic."

Making a Fetish

"Fetish art" is the general name of what we think of as shamanic art in our culture. The making of a fetish is a sacred task, and it is one of the first assignments I give to my women students when they take up the study of female shamanism. A fetish is a conglomeration of found objects, feathers, bones, rocks, beads, hair, leaves, twigs, and anything else that pleases a person and represents the variety of materials found in Nature. It may take a representational form, looking like an animal or a doll, or it may not. Some fetishes look like mobiles or a piece of abstract art. Some take the form of shields. I ask the women to spend time in the wild gathering anything that attracts them, without necessarily having a system of correspondences to explain the intuitive attraction. Choose anything that Nature sends you, including found objects from city streets. The gizmos, gadgets, and whatnots that fall from cars or bikes, or that someone discarded as junk, can become magical when they take a shape or form that appeals to your inner mind and reminds you of an archetype or process in your life. I have made evocative pieces of artwork that included copper rings and metal pieces from auto mechanic shops as well as feathers, beads, and bones of animals found on trails in the hills.

The purpose of a fetish (or yantra) is healing. Probably everyone has seen Zuni fetishes, generally small ceramic or stone sculpted animals that function protectively for the owner. In Africa women make pots that become homes for the spirits that originally made them ill and that will be captured in the pots to be mastered and harnessed for healing. You can set your healing intention and then use the fetish to focus your mind or will on that vow. In the sense that I am describing it, there is no right way to make your fetish. Just enjoy the process and be aware that everything counts. Every knot you tie is a wish made; every stone, bead, bone, or feather means

"I am amazed at how much of what we call interior decorating is just subconscious altar building."
—Luisah Teish

*"God respects me when I work
But he loves me when I sing."*
—Tagore

193

something. But you don't need to know the meaning in some literal, linear way. It's enough just to love the sacred process, trust the magic, and let the artwork begin to speak to you as you produce it. Before you have finished the work, you may have a sense of its name, its purpose, and how you need to relate to it. For instance, some fetishes might "want" something specific, such as to be placed on an altar and given flowers or incense daily. Others will hang in a room and remind you of their purpose every time you pass by. You can make a fetish for protection, then carry it with you or keep it in the room or house you wish to protect. Maybe your fetish will have some other instruction for you. The fetish itself is created as a means of contacting and making yourself available to guidance from the realm of the invisible spirits.

Vicki Noble
Shakti Woman

○ You can find material for a fetish almost anywhere. If you live in the city, bead stores often carry feathers, bits of leather, and quills as well. Twigs, leaves, rocks, and bark may be gathered in a park. Look through your house for things that can be incorporated into a fetish: little bits of metal that were once part of something else, broken thises or thats, half a clothespin, a single earring, a scrap of cloth. Take your collected material and make anything that appeals to you—a statue, a three-dimensional "thing," stuff pasted onto a piece of cloth or wood. Whatever you do, have fun with it. You might start by enlarging the "Messiness is Next to Goddessness" passage, paste it onto colored posterboard, and decorate it with feathers, strings, and messy-looking odds and ends.

Creating religious art is itself a form of worship, a way of connecting with a particular tradition. Tibetan Buddhist art is often highly stylized, with rules and traditional practices sur-

"All the arts are apprenticeship. The big art is life."
—M. C. Richards

"Imagination is more important than knowledge."
—Albert Einstein

rounding its creation. Each painting has an underlying grid which gives specific proportions for each of the symbolic elements. Pictures of the deities, mounted with borders of silk brocade, are called t'hankas.

Phyllis Glanville, an artist who lives in a Tibetan Buddhist retreat center in Northern California, connects with this tradition through its art. The dakinis she draws are seen as existing as a wide variety of feminine spirits (including historical women) on the relative plane and as basic space on the absolute. Like the term Tantra, *the concept of a dakini is often distorted and misunderstood in the West. For more on this complex subject see Tsultrim Allione and Thinley Norbu in this volume.*

"We are born remembering. We are born connected . . . . Every drawing is a quest for origin, a return to the source following the hidden threads in the labyrinthine matrix."
—Meinrad Craighead

Art and Spirituality

Kimberley Snow: Phyllis, tell me about the relationship between your creative process and your spiritual life.

Phyllis Glanville: Until I started doing Tibetan-style art, I hadn't found any subject matter that I connected with. I wanted something that was important enough to express, that had essence, that resonated. I wanted to express my highest ideals so that people would be touched in a way that made them think. I want the art to remind them.

K: The art in the Tibetan tradition is highly structured?

P: Yes, highly mathematical, very precise, and controlled as to how each deity is drawn. Within that gridwork, I can overlay "me" and how it comes through me. When I drew the dakinis of the five Buddha families, I tried to keep in mind both their positive and negative attributes, and it was interesting what would come up in my daily life and in the drawings, too.

K: What do you mean?

P: For instance, if I was working on the Ratna dakini which has to do with the negative emotion of pride, I could see this quality in high relief in my life. It's funny because the Ratna dakini is the one that I've always had a problem drawing. She also represents richness and bounty in life—things that I've denied myself. The Padma dakini seemed like someone I knew pretty well. She was lush, sensuous,

195

"If you bring forth what is inside of you, what you bring forth will save you. If you don't bring forth what is inside of you, what you don't bring forth will destroy you."
—Jesus

into her desires. But I had a hard time with Vajra, the aspect which deals with anger. I've always had a very hard time with anger in myself and in other people. I'm terrified by it. So that is what would come up in my life; I'd see it around me and experience it directly. And I'd flub up on the drawing then try to creatively fix the mistakes because I'd pledged to myself not to start over. In the first set of drawings I did, the dakinis would get wilder and wilder with each mistake—lots of scarves and so forth. When Rinpoche [her Tibetan teacher] took a look at them, he said, "This *what?* Not Buddhist art, this some new art."

K: How does this relate to your spiritual life?

P: My art *is* my spiritual life. It's the closest I come to "official" practice. I don't have the temperament or the heart or mind to do very rigid sitting or visualization. And it's odd because what I depict is exactly what you're "supposed" to see when you sit and visualize, only I don't sit and visualize.

K: Do you do the mantra of the deity you're working on?

P: Sometimes. I've recently started inking drawings and I do mantra to calm my mind, and this calms my hand. Saying the mantra helps to take the "me" out of what I'm doing, at least the judgmental "me" that makes me afraid to put pen to paper.

K: Do you see the dakinis you draw as goddesses?

P: I have a hard time with the term *goddess*. It is one of these loaded terms. Dakinis come from a very different tradition than the goddess movement today.

K: How *do* you see the goddess?

P: I think she is the feminine aspect of spirit that's present in all of us, male and female, just as the male, the god, is present in both men and women. I don't want to identify myself with the goddess movement, any more than I do with a strong patriarchal lineage. Tibetan Buddhism has aspects of the goddess, the feminine, that I connect with and respect, especially the dakini principle as space, as that movement—almost like *chi*—of natural energy, the flow of things, the connectedness. When it's right, you know it. That's the goddess. When you can touch your friend or your partner and at that moment know that there's a healing energy being exchanged, that's the goddess.

K: Tell me about how you first started drawing dakinis.

P: I was living in Mt. Shasta, California, a place that I feel very connected to and which has a lot of feminine energy. I was doing design work and not very happy with it. I asked myself if I could do anything I wanted and not worry about money what would it be? I realized I wanted to be an artist. For a while, I'd had these impulses to go out and buy black paper and colored pencils and draw. It was almost like a food craving, but for art supplies.

I had met a Tibetan lama by this time and was doing traditional practice—formal sitting, visualizing a particular deity, chanting a mantra. But I needed to find a way into the tradition that felt right to me. Part of my practice was to visualize Guru Padmasambhava [who brought Buddhism to Tibet, often called the "Second Buddha"] so I drew him first. Another visualization is of Guru Padmasambhava and his consort in union, so I drew them next. This felt like the ideal expression for me. It wasn't as if I was going to start to draw Tibetan deities for a living, but it just gave me so much pleasure and a way to connect with the practice that I was having a hard time doing.

K: What does it feel like when you are drawing the deities?

P: When I'm clear about what I'm doing—mentally, psychologically, and physically—it's an incredible experience. It's intimate. I get lost in it in a really nice way. When my mind and my hands and my physical body are occupied with a particular task, it allows my mind to expand, and I get little sideways glimpses of how things really are, how it all comes together. I've had that happen when I've worked on design drawings for Rinpoche. Suddenly, I've gotten a shift, a whole different perspective, and it stayed with me. It felt like it was directly from him. I had the same experience when I did some sewing for him last summer. All of a sudden I got a hit. There's some weird sort of connection.

When I showed the first drawing I did of Vajrayogini to Rinpoche he said that the body was nice, that women know women's bodies better than men. Then he looked at the skullcup in her hand [often used symbolically in Tibetan rituals and art], and said, "What's this? Looks like chocolate. And this? Looks like coffee. This what? Looks like smoke."

I was amazed, because when I was doing the drawing I was

"But remember. Make an effort to remember. Or failing that, invent."
—Monique Wittig

197

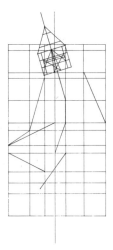

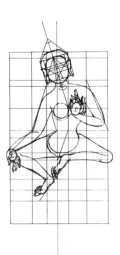

munching on M-and-M's, drinking coffee, and smoking dope! He could look at the drawing I'd done and see what was going on in my head, in my life.

I always asked myself, "How could he see that? How could he tell?" Until one day recently when I was working on a painting and was trying to get the background right—I was trying to draw these radiating lines coming off Buddha's body—and I took a toke. Again, I asked myself, "How did he do that?" when I stepped back from the painting and saw wisps of smoke around the Buddha just as clear as if I as a professional artist had put them there. It was hilarious. I had to stop and thank Rinpoche for pointing it out to me in that moment. I realized if I was going to do that kind of art, I'd better stop smoking dope when I was doing them.

K: Which deities do you connect with the most?

P: The female wrathful deities. I feel them very strongly, in a wild woman kind of way. That wrathful, feminine, direct, explosive, laserlike kind of energy. Even with the male deities, I prefer the wrathful forms.

K: As I understand it, you are working with a fairly rigid form--the proportions are all set out on a grid, there are all kinds of rules and regulations surrounding pictures of the deities. Do you feel any resistance because of this?

P: Not really. In some ways it is rather nice. It eliminates all the decisions that I would have to make about what I want to draw. That's what makes it practice, that overlay of discipline. That's what grounds it, and makes it like what has gone before in that tradition, and the discipline is what lets me tap into it.

In time, I want my paintings to be more expressive of me. But I want to be true to the basic tradition—never knowingly to distort an image deliberately or out of ignorance—but to begin to step out a little. To use a traditional image, but to do it more nontraditionally, perhaps by using a different medium—like these paints that are full of light. Or to draw on a huge scale on canvas.

K: That seems to parallel other trends in Tibetan Buddhism in the United States, such as speaking the prayers in English or putting Christmas tree lights up on the prayer wheel house. Perhaps it is all part of making a bridge to the West. Do you talk to other *t'hanka* painters? What are they doing?

P: I don't *know* any other *t'hanka* painters. Or not any that speak enough English for me to communicate with them. I'm working in a vacuum, and in a sense I don't want to tamper with the vacuum. What I discover on my own has more validity if I don't talk to other people. If this is truly a spiritual path for me, if this is my practice, then it should get me to the same place as everyone else's path. If I can let *it* guide me, then that's a lot more powerful and real than letting other artists guide me. But when I'm working on the deities, they become my teachers. It's just me and them, no middlemen.

I feel there's a need for this art; it's first-generation western Buddhist art by a woman. What makes Tibetan Buddhism a living tradition is that it does come through people's filters. It changes in response to what is needed in the moment. Even if it touches only me, that's something. Hopefully, some power comes through the art and touches others as well.

K: Sometimes I think that all artists, not just painters, are revealers of wisdom, especially poets.

P: I think they are trying to be. It starts with the spirit moving them. But so many artists, especially amateur artists, get side-tracked into dogma and do really predictable work that has no creativity, no spark. Pure spirit—the dakini principle if you will—is what makes a living tradition.

With me, the deities are the core. They are my teachers and I can trust them in a very special way for I'm working with them directly. It's just me and them.

———————————

○ A meditational device is anything that helps to center your meditation. A visual meditational device, called a yantra, can be as simple as a dot on a sheet of paper or as complex as the Wheel of Time mandala. The important thing is that you pick an image or design that has some energy for you, that appeals to you in a way you can't quite explain. Let the spirit work with you as you select the image. Put it where it can easily be seen, and look at it to evoke a sense of peace. Hang your meditational device at eye level, sit quietly, and relax. Don't think about the image, but rather let your mind rest quietly. Simply "go into" the drawing, and let the image work on an unconscious level.

"Our Lord opened my spiritual eye and showed me my soul in the middle of my heart, and I saw the soul as wide as if it were an infinite world, and as if it were a blessed kingdom."
—Julian of Norwich, 1373

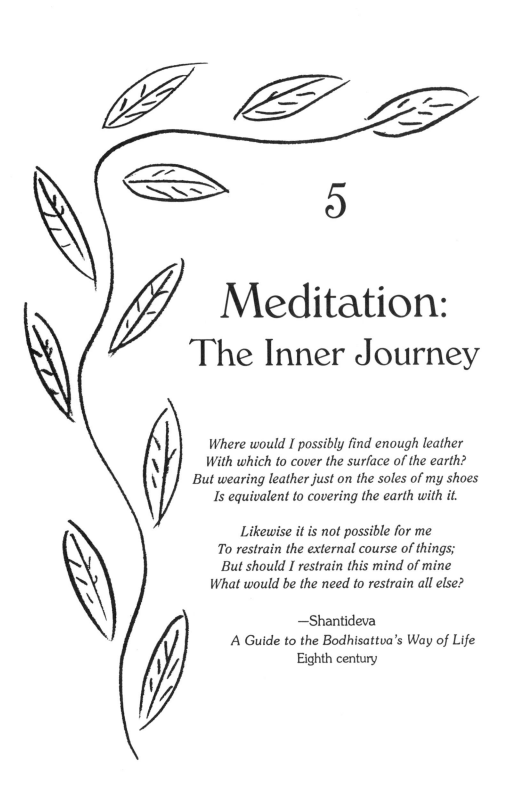

5

Meditation:
The Inner Journey

Where would I possibly find enough leather
With which to cover the surface of the earth?
But wearing leather just on the soles of my shoes
Is equivalent to covering the earth with it.

Likewise it is not possible for me
To restrain the external course of things;
But should I restrain this mind of mine
What would be the need to restrain all else?

—Shantideva
A Guide to the Bodhisattva's Way of Life
Eighth century

It would be almost impossible for me to explain to you the taste of a mango. You have to eat one yourself. Meditation is like that. You just have to try it. Pick the exercise in this section that appeals to you the most and try it for five minutes a day. Part of the process—as in dreamwork—is learning to trust yourself and your own intuition, finding out how to tune into your deeper self. After a week or two, you'll begin to taste the mango. After that, you'll find that your meditation has a life of its own with surprising joys, beneficial side effects, disappointing dry spells, and a host of unpredictable happenings.

Helpful hints: Learn to meditate in a quiet setting, sitting on a cushion or in a chair with spine straight, before you try meditation in action. Don't talk in a light way about your meditation or the fact that you meditate. Try sitting with a group as well as alone; the support is useful. If you start feeling unusually spacey, stop meditating for a while. If you have questions, consult a qualified teacher.

For a comprehensive list of Buddhist retreat centers, see *Buddhist America: Centers, Retreats, Practices,* edited by Don Morreale, John Muir Publications, 1988. For listings of current teachings and publications in Tibetan Buddhism see Snow Lion Newsletter and Catalog, PO Box 6483, Ithaca, NY 14851, and *Shambhala Sun,* 1345 Spruce St., Boulder, CO 80302-4886. For articles on issues concerning Theravadan, Zen, and Tibetan Buddhism, plus announcements of conferences and teachings and listings of regional centers, see *Tricycle: The Buddhist Review,* Dept TRI, Box 3000, Denville, NJ 07834. For Zen information, see *The Ten Directions,* published by the Zen Center of Los Angeles, 923 South Normandie Ave., Los Angeles, CA 90006-1310. And don't forget Tassajara Zen Mountain Center; call (415) 431-3771 for information. For the Sufi Review and Sufi Book Club Catalog, write Pir Publications, Inc., Dept T-1, 256 Post Road East, Westport, CT 06880. For Vipassana retreat information, write Insight Meditation Society, 1230 Pleasant Street, Barre, MA 01005.

Many excellent books on meditation and religion are available by catalog from the following: Shambhala Publications, P.O. Box 308, Boston, MA 02117-0308, (617) 424-0228; Ziji Books and Gifts, 2019 10th Street, Boulder, CO 80302; Bodhi Tree Bookstore, 8585 Melrose Avenue, West Hollywood, CA 90069-5199; Tibetan Treasures, Box 279, Junction City, CA, 96048. For meditation supplies: DharmaCrafts, 199 Auburn Street, Cambridge, MA 02139, and Samadhi Cushions, RR 1, Box 3, Barnet, VT, 05821.

"Meditating means bringing the mind back to something again and again. Thus, we all meditate, but unless we direct it in some way, we meditate on ourselves and on our own problems, reinforcing our self-clinging."
—Lama Yeshe Dorje

Chagdud Tulku escaped from Tibet during the Chinese occupation and came to the United States in 1979, where he founded Chagdud Gonpa which has centers all over the world. For a fascinating account of his life, see his autobiography, Lord of the Dance, Padma Publishing, 1992.

Meditation

To come to an understanding of impermanence and a genuine desire to make others happy in this brief opportunity we have together represents the beginning of true spiritual practice. This kind of sincerity truly catalyzes transformation of mind and being. We don't have to shave our heads or wear special robes. We don't have to leave home or sleep on a bed of stone. Spiritual practice doesn't require austere conditions, only a good heart and the maturity to comprehend impermanence. This will lead to progress.

On the other hand, if we only make a show of spirituality, burning the right incense, sitting the right way, speaking the right words, we're liable to become more proud, more self-righteous, condescending, and faultfinding. Such false practice won't help us or others at all. The purpose of spiritual practice is not to increase our faults. When it's done with a good heart and the knowledge of impermanence, practice can justifiably be called great.

Having heard this once, we may become inspired. It makes us warm inside, makes us happy, to hear such truths. But it's a bit like patching a hole in our clothes: if we don't sew the patch on well, pretty soon it's going to start slipping and the hole's going to show again.

This is where we come to contemplation and meditation. Even though we can be inspired and touched by the simplicity and profundity of a spiritual approach to life, still our habits are very strong and the world remains difficult for us to contend with. Effective practice requires a constant reiteration of what we know to be true.

Meditation is a process of stitching, of reminding ourselves again and again of the deeper truth—impermanence, loving kindness—until the patch is sewn on so strongly it becomes a part of the cloth and strengthens the whole garment.

Then we're not shaken by outer circumstances. There is a kind of ease that comes when we understand the illusory nature of reality, when we comprehend the dreamlike quality of life, this impermanence that pervades everything. Even as it is it isn't, and someday it won't be at all. This doesn't mean that we deny our involvement with life, but that we don't take it quite so seriously; we approach it with less hope and fear. Then we're like an adult playing with a child on the beach: the adult doesn't suffer like the child if the sand castle is washed out to sea. Yet compassion arises in seeing the child's suffering.

Compassion is natural to every one of us, but because we have deep, very self-centered habits, we need to cultivate it by contemplating the suffering of those who invest their dream with solidity. We need to develop a sincere, compassionate desire that their suffering will cease, that they will come to understand the dreamlike quality of life and thus avoid the agony that comes with the inevitable loss of things they value.

For twelve years, a very great Indian scholar and practitioner, Atisha, studied many texts, huge bodies of teachings and commentaries on the doctrine of the Buddha and the realizations of great lamas. After his years of study, he came to the conclusion that every single method—and the Buddha taught eighty-four thousand methods for achieving the transition from ordinary to extraordinary mind—came down to the essential point of good-heartedness.

When we merely talk about purity of heart it seems simple, but in difficult times it's not so easy to maintain. If you are face to face with someone who hates you, someone who would hurt you, it's very hard not to become angry and lose your loving kindness.

"Warning: If you don't have room in your living room for an elephant—don't make friends with the elephant trainer."
—Sufi proverb

207

"There are no impediments to meditation. The very thought of such obstacles in the greatest impediment."
—Ramana Maharshi

It is taught by the Buddha and by beings of infallible wisdom who know all causes and conditions of the past, present, and future that we have all had countless lifetimes. This may prove difficult for some of us to accept, because of course we haven't achieved so high a degree of wisdom: we don't know where we came from before we were born or where we will go after we die. But if we think about it, we live in the midst of today as a consequence of having had a yesterday, and similarly today supplies the basis for our having a tomorrow. It's the same with the sequence of existence. We have this life, which means there was some previous basis for it, while the present itself forms the ground for what will occur next.

If our inherent wisdom were more fully revealed, we'd see that all beings—whether human, animal, or otherwise—at some time throughout countless lifetimes have shown us the kindness of parents, given us a body, protected us, enabled us to survive, provided education, understanding, and some sort of worldly training. It doesn't matter what their roles are now or how difficult our relationships with them may be. It's as if we are playing at make-believe. We're like actors who come to believe we're actually the characters we're enacting.

When we understand this connection between ourselves and every other being, equanimity arises. We regard everyone, whether friend or foe, with consideration. Even though someone may prove difficult, it doesn't mean that person hasn't been important to us before.

When we see one who has once been our parent suffering terribly, our compassion deepens. We contemplate, "How sad—she doesn't understand. If I understand a little bit more, it's my responsibility to help her as much as I can."

A perception like that softens us. Then, when we're in a stressful situation, we think a moment before we react impulsively, responding with patience and compassion instead of anger. We try to be kind and helpful, and refrain from hurtful, self-interested, negative actions and faultfinding.

Applying spiritual practice in daily life begins when you wake up in the morning. Rejoice that you didn't die in the night, knowing you have one more useful day—you can't guarantee that you'll have two. Then remind yourself of correct motivation. Instead of setting out to become rich and famous or to follow your own selfish interests, meet the day with an altruistic intention to help others. And renew your commitment every morning. Tell yourself, "With this day I'll do the very best that I can. In the past I've done fairly well on some days, terribly on others. But since this day may be my last, I will offer my very best; I will do right by other people as much as I am able."

Before you go to sleep at night, don't just hit the pillow and pass out. Instead, review the day. Ask yourself: "How did I do? I had the intention not to hurt anybody—did I accomplish that? I meant to cultivate joy, compassion, love, equanimity—did I do so?" Think not just of this day, but of every day of your life. "Have I developed positive tendencies? Have I been basically a virtuous person? Or have I spent most of my time acting negatively, engaged in nonvirtuous activities?" Ask yourself these things critically and honestly. How does it come out when you really study the tallies?

If you find that you have fallen short, there's no benefit to feeling guilty or blaming yourself. The point is to observe what you have done, because your harmful actions can be purified. Negativity is not marked indelibly in the ground of the mind. It can be changed. So look back. When you see your faults and downfalls, call upon a wisdom being. You don't need to go to a special place, for there is no place where prayer is not heard. It doesn't matter if you consider perfection to be God, Buddha, or a deity, as long as when you objectify it, there is no flaw, no fault, no limitation. From absolute perfection you gain the blessings of purification.

Confess, with that wisdom being as your witness, and sincerely regret the harm you've done, vowing not to repeat it. As you meditate, visualize light radiating from the object of perfection, cleansing you and purifying all the mistakes of your day, your life, every life you've lived.

When you look at your day, you may find that you were able to make others happy. Maybe you gave food to a hungry animal or practiced generosity, patience. Rather than becoming self-satisfied, resolve to do better tomorrow, to be more skillful, more compassionate in your interactions with others. Dedicate the positive energy created by your good actions to all beings, whoever they are, whatever condition they're in, thinking, May this virtue relieve the suffering of beings; may it cause them short- and long-term happiness.

"Meditation allows us to directly participate in our lives instead of living life as an afterthought."
—Stephen Levine

209

During the day, check your mind. How am I behaving? What is my real intention? You can't really know anybody else's mind; the only one you truly know is your own. Whenever you can, contemplate these thoughts: the preciousness of our human birth, impermanence, karma, the suffering of others.

In daily meditation practice we work with two aspects of the mind: its capacity to reason and conceptualize—the intellect—and the quality that is beyond thought--the pervasive, nonconceptual nature of mind. Using the rational faculty, contemplate. Then let the mind rest. Think and then relax; contemplate, then relax. Don't use one or the other exclusively, but both together, like the two wings of a bird.

This isn't something you do only sitting on a cushion. You can meditate this way anywhere—while driving your car, while working. It doesn't require special props or a special environment. It can be practiced in all walks of life.

Some people think that if they meditate for fifteen minutes a day, they ought to become enlightened in a week and a half. But it doesn't work like that. Even if you meditate and pray and contemplate for an hour of the day, that's one hour you're meditating and twenty-three you're not. What are the chances of one person against twenty-three in a tug-of-war? One pulls one way, twenty-three the other—who's going to win?

It's not possible to accomplish what must be achieved in the ground of the mind with one hour of daily meditation. You have to pay attention to your spiritual process throughout the day, as you work, play, sleep; the mind always has to be moving toward the ultimate goal of enlightenment.

There are, of course, established centers where you can hear the teachings of the Buddha, places where you are exposed to a different world view, where you can meditate and contemplate in an environment in which others are doing likewise. It's hard to make progress on your own, hard to change if you hear the teachings only once. It's very helpful to visit such centers, but whether you can or not, you need to sew the patch on your clothes with a care that requires repetition, hearing and applying the teachings again and again.

When you are out and about in the world, keep your mind with what you are doing. If you are writing, keep your mind on the pen. If you are sewing, focus your mind on the stitch. Don't get distracted. Don't think of a hundred things at the same time. Don't get going on what happened yesterday or what might happen in the future. It doesn't matter what the work is if you focus the mind and stay with what you undertake. Hold to it closely, comfortable in what you do, and in that way you will train the mind.

Always check yourself thoroughly, reduce negative thoughts, speech, and behavior, increase those that are positive. Think carefully, and continually refocus, because you can get blurry very easily. What meditation produces is a constant refocusing. You have to bring pure intention back again and again. And then relax the mind, to allow a direct, subtle recognition of that which lies beyond all thought.

It doesn't happen swiftly, but the mind can change. There was once a man in India who decided to measure his thoughts. It wasn't easy, for though one can be determined to watch one's thoughts, many get away, those not seen as they pass by, that come and go without our awareness. So this man started counting his thoughts and determining whether they were good or bad. He put down a white stone for every good, a black stone for every bad thought. At first this produced a huge pile of black stones, but very slowly, as the years went by, the pile of black stones became smaller and the white pile grew. That's the kind of gradual progress we make with sincere effort. There's nothing flashy about the progress of the mind; it's very measured and steady, requiring diligence, attentiveness, patience, and enthusiastic perseverance.

In the tradition of Buddhism there are many profound teachings, but what we've been discussing is the essential sweet nectar of them all. Cultivating good heart throughout daily life, practicing virtue, equanimity, compassion, love, and joy—this is the way to enlightenment.

Chagdud Tulku
Gates to Buddhist Practice

"Meditation is not a means to an end. It is both the means and the end."
—J. Krishnamurti

"Sometimes when they begin meditating, people tell me that it's hopeless, that their thoughts are impossible to control. I assure them that this is a sign of improvement. Their mind has always been unruly; it's just that they're finally noticing it."
—Chagdud Tulku

For more on meditation, see:

Joko Beck, *Nothing Special: Living Zen,* HarperSanFrancisco, 1993.
Hubert Benoit, *Zen and the Psychology of Transformation: The Supreme Doctrine,* Inner Traditions International, 1990.
Thubten Chodron, *What Color is Your Mind?,* Snow Lion, 1993.
Ram Dass, *Journey of Awakening: A Meditator's Guidebook,* Bantam, 1990.
Joseph Goldstein, *The Experience of Insight: A Simple and Direct Guide to Buddhist Meditation,* Shambhala, 1983.
Lama Anagarika Govinda, *Creative Meditation and Multi-Dimensional Consciousness,* Quest, 1976.
Geshe Kelsang Gyatso, *A Meditation Handbook,* Tharpa, 1990.
Tenzin Gyatso, The XIV Dalai Lama, *Kindness, Clarity and Insight,* Snow Lion, 1985.
Thich Nhat Hanh, *A Guide to Walking Meditation,* Parallax, 1985
———, *Being Peace,* Parallax, 1985.
Aryeh Kalan, *Jewish Meditation: A Practical Guide,* Schocken, 1985.
Jack Kornfield, *A Path With A Heart: A Guide Through the Perils and Promises of Spiritual Life,* Bantam, 1993.
———, *Seeking the Heart of Wisdom: The Path of Insight Meditation,* Shambhala, 1987.
Stephen Levine, *A Gradual Awakening,* Doubleday, 1978.
———, *Who Dies? An Investigation of Conscious Living and Conscious Dying,* Doubleday, 1982.
Thomas Merton, *Contemplation in a World of Action,* Doubleday, 1973.
Kathleen McDonald, *How to Meditate,* Wisdom, 1985.
Anthony de Mello, *Sadhana: A Way to God, Christian Exercises in Eastern Form,* Doubleday, 1984.
Paul Reps, *Zen Flesh, Zen Bones,* Doubleday, 1957.
Lati Rinbochay, Denma Locho Rinbochay, Leah Zahler, and Jeffery Hopkins, *Meditative States in Tibetan Buddhism,* Wisdom, 1983.
Kalu Rinpoche, *The Gem Ornament of Manifold Oral Instructions,* KDK Publications, 1983.
Ninian Smart, *Buddhism & Christianity: Rivals and Allies,* University of Hawaii, 1993.
Sogyal Rinpoche, *The Tibetan Book of Living and Dying,* HarperSanFrancisco, 1992.
Lama Zopa Rinpoche, *Transforming Problems into Happiness,* Wisdom, 1993.
Shunryu Suzuki, *Zen Mind, Beginner's Mind,* Weatherhill, 1986.
Chogyam Trungpa, *Cutting Through Spiritual Materialism,* Shambhala, 1973.
Chagdud Tulku, *Gates to Buddhist Practice,* Padma Publishing, 1993.
Tarthang Tulku, *Gesture of Balance,* Dharma, 1977.
Allan Wallace, *Tibetan Buddhism from the Ground Up,* Wisdom, 1993.

Any of the following short meditations will give you "a taste of the mango." The first two are contemplations on impermanence, a central theme in Buddhism. Following the breath is a basic beginning meditation which even advanced practitioners come back to again and again. Naming thoughts is often used in Theravaden or Vipassana meditation, and provides an effective way to learn how your mind works. Walking mindfully is used in many traditions between long sitting meditations. Relaxing the mind by way of concentrating on one of the senses is effective in stopping thoughts.

"We don't see things as they are, we see them as we are."
—Anais Nin

Flower Meditation

Find a flower in its prime. Examine its leaves, petals, and other attributes.

Smell it. Touch it.

Imagine a time before the flower existed. Where was it? A seed? Before it was a seed? A part of a flower that would become the seed of its seed?

Imagine the flower tomorrow, next week. Will the petals be brown, wilted? When will it fall to the ground or be thrown away? Imagine it on the ground, swept up, heaped in garbage, taken away. Where is the flower now?

Bring your consciousness back to the flower. Relate to its beauty, to its impermanence.

Fringe Exercise

Cut out a small square of cloth. Get to know that piece of cloth: its color, its texture, its "clothness." Think about where it came from: visualize cotton growing, being harvested, ginned, cleaned and processed, spun into thread. Or imagine a lamb being born, growing a heavy coat of wool that is sheared, cleaned, and spun into yarn. Imagine the mill where huge spools of thread are woven into cloth, the shuttle going back and forth, back and forth. See the cloth being dyed, rolled onto bolts, sent out to shops.

Now loosen one thread at the corner and pull it out. Continue to pull out the threads from each side all the way around until nothing of the original cloth remains.

At one time, the chair you are sitting on, the house you live in, the tree outside your window—didn't exist. Then certain elements came together and they began to "be." But in the physical world, whatever comes together falls apart; whatever gathers, separates. In time your chair will be sent to the junk heap, your house will be torn down, the tree will die. This may take a long time, but eventually these solid-seeming objects will be gone.

Think about everything in the material world—mountains, cities, your physical body—in terms of this process.

"Breath is the bridge which connects life to consciousness, which unites your body to your thoughts. Whenever your mind becomes scattered, use your breath as the means to take hold of your mind again."
—Thich Nhat Hanh

Following the Breath

The breath connects body and mind, the conscious and unconscious. Focusing on breathing is a common and highly effective meditative technique found in many traditions.

Sit with your spine straight and gently breathe in and out, in and out. As you breathe, follow the inhalation and exhalation with your consciousness. Don't think, just follow the breath. If you find that your mind is wandering (as it will), gently bring your attention back to the breath. In and out. Some people find that it helps to say, "Breathe in, breathe out" in rhythm with the inhalation and exhalation. Brooke Medicine Eagle suggests that we "be breathed" rather than breathe ourselves.

Name That Thought

Sit quietly. Relax your mind and let your thoughts arise freely and without interruption. As you watch your thoughts, name each one as it comes up. At first pick large categories: angry thoughts, planning thoughts, memories, thoughts that are busy, mean, kind, or anxious. After your "sit," you might want to jot down the main categories. The next time you sit, repeat the process. In time, if a particular type of thought keeps asserting itself—anger, for instance—create subcategories. Anger at yourself, anger at your husband, your child, whatever. Or if planning for the future dominates, watch what it is that you are planning for, how often you're living in the future rather than the present. If you do this exercise over a period of time you become quite familiar with your thought patterns, with the types of thoughts that habitually create your reality. Once aware of these thoughts and patterns, you can change them.

"Reality is simply the loss of the ego. Destroy the ego by seeking its identity. It will automatically vanish and reality will shine forth by itself. This is the direct method."
—Ramana Maharshi

Walking Meditation

This meditation is very commonly used on retreats between long sitting meditations.

Center yourself and walk very slowly, being mindful of every move that you make. Right heel comes up, arch is raised, weight onto toe, toe leaves the ground, right foot is raised, leg moves forward, right heel is lowered, touches earth. Weight goes onto whole foot which touches earth. Left heel goes up, and so forth. Put your consciousness in your feet as you walk; don't just talk to yourself. Really feel every muscle move, every tiny sensation in your legs and ankles. To do this over and over with every step develops mindfulness.

Hearing Meditation

Sit quietly outdoors. Do not think, but listen. Do not let your mind get caught up in evaluating or contemplating the sounds ("Bird. I wonder which kind. Maybe a finch. No they make more of a peeping sound"). This kind of evaluation and analysis will lead you to other thoughts ("Mother used to keep two little finches in a cage on the porch. I haven't called her in ages. I really don't feel like it, but . . ."). Pretty soon you're lost in discursive thought and have stopped listening. Likewise, don't react to sounds ("Lawn mower.

I hate that sound. When will it stop?" or "Piano music. I hope it goes on forever"). Don't indulge in attachment or aversion, but listen. Try to hear each sound separately and distinctly.

That's all. Don't think, listen.

Relax the mind. Listen.

"The Tao described in words is not the real Tao. Words cannot describe it. Nameless is the source of creation; named it is the mother of all things."
—Tao Teh Ching

The Tao or The Way is based on a harmonious balancing of yin and yang, of all polar opposites: dark/light, male/female, expansive/contractive. Taoists use nature to remain in contact with the divine, studying animals to understand how they remain healthy. In the following account of the Taoist education of a boy named Saihung, an acolyte named Mist Through A Grove teaches through the example of a cat.

Learning from Cats

The cat was asleep on the edge of the blue quilt, her tail and nose tucked under her folded paws. Mist Through a Grove continued his explanation:

"The early Taoists wanted to remain healthy and retard the aging process. They believed that people aged because their internal energy leaked out. In order to find a way to retain it in the body, they found inspiration in animals like our cat here. They concluded that one way an animal sealed its energy in was by sleeping curled up, effectively closing off its anus and other passages where the energy might escape. This is how our cat sleeps.

"Now look at her abdomen, rising and falling so gently. The cat's breathing is natural and easy. The Taoists also found and confirmed that unhindered breathing filling the entire abdomen was beneficial."

The cat awoke when Mist Through A Grove nudged it. She opened her eyes and pricked up her ears attentively. Mist Through A Grove continued his lesson.

"She wakes instantly, not like humans who are lazy, drowsy, and stiff. See how she stretches. Even the cat knows calisthenics and uses them to maintain her system. The Taoists know that exercise is essential to good health.

"What if our cat gets sick? After all, she eats mice and rats, both very dirty animals. She supplements her diet with herbs and grass in order to clean her system.

"Finally, the cat is spiritual. She meditates. When she sits at the window sill or in front of a mouse hole, she is unmoving and concentrates just like our masters. You've seen her waiting for a rat. Nothing distracts her. Her mind is on only one point. She can sit for almost an entire day at one hole until the rat comes out and she catches it. Yin and yang. Perfect stillness and concentration, perfect action and strength.

"Our cat does not need teachers. The cat teaches itself. It preserves energy, knows the art of breathing, heals itself, and is skilled in meditative concentration. Study the cat, Saihung. Everything you need to learn, she knows already."

Deng Ming-Dao
The Wandering Taoist

"We are sick with a fascination for the useful tools of names and numbers, of symbols, signs, conceptions and ideas. Meditation is therefore the art of suspending verbal and symbolic thinking for a time, somewhat as a courteous audience will stop talking when a concert is about to begin."
—Alan Watts

○ Watch your pet to learn something about staying in touch with the divine. You could perhaps learn devotion from a dog, joy from a bird, patience from a turtle.

○ For an entire day, notice what energy in your life is contractive and which is expansive. Make no other judgment about an event, reaction, emotion, food, landscape, relationship, marriage pattern, whatever you encounter. Pay attention only to what expands and what contracts, what creates a feeling of expansion or contraction when in relationship to you. When is expansive aligned with the male? When with the female? When is female energy contractive? When expansive?

Taoist books that include nature photographs or pictures express the Taoist spirit in a very direct way. Here are some good sources:
John Blofeld, *Taoism: The Road to Immortality,* Shambhala, 1978.

Mantak Chia and Maneewan Chia, *Healing Love Through the Tao: Cultivating Female Sexual Energy,* Healing Tao Books, 1986.

I Ching or *Book of Changes,* trans. by Richard Wilhelm and Cary F. Baynes, Bollingen Series XIX, Princeton University, 1950.

Thomas Merton, *The Way of Chuang Tzu,* New Directions, 1965.

Liu I-Ming, *Awakening to the Tao,* Shambhala, 1988.

Deng Ming-Dao, *The Wandering Taoist,* Harper & Row, 1983.

The Secret of the Golden Flower, Richard Wilhelm, trans., with commentary by C. G. Jung, Causeway, 1975.

Lao Tsu, *Tao Teh Ching,* trans. by Gia-Fu-Feng and Jane English, Random House, 1972.

Alan Watts, *The Watercourse Way,* Pantheon, 1975.

For tapes and courses: The Healing Tao Center, PO Box 1194, 2 Creskill Place, Huntington, NY 11743.

"[Tribal people] say that words are sacred. We don't mean that you are supposed to kneel down and worship them. We mean that you should in your being recognize that when you speak, your utterance has consequences inwardly and outwardly and that you are accountable for those consequences."
—Paula Gunn Allen

The Sufis advise us to speak only after our words have managed to pass through three gates. At the first gate, we ask ourselves, "Are these words true?" If so, we let them pass on; if not, back they go. At the second gate we ask, "Are they necessary?" At the last gate, we ask, "Are they kind?" Here a Buddhist examines how speech produces karma.

Observing Intention

To understand karma, it is essential to see how the motivation or intention preceding an action determines the future karmic result of that action. Thus, if an act is motivated by true kindness, it will necessarily bring a positive result, and if an act is motivated by aggression or greed, it will eventually bring an unpleasant result. Because karmic results do not always bear fruit immediately, it is sometimes difficult to observe this process.

Speech is one area in which karma can be seen in an easy and direct way. For this exercise, resolve to take two or three days to carefully notice the intentions that motivate your speech. Direct your attention to the state of mind that precedes talking, the motivation for your comments, responses, and observations. Try to be particularly aware of whether your speech is even subtly motivated by boredom, concern, irritation, loneliness, compassion, fear, love, competitiveness, greed, or whatever state you observe. Be aware too, of the general mood or state of your heart and mind, and how that may be influencing your speech. Try to observe without any judgment or program of what you should see. Simply notice the various motivations in the mind and the speech that flows from them.

Then, after discovering which motivation is present as you speak, notice the effect of the speech. If there is competitiveness or grasping or pride or irritation behind the speech, what response does it elicit from the world around you? If there is compassion or love, what is the response? If your speech is mindless, as if you were on automatic pilot, what is the response? If there is clarity and concern, how is this received and responded to?

With the law of karma we have a choice in each new moment of what response our heart and mind will bring to the situation around us. In discovering the power of our inner states to determine outer conditions, we are able to follow a path that can lead to genuine happiness and freedom.

> Joseph Goldstein and Jack Kornfield
> *Seeking the Heart of Wisdom:*
> *The Path of Insight Meditation*

"Karma never takes a break."
—Bumper Sticker

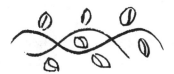

If used with good motivation, concentration on a mantra lessens your focus on yourself, letting you bypass your ego and open into deeper levels of your being, and this, in turn, connects you with something larger than the self.

"Don't do mantra, let it happen to you."
—Ram Dass

Mantra: Protection for the Mind

Through the parallelism of body, mind and speech, the coordination of movement, thought and word, the harmony of feeling, creative imagination, visualization and verbal expression, we achieve a unity of all the functions of our conscious being, which not only affects the surface of our personality— namely our senses and our intellect—but equally the deeper regions of our mind. In the regular performance of such ritual worship, the very foundations of our being are slowly but certainly transformed and made receptive for inner light.
—Lama Govinda

One day, as a young boy, when I was in the synagogue with my grandfather, a very old and pious man came over to say hello. He had always caught my eye as being a uniquely calm and wise-looking fellow, and as he approached he seemed to be mumbling serenely to himself. Coming to stand in front of us, his moving lips vocalized, "The Lord is good" in Hebrew, he had a short chat with Gramps, all the while inaudibly chanting this phrase or mantra over and over behind and between his words. His final audible words to us were the same as his first, and as he left he seemed to glide on this mantric wave as a continuum of steadiness and balance for his mind.

Over the years, we've been introduced to the use of mantra or chanting in every meditative tradition that we've studied. The actual word *mantra* means "mind protection." That is to say that while one is engaged in chanting a mantra, one's mind is protected from dissipating its clarity and power in random or negative thoughts. In many meditative traditions, formal periods of quiet contemplative practice are preceded by a time of devotional chanting or mantric repetition. The repetitive and often sacred nature of these chants can have a calming and stabilizing effect which builds coherence and power in the mind and the subtle nervous system.

The use of such "mind protectors" is an old sacred science. The inner scientist knows and understands the use of sound and vibration as a tool to evoke and refine specific qualities of mind. In Native American traditions a young man or woman would be sent on a vision quest and told to listen for a sacred song or death chant that the Great Spirit would teach to them during this time of alert receptive vigilance. After days of fasting, prayer or other ordeals, a chant would emerge into awareness as a gift or sign from the Great Spirit. From that time on, this death chant would be used to steady and protect the mind at critical times in one's life. Having practiced this chant in the face of adversity millions of times over the course of one's life, one would turn to it whole-heartedly and single-pointedly as one approached the moment of death, allowing it to carry one across the threshold between worlds and into the vastness of Spirit.

In the Tibetan tradition, the repetition of the mantras OM MANI PEDME HUNG, OM AH HUNG VAJRA GURU PEDME SIDDHI HUNG, and OM TARE TUTTARE TURE SVAHA are commonly recited one hundred thousand to one hundred million times in the course of one's life. The subtle psychophysical repetition of such mantric practice provides one with a coherent internal resonance that pervades one's mindbody as well as a continual sense of direct connection with the source of spiritual blessings, power and inspiration. The power of mantras, some say, is related to the cumulative effect of countless conscious repetitions over millennia of their use. By chanting a mantra one's mindbody sympathetically resonates with the cosmic reservoir of its accumulated power and if properly receptive one will experience an infusion of the blessing-energy of that particular mantra.

Clinically we've introduced this meditative practice to people who need to quiet and gentle their minds, with pregnant women and dying patients and loved ones. A friend who is an anesthesiologist often chants mantras in his patients' ears as they drift off on the anesthetic. Throughout a pregnancy, a woman or couple can chant a mantra or sing a song of particular beauty or feeling for them. Gradually the fetus will become imbued with this familiar resonance.

"I will teach you the best way to say Torah. You must be nothing but an ear that hears what the universe of the word is constantly saying within you. The moment you begin to hear what you yourself are saying, you must stop."
—Dov Baer of Mezritch

"Place the name of Rama [God] as a jewelled lamp at the door of your lips and there will be light, as you will, both inside and out."
—Tulsi Das

After birth, this can be chanted to them as a lullaby of reassurance, reducing the trauma of the birth transition. It can also be taught to other members of the family and baby sitters as a sound of comfort from across the room. Children will often respond in an alert and responsive way to these familiar sounds from their time in the womb.

The mantra OM MANI PEDME HUNG has been a final lullaby easing the transition of death for many special loved ones and friends. In the last days of their life, when there wasn't much to say in words, the gentle audible presence of this or other mantras effectively brought balance to their minds as they moved to subtler and subtler states of consciousness.

One of our wisest and kindest teachers, a true master of meditation who has spent nearly a third of his eighty-two years in various contemplative retreats, is continually chanting mantras as he directs his attention and intention of blessing towards countless beings. Used in this way, repetition of mantra is mental target practice in which all living beings are the targets of a heartfelt intention which is projected and carried by the mantra. Christian practitioners might chant the name of Jesus or HALLELUYA, Hebrew practitioners the Shema or SHALOM, Sufis the Zikar, others might work with OM, LOVE, PEACE, JOY ad infinitum. Though there *is* power in the actual vibration and sound of traditional mantras, the mental intention in its use determines the power and magnitude of its benefit.

The actual practice of mantra meditation can be quite simple. You can just sit quietly and mentally recite a mantra or meaningful phrase, resting the mind upon its sound or inner resonance within you. Whenever your mind wanders, simply return to the repetition and keep your attention on what you are doing. To elaborate on this method, visualize waves of light and good vibrations pouring from your heart to others, bringing more light, love and happiness into the world, and dissolving the darkness, pain and fear that fills the minds of so many beings.

When you have a feeling for it, working with mantra can help to calm and focus the mind when you are busy in the world. It is a simple, effective method for strengthening and developing positive qualities of the mind in moments that are ordinarily wasted—driving to work, waiting in line, holding the line on a telephone, walking down the street, and so on—all ordinary activities can be easily integrated into your meditation practice.

The practice of the inner essence of mind protection is more a state of mind than a vocalization. In its deepest essence, it is a state of heart and mind that recognizes the non-duality and interdependent relationship of all beings and things. The response to this is the wisdom that spontaneously wishes to contribute to the well-being of others. This can be demonstrated not only through kind words and helpful actions, but through a resonance of heart and mind that reaches out to others in a deep, quiet and loving way.

When the mind is busy or directed toward superficial appearances, simply chanting a mantra with the intention of creating a more positive atmosphere in the world within and around you can be very helpful. As your mind becomes more subtle and quiet, the repetition of the mantra may likewise become subtler and subtler, until you rest in its innermost essence—silent prayer, a way of simply being natural that brings peace to the world within and around you. In this way, mantra and spoken prayer merge into silence and become the prayer of the heart.

> Joel and Michelle Levey
> *The Fine Arts of Relaxation,*
> *Concentration and Meditation:*
> *Ancient Skills for Modern Minds*

"We must learn to hear the tongue of the Invisible."
—Koran

○ If you've ever gotten a tune "caught" in your head that repeats over and over, you have had a mantra-type experience on a superficial level. With a slight effort of will you can take this capacity for automatic repetition and turn it into something more useful.

Pick a mantra that you feel drawn to, one that gives you a special feeling when you hear it. The Catholic mantra of "Hail Mary full of grace, pray for us now and at the hour of our death" is well known. In addition to the suggestions made by Joel and Michelle Levey, you might pick the Jesus Prayer or a verse of the Bible: "The Lord is my Shepherd, I shall not want" or "Thy will be done." Repetition of the prayer of the twelve-step program: "God grant me the serenity to accept the things I cannot change, the courage to change the things I can, and the wisdom to know the difference," has aided many a person in recovery.

An affirmation is a type of mantra, used for healing or to build self-esteem. Or you might want to pick a mantra that includes other people or even the whole world: "May peace prevail" or "May all beings be happy." "The Goddess is alive, magic is afoot" and "She changes everything She touches, and everything She touches changes" are commonly used by adherents of the Goddess and Wicca movements.

Whatever you pick, make it simple and meaningful for you. Let it find its own rhythm and voice. And stay with it. At first, it will require effort, but gradually it will become second nature. As you repeat a mantra you are slowly, with each repetition, constructing a safety net in your unconscious. If you make a habit of saying mantra when you're prayerful or bored or as an effortful part of your devotion, when you suddenly find yourself in a crisis—say you are dying—you turn automatically to the mantra which will protect and comfort you. So choose well.

A repeated prayer, technically known as hesychasm, is the Christian form of mantra. The "Jesus Prayer" was popularized by the anonymous devotional classic "The Way of the Pilgrim," in which the pilgrim travels from place to place searching for the meaning of Paul's words to the Thessalonians: "Pray without ceasing." One teacher tells the pilgrim that the meaning is an admonition to pray the Jesus Prayer, "Lord Jesus Christ, have mercy upon me." He finds that a ceaseless repetition of the prayer makes him feel close to everyone he meets as though they were "my nearest relative." In time, the prayer becomes second nature to him.

The Way of the Pilgrim

Now I did not walk along as before, filled with care. The calling upon the Name of Jesus Christ gladdened my way. Everybody was

"A prayer in which a person is not aware of whom he is speaking to, what he is asking, who it is who is asking and of whom, I do not call prayer however much the lips may move."
—Teresa of Avila

kind to me, it was as though everyone loved me. . . . And that is how I go about now, and ceaselessly repeat the Prayer of Jesus, which is more precious and sweet to me than anything in the world. At times I do as much as forty-three or -four miles a day, and do not feel that I am walking at all. I am aware only of the fact that I am saying my Prayer. When the bitter cold pierces me, I begin to say my Prayer more earnestly and quickly get warm all over. When hunger begins to overcome me, I call more often on the Names of Jesus, and I forget my wish for food. When I fall ill and get rheumatism in my back and legs, I fix my thoughts on the Prayer and do not notice the pain. If anyone harms me I have only to think, "How sweet is the Prayer of Jesus!" and the injury and the anger alike pass away and I forget it all.

"Prayer is our humble answer to the inconceivable surprise of living."
—Rabbi Abraham Heschel

O Here's how to do the Jesus Prayer: Constantly repeat "Lord Jesus Christ, have mercy on me"; or "Jesus, mercy"; or simply "Jesus." (Or, as Saint Francis did, "Jesu, Jesu, Jesu.") Some insert "Son of the Living God" after the word *Christ*.

At first you may set aside a time in morning and evening—say ten minutes—to repeat the prayer. First, call upon God to be with you in your meditation, then slowly and reflectively say the Jesus Prayer over and over. Think of the words themselves, not the images they evoke. You may say the prayer in rhythm with the in-breath and out-breath or with your heartbeat. Once you've established a habit of repeating the Jesus Prayer in meditation, begin to use it during the day. When you feel stress, when you're waiting in line, when you're dealing with other people, repeat the Jesus Prayer to yourself. In time, you become the prayer itself, embodying the compassion, nonviolence, and love of Jesus.

"My greatest weapon is mute prayer."
—Mahatma Ghandi

"The Life I am trying to grasp is the me that is trying to grasp it."
—R. D. Laing

Shunryu Suzuki Roshi in Zen Mind, Beginner's Mind *advises that when we practice zazen (zen sitting meditation) we should follow the breath. As we inhale, the air comes into the inner world. As we exhale, the air goes into the outer world. Both worlds are limitless. Although we speak of "inner" and "outer" worlds, there is actually only one whole world. Our throat is like a swinging door in that limitless world. If you think, "I breathe," the "I" is extra. There is no "you" to say "I." What we usually speak of as "I" is simply a swinging door that moves as we inhale and exhale. Just movement. When your mind becomes calm and pure enough to follow this movement, there is nothing: no "I," no world, no mind nor body, only a swinging door.*

Beginning Meditation

Simply sit down, close your eyes, and listen to all sounds that may be going on—without trying to name or identify them. Listen as you would to music. If you find that verbal thinking will not drop away, don't attempt to stop it by force of willpower. Just keep your tongue relaxed, floating easily in the lower jaw, and listen to your thoughts as if they were birds chattering outside—mere noise in the skull—and they will eventually subside of themselves, as a turbulent and muddy pool will become calm and clear if left alone.

Also, become aware of breathing and allow your lungs to work in whatever rhythm seems congenial to them. And for a while just sit listening and feeling breath. But, if possible, don't *call* it that. Simply experience the nonverbal happening. You may object that this is not "spiritual" meditation but mere attention to the "physical" world, but it should be understood that the spiritual and the physical are only ideas, philosophical conceptions, and that the reality of which you are now aware is not an idea. Furthermore, there is no "you" aware of it. That was also just an idea. Do you hear yourself listening?

"Don't expect plaudits."
—Atisha

Alan Watts
"The Practice of Meditation"
in *Meditation Manual*

Seventy-year-old Dadi Janki, the speaker in the following, is one of the founders of the Brahma Kumaris (Daughters of Brahma) World Spiritual University. In 1937, a family friend and diamond merchant, Dada Lekhraj, went through a series of transformative experiences and visions, receiving the name "Baba Brahma" from the Father-God Shiva (the creative aspect of the Hindu holy trinity). Baba Brahma quit business and went on to found centers for a spiritual university across India, often placing women in prominent positions as the main teachers and administrators. Dadi Janki, who was nineteen in 1937, became one of his earliest followers and now lives in Madhuban, an ashram in northwest India. Today, the university has approximately a quarter of a million students, and sponsors centers in more than fifty countries.

Raja Yoga

The basis of much of the Raja Yoga philosophy is that perception comes through the senses, which are instruments to carry messages to the mind and from the mind to the soul. The soul receives the message and passes the response back through the same stages and it is thus we communicate with the world. The mind is not the soul. The whole process of communication can happen only through physical matter, but the mind is of much finer matter than the external organs of sense, such as the eyes or ears. When the material of the mind becomes grosser it becomes substance, and when it is grosser still it forms the external material world (and most of us must have noticed that when we become overinvolved with the world in a "gross" way it is difficult to separate our mind from it). Thus intellect and ordinary earth substance are essentially the same in kind and are only different in degree. The soul is the only thing which is nonmaterial; the mind is its tool and the means by which the soul responds to external life. The mind can attach itself to many senses or to only one—when reading a book, for instance, the mind may be oblivious to what it hears or smells—and it is also able to be attached to none of its sense organs and to turn inward to itself. It is this inward vision that the yogi wants to catch. He wants to

"It was important for me that my soul should have a direct relationship with God, without any human intermediary. It was fine to have messengers from God and to share their message, because they had God's power. But I wanted to learn to be a messenger myself. I wanted to take power from God directly."
—Dadi Janki

227

discover the actual composition of the brain and how it behaves in relation to the soul. Above all, he wants to reach the soul.

Another way of understanding this, according to Raja Yoga, is to say that humans are made up of four main attributes, or layers. That which we are most aware of is our body. Next comes our mind and our conscious individuality, what we think of as our mind and our conscious individuality, what we think of as "I." Thirdly there is the soul, the life-force which is the director of "I" and which is also the link with the Supreme Self, and lastly there is the Supreme Self, the Ground of Being, the immense and the eternal. It is the fourth layer which is the goal of Raja Yoga.

Brahma Baba, it is believed, had reached that goal. It is to his teaching, as expressed through mediums (for he died in 1969), that the University students still look for guidance.

"Baba shares information and teaching through the trance messenger. But in fact during Baba's lifetime he himself was the instrument through whom, we believe, God gave the teachings. And so the teachings are the teachings of God. Brahma Baba, not in a trance state but in a fully aware state became the instrument through whom the knowledge was given. We've had meetings with Baba through the trace medium but they haven't provided new information, only further clarification of how to follow the teaching in our life.

"I too am a messenger, but not from any desire for importance in life, just the opposite. The desire to be God's messenger is one in which there is truly no feeling of ego. And yet there has to be a preparation of surrender to God for it is in that way that the human soul itself becomes filled with divinity. It's a very powerful experience being God's messenger. It is only when one has made that preparation to detach oneself from the things of the world, the attractions of the world, that one is able to become the messenger.

"The first and most important way is to go beyond the attitude of male and female, into the awareness of my own eternal identity, and secondly to ask oneself the question, 'What is my role?' Generally for women, there is the feeling of wishing to serve as much as possible through mind, body and wealth. The motivation of service is very strong. 'I am a human being within this female form, what service can I render to others?'

"Women must trim the branches of their emotions so they will not take all the available nourishment . . . . That trimming is necessary before any spiritual development can take place."
—Swami Shivananda Radha

"Last year when I was in Kuala Lumpur, I was interviewed for a local newspaper. I was asked how I overcame the difficulties that I must have experienced in becoming a spiritual server. I replied that many things had happened, but I had never given them any great importance. Things will continue to happen, but I must not be distracted from my aim. If my own aim is clear and I have taken power from God, then nothing can interfere. That is the way in which I can serve.

"For my true aim is to be a lighthouse—to be filled with light and a feeling of lightness—one in which there's no pressure or burden, and because of that one is able to share light with others and show them the path. The lighthouse shows the path of safety. The world is going through such a crisis of suffering, so many negative thoughts, that it's very important that my life as a yogi should be able to guide others to safety.

"What is most needed at this time is a change of perspective, a change of vision in the way we see ourselves, others, and the world. If we just stop for a moment and peel away all the layers of social, cultural and sexual definitions, which up to now have been a restrictive force, it is possible to reach a subtle dimension of the self that is constantly free from all limitations. And while many governments are concerned about the future of the world with an ever-diminishing supply of resources, there lies within each one of us a natural resource which has remained so far virtually untapped. We call that energy the spirit or soul.

"Through meditation we can experience a state of balance, based on the understanding that the personality contained within the soul has both masculine and feminine qualities. When the soul is at peace, both aspects are in harmony. True equality is learning to see ourselves and others as spiritual beings, no matter whether the soul is in a male or female body.

"The life-force is here within the physical form; whatever the physical form is, masculine or feminine, it imposes certain characteristics and traits on the life-force and so we are in a state of dependence or bondage to that. To a soul born in a male costume, as a man, the characteristics are probably going to be bossiness and ego; for a woman it will probably be timidity, dependence and fear. But when the awakening of the spirit takes place, when the soul

"If the mind can get quiet enough, something sacred will be revealed."
—Helen Tworkov

229

the man who is a yogi will have the strength of being a man but it will be tinged with gentleness, humility, so that ego and bossiness disappear. And for a woman, having the experience of detachment from the body and being in yoga brings a lot of strength, a lot of courage so that she is fearless now, not timid and not dependent. In this way the highest characteristics of the soul develop through that connection with God and the detachment from the human body.

"You see, when the soul is in a human body having relationships with other human beings, every relationship is perishable—my mother, my father, my brother, my sister. My relationship with God is the eternal one and this is the experience the soul can have through awareness of itself. Every human being has the power of discrimination, a conscience, but in the state of unawareness we don't know right from wrong. But when we become aware we are not only able to see clearly right from wrong but we're also able to have the link with God, the power with which we can then follow the path which is right. We feel that God is all-power, all-strength that can never perish, and when we're fully conscious of this we can draw it into ourselves and translate it in practical terms as the power of tolerance, the power of discrimination, the power to accommodate, to be flexible, the power to be able to merge, the power of the conscience. There are all different manifestations that I'm able to use in my life in terms of the power I receive from God.

"Our practice can be described very simply as the use of thought to explore and understand our inner worlds. No physical postures are necessary and we do not use mantras to stop the flow of thoughts—instead we examine and contemplate them. Meditation is the essential method of realizing the original pure state of the soul, free from any limitation in understanding or awareness. The power necessary to stabilize this consciousness is gained by using the conscious mind and directing the flow of thoughts towards the highest source of pure energy, the Supreme Soul. This mental link results in a state of inner silence and quietude.

"My one desire is that the attention should be drawn towards God so that souls can experience a personal relationship with God. They should not worry about the future, for the cycle of the world is eternal and will not end, but the world itself is going through

"Our mind is pure and simple. When it is emptied of thought, it enters the pure and simple light of God, and finds nothing but the light."
—Symeon the New Theologian (949-1022)

different phases. It is in the Kali Yuga now, the worst phase, but this will finish and a golden age will come. Instead of worrying, people should start doing positive things now, so that the future can be a good one. And so that we can all cooperate with each other to make a better world. It is very important for people to develop feelings of goodwill for the world, feelings of mercy for the world. The transformation of the world is in our hands."

"Dadi Janki"
in *Weavers of Wisdom: Women Mystics of the Twentieth Century*
by Anne Bancroft

"The first Dalai Lama (1391-1475) would do whatever he did only after he had prayed to the Holy Tara, and thereby his active power to augment the aims of the teachings and of beings became as great as infinite space."
—Stephan Beyer

For many Tibetan Buddhists, a meditation includes visualization of a deity as well as recitation of mantra. The following text is the English version of the Short Red Tara practice from Chagdud Gonpa, a traditional Tibetan Buddhist group under the leadership of Chagdud Tulku, which has retreat centers around the world. Many students use it as an alternative to the full Tara sadhana [sacred text] which is part of the daily worship service performed in Tibetan at these centers.

Tara, the female Buddha, spent many lifetimes as a bodhisattva—one who has pledged not to enter nirvana, but to continue being reborn until all sentient beings are enlightened. After she had worked for many aeons for the benefits of others, her teacher told her to pray for rebirth as a man so that she could achieve buddhahood. She refused to do so, saying that she would always be reborn as a female and would achieve liberation in a female body. This she did and became known as the female buddha. The Dalai Lama has called her the first feminist.

Like Catholics who experience a personal relationship with the Virgin Mary, many Buddhists feel a strong heart connection

231

with Tara. She manifests in all the colors of the Buddha families: White Tara, Green Tara, Red Tara, and so forth. For a picture of Red Tara, see page 200.

Red Tara Practice

Begin by visualizing Tara in front of you: ruby red, luminous, and exceedingly beautiful. She is smiling. Half of her hair is in a knot at the crown of her head, the other half cascades down her back. She is dressed in flowing silken garments, with many jewels and ornaments. In her right hand she hold a long-life vase, in her left she holds a red utpala flower by the stem; inside its petals rests a bow and arrow made of delicate lotus blossoms.

In the space in front of me the mother of all the victorious ones, Arya Tara, actually appears and to her I pray:

Now, as I and countless others are lost in the ocean of samsaric suffering,
I seek buddhahood to gain temporary and ultimate happiness for myself and all living beings.
For this reason I take refuge in Arya Tara, embodiment of pure awareness,
inseparable from all perfect qualities of buddha, dharma, sangha, lama, yidam and dakini.

From the depths of my heart I pray, evoking from Tara's forehead, throat and heart
a brilliant surge of rainbow light.
As the light rays touch me and all other beings, the poisonous fruits of negative karma—
sickness, demonic afflictions and obstacles—evaporate like dew in the morning sun.
Merit, wisdom, glory, wealth and longevity increase beyond measure.
JE TZUN P'HAG MA DROL MA KHYED KHYEN NO
GAL KYEN KUN SEL SAM DON NYUR DRUB DZOD

Illustrious Tara, please be aware of me. Remove my obstacles and quickly grant my excellent aspirations.

(Repeat many times)

OM TARE TAM SOHA

(Repeat many times)

By the power of having prayed thus from the heart, may the enlightened mind be mastered
and appearances perceived purely as the deity's body.
May the meaning of the developing and completion stages be naturally internalized.
May conditions inauspicious to the perfect path be pacified, and all conceivable auspicious conditions and aspirations be fulfilled.
May the stains and obscurations of nonvirtue be cleansed, and harm from other beings and bad dreams be averted.
Grant the blessing of protection from the fear of lower existences.
May rebirth not occur in the eight states devoid of leisure to practice.
May all lifetimes be remembered and faculties be clear.
May discipline be pure and the mind attend to dharma.
From the ripening of karma caused by delusion, grant the blessing that shields, protects and conceals.
May the malignancy of enemies, demons and ghostly interferences,
the harmful effects of untimely death, epidemics and illnesses caused by poison,
all be pacified and purified, and may the wisdom and activities of Tara be revealed.

OM AH HUNG
In the pure realm of the victorious ones, the spontaneous presence of the three kayas,
is she who gives birth to the victorious ones of the three

times, a cloud of inexhaustible bliss of the three secrets. I bow to you, O sublime guide of the three realms of existence.

From now until I reach enlightenment, I will rely on you as my sole source of refuge and protection.

In accordance with your former aspirations and committments, do not waver in your compassion.

Fully bestow on me your powers, blessings and siddhis.

Whosoever sees me, hears me, touches me or remembers me—

by these four means of liberation and by the most sublime siddhi,

may I be capable of freeing all those connected to me, and may my attainment become equal to yours.

Without relying on the power of magnetizing, how could one gain the necessary qualities to care for others?

May I influence all those to be tamed, positive and negative without exception,

by inspiring in them the four kinds of devotion.

Furthermore, upon mastering positive qualities within a state of liberation,

may all beings quickly attain the actual form of the victorious ones,

resplendent with the major and minor marks of perfection.

Until such time, may we be free from the eight great fears and from malevolent influences.

May such favorable qualities as longevity, glory and excellence flourish.

May the yogas of the two stages be mastered, and may we be free from obstacles.

In all countries may disease, war and famine be pacified.

May all beings have bliss, happiness and engage in the dharma.

May the Buddha's teachings be propagated,

and may all beings come under the guidance of Tara, mother of the victorious ones.

DEDICATION

Throughout my many lives and until this moment, whatever
virtue I have accomplished,
including the merit generated by this practice, and all that I
will ever attain,
this I offer for the welfare of sentient beings.
May sickness, war, famine and suffering be decreased for
every being,
while their wisdom and compassion increase in this and
every future life.
May I clearly perceive all experiences to be as insubstantial
as the dream fabric of the night
and instantly awaken to perceive the pure wisdom display
in the arising of every phenomenon.
May I quickly attain enlightenment in order to work ceaselessly for the liberation of all sentient beings.

PRAYERS OF ASPIRATION

Buddhas and bodhisattvas altogether:
    whatever kind of motivation you have,
    whatever kind of beneficial action,
    whatever kind of wishing prayers,
    whatever kind of omniscience,
    whatever kind of life accomplishment,
    whatever kind of benevolent power, and
    whatever kind of immense wisdom you have,
    then similarly I, who have come in the same way to
    benefit beings,
    pray to attain these qualities.

THE AUSPICIOUS WISH

At this very moment, for the peoples and the nations of the
earth,
may not even the names disease, famine, war and suffering
be heard.

235

Rather may their moral conduct, merit, wealth and prosperity increase,
and may supreme good fortune and well-being always arise for them.

Red Tara
Translated from the Tibetan under the direction of Chagdud Tulku

"Tara is the flawless expression of the inseparability of emptiness, awareness and compassion. Just as you use a mirror to see your face, Tara meditation is a means of seeing the true face of your mind, devoid of any trace of delusion."
—Chagdud Tulku

See also *Red Tara Commentary,* by Jane Tromge, Padma Publishing, 1994. This book, as well as Chagdud Tulku's autobiography, *Lord of the Dance,* and his oral teachings, *Gates to Buddhist Practice,* are available from Tibetan Treasures, Box 279, Junction City, CA 96048. *The Wind Horse,* a newsletter listing empowerments of Red Tara as well as retreats, events, and other activities of Chagdud Gonpa, is available from the same address.

Michelle Levey and her husband, Joel, teach meditation and conduct workshops on the sacred dimensions of the helping professions, enhancing creativity, and affecting the heart of business. She is co-founder of InnerWork Technologies, Inc., a Seattle-based training and consulting firm that specializes in enhancing the synergy of individual, team, and organizational effectiveness. She has worked with such diverse groups as NASA and the U.S. Army Green Berets.

Twelve Moons of Meditation

"Always keep the Buddha with you, like an umbrella."
—Gen Lamrimpa

When I turned forty I had the rare and precious opportunity to devote an entire year of my life to polishing the mirrors of my heart and mind in silent meditation. I was part of a team of inner explorers, which included my husband and a group of friends.

Our retreat, led by the Venerable Gen Lamrimpa, took place at Cloud Mountain in the Pacific Northwest under the auspices and with the many blessings of His Holiness the Dalai Lama. It was truly a unique experiment for our time and culture, both as to its nature and length of duration.

Designed specifically for the purpose of cultivating the development of a state of mind characterized by profound and single-pointed concentration, our practice led us along the various stages of a path toward what is known technically as "access concentration," or "shamatha" in Sanskrit and "shine" in Tibetan. This rarefied state of absorbed focus, termed "calm abiding" in English, refers to a sustained unwavering concentration in which all mental and emotional turbulence is completely subdued. It produces a quality of mind that leads to a nondual state of intuitive insight in which the meditator and the object of meditation merge and become one.

Another unique aspect of our retreat was that although it took place within the context of a group, in actuality it was very much a solo experience. Each meditator practiced in his or her own "retreat hut," a little room about eight feet by nine feet, furnished only with a simple bed, our own handmade meditation platform, makeshift altar, propane light and heater. And though we were all engaged in the practice of shamatha meditation, the actual specific focus of concentration was chosen by each meditator and varied from individual to individual. While some people chose to concentrate on their breath, others selected a visualized image, and some contemplated the nature of mind itself. Ultimately, I chose to work with a traditional Tibetan shamatha object: the visualized mental image of the Buddha Shakyamuni. Our teacher explained that there were special purposes and benefits in focusing on the image of the Buddha. Even if one didn't attain shamatha, it would leave very good and wholesome imprints that would be especially helpful at the moment of death.

Our expedition party was composed of five women and three men, with my husband Joel and I the only married couple making the journey of the whole year together. Though we lived in separate rooms, were celibate, and had very little contact, we both felt that in many ways it was the most intimate year of our lives. Not busy

"As a culture we tend to be strongly outer-directed; we are not trained to venture inward to find the next steps of our growth. As a result, much truth lies hidden within us, in the depths of our self. Of that unknown, hidden self, there is much that must be unfolded in order for us to embody the truth of divinity."
—Charles Bates

distracting ourselves with the superficial details, demands, and conflicting desires of ordinary daily experience, we were able to stay connected with an intimate sense of attunement at the very depths of our being.

Even the physical wall that we shared between our two rooms seemed transparent and nonexistent to our psyches, and often I would awake from my dreams surprised to find it there, so absent was it in psychological reality. Joel and I had agreed before the retreat started that we would set aside a special time each day to "sit" with each other. Each in our own room, on our own meditation cushion, we had a date every day at 5:30 P.M. that we kept faithfully.

What a pleasing punctuation it gave to the day to shift from wherever we were and focus in on each other. For this stop in time, we would bring the power of the concentrated mind we had been building all day and beam it in with love to interpenetrate each other's being in our hearts. Often it was the sweetest part of the whole day, and one that we really looked forward to. We both still feel that sitting together in this way throughout the year helped to nurture and nourish the bond between us. There is a level of touching and connection that can be tasted and known in silence that speaking can never compete with, for it far transcends and is more powerful than any words can ever be.

Not only was this the most intimate year of my life, it was also, subjectively, the shortest! In fact, if I hadn't actually witnessed the marvelous changing of the four seasons, I wouldn't have believed that twelve months had already flown by so quickly. We all perceived this accelerated warp of time perception.

Early morning turned out to produce my best meditations, and be my "power time" in general, so I usually rose well before dawn. When the weather permitted, I would often be perched on a little outdoor meditation platform, looking out across the forest toward Mt. Saint Helens, ready to greet the sunrise in meditation until about 7:30 A.M.

By the second month most of us had turned off our propane heaters because we found the noise they made too disturbing, so the walk to the bath house in the brisk Northwest morning air to warm up with a hot shower was another of our life's simple joys! Then there was breakfast, available from about 8 to 9 A.M. As the retreat

"We can live any way we want. People take vows of poverty, chastity, and obedience—even of silence—by choice. The thing is to stalk your calling in a certain skilled and supple way, to locate the most tender and live spot and plug into that pulse."
—Annie Dillard

progressed, many of us simply picked up our meals and carried them back to our rooms in order to minimize distraction. By eating privately, we were able to stay more focused and less likely to become involved in the extraneous activities around us. For the same reason we were encouraged not to receive mail or make phone calls, but the choice was left up to us. This was an accelerated course in fostering individual responsibility.

Being in charge of our own individual meditation schedules required a certain level of spiritual maturity and disciplined self-direction. Not sitting in the same physical space and predetermined time schedule of a group gave us both a greater degree of freedom and an equally greater challenge of responsibility. Sometimes I missed the supportive energy I was accustomed to sharing in a group sitting context, but I appreciated the impetus I gained getting to discipline myself in a new way. Since no one but I (and the Buddha!) would know whether I was really meditating in my own room or not, this really turned up the heat on my own motivation and commitment to the practice.

Our meditation teacher had advised us, in keeping with Tibetan tradition, to begin with short sessions of high quality, and only very slowly and gradually to increase the time periods of our sittings. Accordingly, we all started with ten-minute sessions, followed by a very short break to rest and refresh the mind. When we found that we could concentrate for ten minutes with very little mind wandering, we could then add another five minutes, and so on. The rest of the day went by as a series of concentrated sitting sessions, gradually increasing in length, with periods of relaxation, walking meditation, and inspirational reading. Lunch was available over a two-hour period, from about 12:30 to 2:30 P.M., to allow for the varying and unique schedules of each retreatant. The afternoons followed the same essential pattern as the mornings: sitting—break—sitting—break. At 5:30 P.M. I'd "sit" with Joel, and then go off to get some tea and supper and settle back in for the night until about 10 P.M., when I'd dedicate the merits of the day's practice with prayers that the positive energy generated would bring benefit to all beings. Having dedicated and radiated all the good energy of myself and others, I was ready for sleeping meditation and dream yoga.

Our teacher, Gen Lamrimpa, was generally available to us as

"Meditation is a process of lightening up, of trusting the basic goodness of what we have and who we are, and of realizing that any wisdom that exists, exists in what we already have."
—Pema Chödrön

239

> *"For the ordinary mind, whose mind is a checker-board of crisscrossing reflections, opinions, and prejudices, bare attention is virtually impossible; one's life is thus centered not on reality itself but in one's ideas about it."*
> —Philip Kapleau

much as we needed. There were no scheduled interviews, and it was totally up to us to request time with him to ask questions and check our navigational course correction. Sometimes I'd go to see him very often, other times weeks would pass with very little interaction other than a warm smile and a wave on the way to lunch. Gen-la, as we called him respectfully, is an extraordinary yogi and remarkable lama who has spent more than seventeen years of his life in retreat in the mountains above Dharmasala, India, after escaping from Tibet in the mass exodus that followed the Chinese invasion and takeover in 1959. It is to this kind, compassionate and very wise being that I give my heartfelt gratitude, for without him, the year that changed my life could never have happened.

Everything was set up to create the most conducive circumstances possible to support the success of our practice. Our sole job was simply to practice single-pointed concentration on our chosen object, and we were not required to do any chores. We lived in a sheltered and generally pampered universe, shielded from the harsh realities of the mundane world. The Presidential election came and went. Barely noticed. Breathing in and Breathing out. Living with the Buddha. These were our main concerns.

Then in the eleventh month of the retreat, I received word that my father was in critical condition in the intensive care unit, having suffered a serious heart attack, and that my mother was desperately distressed. The question of whether to leave the retreat—which had reached a critical stage—to be with them tugged on my mind with painful and vivid intensity. It was time to see the Lama and seek his advice. After much discussion and deep inquiry, it became clear that if I could get there in time to guide my father through the dying process and be of benefit to my parents, there would be much greater positive energy generated by that than by staying in retreat and not helping directly. After all, why did I go into retreat anyway, if not to be able to be of greater service when I came out?

Now can you imagine what it must have been like to emerge from the purity of those eleven months of silent meditation and into the bustling frenetic energy and noise of New York City, one of the craziest cities on this planet? But what you might not have been able to imagine was the incredible grace and mantle of protection that continued to surround and bless me throughout that whole amazing journey. The Buddha was my constant companion and kept me company through it all, and everyone I met was the recipient of his gracious kindness, compassion and blessing.

I was able to stay with my father for seven days and to be with him at the actual time of his death—our final gift to each other. During those seven days much miraculous healing and opening of levels of love and communication took place that had not happened during the course of a lifetime. And I know that much of what I was able to give my parents at that pivotal time came as a direct fruit of my year of meditation. My father's last words to my mother and myself, waved with a gesture of his hands in our direction was, "Be peaceful." Being peaceful—the essential meaning of "shamatha." My mother surprised me by asking me to conduct the funeral services, and I was able to share the Dharma in this spirit of peace and joy with the rest of our family. What a blessing! Somehow, through this whole process, my mother and I entered into a transformed relationship of heightened respect, compassion and mutual acceptance.

Looking back, I cannot say that I attained any great state of Realization or concentrative absorption, but the benefits of those twelve moons of meditation changed me in many important ways. A deeper faith, a little more patience, compassion and mindful awareness, a clearer sense of priorities, and a much closer relationship with the Buddha within me, are among the jewelled treasures that I carry from this year. And as Gen-la said, "If you don't get shamatha, but you do get more patience and more compassion, that is the real Dharma fruit."

May all beings enjoy its sweet taste!

> Michelle Levey
> *Living with the Buddha:*
> *A Journey of Twelve Moons*
> [Work in progress]

"The common belief that to follow the Buddha's teaching one has to retire from life is a misconception. It is really an unconscious defense against practicing it."
—Walpola Rahula

○ Here's a practice, called The Paintbrush, that you might want to try. Your consciousness is a paintbrush with which you are going to paint your body. Begin at the crown, brushing your head with small, overlapping strokes. Feel your consciousness touch your scalp, fanning out from the crown to methodically cover the back of the head, then begin again at the crown, cover the forehead, around the eyes, the nose, the mouth, and the chin. Continue down your neck, your shoulders, upper arms, elbow, forearms, wrists, palms, and fingers. Section your back into left and right halves, stopping at the waist; first paint one half, then the other. Continue the process on the front, painting one half, then the other. Track across the waist, back and forth until you've reached the groin area, then switch over to the back, going back and forth until you've covered your backside. Do both legs: thighs, back and front, knees, calves, ankles, feet. From the feet go to the crown of the head again and rest. If you feel resistance in any area of the body, go over it several times to release the energy.

"To live is so startling it leaves little time for anything else."
—Emily Dickinson

A thirteenth-century German mystic here sees the senses as the means by which God is embodied on this earth. For an updated version of this idea, see Diane Ackerman's A Natural History of the Senses, *Random House, 1990.*

How God Gives His Senses to the Soul That It May Use Them

She once begged the Lord to give her something that would always cause her to remember him. Thereupon she received from the Lord this answer: "See, I give you my eyes, that you may see all things with them, and my ears, that you may hear all things with them; my mouth I also give you, so that all you have to say, whether in speech, prayer, or song, you may say through it. I give you my heart, that through it you may think everything and may love me and all things for my sake." In these words God drew this soul entirely into him and united with it in such a way that it seemed to her that she saw with God's eyes, and heard with his ears, and spoke with his mouth, and felt that she had no other heart than the heart of God. This she was given to feel on many later occasions.

Mechtild Von Hackborn (1242-1299)

○ Pick an object—a piece of fruit, a statue, a seashell—and place it before you. Don't think about it, but sit quietly and absorb it. Look at it from all angles, inspect the object's texture, color, shape. Feel the weight and heft of it, watch the way it reflects light, see if it casts a shadow. Examine it minutely: the larger outline as well as its tiny bumps and crevices. Try to see it as it exists in itself without any connection to you.

Close your eyes and recreate the object. Try to draw it. Go from room to room "seeing" things in this way.

_____

Barbara Mearns is a psychotherapist who currently lives in Hawaii. Especially interested in the way in which the body holds tension and trauma, she plans to combine yoga with other forms of therapy. Yoga, known in the west mainly as an exercise program, actually incorporates breathing, meditation, postures, and diet.

The Body Remembers

Kimberley Snow: I want to talk about spirituality and the body. I'll start by asking you how you got into yoga.
Barbara Mearns: I was raised as a Jehovah's Witness and when I left that in my early twenties, I felt that there was no way I could do anything with organized religion. At that time I equated religion with spirituality, so I thought of myself as pretty much nonspiritual.

Then I wanted to lose weight and a friend recommended a yoga

"We have attempted to separate the spiritual and the erotic, thereby reducing the spiritual to a world of flattened affect, a world of the ascetic who aspires to feel nothing."
—Audre Lorde

243

"For the body is not the dwelling place of the spirit—it is the spirit."
—Paula Gunn Allen

class. I was very out of my body at the time; I didn't exercise much, so I started to take a very soft yoga. It was okay, relaxing. But then I met one teacher who did a more energetic form of yoga called Iyengar yoga, named for the teacher who had started it. Iyengar yoga brings awareness of different parts of your body through precision. It's very cerebral in some ways and appeals to people who are usually in their heads, but also in their bodies, so yoga serves as a link to let them move energy around.

I connected to it very strongly. I felt that I'd come home. I experienced an opening in my body, an awareness that was amazing. That's how I refound spirituality. It was totally undeliberate, like coming in through the back door. I just loved doing it.

K: How is Iyengar different from traditional yoga?

B: They are both forms of Hatha yoga, but in Iyengar there is more emphasis on bringing awareness into an isolated area, getting deeply into a specific part of the body. But all yoga teaches an appreciation of the body, of how to be in the body joyfully. In doing standing poses, for instance, there's a certain way to have the feet positioned and a particular way to move your muscles. For example, when doing the triangular pose, you want to have the back heel in line with the arch, you don't want to have them out of line. People usually have a tendency to lock the knee, but you need to use the thigh muscle to open up the hip socket. The more you can contact different areas of your body, the more you become aware of the body as an organism, as part of you rather than something that *you* have. A lot of it is about opening up the chest. Many people have dead areas in their backs between their shoulder blades that could also be opened up. In fact, most of us are walking around with a lot of dead areas in our bodies. Yoga is a discipline to open up these areas and bring awareness into them. The more I did that, the more I could feel my body, be aware of my energy, the more it took me out of my head, brought me out of my self and put me back in touch with my spirituality. It was direct: it had nothing to do with dogma or theory, but the feeling of connectedness that I had in my body once I got in touch with it.

K: Connected with . . . ?

B: Everything. Once you bring in that awareness, it is almost as if the body dissolves. It's like in meditation when you concentrate on the breath, when you focus on one part of your body, everything slows down. Ideally your consciousness comes down out of your head and lives in the part of your body you're concentrating on. The way I've experienced it, the body has its own intelligence. So I try to get out of the mind when doing the poses and get into the body's intelligence because the mind usually screws up the poses, but the body remembers. A person will come to yoga class for the first time and everything is hard—she or he looks and feels awkward. But by the second time, the body remembers the first lesson and integrates it. The body is doing it, not the mind.

K: Do you think the body has its own will?

B: The body has its own life. It's connected to the mind, but I think it is a truer part of who we are because it holds all our own memories and our traumas. That comes out in yoga.

K: How?

B: When people have had a lot of sadness or grief, they close down. Yoga poses get into those areas, get into those blocks, and release emotion. Sometimes you may not remember anything specific, just a general malaise when you begin to work on certain areas. Or sometimes there are tears when you get in to where the trauma is held.

When a person does back bends, for instance, a lot of anger can come up. Sometimes a student doesn't like a particular pose or doesn't like the other people in the group. They feel resistance—just like in psychotherapy. Sometimes there's a good reason for the resistance, and you have to honor that and not just break through it. I believe in being gentle, for each body has its own pace. The kind of yoga I teach emphasizes building up strength—it's hard work. Your body has to be strong enough to let go of all that stuff. So much is happening with each of us—spiritually, emotionally, physically. A lot of yoga is just being present in the moment in the body and letting awareness come into that. A sense of being here and being full. As long as we're disembodied, we don't feel that. In a pose, when I do feel 100 percent present, then I feel connected with everything around me. I'm not in my head, but conscious of every part of myself, and I can feel that energy moving. It's a strong openness.

K: What about when you're not doing the poses?

B: It carries over. It calms the mind and that focus is like meditation.

"Spirituality is, after all, trying to understand something called life. That life resides in the body. I believe that when the body is no longer a suitable place for the soul, it will leave."
—Chandra Patel

*"Don't think about
the future.
Just be here now.
Don't think about the past.
Just be here now."*
—Ram Dass

It *is* meditation, a moving rather than a sitting meditation. Rather than being so caught up in the drama of my life, I observe what's going on. Just as I can watch what is happening when I move the energy in my body, I can watch what happens, observing, and accepting. Being where you are—I think many of the disciplines teach that.

K: Tell me more about teaching yoga.

B: A lot of yoga is just moving energy through. In class, I tend to adjust poses a lot by putting my hands on students. I like to get energy moving through the sacrum, that's another place where people tend to have problems physically. A new student usually doesn't have energy there so I try to move energy into that part of the body. Once the energy comes in, the body changes. Like your cat here sitting on my lap. She has no blocks, you can feel her energy coming through.

K: Did you learn how to move energy in other people when you studied with Iyengar in India?

B: Not really. I don't know how I learned. It started through adjusting people's poses technically, then it just came. I can see it as well as feel it. Blocked areas look like dead flesh. If there's energy, it looks alive, has a different color. I think we all work with energy intuitively—touching, hugging—but it often remains unconscious. It's such a shame that in the West we just don't relate to the body; many people would be happy to cut themselves off at the neck, and live from the neck up.

K: The Judeo-Christian traditions don't do much with the body, do they? There is nothing comparable to yoga there that I know of.

B: No. When Jews or Christians mention the body it is usually in negative terms. It is all very sinful. When I was a kid—a Jehovah's Witness—I had some mystical experiences although I didn't recognize them for what they were. But I'd sit and try to understand what everything was all about, so I'd say "me me me" over and over again; then I'd dissolve. I didn't tell anyone about it. If I'd told my mother she would have said it all came from Satan, but it felt pure to me. In some ways, yoga got me back to that sense of oneness and purity.

K: Were these childhood experiences bodily sensations?

B: Yes. It was almost like an orgasm, but more total. It was a tingling all over but also dissolving.

K: What made you say "me" over and over again? It's wonderful that you did.

B: I was trying to understand that I was alive. I'd just say "me" and think about what that meant. I think these experiences saved me from being a Jehovah's Witness. They saved my life.

K: Tell me about yoga breathing.

B: A lot of the breathing is to open the chest. There are different phases to go through in yoga, the *asanas* or the poses are one phase, the *dhyana*—removing the senses—is another phase, observing everything, moving into a more meditative state. The *pranayana*—the breathing—is considered the link between the body and the mind. Even if at the beginning the student can't do it, it's important to know that the breath is there, not to hold the breath.

K: If you were giving instructions to your class on breathing, what would you tell them?

B: To try to keep the breath down in the lower abdomen, the *hara* region, and to breathe into that softly, lengthening the inhalations and exhalations, feeling the openness coming from that area. I find that most people clench in the pelvis and the energy can't move through. At the beginning, it is good to keep awareness in the belly rather than the chest for this tends to relax the poses. They are physically challenging, but it is important to relax into them, to surrender and let go of the mind. To keep the consciousness in the belly and with the breath is not traditional. Traditional *pranayana* sucks the abdomen in and moves the breath up into the chest so that the abdomen is kind of hard and moving in. But I don't like that. I think it's very yang. I think women tend to hold emotional trauma in their abdomen. We're taught to hold it in, but I like releasing it.

K: Bernadette Roberts makes the point that most traditional religions were formulated to try to counteract or control the male ego. Thus, when the female enters these disciplines, she is trying to control something she may not even have.

B: That's why females have to make them their own. There's a lot of good in these traditions, but a lot we can't use. Certainly Iyengar is very patriarchal, and has been criticized for being too hard, too rigid. I try to bring a softness to it without throwing out the whole thing.

K: Certain Buddhist techniques stress relaxing the mind. They say

"We have been raised to fear the yes within ourselves, our deepest cravings."
—Audre Lorde

"To know truth one must get rid of knowledge; nothing is more powerful and creative than emptiness."
—Lao-Tzu

that if you relax the mind, the body will follow.

B: Hatha yoga goes the other way: Relax the body, and the mind will follow. The body is just so wonderful, it's like a universe inside. Going in, with yoga, it's endless. I can do a pose a thousand times, and when I do it again, and go in, I can find something new.

K: What do you find?

B: Space. Space within. Allowing the spine to lengthen and allowing that space just to be. It's already there, but we try to compress it, make it solid. Part of yoga is allowing that space and rejoicing in that space.

Because yoga, like meditation, should be experienced, you might want to take a yoga class or use a videotape at home. Some good videotapes are available through Pyramid Books, the New Age Collection, PO Box 3333, Chelmsford, MA 01824-0933; *Yoga Journal* Video Series—Healing Arts, 321 Hampton Drive, S-203, Venice, CA 90291; and *Signals,* WGBH Educational Foundation, PO Box 6442,; St. Paul, MN 55164-0428.

An audiotape with B. K. Iyengar called "Yogafire" (#1895) is available from New Directions, PO Box 410510, San Francisco, CA 94141-0510, (415) 563-8899.

Books can also be helpful when they include exercises and pictures. A few suggestions: *Gentle Yoga: A Guide to Gentle Exercise,* Lorna Bell and Eudora Seyfer, Celestial Arts, 1987; *Yoga for Health,* Richard Hittleman, Ballentine, 1985; *Tree of Yoga,* B.K. Iyengar, Shambhala, 1989; B.K. Iyengar, *His Life and Work,* Timeless Books, 1987; *Hatha Yoga for Total Health,* Sue Luby, Prentiss Hall, 1977; *Simplified Course in Hatha Yoga,* Walter Slater, Quest Books, 1967; *Yoga for Me,* Susan Terkel, Lerner Publications, 1982.

"Remembering" your connection with the Divine is a central aspect of Sufism, the mystical branch of Islam, as well as in Gurdjieff work, where it is referred to as "self-remembering." Buddhist meditation stresses mindfulness or meditation in action. Here the speaker is a Western woman.

Remember

Remember the sky that you were born under,
know each of the star's stories.
Remember the moon, know who she is. I met her
in a bar once in Iowa City.
Remember the sun's birth at dawn, that is the
strongest point of time. Remember sundown
and the giving away to night.
Remember your birth, how your mother struggled
to give you form and breath. You are evidence of
her life, and her mother's, and hers.
Remember your father, his hands cradling
your mother's flesh, and maybe her heart, too
and maybe not.
He is your life, also.
Remember the earth whose skin you are.
Red earth yellow earth white earth brown earth
black earth we are earth.
Remember the plants, trees, animal life who all have their
tribes, their families, their histories, too. Talk to them,
listen to them. They are alive poems.
Remember the wind. Remember her voice. She knows the
origin of this universe. I heard her singing Kiowa war
dance songs at the corner of Fourth and Central once.
Remember that you are all people and that all people
are you.
Remember that you are this universe and that this
universe is you.
Remember that all is in motion, is growing, is you.
Remember that language comes from this.

Remember the dance that language is, that life is.
Remember
to remember.

Joy Harjo
She Had Some Horses

*"What do you teach?"
someone asked Gurdjieff. "I
wish you to know that when
rain falls streets are wet"
was the answer.*

○ Write a poem or reflection about remembering your connection to the sacred.

———————————

G. I. Gurdjieff, born on the Russian-Turkish border in 1877, spent a number of years studying esoteric spiritual traditions in Central Asia and the Middle East. He gathered many pupils, first in Moscow and finally in Paris, where he opened his Institute for the Harmonious Development of Man in 1922. When Mrs. Staveley studied with Gurdjieff many years ago, she had "the sensation of something that had been crushed and buried" in her coming into the light. "Someone knows how it is, really knows," she later wrote. "I won't have to pretend anymore." In Themes *she presents exercises for those who are interested in learning how to "do" the Gurdjieff work rather than simply talking about his ideas—many of which were adapted from Sufism.*

Awareness

Yesterday we spoke of self-observation in a general way—trying to let "it" be and do, and "it" always is and does, while trying to keep a point of awareness deeper inside. We found there were many difficulties: the preconceived notion of what it was we were observing, the thinking one knows it all already, the fear, the common or garden variety of resistance to any effort that does not bring an immediate result or reward, and so on and so forth. Perhaps most of all, the difficulty of remembering to try at all.

Maybe some of us had a glimpse of the deadness of the machine. Most of the time I move about as if I were dead. There is no one at home in my inner world. I do not see what I look at; I do not listen to what I hear; all my senses, all the parts of me through which I am related to the world around me are dull and as if blocked. What blocks them? It seems to be this false sense of myself through which everything is perceived.

Can I do something about this state of affairs? Yes, something is possible. I can begin to put this instrument which is my body in better order. I can be more aware. When I speak to another person I can really try to see him instead of my reactions to him. I can cut down my own talking by half and listen—not only to what is said but to how it is said. I can begin to learn to use this wonderfully subtle instrument which is my body. If I am aware of the world about me I am more alive. If not, I am already dead.

The world has been here a long, long time with all its mystery and wonder. It will continue to be here. But I will not. There is no more time for sleep.

Let me take one thing to practice awareness on today—my hands. They connect me with the world in many ways. They have their own intelligence. I will not identify with them—call them my hands—but will strive to be aware of them as a thing in themselves. Know their strength, their sensitivity, their intelligence, and what else? All the things I really do not know about them.

A. L. Staveley
Themes

"When we pay attention, whatever we are doing—whether it be cooking, cleaning or making love—is transformed and becomes part of our spiritual path. We begin to notice details and textures that we never noticed before; everyday life becomes clearer, sharper, and at the same time more spacious."
—Rick Fields

O The above "hands" exercise is a powerful one, especially when kneading dough. You may also want to try it when driving or gardening.

For more about the life and teachings of Gurdjieff, consult:

J. G. Bennett, *Gurdjieff Making a New World*, Bennett, 1993.

_____, *Is There "Life" on Earth? An Introduction to Gurdjieff*, Bennett, 1989.

J. G. and Elizabeth Bennett, *Idiots in Paris*, Samuel Weiser, 1991.

G. I. Gurdjieff, *Life is Real Only Then, When "I Am"*, Dutton, 1978.

_____, *Meetings with Remarkable Men*, Dutton, 1963.

_____, *Views from the Real World*, Dutton, 1973.

Kathryn Hulme, *Undiscovered Country in Search of Gurdjieff*, Little, Brown, 1966.

P. D. Ouspensky, *In Search of the Miraculous*, Harcourt Brace Jovanovich, 1977.

_____ , *The Psychology of Man's Possible Evolution*, Vintage, 1974.

Kathleen Riordan Speeth, *The Gurdjieff Work*, Jeremy P. Tarcher, 1989.

Charles T. Tart, *Waking Up: Overcoming the Obstacles to Human Potential*, Shambhala, 1986.

Some sources for books on Gurdjieff and his work:

Bennett Books, PO Box 1553, Santa Fe, NM 87504.
By the Way Books, PO BOX 1417 G, Lawrenceville, GA 30246.
Claymont Communications, PO Box 112, Charleston, WV 25414.

For movement classes and seminars based on Gurdjieff's teachings, contact: Larry Altman, 71 Reposo Drive, Oakview, CA 93022.

> *"Although meditation is actually very simple, it is easy to get confused by the many different descriptions of meditative practices. Forget them all and just sit quietly."*
> —Tarthang Tulku

Lectio Divina *means "sacred reading" and is a simple method of praying the Scripture.*

Lectio Divina

Begin by stilling yourself—lighting a candle, praying, sitting quietly—then pick up the Scripture or any spiritual classic and slowly begin to read aloud. If a particular phrase attracts you, stop and repeat the text. Listen to the Word. Absorb it fully. Contemplate how you can apply it to your life. Continue for about fifteen or twenty minutes, then close the session by blowing out the candle and repeating a short prayer.

After completing a practice session, it is a good idea to do what is called "dedicating the merit"—mentally wishing that everyone will benefit from whatever energy you generated through your prayer or practice. Giving away the benefit in this way helps to keep your ego from getting puffed up because you are doing spiritual practice and also extends your practice to others.

The following guided meditation was written for a group of retreatants preparing themselves for the season of Lent, its metaphors drawn primarily from the Judeo-Christian scriptures, its theme centering on creation and reconciliation.

"Dwelling means place, presence, rest—and we live out this dwelling not only in actual places but, at a deeper level, in symbolic, centering spiritual locations which turn out to be within ourselves."
—Maria Harris

Guided Meditation at Lent

You are going back now, back in time, back to the beginning, when there was no time, before telephones or automobiles, before the invention of machines. You are going back to the beginning, before the creation of mountains or oceans, deserts, animals, human beings or plants. You are going back to the moment of vast open space.

. . . Silence . . .

Begin now to experience this emptiness.

You have come home.

As you gaze about, you see moving universes come into being as soundless explosions that quiet until order returns.

. . . Silence . . .

You are now able to see planet earth, where a divine wind sweeps over the waters. You experience earthquakes, the birth of mountains, the hot lava of erupting volcanoes. Plants, trees, and flowering vegetation push their way up through the earth's crust. Slowly the process of humanization begins. Slowly now your spirit becomes enfleshed, consciousness finding a material home.

Slowly you awaken to a vision of a garden, with waterfalls, rivers, swarms of living animals, some with fins, some with wings, some with legs. You run across the earth with the gazelle. You follow the

253

flight of the eagle. The trees are laden with tender fruit of all kinds. Birds and flowers join with all creation singing an unending hymn of praise. The spirits of the dancing ground, musical waters, and warm sun embrace all that exists with unconditional love.

You move through childhood in the garden of the Deity, growing, changing within the garden of your birth. No matter where you go the hymn of the Godhead is available to you, washing your heart with laughter.

One day you come upon a part of the garden you have not seen before. There stands a tree unlike any other. Whirling lights of music surround it. All becomes electrified with the same cosmic intensity the tree is bathed in, and then you hear the voices of the life force saying:

YOU ARE FREE TO EAT OF ALL THE TREES IN THE GARDEN . . . BUT OF THE TREE OF KNOWLEDGE YOU ARE NOT TO EAT . . . FOR THE DAY YOU EAT THAT, YOU ARE DOOMED TO DIE.

This is the voice of truth, of power and majesty. Understanding, acceptance and love bring you into intimate union with the intrinsic purity of the moment. As you leave this holy place you bow with outstretched arms.

But as time passes, you sense a new stirring in your consciousness. For the first time in your life you experience conflict, for you have never known desire before. The mystery of the magical lights and fruit of the tree hold you mesmerized. You are forever changed. You cannot forget the tree of light.

Feeling discomfort of body, of mind, each day you return to the tree, and each day the yearning grows stronger. Finally it becomes a passion, like a coiled serpent brought to life and ready to spring. Then the rationalizations begin:

"If God really cared to forbid the fruit, then why would I feel such discomfort tormenting my soul, tearing my heart apart, confusing my mind?" The voices in your head begin to multiply. "Knowledge, what knowledge was God talking about?" "Why can't I have this knowledge?" "Why should knowledge be the cause of my death?"

"I want it. I am afraid of it. I will never go back to that tree. I keep

"Fear is created not by the world around us, but in the mind, by what we think is going to happen."
—Elisabeth Gawain

254

going back. I, me, mine. Why can't I have it? Stupid, eating one piece of fruit can't kill me."

The craving becomes anger. Then greed, even lust finds it's way into your heart. One day you feel the conflict tearing at you so strongly you return to the tree full of a force of rebellion so strong you can't resist. You are going to eat the forbidden fruit. Your head is filled with red-hot voices, the clamor is loud, driving, convincing. You no longer walk with God in the cool of the evening; there is no space left in your mind, no space between thoughts, no space for the Deity's voice to be heard. So seductive, so risky, the dominating voices of your ego drive you into the sacred space surrounding the tree. You reach up and take hold of the precious fruit and bite into it. Your mouth bites into the luscious, sweet, cool, crisp flesh of the fruit. The juices of creation spill out of your mouth, down your chin, over your hand, onto your chest, then drip over your stomach.

With a bolt of lightning, your eyes open to the truth. At once you understand, at once you gain the knowledge of adulthood and you feel more naked then you have ever felt before. You begin to run away, farther and farther away from this awful place; you race grabbing at leaves to cover yourself; you feel afraid. Trembling, panicked and ashamed, you crouch down trying to hide. No matter where you go, no matter how you try to forget, the pain and the awareness stays with you. Everywhere you go, no matter how far you run, you hear the familiar sound of God's footsteps echoing throughout the garden. You hear Creation's voice calling you, "Where are you?". . . Finally in a choked voice you reply, "I heard you Lord, but I was afraid, so I hid."

You have left the garden of your youth behind while entering the wilderness of adulthood. In the process you and Deity have been separated. Now the struggle begins as you try to regain that which has been lost. Now you must strive to separate God's voice from the myriad interior voices clamoring for attention. No longer will your life be one of carefree abandon. No longer will you run with the innocent beasts across the dancing ground. Now you must think about all your actions. Think what to do, what not to do. Think about right and wrong. Now you must search day in and day out for truth. Now you are responsible for your destination, since the naive child has died.

You weep, your tears pour forth. Your suffering continues unabated down through the ages. As you weep, however, you become aware of

"Most people are unaware of the beliefs with which they guard the boundaries of their experience."
—Baba Cooper

"God wants nothing of you but the gift of a peaceful heart."
—Meister Eckhart

a cleansing taking place. The great separation you felt when crouched down hiding, the fear and shame, begin to dissolve. Exhausted from weeping, your mind quiets. Blessed space appears between your thoughts. Your tears carry the pain-filled memories farther and farther away. Your heart opens once again; washed clean by tears, you once again see in the distance a garden of lights. You hear clouds of music, you smell the pungent aroma of perfumed flowers. Off on the horizon, you hear waters of baptism crashing down from ice-capped mountains, tumbling over rocks though meadows and valleys on the way to the vast mother ocean. Softly you hear the voice of the Godhead. It is the voice of radiant energy vibrating from the life source, the voice of quiet peace and exuberant joy.

You hear God's words—"Where are you?" This time you embrace the source of unconditional love by opening your arms out wide. Falling on your knees you reply, "Here I am Lord, it is I, Lord. I have heard you calling in the night, I'll go Lord, if you need me. I will hold creation in my heart."

Once again you have come back home, you have reached your final destination; the love and peacefulness of the energetic moment continues as the voice of the cosmos speaks:

As I am in you
So are you within me
When you become heavily burdened
I will refresh you
Go then to a sacred place and call me
I will answer
Follow only my voice for I am the light,
I am the life, I am the resurrection
Those who believe in me, even though they die,
They will live
and those who believe in me will never die.
Go now and know that you are loved.

. . . PAUSE . . .

It is now time to return to the present.
When you feel ready, stretch your legs and arms.

Discussion can follow these meditations, or silence and music. It is important to bring people fully back to the moment if they will be driving cars or negotiating subway systems.

Mary Ann McGuire
Christian minister

○ Create an atmosphere for this meditation by lighting candles, making an altar, playing soft music, and lighting incense; then read it aloud to a small group.

———————————————

Thus I was taught that love is our lord's meaning. And I saw most surely in this and in all, that before God made us he loved us, which love was never slaked nor ever shall be. And in this love he has done all his works and in this love he has made all things profitable to us, and in this love our life is everlasting. In our creation we had beginning, but the love in which he made us was in him from without beginning. In this love we have our beginning, and all this shall we see in God without end."
—Julian of Norwich

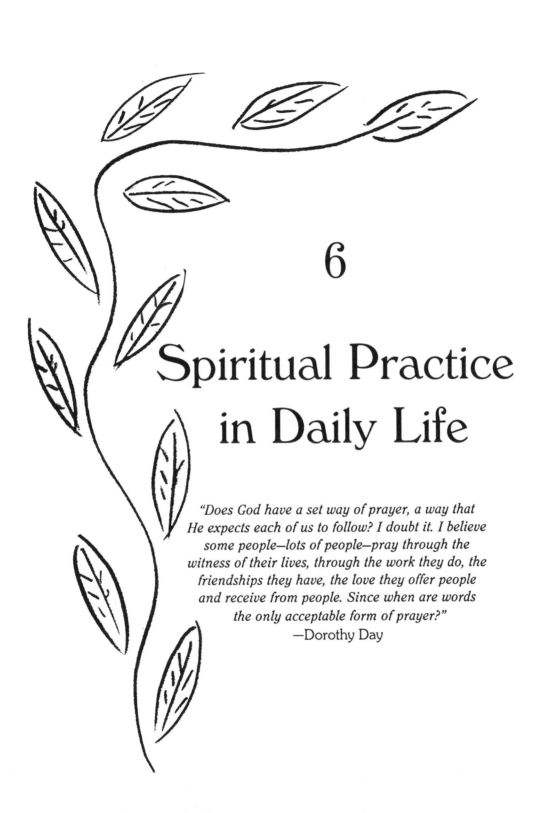

6

Spiritual Practice
in Daily Life

*"Does God have a set way of prayer, a way that
He expects each of us to follow? I doubt it. I believe
some people—lots of people—pray through the
witness of their lives, through the work they do, the
friendships they have, the love they offer people
and receive from people. Since when are words
the only acceptable form of prayer?"*
—Dorothy Day

Art, gardening, writing, contemplation, mindfulness, cooking, mothering, loving kindness, communing with nature, yoga, social action, nursing, and other forms of service all function as daily practice for women. So does nightly praying, keeping the Shabbat, sitting meditation, repeating a mantra, fasting, and other practices traditionally prescribed by religious groups. The important thing is to bring a conscious, ongoing awareness into your chosen activity, acknowledging that it forms a part of your spiritual path. This intent, this consciousness, helps to stabilize and deepen your experience.

It is best to connect with a practice from the heart, not because someone else recommends it. When you find one that speaks to you, use it regularly. A daily—or at least an ongoing—habit of consciously connecting to the spirit by a specific method creates a pattern in the body and in the unconscious which will carry you through when the mind is exhausted. Consistent practice automatically leads you to spiritual renewal and revitalization.

Retreats, seminars, and workshops help to broaden and strengthen spiritual practice and introduce you to others on the same path. In time, you may wish to find a teacher or become part of a community, but the first step is to establish an ongoing practice.

Ayya Khema, a Theravadan Buddhist nun, was born in Germany and as a child escaped the Nazis by fleeing to China with her family. Along with other Jewish refugees, she was put into a Japanese prisoner-of-war camp where her father died. She eventually married and had two children, but managed to meditate as a householder. Before she became involved with Buddhism, she learned meditation at the Aurobindo ashram in India from the Mother, and studied Advaita at Ramana Maharishi's ashram. She has established Buddhist centers in Germany, Australia, and Nun's Island in Sri Lanka, and is the author of Being Nobody, Going Nowhere.

"It is more difficult to be a complete human being than a saint. It means nothing can be excluded or suppressed."
—Stephen Levine

Nothing Special

Spiritual practice is often misunderstood and believed to be something special. It isn't. It is one's whole body and mind. Nothing special at all, just oneself. Many people think of it as meditation or ritual, devotional practice or chanting to be performed at a specific time in a certain place. Or it may be connected with a special person without whom the practice cannot occur. These are views and opinions which lead to nothing.

In the best case they may result in sporadic practice and in the worst case, they lead to fracturing ourselves, making two, three or four people out of ourselves when we aren't even one whole yet. Namely, the ordinary person doing all the ordinary worldly chores and the other one who becomes spiritual at certain times in diverse ways. Meditation, rituals, devotional practice, chanting, certain places, certain people can be added to our lives but they are not the essence of our spirituality.

Our practice consists of constant purification; there's nothing else to be done. Eventually we will arrive at a point where our thought processes and feelings are not only kind and loving but also full of wisdom, bringing benefit to ourselves and others.

Ayya Khema
Little Dust in Our Eyes

○ Is there a special "spiritual" you that stands apart from your other persona? Examine the ways in which this part of your personality is kept separate (untouched?) from your "normal" self. Becoming conscious of this division is perhaps the first step toward integration.

———————————————

Most religions offer some way of purifying past actions through confession of wrong and commitment to improved behavior in the future. In the following exercise, adapted from Tibetan Buddhism, one confesses to and receives absolution from a source of light visualized above the head. Although this light can be seen to represent divine forgiveness and compassion, these forces—projected by your own psyche—are also inner.

Purification

Visualize a source of light about six inches above your head. Take a moment to relate to this pure and healing source of light. Confess—to yourself, to the light—something you've done wrong. Contemplate the consequences of your action, not just on yourself, but on others. Feel deep regret for your action. Vow not to repeat it. Experience the light above you streaming down through the crown of your head and flowing through your body, pushing out the impurities caused by your action; feel the negative residue leave your body through your pores, through the soles of your feet. Repeat this process until you feel filled with light. Sincerely wish that others can benefit from this light.

Taking and Sending

After you've used the light-purification exercise over a period of time, you come to feel that you're filled with healing light which you wish to share with others. When you are standing next to someone— say an impatient person in front of you in the grocery line—visualize that you breathe in their energy which is dark and smoky. Bring it

"What happens when there is no transformation [of consciousness] is very subtle: unknowingly the ego uses religion to preserve itself, defend itself, change the world for itself, and thus religion becomes the servant of the ego, its cloak and its mask. This is the most powerful position the ego can possible assume, because it is all in the name of the divine and ultimate truth."
—Bernadette Roberts

into your light-filled being, and breathe it out clear and fine. Match your breathing to the distressed person's, breathing in dark, breathing out light. Concentrate on doing this whenever you are with others. By controlling the way in which their energy is absorbed and processed, you will be able to remain centered yourself as well as helping others in distress. It is surprising how this technique calms others down.

"There have been thousands upon thousands of people who have practiced meditation and obtained its fruits. Don't doubt its possibilities because of the simplicity of its method. If you can't find the truth right where you are, where else do you think you will find it?"
—Dogen

To take in pleasure and push away pain is logical to the ego. The practice of taking and sending, called tonglen *in Tibetan, reverses this process. Pema Chödrön, a Buddhist nun, is the director of Gampo Abbey in Cape Breton, Nova Scotia.*

Start Where You Are

There are two slogans that go along with the tonglen practice: "Sending and taking should be practiced alternately. / These two should ride the breath"—which is actually a description of tonglen and how it works—and "Begin the sequence of sending and taking with yourself."

The slogan "Begin the sequence of sending and taking with yourself" is getting at the point that compassion starts with making friends with ourselves, and particularly with our poisons—the messy areas. As we practice tonglen—taking and sending—and contemplate the lojong slogans, gradually it begins to dawn on us how totally interconnected we all are. Now people know that what we do to the rivers in South America affects the whole world, and what we do to the air in Alaska affects the whole world. Everything is interrelated—including ourselves, so this is very important, this making friends with ourselves. It's the key to a more sane compassionate planet.

What you do for yourself—any gesture of kindness, any gesture of gentleness, any gesture of honesty and clear seeing toward yourself—will affect how you experience your world. In fact, it will transform how you experience the world. What you do for yourself, you're doing for others, and what you do for others, you're doing for yourself. When you exchange yourself for others in the practice of tonglen, it becomes increasingly uncertain what is out there and what is in here.

If you have rage and righteously act it out and blame it all on others, it's really you who suffers. The other people and the environment suffer also, but you suffer more because you're being eaten up inside with rage, causing you to hate yourself more and more.

We act out because, ironically, we think it will bring us some relief. We equate it with happiness. Often there *is* some relief, for the moment. When you have an addiction and you fulfill that addiction, there is a moment in which you feel some relief. Then the nightmare gets worse. So it is with aggression. When you get to tell someone off, you might feel pretty good for a while, but somehow the sense of righteous indignation and hatred grows, and it hurts you. It's as if you pick up hot coals with your bare hands and throw them at your enemy. If the coals happen to hit him, he will be hurt. But in the meantime, you are guaranteed to be burned.

On the other hand, if we begin to surrender to ourselves—begin to drop the story line and experience what all this messy stuff behind the story line feels like—we begin to find bodhichitta, the tenderness that's under all that harshness. By being kind to ourselves, we become kind to others. By being kind to others—if it's done properly, with proper understanding—we benefit as well. So the point is that we are completely interrelated. What you do to others, you do to yourself. What you do to yourself, you do to others.

> Pema Chödrön
> *Start Where You Are:*
> *A Guide to Compassionate Living*

Also see Pema Chödrön's excellent book *The Wisdom of No Escape*, Shambhala, 1991.

"Always meditate on whatever provokes resentment."
—Atisha

Many women, feeling a lack of meaning in their lives, spontaneously invent rituals, use "recipe" books from Wicca or the goddess movement, or a combination thereof. Diane Mariechild explains the importance of rituals in our lives.

"Ritual is a statement of what we want and a remembrance of the great cycles of things."
—Brooke Medicine Eagle

Rituals

To become whole we need to find a center, a space where we can gather and focus our inner energy so that we are not continually shaken by criticism, demands or stressful situations. Traditional religious beliefs have mistakenly identified this as perfection, when what is really necessary is wholeness. My personal search has led me into feminism, psychic development, meditation, reincarnation, Wiccan rituals, yoga and a study of matriarchal consciousness. Out of this search I have created my own rituals that strengthen and center me. I borrow from many traditions, but for the most part the rituals well up from an inner source. And later, to my surprise and excitement, I find how similar they are to ancient traditions.

A ritual is a stylized series of actions, whether physical or mental, that is used to change one's perception of reality. It is a symbolic event that attempts to concretize an inner event. A ritual often begins and is performed long before an awareness of the meaning develops. A transformation of personality is implied in every ritual and a ritual is implied in every magical process.

The art of ritual is the discovery of how to make the best use of energy flows. There is strength in ritual. There is power in clarifying our actions, making them precise and then using repetition of sounds and movements to build the energy. We bring our energy in tune with the universal energy, thus experiencing our connections with the whole of the universe.

A ritual may be as simple as the lighting of a candle, or it may involve elaborate preparations. Ritual may include the use of some or all of these things: stylized movements, repetitive words, chants or song, objects, costumes, tools, foods, beverages or drugs. Each action, whether it is a repeated series of words, a gathering of special objects, a way of dressing, or holding the body in dance or repose, is meditated on, chosen and executed carefully and thoughtfully. Rituals may happen spontaneously, or each detail may be planned in advance. Most rituals contain elements of both.

In ritual you create in the microcosm what you desire in the macrocosm. Before performing a ritual you need to have your purpose and the reasons behind it clearly in your mind. These questions might be helpful in assessing your purpose: What do I want? Why do I want it? What will happen if I achieve my purpose? What will happen if I don't? How will my success or failure affect other people? Do I want it so much that I become fearful or tense and block the energy I need to achieve it? Do I really believe I can achieve it? Do I think I deserve to achieve it? Do I have whatever is necessary (energy, self-confidence, tools, time, material resources) to achieve it?

Once your purposes are clear you can begin to plan the ritual. There are several steps involved in planning and performing rituals, and each is important in its own right. The first and second steps are planning and preparing materials for the ritual. And the third and fourth steps are the inner preparation (meditation and/or fasting and purification) and the ceremony itself.

There are varying situations in our lives that we might want to ritualize: holidays or celebrations of special feelings we wish to keep positive. We might also ritualize situations we wish release from: pain or fear, sorrow over the death of a friend, confusion over the breakup of a relationship. Rituals might also be used to change a negative situation into a positive one such as self-healing or changing from a jobless state to an employed one.

. . . The first [ritual] is a self-blessing, a ritual of affirmation that can be performed monthly or whenever you feel the need or desire.

. "The power to regain our own life comes from the discovery of the cosmic covenant, the deep harmony in the community of being in which we participate."
—Mary Daly

SELF-BLESSING

Gather together a white candle, a small bowl or cup of water and a stick of incense. Pick a quiet time and space. Light the candle and incense and sit quietly, letting all tension slip away and all worried thought leave your body/mind.

Dip your fingers in the water and touch your eyes saying, "Bless my eyes that I may have clarity of vision."

Dip your fingers in the water and touch your mouth saying, "Bless my mouth that I may speak the truth."

Dip your fingers in the water and touch your ears saying, "Bless my ears that I may hear all that is spoken unto me."

Dip your fingers in the water and touch your heart saying, "Bless my heart that I may be filled with love."

Dip your fingers in the water and touch your womb saying, "Bless my womb that I may be in touch with my creative energies and the creative energy of the universe."

Dip your fingers in the water and touch your feet saying, "Bless my feet that I may find and walk on my own true path."

Quietly reflect on the words you have spoken and feel yourself filled with a peaceful, loving energy.

When you feel complete, put out the candle. Empty the bowl and wash it carefully.

Diane Mariechild
Motherwit, Rev. Ed.

"When you take a dirty floor, scrub it and make it spotlessly clean, and then polish it until it shines, it radiates back to you the love which you poured into it. The divinity of that floor has been drawn forth."
—Eileen Caddy

Numerous books on rituals are in print. To find one that suits you, go to a woman's bookstore, scan the titles of the "recipe" books to see which one "shines" at you or draws your attention in some way, then flip through it. If you stand there reading for some time, you've found the right book.

Diane Mariechild has a number of other books out, as does Z. Budapest. Budapest's include *Grandmother Moon: Lunar Magic in Our Lives*, HarperCollins, 1991, and *The Grandmother of Time*, HarperCollins, 1989.

Other good ones are:

Sedona Cahill and Josh Helpern, *The Ceremonial Circle: Practice, Ritual and Renewal for Personal and Community Healing*, HarperCollins, 1990.

J. C. Cooper, *The Aquarian Dictionary of Festivals*, Aquarian, 1991.

Marian Green, *A Calendar of Festivals*, Element Books, 1991.

Richard Heinber, *Celebrate the Solstice: Honoring the Earth's Seasonal Rhythms through Festival and Ceremony*, Quest, 1993.

Shekhinah Mountainwater, *Ariadne's Thread: A Workbook of Goddess Magic*, Crossing, 1991.

Starhawk, *The Spiral Dance*, Harper & Row, 1989.

Barbara Walker, *Women's Rituals: A Sourcebook*, Harper & Row, 1990.

The author, initially drawn by the quiet simplicity of their quilt designs, spent much time with the Amish. Although she found that she couldn't live as they did, she discovered a world in which the sacred and everyday were seamlessly integrated, where people didn't talk about their values, but lived them.

Learning from the Amish

Everything was a ritual.

Doing the dishes, mowing the lawn, baking bread, quilting, canning, hanging out the laundry, picking fresh produce, weeding. Friday: housecleaning; Saturday: mowing the lawn; Monday: washing. Emma, Lydia, and Miriam, three generations of women living side by side, knew exactly what had to be done and in what order. Nothing had to be explained.

No distinction was made between the sacred and the everyday. Five minutes in the early morning and five minutes in the evening were devoted to prayer. The rest of the day was spent living their beliefs. Their life was all one piece. It was all sacred—and all ordinary.

Sue Bender
*Plain and Simple:
A Woman's Journey to the Amish*

O Think about doing one thing today that will simplify your life. Now do it.

Simple Living is a newsletter centered on the concept of voluntary simplicity. To subscribe, contact Simple Living Press, 1802 North 54th Street, Seattle, WA 98103.

"Simplicity of living means meeting life face to face. It means confronting life clearly, without unnecessary distractions, without trying to soften the awesomeness of our existence or masking the deeper manifestations of life with pretentions, distractions and unnecessary accumulations."
—Duane Elgin

Ancestor reverence—even a simple appreciation of different material aspects of the world we have inherited—is another way to feel connected with the great web of life.

"We are tomorrow's past."
—Mary Webb

Homage to Ancestors

Africans believe that those who go before us make us what we are. Accordingly, ancestor-reverence holds an important place in the African belief system. Through reverence for them we recognize our origins and ensure the spiritual and physical continuity of the human race. . . .

If you are serious about your spirituality, you will see that white women must stand in support of their Mother [Africa, where humans originated] and see Black women as their mothers-sisters. And Black women must look beyond the five-hundred-year-old veneer of distorted history and recognize their sisters-daughters. We are children of a common womb. In the spiritual sense everyone on the planet—black and white, female and male, gay, straight, and bisexual—is "kin incarnate." Were we not that, we would be "kin in spirit" on another plane.

So take the time now to give racism a dishonorable burial. Let us starve him out, deprive him of his spirit, eradicate his name.

Also, practice fidelity to the principle of reverence. Look around you. Is your dress made of Japanese silk? Yes? Then revere those ancestors. Having cornbread with dinner tonight? Recognize the work of the Native Americans. Is that salsa music playing on your radio? If you just love the stuff, then salute your Latin ancestors.

We can no longer afford to be "tribal." There has already been too much physical and cultural interchange for that—thank Goddess! What we must do now is turn to Mother Earth and salute Her for allowing us to live on Her body. We must feed Her, sing to Her and regard Her and all Her creations with loving reverence. For example, I praise the Wind Goddess and the Wright brothers every time I board an airplane. Speaking from experience, I assure you that if you internalize this attitude you will be rewarded with a feeling of never walking alone.

Luisah Teish
Jambalaya: The Natural Woman's Book of Personal Charms and Practical Rituals

○ Honor your ancestors, as Teish suggests. Also, relax your mind and remember things of beauty that you've seen: faces, mountains, rooms, fabrics, flowers. Go deeply into your past and let the images come forth. Without grasping, simply appreciate the beauty you've witnessed.

Ram Dass, once a colleague of Timothy Leary at Harvard, authored Be Here Now *in 1971. This spiritual guide with its large format and brown paper with crazy-looking type styles and illustrations introduced Eastern, especially Hindu, ideas in an approachable way to a whole generation of students. And that was just the beginning.*

"Spiritual growth may be measured by a decrease of afflictive emotions and increase of love and compassion for others."
—Chagdud Tulku

Compassion in Action

In pursuing the path of action, I have begun to see recognizable stages in the transformative process. At first I saw myself as a separate entity full of needs and desires. My identity with these desires left me very attached to the fruits of my actions and thus willing to manipulate things and people, as if they were objects, to realize my goals. Then, with just a little awakening, I saw that the desires were unending and even the gratification of them was leaving me in an unsatisfactory alienated state. I saw that I would always be dissatisfied as long as I was caught up in my desires, and that under these conditions my actions could not express the highest level of compassion.

As I understood my predicament more clearly, the desire for liberation started to supplant other desires. This was the beginning of the path of action. Through mindfulness training I began to cultivate the part of me that was not identified with the desires. Desires arose and passed by with little clinging on my part to them. During this period my aversions and attractions, born of desires that remained, became painfully apparent. At first I was hard on myself for being so caught in the desire mind. With time, however, compassion toward myself began to develop, and I was able simply to note the arising of these various feelings of attraction and aversion. I found myself less affected by the success and failure of my efforts in each task. The ability to witness my reactions to these results increased. A quality of equanimity began to arise. I also noticed that each time an action was carried out even partially selflessly, it strengthened an identity with some force greater than myself and helped to free me from thinking of myself as separate.

Now I notice two things developing simultaneously. The first is an impersonality in my actions, almost as if someone else were performing them. There is a sense of my being an instrument of some compassionate force or mind deeper or higher than my own separate mind. It is difficult to describe. Sri Aurobindo, a great Indian holy person, spelled out in precise detail just how our minds surrender into and are supplanted by the higher, more universal mind. One way of describing what I experience is that it is as though I am a node in a large network of compassion. The biblical expression "Not my will but thine" reflects this moment-to-moment experience.

The other emerging quality is an intensification of the love that permeates actions. The universe of forms has become increasingly imbued with a radiance, an awesome, often bittersweet beauty, that makes each of my actions in the world feel like an act of devotion. Because it is new to me, I am often surprised by the feeling of love for other people, animals, and the earth that arises, often when I least expect it.

This feeling of treasuring other beings and serving them as the beloved makes me want to perform my acts even more skillfully, making each act an offering of beauty. The act of love draws me closer to whoever or whatever is before me, and with this closeness comes an intensification of empathy and joys and sufferings. Out of this arises a desire to alleviate suffering in the best possible way. Whether I am at the checkout counter in the supermarket, sharing a moment with a person facing a terminal illness, protesting in a political action, or dealing with a policeman who has stopped me on the highway, it is all a dialogue with the beloved, our interaction being a vehicle through which we meet and are together. This love grows until, as mystic poets have suggested, it could "start to equal the love that a mother has for her baby, that a miser has for her or

"Love is the choice to experience life as a member of the human family, a partner in the dance of life, rather than as an alien in the world or as a deity above the world, aloof and apart from human flesh."
—Carter Heyward

his money, that a person has for her or his lover."

Seeing the world as the many faces of the beloved, and experiencing myself as an instrument of some higher compassionate force of mind, feels at times as though the beloved is serving the beloved. Where am I in this process? In the beginning, I felt that I was doing it. Then I felt that I was observing it. And now I sometimes find myself absent and the compassionate action just occurring, rising out of the momentary conditions of the situation, having little to do with me at all. Reflecting upon these moments, I have a better understanding of the mystical adage "Out of emptiness arises compassion."

Ram Dass and Mirabai Bush
*Compassion in Action: Setting
Out of the Path of Service*

"The question, 'What shall we do?' is the wrong question. The question, then, is 'How shall we be?'"
—Sonia Johnson

O Before you begin an exercise, it is a good idea to slow down, quiet yourself, and center by concentrating your energy in your chest or abdomen, or on your breathing. The following exercise, called "Loving Kindness Meditation," is an extremely powerful tool in opening the heart and developing compassion.

Visualize a lotus in your heart. Feel it open and send out rays of love-filled light. Direct this stream of love first to yourself, then to those around you, to specific members of your family, your friends, and to people you see casually every day—the mail carrier, the clerk at the supermarket. Feel the loving kindness from your heart overflow the room you are in and spread out into your neighborhood, then the city where you live. It grows and swells until your loving kindness covers the state, country, continent, finally the entire globe. As you visualize the earth as a whole, bring it back into your heart where it becomes a lotus. Relax the mind, and rest in this state as long as possible.

273

When you spontaneously give your ice cream cone to a little boy who has just dropped his, when you drop a coin in an "expired" parking meter so a stranger's car won't get a ticket, or whenever you do anything spontaneously kind or generous, you have committed a "random act of kindness." Imagine what would happen if every day were filled with these acts, if there were a rash of such outbreaks worldwide . . .

"My religion is very simple—my religion is kindness."
—the Dalai Lama

Random Acts of Kindness

When I graduated from college I took a job at an insurance company in this huge downtown office building. On my first day, I was escorted to this tiny cubicle surrounded by what seemed like thousands of other tiny cubicles, and put to work doing some meaningless thing. It was so terribly depressing I almost broke down crying. At lunch—after literally punching out a time clock—all I could think about was how much I wanted to quit, but I couldn't because I desperately needed the money.

When I got back to my cubicle after lunch there was a beautiful bouquet of flowers sitting on my desk. For the whole first month I worked there flowers just kept arriving on my desk. I found out later that it had been a kind of spontaneous office project. A woman in the cubicle next to me brought in the first flowers to try to cheer me up, and then other people just began replenishing my vase. I ended up working there for two years, and many of my best, longest-lasting friendships grew out of that experience.

Editors of Conari Press
Random Acts of Kindness

○ Practice random acts of kindness whenever you can. You'll find you benefit as much or more than the recipient.

Compassion easily flows toward our family and circle of friends, but Teresa of Calcutta points out that this isn't enough: Community is a global matter.

Community

It is not enough for us to say: I love God, but I do not love my neighbor. Saint John says you are a liar if you say you love God and you don't love your neighbor. How can you love God whom you do not see, if you do not love your neighbor whom you see, whom you touch, with whom you live. And so this is very important for us to realize that love, to be true, has to hurt. It hurt Jesus to love us, it hurt him. And to make sure we remember his great love he made himself bread of life to satisfy our hunger for his love. Our hunger for God, because we have been created for that love. We have been created in his image. We have been created to love and be loved, and then he has become man to make it possible for us to love as he loved us. He makes himself the hungry one—the naked one—the homeless one—the sick one—the one in prison—the lonely one—the unwanted one—and he says: You did it to me. Hungry for our love, and this is the hunger of our poor people. This is the hunger that you and I must find, it may be in our own home.

Teresa of Calcutta
Nobel Prize Acceptance Speech, 1979

"Caring for other people is the very essence of Islam. Even a basic aspect of Islam, like prayers, should be curtailed if a human need has to be fulfilled. Prayers should not cut us off from people's needs; instead they should make us more sensitive."
—Kaukab Siddique

Today motherhood is seriously undervalued as an occupation, much less a spiritual path. Nonetheless, there are few things that challenge and stretch a woman quite as much as being a mother—a fact which is more fully appreciated in other cultures and in other times.

"On a spiritual path one may discover that the feminine principle embodied in motherhood is a stepping stone to our Christ-self, our Buddha-self, our divine self."
—Qahira Qalbi

Selflessness

Everything which endures can only do so because Eternal Consciousness gives it sentience.

A mother who gives herself completely to her infant meets herself in the dark and finds fulfillment.

In the hours between midnight and dawn, she crosses the threshold of self-concern and discovers a Self that has no limits. A wise mother meets this Presence with humility and steps through time into selflessness.

Infants know when their mothers have done this, and they become peaceful.

Who, then, is the doer? Is it the infant who brings its mother through the veil of self-concern into limitlessness? Is it the mother, who chooses to hold sacred her infant's needs and surrender herself? Or is it the One, which weaves them both through a spiraling path toward wholeness?

You can sit and meditate while your baby cries himself to sleep. Or you can go to him and share his tears, and find your Self.

Vimala McClure
The Tao of Motherhood

○ Think of the kindest person you have ever known. Remember

that person in detail, recalling each act of kindness shown to you and to others. What is this person's history? How did he or she become so kind? Engage in a dialogue with this person about kindness.

————————————

Fasting is a traditional way to purify the body and spirit; here it is dedicated to world peace.

"What is the necessity of giving up the world altogether. It is enough to give up the attachment to it."
—Ramakrishna

A Reflection on Fasting

In their pastoral, *The Challenge of Peace,* the U.S. Catholic bishops call the Christian community to fast for the cause of peace.

As a tangible sign of our need and desire to do penance, we, for the cause of peace, commit ourselves to fasting and abstinence on each Friday of the year. We call upon our people voluntarily to do penance on Friday by eating less food and by abstaining from meat. This return to a traditional practice of penance, once well observed in the U.S. church, should be accompanied by works of charity and service toward our neighbors. Each Friday should be a day significantly devoted to prayer, penance and almsgiving for peace.

The New Testament's answer to the question, "Why should we fast?" is "As a sign of your love." Fasting is not an end in itself. Love has to do with relationships, and fasting can lead us to a better understanding of our essential relationships with ourselves, with others, with the planet earth, and with God. Fasting and abstinence may well be a starting point for spiritual growth toward greater love among the well-fed congregations in this affluent society, protected by a bloated nuclear arsenal.

The New Testament does not guarantee a positive outcome for fasting. Fasting can get side-tracked into dieting. Fasting which will result in deepening love must begin in love and abide in it. Yet a loving decision to forego the joy of uncontrolled eating for a single day out of each seven can put us in touch immediately with our dependence on our own gratification for a sense of well-being. Our initial efforts to fast may reveal that we do indeed live "by bread alone." What then?

*"Emptiness is the fasting
of the mind."*
—Chuang Tzu

A time of fasting is a time of testing human readiness to wait on God. Do we trust that God lives, that God cares, that God loves and keeps the earth and all who live on it? Have we the humility to yield control to God? Fasting in faith can lead us more deeply into the mystery of God with us and in us, and so restore human hope grown weary, love grown cold.

The New Testament regularly associates fasting and prayer and almsgiving. So does the peace pastoral. Both prayer and almsgiving move the center of our fasting beyond our preoccupation with ourselves toward a center of love. If we dare to discover hunger symbolically through a day of fasting each week, a further decision to complement that fast with almsgiving will force us to look around for hungry people.

A day of fasting and involvement with the hungry can draw us further into understanding the complexity of our social reality. We might become more curious about the fat defense budgets and their relationship to unemployment, underemployment, inflation, empty stomachs. We might get more interested in the chain of world food production, which keeps our supermarkets and tables loaded while keeping the world's agricultural workers malnourished, feeding instead the workers' resentment of us and our way of life.

This simple discipline, practiced and continually reflected on, can be a sign of our deepening conversion to the mystery of a love powerful enough to redeem the world.

Mary Collins OSB
in *The Fire of Peace: A Prayer Book*

○ Try fasting for half a day. Then a day. Fasting helps to break our attachment to everything we cling to, not just food.

In Islam, fasting from sunup to sunset is required during Ramadan, roughly one month out of the year. It is recommended at other times to allow a person to detach from desires and rest in dhikr. *The basic principle of* dhikr, *which is remembrance or invocation of Allah, is to bring a person into a state where there are no thoughts, thereby becoming neutralized or cleansed.*

The Prophet on Fasting

The Prophet said, "For how many people does fasting bring nothing other than hunger and thirst?"

The Prophet once heard a woman neighbor cursing her servant. He sent her some food, and she sent back a message saying that she was fasting. He said, "How can you be fasting, and yet curse your servant? What is the use of your fast?" We cannot take just one portion of our path. We cannot take only the outer practices without the inner meaning. What is the inner meaning of fasting? The real meaning, the inner secret, is for one's heart to fast from anything other than Allah.

Shaykh Fadhlalla Haeri
Living Islam: East and West

"You are not a Muslim if there is one person in your neighborhood who goes to sleep hungry."
—Muhammed

Because women are so often the ones in charge of preparing food, it is only natural that reform concerning the rules and regulations that govern the kitchen should start with them.

Kashrut

The creation of new kinds of community is one vital component of a feminist Judaism. Within Jewish communities seeking to connect faith and politics, new content poured into traditional

"Firstly, if our transforming of Judaism is to be authentic, I believe we must start where Judaism is now, not from Biblical times . . . . Secondly, how do we define what is authentic Jewish practice? Is it what the rabbis say, or is it what the people do?"
—Alix Prani

Jewish ceremonies and forms often provides connections between visions of social and religious transformation and the basic rhythms of everyday life. The consonance of purpose between law and prophecy—to connect faith with the whole of reality—can be enacted in ritual and law attuned to the demands of justice. Thus, coming out of new Jewish communities, a number of Jewish feminists and other progressive Jews have called for a set of dietary laws (*kashrut*) that reflect the feminist value of connection to other persons and a wider web of life. *Kashrut* is already a system reminding us of the sanctity of animal life, and some have suggested that, for the sake of this sanctity as well as for the sake of preserving grain for the hungry, we extend this reminder to a full vegetarianism. *Kashrut* already tells us that "we are what we eat," and many values central to contemporary progressive food practices and to feminist concerns about sexuality and embodiment can be included in an expanded system of *kashrut*. Concern for protecting our bodies might take the form of prohibiting foods that are grown with pesticides or that contain carcinogens or hormones. Concern over the rise of hunger might be expressed in the form of a special blessing before or after meals and a commitment to set aside a proportion of the cost of all meals to feed the hungry. Concern about the exploitation of workers and planting of monocrops on lands needed for local agricultural production might lead to forbidding foods that are the product of exploitation and oppression. In these ways, *kashrut,* which has been a central dimension of Judaism as a system of separations and distinctions, can also be a vehicle for connecting Jews to others without losing its meaning as a marker of Jewish distinctiveness and identity. Such a new *kashrut* would turn the simple everyday act of eating into an aspect of the continuing quest for justice.

Judith Plaskow
Standing Again at Sinai

○ At mealtimes in Soto Zen monasteries, monks and laypeople chant: "Seventy-two labors brought us this food. We should know how it comes to us." The number seventy-two refers to the posts within the monastery, including those of abbot, administrators, cook, and so on. Simultaneously, the number represents all efforts that contribute to life inside and outside the monastery, past or present. This little chant expresses appreciation for benefits being received, and dedicates the merit generated by their use back out into the world.

Abbess Koei Hoshino practices shojin *cooking, a method of cooking vegetarian food developed by Zen monks and nuns to aid their spiritual practice. The word* shojin *is composed of the Chinese characters for "spirit" and "to prepare." The tradition includes not only the immediate preparation of food in a mindful way, but every aspect of the process from the cultivation of plants to placing the food on the table. Perhaps you can use this method as you prepare food to become more mindful in and out of the kitchen.*

Shojin Cooking

Every aspect of life is spiritual practice. In Zen we say, "always, everyday life." This means that everything in life is training. That's how I have lived my life. So I never think of cooking as something separate from spiritual life. . . .

In the beginning of the process, I think of those who will be given the food to eat. But then, as the process of preparing food takes over, there is *mu* (nothingness), as we say in Zen. I don't think of anything. The mind enters a state in which it is not caught up in anything. It is then that one is able to do one's best cooking. So, if you are thinking, "Let's prepare this well for others" or "Let's offer our affectionate heart in preparing this food" you will know your practice is still shallow. When you are doing your best, you get to the point where you are just doing your best, not thinking of it.

Abbess Koei Hoshino
from an interview with Theresa King
in *The Spiral Path*

"On special days [at the Monastery] I took the extra discipline offered to women—'one bowl-one meal-one sitting.' This literally meant that I was allowed one meal a day in one bowl, at one sitting. The object of this discipline was to bring greater awareness and sensibility to the act of eating. I felt thankful to all of those who participated in the growing, harvesting, preparing and serving of the food."
—Jacqueline Mandell

"When you prepare food, do not see with ordinary eyes and do not think with ordinary mind. Take up a blade of grass and construct a treasure king's land; enter into a particle of dust and turn the great dharma wheel. Do not arouse disdainful mind when you prepare a broth of wild grasses; do not arouse joyful mind when you prepare a fine cream soup."
—Dogen

❍ Cooking Exercise: The next time you cook, pay close attention to every single action that you perform in the kitchen. Don't think about what you have to do later in the day or what you did that morning. Think about the potato you are peeling, the carrot you are cutting in long, thin strips. Look at the color of the vegetable in your hand, examine its various features. Cut it open and appreciate its complexity and variety—the seeds or the pattern. Taste it, feel its texture. Think about where it came from, how it grew in the sun, how it was washed with the rain. Contemplate its harvest, its journey from the field to the store. Appreciate every item of food that you prepare. Be with the food; don't be somewhere else. Cut it carefully. Cook it mindfully. Pay attention.

❍ Dishwashing Exercise: As you wash dishes, keep your consciousness focused on your actions: your hand as it turns on the tap, as it pours out the soap. With a relaxed, open mind, be aware of yourself putting each plate into the water, wiping it clean, rinsing it, putting it on the rack to dry. This sounds easy to do, but is surprisingly difficult. The mind tends to "space out" after a few dishes and forget all about doing the exercise. When you remember, simply bring your consciousness right back to the task at hand. No need to tell yourself that your mind is like a flea the way it hops around or that you really should learn to concentrate. Just bring the mind back into focus. By doing this as daily practice, you can train the mind to concentrate—and also get a lot of dishes done.

Also see Bettina Vitell, *A Taste of Heaven and Earth: A Zen Approach to Cooking and Eating*, HarperCollins, 1993.

Macrobiotic cooking provides a deeply spiritual approach to food, stressing harmonious balancing of yin and yang as well as mindful attention to ingredients and their preparation. Vivian Eggers, who lives on Maui, began her studies at the Omega Institute in Rhinebeck, New York, and continued them at the Kushi Institute in Boston. She often cooks for religious retreats.

Harmony Through Macrobiotics

Kimberley Snow: What's the theory behind macrobiotic cooking?
Vivian Eggers: Basically, it's the understanding of the principle of yin and yang and its application to food and the condition of the body. Yin is basically expansive energy and yang is contractive energy, and there are many different words to describe the qualities of expansion and contraction: lightness and darkness, male and female. One of the most basic points for understanding this is through the seasons and the transformation of the seasons. Summer is hot, everything is lush and green, the birds are out singing every day. It's an expansive time. Then this changes and shifts and goes all the way around to its opposite in the winter when the leaves are gone, it's barren and cold, the land is frozen. We stay inside trying to keep warm and retain heat. Yin and yang are very real, very manifest in daily life. So when you start thinking in terms of yin and yang it's like being given new tools for seeing.

Within that energy system, there are many correlations with the body, each organ corresponds to each of the five elements--fire, earth, water, air, and metal. And each element has a particular energy. That's what one studies in acupuncture or shiatsu as well as macrobiotic cooking so that you understand the sensitivity of the organs to a particular time of year, to a particular time of day, to a particular color, to a particular emotion, to a particular food. In macrobiotic cooking, you study the whole body, not just how to cut up carrots.

K: You just spoke of metal energy. What is it?
V: We're sitting here now in a country setting where there's a lot of earth energy, but in the background, we hear a truck on the highway. That's metal energy. It moves very quickly; it cuts through air energy, through earth energy. Look at these scissors, they're made of energy, strong, solid, cutting. They're good example of metal energy.

K: What food has metal energy?
V: Brown rice, for instance. It's strong, and supports metal energy in the human body.

K: Let's take one day in the life of a macrobiotic cook. How would you approach cooking for a family?
V: First, an assessment of my own condition, by checking in with

"Macrobiotics does not require any change in your religion, way of thinking, or personal lifestyle. It requires only that you eat in harmony with your environment."
—Aveline Kushi

"In many ways, the kitchen is like a shrine or a temple where the cook, or creator, directs the health and happiness of the family and of society."
—Wendy Esko

"The foods that people eat become part of them, and creating a total balance in each meal can be a practical, positive step towards creating a balance in all aspects of life."
—Andrea Bliss Lerman

myself in the morning to see how I feel. What color is my skin? What's going on with my eyes? How's my tongue? Are my fingers or toes cold? All those little things. If there's a complaint—a headache, menstrual cramps—your body will let you know immediately. So this influences what I'm going to ingest throughout the day. If I'm cooking for children, then I go and be with them: Hello, how are you? How did you sleep last night? What's going on with your body?

K: You have to be conscious of not only what's being prepared and how it's presented, but also who is going to eat it and how it effects them on an internal level?

V: Absolutely. Initially, it sounds like a lot of work, but it's not. It's as easy as riding a bicycle. When you first teach a child how to ride a bicycle, you tell her that she needs to sit on the seat, to balance, to pedal, to hold onto the handle bars and steer, go at a certain speed, so on and so forth. But doing it is really easy. And of course, the more you do it, the more you learn. This is a study I've been involved with for maybe fourteen years now and every time I cook for a group of people or go through a process with my own health, I'm still learning. It's an expansion process, like being handed a flower that gradually unfolds over a period of years.

K: What all is involved?

V: In addition to nutrition, macrobiotics deals with the energetics of food, the energy of the cook and how important that is. Being aware that you're not putting anger in the food, and so forth. Plus the style of cutting and how that influences not only the taste of the dish, but its energy.

If you're cutting carrots, for instance, the way you cut creates a particular energetic quality. If I take the carrot and make big diagonal cuts by turning the carrot every inch, I end up with large triangular pieces, suitable for a stew. If I take the carrot and make quick short cuts on the diagonal, say an eighth of an inch, then turn these pieces over and cut them very finely, I end up with long fine match-stick shaped carrots. Now if I put them both into a large stew pot and cook them for an hour, the large pieces will be tender, the skin of the carrot will have lightly separated from it. However, the match-stick carrots will be completely exhausted. On the other hand, if I saute both of them in a skillet, the match-sticks will be done in a matter of minutes, where the others will be somewhat warmed and seared on the outside, but completely raw on the inside. So one of the fundamentals of macrobiotic cooking is knowing how to use a knife to chop vegetables so there is a uniform cut and consistency to them. Also, when you cut, you put your own *ki* [energy] into them as opposed to using a Cuisinart where you get a consistent cut, but no *ki* energy. If you want to give someone your *ki*, then the stronger food is the one you've cut by hand and put your energy into.

Food preparation becomes a form of meditation because of your focus and awareness and intention to sustain those you feed, not just to get the meal out of the way. When I'm cooking for retreats, it becomes part of my practice. I try to go into the kitchen and remain centered and aware, creating the most peaceful food that I can, even if it's for a hundred and fifty or more people.

K: So instead of planning the menu a week in advance, you have to be constantly mindful of what you need, of what your body needs, what other people need.

V: Absolutely. You develop that, and it's quite easy. It just comes. I couldn't go back to the other way of cooking. Now I always consider who am I cooking for and what is the intention. It has become second nature. When I cook I'm always in a place of joy and pleasure internally.

K: How do you know if food is yin or yang? Does it change depending on how it is prepared?

V: Yin and yang are relative to each other. In the Taoist symbol, one area is predominately black, with a little dot of white, and vice versa. This perfectly depicts yin and yang in that they're connected to each other and even though a particular thing may have a predominantly yang quality, it still has a little bit of yin. Certain substances are very yang—salt and beef, for instance. But when you want to get into a fine comparison, you have to look at one food in relation to another.

The recommendation in macrobiotics is a grain-based diet. The main food you eat are grains, for they are our most gentle, peaceful, nurturing food, the ones with the most to give to sustain and develop human life. Within grains, brown rice is the focal point, the centering food. The rest branches out and develops around it.

K: Was all this developed before the theories about eating low on the food chain?

V: Long before, but it meshes beautifully with it. A cow is a large animal with its own digestive system, with a heart of its own, a

"The relation between man and nature is like that between the embryo and its placenta. The placenta nourishes, supports and sustains the developing embryo. It would be quite bizarre if the embryo were to seek to destroy this protector organism."
—Muchio Kushi

"I take the position that every disease is produced by excess in diet. Bad nutrition is rather exceptional . . . . Chew each mouthful of food at least thirty times. By chewing each mouthful completely, you will automatically decrease excessive food intake because the stress on your jaws will prevent you from overindulging."
—George Ohsawa

circulatory system, a nervous system, and so on. Before you can ingest it, you have to take its life in one way or another, then take the meat from its body in a good clean way and prepare it in a certain way, otherwise it becomes poisonous. Look at the activity that's involved in all of that. Of course in this modern day and age, we just go to the supermarket and run the cart down the meat aisle and choose a shrink-wrapped package. It's not like it was several generations ago when people were involved in a personal way in taking the lives of the animal they would then eat. The modern meat industry has separated us from that process altogether. It's yet another way in which we are divorced from our bodies.

K: And perhaps from the sacred. Many native traditions honor the deer for giving its life so that the two-leggeds might eat. And from the way you talk about macrobiotic cooking, even vegetables seem filled with an almost animistic energy.

V: Absolutely. The mundane world becomes very precious. Macrobiotic cooking requires constant mindfulness. The meals that I would feed a troupe of exotic dancers from Armenia wouldn't be the same food that I would feed to a group of nuns on retreat. There would be adjustments of the food, of the preparation, and the cooking technique.

Take grain, for instance. Most people take their grain in the form of bread. Even in whole-grained bread, the grain is crushed, ground into flour. Then it usually sits around a very long time until it is baked. By the time you get it, the grain has gone through quite a process. Where's the *ki* energy in it? As opposed to going to the store and buying brown rice, cooking it in your pressure cooker, then eating it by crushing the grain in your own mouth.

Digestion begins in the mouth, so macrobiotics recommends that each mouthful be chewed twenty-five to fifty times to bring out the sweetness of the grain, also to really taste the grain. Many people completely miss the experience of truly tasting food. There is a textural change that occurs as well in long chewing so that digestion is much easier since the food liquifies. If you take time to just sit and eat slowly, you'll find that the food you are eating can be better utilized and that you'll eat less. You can eat smaller portions of food and be satisfied.

Macrobiotics is about having a rich, full, deep, healthy, independent life. Part of the reason for eating this way is to remove yourself from the dependency on drugstores and doctors or even holistic practitioners. In studying macrobiotics, you are removing yourself from all of this for you are studying your body and its relationship to this earth, to the elements. In choosing your foods with such awareness, many deep and profound changes occur within the body.

K: I think that most people's idea of macrobiotic food is that it is a very boring diet of brown rice.

V: Yes. Everywhere I travel people will say, "Oh, I did that macrobiotic diet." When I ask them what they ate, they say they cooked brown rice and miso soup. That's all I hear. Maybe they add aduki beans. That *is* pretty boring. But that isn't what macrobiotics is about and it's a great misunderstanding. Initially, Michio Kushi, who helped to popularize macrobiotics, promoted a basic macrobiotic diet consisting of a certain proportion of brown rice to beans to a sea vegetable to a root vegetable to a pickle accompanied by miso soup. That's what I call the training wheel diet. So this is a guideline. The foundation is brown rice and miso soup, but true macrobiotic cooking spins out from there very, very quickly. To prepare a macrobiotic meal is a real spontaneous dance.

K: How would someone learn to cook macrobiotically?

V: They could start by seeking out a macrobiotic cook or center. There are people all over the United States. Also books are an excellent starting place. They provide information, bring up questions. The basic recipe book, *Introducing Macrobiotic Cooking* by Wendy Esko, is a primer that is very easy to understand; it teaches all the dishes in a straightforward way.

K: When I worked as a chef, I'd find myself having long, nonverbal conversations with food. Do you talk to food? Does it talk to you?

V: Absolutely.

○ Macrobiotic advocates teach that eating in harmony with your environment creates a balance and peace in your life that can be extended to your family, community, and eventually the world. Keep this in mind the next time you sit down at a table for a meal.

○ Anyone who has ever been on a strict diet is familiar with the following eating meditation: Take a small handful of raisins or nuts. Eat them one at a time, paying strict attention to taste, smell, texture.

"All that I have said smacks of rigidity; this diet appears to be one of very stringent, restrictive discipline. Yet do not be seduced into fanaticism. And, above all, do not fall a victim to anxiety. Nothing is absolute save the laws of relativity and change. I cannot urge you enough to be flexible and unafraid, seek to know yourself and your needs."
—Michel Abehsera

Don't let your mind wander, but concentrate on each little morsel of food as it enters your mouth, as you chew and swallow, savoring the taste. Let the taste sensation completely disappear before you place another bite in your mouth. Compare this with the way you normally eat a handful of raisins or nuts. Try to eat an entire meal with this type of careful attention to what you are eating, chewing, swallowing.

"I believe in my body's own regenerative powers . . . . I can cooperate with nature's great forces to heal myself."
—Kristina Turner

To learn more about the macrobiotic communities contact The International Macrobiotic Directory, 1050 40th Street, Oakland, CA 94608. Michio and Avaline Kushi, who run the Kushi Institute in Boston, have a number of cookbooks out, including Michio Kushi's *Standard Macrobiotic Diet,* One Peaceful World, 1992, and *The Macrobiotic Way,* Avery Publishing Group, 1985; and, with the East West Foundation, *The Macrobiotic Approach to Cancer.* See also Aveline Kushi's *Complete Guide To Macrobiotic Cooking* (Warner Books, 1985), and *Introducing Macrobiotic Cooking* by Wendy Esko (Japan Publications, 1987). Aveline Kushi and Wendy Esko co-authored *The Changing Seasons Cookbook* (Avery Publishing Group, 1987), and *The Macrobiotic Cancer Prevention Cookbook.* Cornelia Aihara, who—with her husband Herman—runs the George Ohsawa Macrobiotic Foundation and Vega Study Center in Oroville, CA, is the author of *The Do of Cooking,* GOMF Press, 1971, and the *Chico-San Cookbook,* Chico-San, Inc., 1972. Herman Aihara authored *Basic Macrobiotics,* Japan Publications, 1985, which includes a summary of George Ohsawa's philosophy. Andrea Bliss Lerman's *The Macrobiotic Community Cookbook,* Avery Publishing Group, 1989, features recipes and short sketches of the chefs involved. Other fine books include *Cooking with Sea Vegetables,* Thorsons Publishing Group, 1987; Annemarie Colbin's *The Book of Whole Meals,* Ballantine Books, 1983; East West Journal's *Sweet and Natural Desserts,* East West Health Books, 1986; Mary Estella, *Natural Foods Cookbook,* Japan Publications, 1984, and *The Art of Just Cooking,* Autumn Press, 1974; Marcea Weber, *The Sweet Life: Natural Macrobiotic Desserts,* Japan Publications, 1981; and Kristin Turner, *The Self-Healing Cookbook,* Earthtone Press, 1987.

For a book from a completely different perspective about the kinds of energy that can be put in food, read *Like Water for Chocolate,* by Lauro Esquirel. Also be sure to see the wonderful film *Babette's Feast* which is based on an Isak Dinesen short story.

The next time you need a chef for a retreat, contact Vivian Eggers, RR2 Box 755J, Kula, HI 96790 (808) 878-3836.

Many people feel the presence of God or spirit more fully in a garden than anywhere else.

Gardening

This very evening, in the dusk, I was walking in my garden alone. The air was full of sweetness from great walls or cascades of the mock orange, from heavy peonies in full bloom, whose white or rose-colored petals weighed the plants almost to the ground, from valerian or garden heliotrope, white with flowers. Outside the wall of green made by tall spruces, I heard voices. One said: "Do look at those peonies—aren't they wonderful!" I called to the strangers, asking them to enter, to wander where they would. In they came, and we spent a few moments together enjoying the soft sight of many blooming flowers, the sweet scents in the dew, the rich greens of foliage and turf in the fading light; then I left them still exclaiming over the beauty of what they saw. But we had had together, these three unknown women and I, that satisfaction of the common beauty of the common things of the common life; and such moments leave one happier. They make for friendships through a common, fine interest, an interest in the things that grow, an interest than which there is no better for body, mind, or spirit. Each one has his own most real thing. Mine is the garden. And the best wish I can wish for anyone is that he may have a garden of his own, a little garden in which, through work and sweet imaginings, he may find a creative happiness unknown to those without this dear possession.

Louise Yeomans King
Chronicles of the Garden

"I think it pisses God off it you walk by the color purple in a field somewhere and don't notice it."
—Alice Walker

For more on women's connection with spirituality through nature, see Lorraine Anderson's *Sisters of the Earth*, Vintage, 1991, which contains an excellent bibliography of both prose and poetry. Also see Ellen Bernstein's *Let the Earth Teach You Torah: A Guide to Teaching Jewish Ecological Wisdom*, Shomrei Adamah, 1992, and Stephen Rockefeller and John Elder's *Spirit and Nature: Why the Environment is a Religious Issue*, Beacon, 1992.

In almost all traditions, a constant examination of one's mind and motivation provides an ongoing daily practice. Here are some practices on habits.

"Only a minute to minute relentless struggle can balance one's natural but stupefying insistence to remain unchanged."
—Taisha Abelar

Breaking the Hold of Bad Habits and Developing Good Ones

Our mind and body run by habit. Half of the time, we're not conscious of what we're doing, but go from one end of the day to the other with the help of our habits. Some habits—like hitting the same keys with the same fingers as we type—save us enormous amounts of time and energy. Other habits—like a tendency toward negativity—are just as automatic, but very destructive to ourselves and those around us.

In order to change our habits, we must first know what they are. We find out what they are by paying attention to how we think, how we react to the world around us. Once we begin to discern a habitual pattern that is confining us—the tendency to withdraw, for instance—we make a conscious effort to do the opposite—to respond instead of withdrawing. We can't, of course, change our habits overnight, but we can begin whittling them down little by little as we apply an antidote.

One way to try to break the hold of a bad habit is to go on a fast. Usually a fast is connected with eating, but there are other things that we can give up: habitual emotional responses such as anger, defensiveness, jealousy; verbal tendencies such as gossiping, speaking harshly to or critically of others; ingrained work patterns that can range from chronic procrastination to obsessive overachievement. (The list of bad habits can be very long.) Pick a habit that you feel is counterproductive and make a commitment not to indulge in that habit for a relatively short period of time, say, ten or twelve hours. Noting every time you "almost" break the fast is helpful.

(As in a food fast, I usually find that the first few hours are inspiring and relatively easy, with any discomfort offset by a glow of virtue. But as the day wears on, my vigilance and resolve wears thin and I want to drop back into a more automatic way of behaving, deciding that it's not much fun to try to modify my habits.)

Take a moment in the morning to develop the aspiration not to harm others throughout the day. At night, review your day, honestly admitting what you did to harm others, how you could have done better. Also review the things you did right during the day, things that make you glad. Develop morning and evening sessions as habits, then try to extend the mindfulness within these sessions throughout the entire day.

Irina Tweedie went to India in 1961 hoping to get some instruction in Yoga, some wonderful teachings. She found a Sufi Master, and, she says, what he "mainly did was force me to face the darkness within myself, and it almost killed me." By using violent reproof, her teacher kept her off balance until she had to come to terms with that within her which she had been rejecting all her life. The following appears very early in her book, which chronicles the process she underwent and her intricate relationship with her teacher.

"When someone beats a rug with a stick, he is not beating the rug—his aim is to get rid of the dust. Your inward is full of dust from the veil of I-ness and that dust will not leave all at once. With every cruelty and every blow, it departs little by little, from the heart's face, sometimes in sleep and sometimes in wakefulness."
—Rumi

A Sufi Teacher

6 October

Doubts kept creeping into my mind. Many doubts. Such ordinary surroundings. Such ordinary people around him. Is he a Great Man? There seems to be none of the glamour of a great guru about him as we are used to reading in books. He seems so simple, living a simple, ordinary life. Clearly, he takes his household duties seriously. I could see that he was the head of a large family—six children, and his brother and his family living also in the same house, all sharing the same courtyard. And I saw also other people there, a few other families. The place was full of comings and goings, all kinds of activities, not to count his disciples of whom there seemed to be many.

Decided to speak to L. [roommate] about it. She will soon be back. In the meantime, I resolved to stay away as much as possible. Went there after 6 P.M. He was writing letters seated cross-legged on his tachat. I tried to read a book I had brought with me. Soon he looked up and asked me if I felt uneasy, if I felt any pain. Told him that if my foot is not better, I will not come tomorrow. (I could hardly walk because of an infection.) He made some sympathetic noises. While speaking, I secretly hoped that he would cure it instantly. He looked at my foot; "It will come right by itself," he said as if aware of my thoughts. "Rest is useful," he added, and continued to write. Did not stay long and went home.

9 October

Pushpa's house is roomy and comfortable. Ceiling fans are in every room. With my infected foot as an excuse, I did not go to the guru last night. But I went this morning. He was talking nearly all the time about his guru, and how much money he spent on him. I wonder if he knows my thoughts about him and talks like this because of it. I have now every possible suspicion about him. Stayed for a very short while. I did not return in the afternoon as it was raining heavily. Will try to keep away from him until L.'s arrival. So much hope shattered. . . . Did I expect too much perhaps? It all seems so commonplace; and he hardly bothers to answer my questions.

"You will know one day."

Why and how? What prevents him from explaining? What an attitude!

A feeling of great loneliness. . . . Dark, endless longing. I do not know for what. Much disappointment and much bitterness. Who are you, Bhai Sahib? Are you what L. told me? A Great Teacher, a man of great spiritual power? Or are you just one of so many pseudo-gurus one meets here in India? Are you a Teacher at all? You seem to have many disciples. From what I have heard from L., you must be a Great Man. But are you?

10 October

It was raining in the morning. Went about 5 P.M. There were no visitors. Then a professor of mathematics arrived and sat with us. Later Bhai Sahib suggested that we might like to go to a learned discussion which was being held in the park. I refused. I wanted to be punctual at the *Kirtan* [singing of devotion hymns in praise of the Deity] which was being held at Pushpa's place at 7 P.M.

"A Guru is like a fire. If you are too far away, you don't feel the warmth, if you are too close, you get burned."
—Tibetan Proverb

"Don't expect plaudits."
—Atisha

Left with the professor of mathematics, who was also going to the Kirtan. Walking along he asked me what this discussion at the park was supposed to be about. I said it concerned the Avatar [divine incarnation] of Ram, one theory being that he was the only real incarnation of Vishnu [the Second Person of the Hindu Trinity: the Preserver].

Then I began to tell him about my doubts. "Is there any purpose in going to Bhai Sahib at all? Is it not a waste of time?" He listened with great seriousness.

"If you are convinced that your guru is always right, that he is the only Great Man, then you will progress. Your guru may not be great at all, but you think that he is, and it is your faith which will make you progress. It is the same with Ram; what does it matter if he is the only incarnation of God or not? For the man who believes it, he is. So why discuss? I refuse to participate in intellectual acrobatics."

I agreed with him. "What disturbs me most with Bhai Sahib," I went on, "is the fact that he does not answer questions. Every time I want to know something, he will say, `You will know it one day yourself.' Now who can tell me if I will really know? Maybe I never will; so why not simply answer it? I want to know NOW, not sometime in a hypothetical future! I begin to wonder if I am wasting my time!"

"You know," he said, "just to give an example: a son of a rich man inherits the wealth of his father and then he will have more than you or me. Now, here it is the same in this place. This man has a certain power which will reveal in time something very wonderful within yourself. It happened to others, it happened to me. I have been here for the last twelve years, I speak from experience. I don't know how it happened: I have no explanation for it. I don't know how one can inherit such a thing, but it is a fact. Stay here for a month and you will be in the same state L. is in, and we all are, and then you will think differently. L., when she came years ago, spoke as you do now." I said I was sure it would take longer than one month.

"Of course, it takes years," he agreed, "but after one month you will be able to form a judgement."

I told him I had decided at any rate to stay here until March, and he answered that it would be wise to do so.

"If a pickpocket meets a Holy Man, he will see only his pockets."
—Hari Dass Baba

*"The first step is to under-
stand your own
consciousness."*
—Dhyani Ywahoo

"I have seen strange and wonderful things happen to human beings here. Dhyana is definitely NOT a mediumistic trance; it is a Yogic state; it has nothing to do with mesmerism either."

We were entering Pushpa's gate. The veranda was brightly lit; many people were already there. "Dhyana is complete abstraction of the senses." He repeated, "A Yogic state."

As we entered the music started. I was in deep thought. So, that was it. Somehow I felt that this conversation represented a turning point. An intelligent man with a balanced mind, normal and reasonable, gave me his opinion. I liked and trusted him from the first moment I saw him, a few days ago. In my heart I felt I should give it a try, accept the situation as it presents itself and see what will happen. . . . Why not?

Lights were burning in front of the pictures of Rama, Shiva and Parvati [Hindu deities]. The room was crowded, everyone seated on the floor, their faces full of devotion; my heart kept rhythm with the ancient melody. . . . "Hari Rama, Hari, Hari . . . ," and I was thinking and thinking.

And I was still thinking deeply when in my room, hardly aware of howling dogs roaming the streets and the evening noises of a busy Indian street. "Is dhyana just sleep?" I asked.

"If you think that it may be sleep, then it is sleep. If you think it is not, then it is not." His face had been stern, but with a faint suspicion of a twinkle in his eye, a hidden laughter.

12 October

I feel well and my foot has healed completely.

Arrived about 5 P.M. Nobody was in the room. Sat down in my usual place in the chair opposite his tachat. His wife came in, searching for something in recess amongst the books. Then he entered. I do not remember how we started to talk about dhyana, but probably I began because it kept worrying me. As soon as I had stepped into his room, the thinking process had slowed down and I felt sleepy; I told him so and he translated it to his wife. She said that I was not the only one; it happened to her too.

"I never sleep during the day," he remarked.

"How can you stay awake in this place?" I wondered; "I feel sleepy as soon as I sit down!" He laughed. Then he began to tell me that in 1956 he was very ill, desperately ill, and many people came who could be of some help, in one way or another. But they all sat there fast asleep, and his wife used to ask: "What have they all come for—just to sleep?"

"So dhyana does mean to be asleep after all? Are dhyana and sleep the same thing?"

"No they are not. They could be similar at the beginning. But if you remain too long unconscious, without being conscious some-where else, then you are not normal, then something is wrong with you."

"Do you mean to say that one becomes conscious somewhere else when unconscious on the physical plane? You may remember that I asked you several times about it but you never answered!"

"Of course!" He laughed merrily. "It comes gradually, little by little. It takes time. But before you can do it you must forget everything. Leave everything behind."

It seemed to be a frightening thought. He laughed again softly and gave me a look of kindly amusement. "How do you swim?" he began after a silence. "You throw water behind and behind you; that's how you propel yourself. Spiritual life is the same; you keep throwing everything behind, as you go on. This is the only way; there is no other."

"Is there not a danger of becoming stupid by forgetting every-thing?" I wondered.

"Why?" he retorted; "If you have ten rupees in your bag and you get ten thousand, you will forget the ten rupees will you not? The ten rupees are still there aren't they? But you don't think of them anymore." I could see what he meant and also that he was right.

Later I mentioned a discussion I had with L. about spiritual life. She was of the opinion that I could not go on further by myself alone, or progress more than I had already done; that a guru was absolutely necessary.

"A guru is a short-cut, a short-cut and a sharp one. But not a guru; a friend, a Spiritual Guide. I have nothing to teach."

"What do you mean by a system?" He often used the expression in conversation. I was not quite sure if I understood its meaning.

"A system is a school of Yoga, or a path to Self Realization; the meaning is the same. We are all called Saints but it is the same as Yogis; in Wisdom there is no difference. The colour of our line is golden yellow, and we are called the Golden Sufis or the Silent Sufis,

"Guru, God, and Self are One."
—Ramana Maharshi

"Who realizes what? That is realization."
—Hari Dass Baba

because we practice silent meditation. We do not use music or dancing or any definite practice. We do not belong to any country or any civilization, but we work according to the needs of the people of the time. We belong to Raja Yoga, but not in the sense that it is practiced by the Vedantins. Raja means simply 'Kingly,' or 'Royal'— the direct road to absolute truth."

"And why is it that one cannot go on by oneself any further and one needs a guru?"

"Because by yourself alone you can never go beyond the level of the mind. How can you vacate?"

"You mean to empty the mind, to clear it of any thought?" I asked, not being sure what he meant by "vacate."

"Yes, how can you vacate, clear out your mind, if you are constantly working through the mind? How can the mind empty itself of itself? You must be able to leave it, to forget everything and this one cannot do alone. For the mind cannot transcend itself."

"Will I ever be able to do it, as I am afraid of this idea," I said, doubtfully. He laughed again looking at me sideways.

"If you are ill, who does the work? Others, of course! If you are unconscious, be sure there will be many people to look after you!" I said that it may be true in theory; but if, for instance in deep *samadhi* [a superconscious state, a merging into Universal Consciousness], I could easily be robbed.

"No," he retorted; "then you are not in samadhi. If you are in samadhi, you go to your Creator, and the Creator will look after you. And even if you are robbed, it is not because you were in samadhi, but because it was your destiny to be robbed, and it is of no importance to you once you have reached this state of consciousness. When we travel together, you will see that I take nothing with me, I am not afraid."

"But if you travel and have no money, somebody has to travel with you and keep the money and be careful that it is not lost; otherwise both of you will be in trouble," I insisted.

"Yes, that could be true; but not necessarily so. Perhaps I could travel free, or the money will be forthcoming; God works through many channels. At any rate, I affirmed that to him who is in samadhi nothing happens, and if it does, he does not care." He fell silent. After a while he said thoughtfully: "You have your knowledge. You will forget it all. You MUST forget it before you can take any further step."

I wondered if this is what the scriptures mean; one should forget all books and leave all acquired knowledge behind; only then can one make the big leap into the Unknown beyond the mind? He agreed.

"There are only very few people in the world nowadays who can teach you the Sufi method. The Sufi method represents complete freedom. You are never forced. To put somebody in dhyana can be done, but it would only show that my will is stronger than yours. In this case it would be mesmerism; there is nothing spiritual about that; and it would be wrong. When the human being is attracted to the Spiritual Guide and wants to become a *shishya* [disciple], there are two ways open to him: the path of the dhyana, the slow but the easier way; or the path of *tyaga* [complete renunciation, the Road of Fire, the burning away of all dross]. And it is the Guide who has to decide which way is the best suited in each individual case. The path of dhyana is for the many, the path of tyaga is for the few. How many would want to sacrifice everything for the sake of Truth? The shishya has every right to test the Guide, (here he laughed his young and merry laugh) then the Guide can take over and the disciple has no free will for a while."

He contradicts himself, I thought, but said nothing. Then he began to speak about his guru, the Great Sufi.

"He is always with me," he said.

"Do you mean that you see him?" I asked.

He had a tender, far-away look. "If I say that I see him with these physical eyes, I would be lying; if I say that I don't see him I also would be lying," he said after a brief silence. I knew what he meant: he could reach him in his higher states of consciousness.

Well perhaps it is a good thing after all, that I came here. And I was thankful for the opportunity of this conversation.

> Irina Tweedie
> *The Chasm of Fire: A Woman's Experience of Liberation Through the Teachings of a Sufi Master*

"The Grace of the Guru is like an ocean. If one comes with a cup he will only get a cupful. It is no use complaining of the niggardliness of the ocean. The bigger the vessel the more one will be able to carry."
—Ramana Maharshi

The Sufi Review is by far the best resource for Islamic mysticism and the Sufi Path of Love, offering reviews, articles, and book listings. *The Sufi Review* is published by Pir Publications, Inc., Colonial Green, 256 Post Road East, Westport, CT 06880, (203) 221-7595. Also available from Pir: *The Sufi Book Club.*

———————————

Vedanta, based on the Ramakrishna movement within Hinduism, sponsors a number of convents in the West. In these convents all four of the yogas are blended together in the daily life of the nuns: Karma Yoga through selfless action and social service; Jnana Yoga through lectures, classes, and study of the scriptures; Bhakti Yoga through ritual worship, singing, and other devotional practices; and Raja Yoga through daily meditation.

Vedanta Convents

One of the special features of the Ramakrishna Movement is the unique place which women occupy within it. Sri Ramakrishna accepted a woman, the Bhairavi Brahmani, as one of his Gurus, worshipped God in the form of a woman, Kali, the Divine Mother, and looked upon his own wife and mother as visible manifestations of the Divine Mother, even worshipping his wife, Holy Mother, in the form of the Goddess, Shodasi. After the passing away of Sri Ramakrishna, Holy Mother was looked upon by Sri Ramakrishna's devotees and monastic disciples as the spiritual guide and inspiration for the Movement, and she herself gave initiation to many sincere seekers of God. Thus a great feeling of reverence for women as special manifestations of the Divine has existed in the Ramakrishna tradition from its very beginning. . . .

The monastics in any religion or in any country are the true rebels of society. They have renounced what society holds most dear—marriage, family and career—to devote themselves wholeheartedly to the pursuit of the ultimate goal in life. In America this rebellion is even more pronounced since, unlike countries with a rich spiritual heritage, there is very little understanding of monasticism or renunciation in America. Another concept foreign to the average

American is the relinquishing of one's personal freedom to live in a highly disciplined religious community. Americans are fiercely independent. They prize their freedom above all else—the liberty to do what you want, when you want. Those who accept the discipline of monastic life aspire after the highest Freedom—Spiritual Realization.

The unifying thread that runs through all the convents is community life. In a convent, the community is the nun's biggest protection. The company of other nuns continually reminds her of her vocation. She knows that as long as she is sincere in her spiritual life, she will always have the support of the group. If she falters or begins to veer off the track, her sisters will steer her to the right path. This mutual love and respect is much cherished by community members.

This does not means, however, that community life is always a pleasant experience. Many nuns consider group living their greatest austerity. The friction created by a group of women living together from different backgrounds and with different outlooks and personalities can be very difficult to live with on a day-to-day basis. But it is in and through community life that monastics grow spiritually. The group acts like a mirror, reflecting back your weak points and strong points so you can look at yourself objectively and correct the weaknesses and reinforce the strengths.

Successful living in a community requires adjusting your needs to the needs of others. You cannot be completely selfish and live in a group. There has to be a certain amount of individual sacrifice for the group to remain cohesive, and this entails the curtailing of individual freedom. Aside from selflessness, community life is a fertile ground for the cultivation of other sterling qualities such as patience, tolerance, compassion, acceptance, and contentment.

But above all, living in a monastic community provides the rare opportunity to practice the lofty ideals of Vedanta without the distractions of the world—to practice meditation and concentration, continence and truthfulness, to intensify faith in and love of God, to practice discrimination between the real and the unreal, to practice seeing God in everyone and feeling His living presence. . . .

When American nuns are asked, "What is your goal in life?" the most common answer is "to realize God." When asked for further clarification, however, a wide variety of answers come forth. It is the

"An inner effort must always be undertaken in a deep state of surrender, in order to create a space within the person to receive the flow of higher energy. While the nature of surrender is essentially open and passive, the process of energy absorption is active."
—Swami Rudrananda

"Let us recall that the 'nature of things' is for us the best, the most affectionate, and the most humiliating of masters; it surrounds us with vigilant assistance. The only task incumbent upon us is to understand reality and to let ourselves be transformed by it."
—Hubert Benoit

beauty of Vedanta that the same Reality can be approached in so many different ways according to the nature of the individual. Some define God in monistic terms, and likewise their goal is to experience the eternal oneness and to see the divinity in everything. Others prefer the dualistic approach to God and, as such, their goal is to see their Chosen Ideal and feel His presence always. Some seek to acquire certain characteristics such as selflessness, desirelessness and fearlessness. Others prefer social service, serving God in man.

A further reason for Vedanta's special appeal to women monastics has to do with its teachings regarding the oneness of all existence and the impersonal, or sexless, nature of the Self. Swami Vivekananda gave much emphasis to this teaching and went to great pains to see it translated into action in the social realm. This meant, for him, an end to all privilege and tyranny, whether of the rich over the poor, the priestly class over the lower classes, or men over women. Regarding the latter he wrote, "I shall not rest till I root out this distinction of sex. Is there any sex-distinction in the Atman? Out with the differentiation between man and woman—all is Atman!" And despite prejudices at that time against women pursuing higher education and embracing monastic life, Swamiji encouraged his women-disciples, both in India and abroad, to take to a life of renunciation and study. He was convinced that renunciation was necessary for women, just as it was for men, both for their own sake and for the sake of the world.

Swami Swahananda
The Vedanta Kesari

Also see Swami Ghanananda's *Women Saints East and West,* Vedanta, 1955.

Mary Baker Eddy, founder of the Christian Science Church, restored the concept of healing to the Christian tradition. As we see here, healing is a form of worship.

Christian Science Healing

The purpose of spiritual healing is never simply to produce physical ease. It is rather to put off a limited, physical concept of man which binds thought to matter, and thus bring to light Paul's "new" man. This is the man whom Christian Scientists understand to be the "real" man, created by God in His own image, spiritual and whole.

Here is the reason Christian Scientists do not turn to a doctor if they are not quickly healed through their own or a practitioner's prayers. Bodily conditions they view as effect rather than cause—the outward expression of conscious and unconscious thoughts. On this premise what needs to be healed is always a false concept of being, not a material condition. The purpose of turning to God for healing is therefore not merely to change the evidence before the physical senses but to heal the deeper alienation of human thought from God. . . .

Christian Science healing is in fact one way of worshipping God. It is an integral part of a deeply felt and closely reasoned view of ultimate reality. This very fact sometimes causes its use of the words "real" and "unreal" to be misunderstood. For when Christian Scientists speak of sickness as unreal, they do not mean that humanly it is to be ignored. They mean rather that it is no part of man's true, essential being but comes from a mortal misconception of being, without validity, necessity, or legitimacy. Like a mathematical error which has no substance and no principle to support it, sickness is not to be ignored but to be conscientiously wiped out by a correct understanding of the divine Principle of being. This is the metaphysical basis of Christian Science practice.

Editors
A Century of Christian Science Healing

"To the Christian Science healer, sickness is a dream from which the patient needs to be awakened."
—Mary Baker Eddy

For an excellent treatment on the mind/body connection, see "New Dimensions in Healing" in *As Above, So Below: Paths to Spiritual Renewal in Daily Life,* edited by Ronald S. Miller and the editors of the *New Age Journal,* Jeremy P. Tarcher, Inc. 1992. This volume, like their earlier *Chop Wood, Carry Water,* covers a wide range of spiritual topics in a comprehensive yet readable form, and includes bibliographies, workshops, and other resources.

Also of interest: Jeanne Achterberg, *Imagery in Healing: Shamanism and Modern Medicine,* Shambhala, 1985; Richard Carlson and Benjamin Shield, *Healers on Healing,* Jeremy P. Tarcher, 1989; Dora Lunz, ed., *Spiritual Aspects of the Healing Arts,* Theosophical Publishing House, 1985; Diane Stein, *All Women are Healers: A Comprehensive Guide to Natural Healing,* Crossing, 1990.

> *"Only when one is connected to one's own core is one connected to others. And, for me, the core, the inner spring, can best be refound through solitude."*
> —Anne Morrow Lindberg

Retreat centers often feature hot springs or other means of purifying the body. Here, Susanne Fairclough, an editor and freelance writer who lives in Massachusetts, describes her experience in a sweat lodge, a traditional Native American method of cleansing the body and spirit.

Sweat Lodge

Our group of twenty-five men and women is packed tightly in the sweat lodge. We can barely sit cross-legged on the cold earthen floor inside this Tunkan tipi, or birth age house. Heated stones are placed in a hole in the center of the ten-foot-diameter dome of the lodge. My back leans against the frame of the three-foot-high sapling structure, which is covered by thick layers of cloth.

Wallace Black Elk, a Lakota Indian, is leading this purification lodge, or Stone People lodge, as he prefers to call it—one of seven Lakota rituals. Our purpose is to open up communication with Grandmother Earth who is in touch with all the spirits of the universe.

Above our heads along the wooden framework, each of us places our string of prayer ties, bundles of tobacco—a suitable offering to the spirits—wrapped in multicolored squares of cloth, which we have made earlier in the day. For each bundle I tied, I made a prayer. Wallace tells us to pray from the heart. He points to his head and says, "There's too much traffic up here." Hence the confusion that results. Even our English language is full of doubt, he says: *maybes, I assumes,* and *ifs.* Pray with certainty, saying, "Give me health," or if confused, say, "Give me wisdom to know what is right to do."

Through the doorway, Wallace calls out to the "firemen," who are chosen to tend the fire which heats the stones outside the lodge. "Bring in seven stones." A glowing stone is removed from the fire with a shovel; the coals are knocked away and sparks brushed free with a pine bough. Thus cleansed, each head-sized stone is brought through the doorway and placed in the pit in the center of the lodge. Cedar is sprinkled on each stone; its fragrance soothes the tightness in my chest. Wallace calls out for nine more stones, and I wonder if I can stand the heat, the claustrophobia. As the rocks are placed in front of us, the tension builds.

The intensity of the sweat lodge soon pushes me beyond the secure vantage point of an "interesting experience." Wallace tells us the lodge helps develop patience, courage, endurance, and under-standing--qualities we need to become real Earth people, to become true humans.

The door flap is closed. Even on a moonless night, I've never seen so thick a blackness. Deprived of my sight, my other senses come alive. I notice the prickling heat against my skin. The rise and fall of my chest, breathing. Wallace takes a dipper of spring water from a bucket and pours in on top of the stones. They sizzle, and the steam sears my nostrils and lungs.

Wallace speaks with the Stone People, explaining our purpose, and relays to us what they have to say—they say our energy is positive, seeking good. Wallace's nephew, Bernard Ice, beats a drum and the lodge reverberates as though we are sitting inside a universal drum. He chants in the ancient language which is said to have been common to all men and animals a long time ago. The sounds easily flow from my throat and I join with others in the chant, praying to know what is helpful and true. Together our song seems powerful and hopeful.

In blackness like that at the beginning of time, my greatest fears are conjured: isolation, annihilation, death. Sparks of light flash in the dark. The Stone People are said to speak in such a manner. I envision myself sitting under a vast desert sky, starlit. With me are

"Our own life is the instrument with which we experiment with truth."
—Thich Nhat Hanh

303

all my relations. A radiant dancing fire warms us. A drum resounds like the heartbeat of the earth.

Our chant together seems a thread in timeless space, weaving a robe of life to wear. Harmonic sound grows and subsides in waves. I feel connected to the Earth and all the life upon it. In this place that I envision to be between death and rebirth, I feel that we uphold one another with our prayers. We protect one another with robes of kindness. Eyeless, in the darkness of the Stone People lodge, I journey beneath the surface of things, and experience the center of the circle where everything connects.

The door flap is opened and closed four times during the ceremony. "We tell our little problems, so we contaminate the air. Then when we open the door, all that contamination goes out, and new pure air comes in," Wallace explains to William S. Lyon in *The Sacred Ways of a Lakota*. When the door is closed for the last time, Wallace prays for the sick and the suffering, for people who have committed suicide and for the homeless.

When I emerge after an hour and half in the lodge, I feel calm, energized rather than drained from the heat. All my sense are alive. The wet grass is cold on my bare feet. A chain of tiny white lights along the path to the farmhouse guides me like a boat into the harbor. I share my experience with others. Each person tells a different story.

Joseph, who works caring for the elderly, had found what he had come for, a way to "open his heart." Sister Marghoretta, a Benedictine nun who teaches second-grade children, came from her convent in Pennsylvania to heal a wound. She entered the sweat lodge clothed in her black nun's habit and sat next to Wallace. When he passed the gourd to her she said: "I am here because I and others of the church wish to repair the harm that was done to your people who were prohibited from practicing your beliefs; and to repair the harm done to ourselves because we did not stand by your side at the beginning and learn from you." From within the darkness of the lodge, feathers brushed her hand. She felt her prayer was heard.

We all stand in a circle around the fire, Wallace lights the pipe and gives it first to a woman, he says, because the pipe belongs to a woman, the Earth. Each person draws in on the thick, sweet mixture of smoke, linking us together. A fireman carries the bucket of spring water around, and we each drink a dipperful.

"Through life it's important that we all make our circle within the mind, and that we stay within that circle, because that's our sacred space."
—Twylah Nitsch

The next morning after breakfast, Wallace thanks us for coming and teaching him. He asks, "How does one say thank you?" In his Lakota way he circles through several stories to teach us how. Perhaps we will feel regret once it is too late and we have destroyed our planet, Wallace warns. He repeats the question, "How do you say thank you?" as though this is a very important key which we have forgotten. He tells us: To appreciate our world we need to learn about it; we need to say thank you to the Fire, Earth, Water, and Green (living things) that sustain our lives.

Again we make a circle, this time to say goodbye to one another. Each person goes round the circle shaking hands until we all have said hello for the first time, or goodbye, or thank you. In Lakota, the circle is important, exemplified in the teepee—each person is at the center of the universe connecting with everything else.

I feel refreshed. Each moment seems precious, rich, and vivid—the yellow maples along the roadside and the stand of white birches at a river's edge, the rich scent of late October sunshine on strewn leaves, conversations with fellow travelers in the sunny kitchen smelling of gingery muffins. All thoughts and troubles subside temporarily into the simple beauty of what is happening, now. As I drive home, a silvery moon drifts above the bronze-gold mountains, the day almost finished, and I feel as though I've been awakened again to the world.

> Susanne Fairclough
> "All My Relations: A Spiritual Retreat"
> *Natural Health*, March/April 1992

"Your religion was written on tablets of stone by the iron finger of an angry God, so you would not forget it. The red man could never understand it or remember it. Our religion is the ways of the forefathers, the dreams of our old men, sent them by the Great Spirit, and the visions of our sachems. And it is written in the hearts of our people."
—Chief Seattle

To find a retreat center, consult the following:

Patricia Christian-Meyer, *Catholic America: Self-Renewal Centers, and Retreats*, John Muir Publications, 1989.

David A Cooper, *Silence, Simplicity, and Solitude*, Bell Tower, 1992.

Jack and Marcia Kelly, *Sanctuaries: A Guide to Lodging in Monasteries, Abbeys, and Retreats of the United States*, Bell Tower, 1991.

Donald E. Morreale, *Buddhist America: Centers, Retreats, Practices*, John Muir Publications, 1988.

Martine Rudee and Jonathan Blease, *Traveler's Guide to Healing Centers and Retreats in North America*, John Muir Publications, 1989 (lists more than three hundred nonsectarian centers).

Refuges known as Peace Villages were scattered throughout the southern United States until the 1800s. The Tsalagi (Cherokee) people used these villages as sanctuaries where, through diet and meditation, the inhabitants radiated peace of mind. No blood was shed, nor was harm done within their boundaries. Each Peace Village was guided by the Peace Chief, who remained committed to protecting life and transforming consciousness.

"In the West we have a deep conviction that any problem can be solved. For many aspects of our life this is true. However, the fundamental problem of our existence can never be worked out by ourselves because we are the problem."
—John H. Mann

Peacekeeping

The Peacekeeper holds the vision of peace for all beings in all worlds, as beauteous expression of harmony and balance resonating through thought, word, and deed.

The Peacekeeper sees all in good relationship, perceiving the underlying unity of creation.

The Peacekeeper knows that each being is empowered by will to choose, wisdom to see, and intelligence to act, all being together weaving the dream of our shared reality.

Recognizing that patterns of mind manifest as one's individual, family, clan, national, and planetary relationships, the Peacekeeper turns aside anger, doubt, and fear, harmonizing conflicting emotions through complementary resolution.

The Peacekeeper acts with consideration for future generations, with the mind of preserving life and that which enriches living . . . .

Peacekeeper mind is an integration of light and dark within oneself. It is to choose to empower oneself, to be what one is rather than reacting in the patterns of the past or to the expectations of others. It is to recognize ourselves in the moment. As a nation, as a planet, we are growing. Many of the ideas that have been important in our development and learning as a human race have been outer explorations: scientific means, inventions, methods of healing. Now we are coming again to the inner exploration. We are seeing the whole cycle, the cycle of things. In this cycle it is our thought that is most significant. Even the plants and the land show us that. When people take the time to create a space of love in their homes, a place and time for prayer and meditation, a vortex of energy is created that actually strengthens the electromagnetic fields of their bodies and the land where they live. This lesson was clearly demonstrated at Findhorn, the spiritual community in Scotland renowned for its magnificent, almost "miraculous" gardens. The power of attunement to the land and to the flow of abundance in one's own mind can manifest miracles of abundance on Earth. So a stream of clear thinking is most important. We are co-creators.

Being present in the moment means acknowledging whatever energy is being experienced and bringing it to resolution, by calling forth balance. When there is anger or frustration in you or around you, instead of focusing on the anger, focus on the seed of compassion, focus on love and resolution. The thought form of resolution in itself sets up a resonant field that enables the mind to perceive methods of resolution.

Dhyani Ywahoo
Voices of our Ancestors

"The final and most important basepoint for a feminist moral theology is the centrality of relationship."
—Beverly Wildung Harrison

O Make yourself a modern-day peacekeeper. As Dhyani Ywahoo suggests, focus on the seeds of compassion, love, and resolution when there is anger around you. Breathing in another person's anger and breathing out love is a challenging place to start.

———————————————

Contemplating impermanence helps you to realize that the true nature of reality is change. Since everything is passing, fleeting, moving, why get so upset over every little thing?

Contemplating Impermanence

Set up a signal to yourself—every time you open the car door, for instance—as a time to contemplate impermanence. Remember that you won't be here for long, that everything that comes together falls apart, that meeting implies parting, that with birth comes death. Every time you open that door, *feel* the truth of impermanence. This helps to loosen not only self-clinging, but the importance we place on every tiny situation during the day.

"How do geese know when to fly to the sun? Who tells them the seasons? How do we, humans, know when it is time to move on? As with the migrant birds, so surely with us, there is a voice within, if only we would listen to it, that tells us so certainly when to go forth into the unknown."
—Elisabeth Kubler-Ross

Often women's expression of spirituality involves taking care of the sick and the dying. Their experiences are not limited to a deathbed scene, but can involve the long, slow business of illness and decline that precedes death. Here, a woman writes of her mother's final sickness. The author, a Mormon and naturalist, weaves together the story of a bird refuge endangered by the rising levels of Great Salt Lake with that of her relatively young mother's illness and death. Her mother, who had been exposed to nuclear fallout from atomic testing in Utah in the 1950s, was one of five women in the immediate family to die from cancer.

Helping Mother to Die

"I don't want everyone hovering over me as though I have a day or two to live. Besides, this is terribly boring."

"I'm not sure I would use the word, *boring.* . . ."

"Illness is boring," she said. "Take my word."

"You seem to have a different attitude, Mother. Is that true?"

"It feels good to finally be able to embrace my cancer. It's almost like a friend," she said. "For the first time, I feel like moving with it and not resisting what is ahead. Before, I always knew I had more time, that the disease was outside of myself. This time, I don't feel that way. The cancer is very much a part of me.

"Terry, I need you to help me through my death."

I laid my head on her lap and closed my eyes. I could not tell if it was my mother's fingers combing through my hair or the wind . . . .

Walking into her room, I could see death was imminent, and I was surprised to see the physical changes from the night before. Her color had changed—especially around the mouth and nose. Her face was waxen. Her feet were cold. It was as though dying moves from your toes upward.

Mother's breathing was regular, but strained as she exhaled. So much going out. So little coming in. I knelt at the foot of her bed with the soles of her feet pressed against my forehead. It was the only place I could feel her pulse. I rubbed her legs under the mohair blanket. They were like ice. Dad paced the room, occasionally sitting next to her to hold her hand. We took turns.

From one until four in the afternoon, we sat near her. A meditation. Her breaths could now be heard as moans. Her eyes were haunting, open, and clear. Time was suspended like watching a fire. Gradually, Mother's breaths became a mantra and the death mask we feared was removed.

Dad spoke of what it had meant to him to "take care of our own." In these hours, we began to realize the magnitude of these past weeks, months, years. Talk of everyday life crept in, basketball scores, the day's news, even laughter, and there, Mother lay dying. I never doubted her presence.

The light in the room deepened. It occurred to me that Mother would wait until after sunset. And it was an exquisite one. An apricot aura radiated above the purple Oquirrh Range. I told Mother what a beautiful sunset it was—I recalled her applause [at a similar sunset].

We turned a small lamp on. Mother's color looked better and, for a moment, we believed she would never die. The belabored breathing continued. We took turns holding her hands. Rubbing her forehead. Moistening her mouth. And we could feel the cold moving up her body. Her head was turned now, and with each breath her head drew back, reminding me of the swallow I beheld at Bear River, moments before it died.

Dad began to get nervous. He worried that Mother could go on for a few more days, that we had kept vigil too many times. He smiled with an anxious grin, saying, "Diane, you may outlast me yet . . . ."

He wanted to be there when she died, and yet he didn't. He was afraid he would not be able to survive it. After a few minutes of wavering, Dad decided to pick up his car downtown. Brooke said he would drive him.

Dan left. Steve and Ann disappeared to other parts of the house. Hank was gone. I was alone with Mother.

Our eyes met. Death eyes. I looked into them, eyes wide with knowledge, unblinking, objective eyes. Eyes detached from the soul. Eyes turned inward. I moved from the chaise across the room and sat cross-legged on the bed next to her. I took her right hand in mind and whispered, "Okay, Mother, let's do it. . . ."

I began breathing with her. It began simply as a mirroring of her breath, taking the exertion of her exhale, "ah . . . ," and reflecting back a more peaceful expression, "awe. . . ." Mother and I became one. One breathing organism. Everything we had ever shared in our

"I died as a mineral and became a plant,
I died as plant and rose to animal,
I died as animal and I was a Man.
Why should I fear? When was I less by dying?"
—Rumi

"For, as in the Taoist description of the wheel in terms of the strong, empty spaces between the spokes, one's future depends not only on the visible spokes of the present, but also on those invisible elements from the past, those things we are missing, are grieving for, have forgotten and left behind, so that they may be recovered."
—Tess Gallagher

lives manifested itself in this moment, in each breath. Here and now.

I was stunned by the way her eyes fixed on mine—the duet we were engaged in. At other times, I just closed my eyes and merged with her, whispering once again, "Let go, Mother, let go . . ." But mostly, it was just breath . . . slowing down, quieting down, until only the sweetest, faintest expression of breath remained.

Steve and Ann walk into the room. They can feel her spirit: Mother's wisps of breath creating an atmosphere of peace.

I feel joy. I feel love. I feel her love for me, for all of us, for her life and her birth, the rebirth of her soul.

I say to Steve, "She's going . . . she's going . . ."

He sits next to her and takes her other hand. Faint breaths. Soft breaths. In my heart I say, "Let go . . . let go . . . follow the light . . ." There is a crescendo of movement, like walking up a pyramid of light. And it is sexual, the concentration of love, of being fully present. Pure feeling. Pure color. I can feel her spirit rising through the top of her head. Her eyes focus on mine with total joy—a fullness that transcends words.

Just then, we hear the garage door open. Dad and Brooke are home. A few more breaths . . . one last breath—Dad walks into the room. Mother turns to him. Their eyes meet. She smiles. And she goes. . . .

In Mormon theology, the Holy Trinity is comprised of God the Father, Jesus Christ the Son, and the Holy Ghost. We call this the Godhead.

Where is the Motherbody?

We are far too conciliatory. If we as Mormon women believe in God the Father and in his son, Jesus Christ, it is only logical that a Mother-in-Heaven balances the sacred triangle. I believe the Holy Ghost is female, although she has remained hidden, invisible, deprived of a body, she is the spirit that seeps into our hearts and directs us to the well. The "still, small voice" I was taught to listen to as a child was "the gift of the Holy Ghost." Today I choose to recognize this presence as holy intuition, the gift of the Mother. My prayers no longer bear the "proper" masculine salutation. I include both Father and Mother in Heaven. If we could introduce the Motherbody as a spiritual counterpoint to the Godhead, perhaps our inspiration and devotion would no longer be directed to the stars, but our worship could return to the Earth.

My physical mother is gone. My spiritual mother remains. I am a woman rewriting my genealogy.

> Terry Tempest Williams
> *Refuge: An Unnatural History*
> *of Family and Place*

Two other books along these lines will also be of interest: *Loss of the Ground-Note: Women Writing About the Loss of Their Mothers,* edited by Helen Vozenilek, Clothespin Fever Press, 1992, and *Women and Authority: Re-emerging Mormon Feminism,* edited by Maxine Hanks, Signature Books, 1993.

○ Here's a bedtime meditation. Imagine yourself in a hospital bed, dying. Be aware of how you came to be in the bed, what disease you suffer from or what trauma brought you there. Feel what it is like to have everyone around you thinking of your death. What are they thinking? What are they feeling? Visualize yourself getting weaker and weaker, your body getting heavy, your senses failing. Everyone seems very far away from you. Feel yourself dying, leaving your body.

If you perform this visualization every night, your fear of death lessens as it prepares you for your actual death. It also heightens your awareness of impermanence which gradually lessens ego-clinging, allowing you to live more in the moment, more in process. Undeniably, performing this meditation on a regular basis makes you appreciate whatever time you have left.

"Only one breath separates us from the next life. If we do not reflect on death in the morning, we will waste the day; if we do not reflect on death in the evening, we will waste the night."
—Karma Lekshe Tsomo

Therapy, personal growth, and inner work often become the first step of a spiritual journey. Visualizing a situation, imagining something into being in order to work with the evoked elements, is frequently used by psychologists for healing or for growth. Jungians call the conscious use of the imaginative faculty "active imagination." It involves the conscious ego-mind entering into dialogue with the images that arise in one's imagination and/or participating in the action or stories being created there. The conscious awareness transforms this activity from passive fantasy into a very useful psychological tool. No doubt trancing functions in a similar way. For more on this technique, see Robert A. Johnson's Inner Work, *HarperSan Francisco, 1986.*

For now, use your active imagination in the following exercise which not only helps you to prepare for death, but brings you face to face with unfinished business that may be creating an obstacle to your spiritual development.

"Ours in not an inert universe, it's an alive universe; so what we call birth and death are just temporary states, temporary transformations, names for our true self at one time, and in one situation."
—Philip Kapleau Roshi

Attend Your Own Funeral

Laura Huxley, in *You Are Not the Target* (Farrar, Strauss and Giroux, 1963), suggests this exercise. First, make sure that you will not be disturbed for a few hours. Lie down in a darkened room. Imagine that you have died. You cannot speak or move; your body is lifeless. It is time for your funeral and your friends are filing by. What do they remember about you? How do they feel? If looking at any of them makes you want to cry, go ahead and cry—freely. If you could speak, what would you say to them?

What unfinished business do you have with these people at your funeral? With yourself? What do they say at the eulogy? Is it true?

Turn to the person who irritated you the most in your life. Do you have anything to say to him or her? Say it.

Look at the ones you've loved the most. Tell them how you feel. Say goodbye to them. If you can't say it in words, let your emotions come through as cries.

This is your last party. Tell everyone what your life has been about, the mistakes you've made, the secrets you've kept. There is no longer any reason for protection or armor. Let it all go.

Now it is over. Come back to your living body. Acknowledge and respect what you've learned. Rest in that knowledge.

Death & Dying Workshops:

Life, Death, and Transition Workshops with Elisabeth Kubler-Ross: The Elisabeth Kubler-Ross Center, South Route 616, Head Waters, VA 24442, (703) 396-3441.
Conscious Living/Conscious Dying workshops with Stephen and Ondrea Levine: c/o Daniel Barnes, The Access Group, 4 Cielo Lane, #4D, Novato, CA 94949, (415) 883-6111.

"The moment you find a technique, you become attached to it and there is no longer any open listening. The mind clings to methods because it finds safety in them. Real questioning has no methods, no knowing—just wondering freely, vulnerably, what it is that is actually happening inside and out. Not the word, not the idea of it, not the reaction to it, but the simple fact."
—Toni Packer

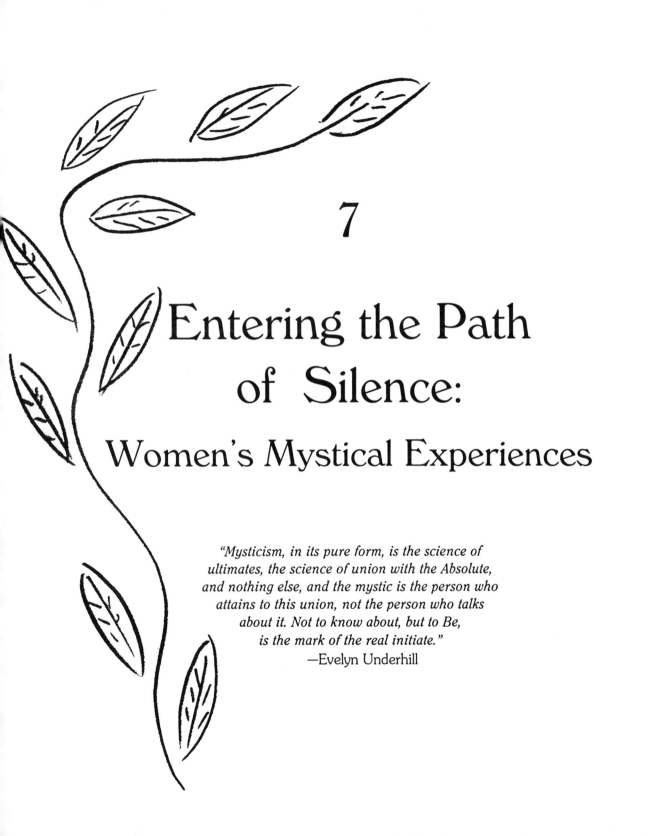

7

Entering the Path
of Silence:

Women's Mystical Experiences

*"Mysticism, in its pure form, is the science of
ultimates, the science of union with the Absolute,
and nothing else, and the mystic is the person who
attains to this union, not the person who talks
about it. Not to know about, but to Be,
is the mark of the real initiate."*
—Evelyn Underhill

Mystical experience almost always involves a loss of the self and a connection with something larger. These moments may be fleeting or sustained. D. T. Suzuki, who was instrumental in bringing Zen Buddhism to the West, told Roshi Jiyu Kennett that "once or twice" he had the great experience of Kensho or "seeing into his own nature," but "a million times the little moments that make one dance."

Evelyn Underhill, in *Mysticism,* holds that spiritual history reveals two distinct and fundamentally different attitudes toward the unseen, and methods for getting in touch with it. She calls these methods the "way of magic" and the "way of mysticism." The fundamental difference between the two is that "magic wants to get, mysticism wants to give—immortal and antagonistic attitudes, which turn up under one disguise or another in every age of thought." She points out that mysticism is nonindividualistic, and rather implies the abolition of individuality, of "that hard separateness, that 'I, Me, Mine' which makes of man a finite isolated thing." Essentially, she concludes, mysticism is a movement of the heart which seeks to transcend the limitations of the ego in order to surrender itself to ultimate reality for no personal gain.

Most religions focus on the heart rather than the head when it comes to union with the divine. Christianity is based on connection to Christ and to others through love, and many Medieval women mystics spoke of their union with Christ in sexual terms. Buddhism puts the seat of intelligence in the heart, and it is from that center that we reach out. The Sufi mystic is in love with the Absolute—not in some weak, sentimental way but with the entire force of the will—and seeks for this beloved in every aspect of earthly phenomena. For the modern Taoists, love is the Way. *Ecstacy* is a word often used when this contact has been established, but *stillness, silence, deepening,* and *peace* also describe this union.

Mystical experiences may arrive spontaneously or be actively sought through a lifetime of meditation and devotion. Silence and letting go seem to form an intrinsic part of the experience. As Martin Buber put it, "When we are quiet to the Lord, he makes his dwelling with us; we say Lord, Lord, and we have lost him." Because the experience is essentially beyond language, fundamentally ineffable, the attempts to describe union are sometimes overdramatic, even hysterical. This excess of language perhaps leads people to believe that communion with the divine involves whipped-up emotions and the whir of angel wings—something they aren't capable of or don't deserve. It could be, however, that the mystical experiences written about—or at least anthologized—represent only one type of union, and that Suzuki's "million moments that make one dance" are much more commonly experienced than generally acknowledged. Women throughout the ages have often lived in this dancing light, but may never have felt the need to write or speak about it because they were never separate enough from the experience to require that it be put into language to make it seem real to them.

We've all had these moments of connection, of touching down deeply to feel our spiritual roots: a sudden stillness in the woods where we forget ourselves completely and "become one" with nature; contact with another person in which we so fully embody ourselves that our soul bypasses our ego to directly commune with their soul; moments of utter clarity when delusion falls away, leaving only naked awareness. These moments—which can be described as contact with the Tao, "letting go" in Zen, self-remembering in Gurdjieff work, and so on—give meaning to our lives and provide felt connection with the rest of the world. They also shape our spiritual path, for after we start paying attention to such dancing moments, worldly compensations no longer satisfy, we want the authenticity and validity of the Tao contact to last. And it can, but we need to have faith in our own experience, slow down, pay attention, and let go.

Psychologist Jean Shinoda Bolen, author of Goddesses in Everywoman, *connects the Eastern concept of the Tao with C. G. Jung's theory of synchronicity, which finds deep spiritual roots beneath what may appear to be a coincidental meeting or event. True moments of synchronicity have an emotional charge, a sense of knowing, that is absent in chance happenings. Anyone who has worked with the* I-Ching (Book of Changes) *and felt herself to be part of a larger design has experienced synchronicity—and the Tao.*

The Tao

The experience of the Tao or of a unifying principle in the universe to which everything in the world relates, underlies the major Eastern religions—Hinduism, Buddhism, Confucianism, Taoist, and Zen. Although each religion may call the experience by a different name, the essence of all varieties of Eastern mysticism is the same. Each holds that all phenomena—people, animals, plants, and objects from atomic particles to galaxies are aspects of the One. . . .

The Tao experience conveys a profound awareness of being part of something far greater than ourselves, of being included, loved, and in touch with an invisible, eternal reality. In that timeless moment, when the Tao is experienced, we know that this is more significant than the tangible world around us and far more meaningful than our usual, everyday concerns. At that moment, everything and everyone seems synchronistically connected, linked by an underlying spiritual meaning.

What is known intuitively, through experience of the Tao, is that we are not lonely, isolated, insignificant, and meaningless creatures, accidently evolved from organic rubbish on a minuscule dot in the vast cosmos. Instead, the Tao experience gives us the direct knowledge that we are linked to all others and to the universe, through that which underlies everything and which some call God. Synchronistic events are glimpses into this underlying oneness, which is the meaning conveyed through an uncanny coincidence. The unseen linkage moves us; the synchronistic event tells us we are not alone.

Jean Shinoda Bolen
The Tao of Psychology: Synchronicity and the Self

"Unfortunately our Western mind, lacking all culture in this respect, has never yet devised a concept, nor even a name, for the 'union of opposites through the middle path,' that most fundamental item of inward experience, which could respectably be set against the Chinese concept of the Tao."
—Carl G. Jung

"There is a true secret about starting practice. The operation is as different for men and women as sky from sea. The principle for men is refinement of energy, the expedient for women is refinement of body."
—Liu-I-Ming

Women who became adept at Taoist practices were called *"Immortal Sisters"* and were often given the honorific title of *"Real Human." Sun Bu-er lived in the twelfth century in China and began a serious study of the Tao when she was fifty-one, after raising three children. In her set of fourteen poems, a classic of Taoist practice, she advocated that women "cut off the dragon," that is, stop the menstrual flow, so that "the alchemical energy returns to the furnace." Much of esoteric Taoism includes working with the inner forces of yin and yang, sexual energy, and inner alchemy. In the following poem—not a part of the work mentioned above—brambles are a metaphor for compulsive emotional reactions, whereas the lotus blossom, which grows in mud yet remains pure, symbolizes pristine mind.*

Immortal Sister's Poem

Brambles should be cut away,
Removing even the sprouts.
Within essence there naturally blooms
A beautiful lotus blossom.
One day there will suddenly appear
An image of light;
When you know that,
You yourself are it.

Sun Bu-er
from *Immortal Sisters: Secrets of Taoist Women*, translated and edited by Thomas Cleary

For more on women mystics, see:

Ann Bancroft, *Weavers of Wisdom: Women Mystics of the Twentieth Century*, Arkana, 1989.

Carol Lee Flinders, *Enduring Grace: Loving Portraits of Seven Women Mystics,* Harper & Row, 1993.

Meditations With series, edited by Matthew Fox, Bear & Company (includes writings of such female Christian mystics as Hildegard of Bingen, Julian of Norwich, and Teresa of Avila).

Leonore Friedman, *Meetings with Remarkable Women,* Shambhala, 1987.

Swami Ghananada and Sir John Stewart-Wallace, eds., *Women Saints: East and West,* Vedanta, 1979.

Mary Giles, ed., *The Feminist Mystic,* Crossroad, 1982.

Daniel Goleman, *Varieties of Meditative Experience,* Dutton, 1977.

William James, *The Varieties of Religious Experience,* Modern Library, 1988.

Roshi Jiyu Kennett, *How to Grow a Lotus Blossom,* Abbey, 1977.

Ellen Sidor, ed., *A Gathering of Spirit: Women Teaching in American Buddhism,* Primary Point, 1987.

Bernadette Roberts, *The Path to No-Self,* Shambhala, 1985.

Eveyln Underhill, *Practical Mysticism,* Dent, 1914.

Simone Weil, *Waiting for God,* Routledge & Kegan Paul, 1951.

"I feel this communion, this strange attunement, most readily with large white pines, a little less with big spruces, sugar maples, beeches, or oaks. Clearly white pines and I are on the same wavelength. What I give back to the trees I cannot imagine. I hope they receive something, because trees are among my closest friends."
—Anne Labastille

The author was eight years old when she experienced the following event.

The Glade

The incident happened during a nature walk in the Maine woods where I was at summer camp. I was last in line; I had fallen back a bit and was hurrying to catch up when, through the trees, I saw a glade. It had a lush fir tree at the far side and a knoll in the center covered in bright, almost luminous green moss. The rays of the afternoon sun slanted against the blue-black green of the pine forest. The little roof of visible sky was perfectly blue. The whole picture had a completeness, an all-there quality of such dense power that it stopped me in my tracks. I went to the edge and then, softly, as though into a magical or holy place, to the center, where I sat, then lay down with my cheek against the freshness of the moss. It is here, I thought, and I felt the anxiety that colored my life fall away. This,

"Sometimes I think I am half mad with love for this place . . . . My center does not come from my mind—it feels in me like a plot of warm moist well-tilled earth with the sun shining hot on it."
—Georgia O'Keefe

at last, was where things were as they ought to be. Everything was in its place—the tree, the earth underneath, the rock, the moss. In autumn, it would be right; in winter under the snow, it would be perfect in its wintriness. Spring would come again and miracle within miracle would unfold, each at its special pace, some things having died off, some sprouting in their first spring, but all of equal and utter rightness.

I felt I had discovered the missing center of things, the key to rightness itself, and must hold on to this knowledge which was so clear in that place. I was tempted for a moment to take a scrap of moss away with me, to keep as a reminder; but a rather grown-up thought prevented me. I suddenly feared that in treasuring an amulet of moss, I might lose the real prize: the insight I had had—that I might think my vision safe as long as I kept the moss, only to find one day that I had nothing but a pinch of dead vegetation.

So I took nothing, but promised myself I would remember The Glade every night before going to sleep and in that way never be far from its stabilizing power. I knew, even at eight, that the confusion of values thrust upon me by parents, teachers, other children, nannies, camp counselors, and others would only worsen as I grew up. The years would add complications and steer me into more and more impenetrable tangles of rights and wrongs, desirables and undesirables. I had already seen enough to know that. But if I could keep The Glade with me, I thought, I would never get lost.

That night in my camp bed I brought The Glade to mind and was filled with a sense of thankfulness, and renewed my vow to preserve my vision. And for years its quality was undiminished as I saw the knoll, the fir, the light, the wholeness, in my mind every night.

Jean Liedloff
The Continuum Concept: Allowing Human Nature to Work Successfully

As in Native American and other shamanic traditions, the connection to the invisible world here ties closely to nature. The spirit-driven wind is very similar to descriptions of the African goddess Oya, often experienced as a gale force wind or even a tornado.

The Presences

She appeared in white, garbed in white, standing white, pure white.
—Bernardino de Sahagun

On the gulf where I was raised, *en el Valle del Rio Grande* in South Texas—that triangular piece of land wedged between the river *y el golfo* [and the gulf] which serves as the Texas-U.S./Mexican border--is a Mexican *pueblito* [little village] called Hargill (at one time in the history of this one-grocery-store, two-service-stations town there were thirteen churches and thirteen *cantinas* [bars]). Down the road, a little ways from our house, was a deserted church. It was known among the *mexicanos* that if you walked down the road late at night you would see a woman dressed in white floating about, peering out the church window. She would follow those who had done something bad or who were afraid. *Los mexicanos* called her *la jila*. Some thought she was *la Llorona*. She was, I think, *Cihuacoatl*, Serpent Woman, ancient Aztec goddess of the earth, of war and birth, patron of midwives, and antecedent of *la Llorona*. Covered with chalk, *Cihuacoatl* wears a white dress with a decoration half red and half black. Her hair forms two little horns (which the Aztecs depicted as knives) crossed on her forehead. The lower part of her face is a bare jawbone, signifying death. On her back she carries a cradle, the knife of sacrifice swaddled as if it were her papoose, her child. Like *la Llorona*, *Cihuacoatl* howls and weeps in the night, screams as if demented. She brings mental depression and sorrow. Long before it takes place, she is the first to predict something is to happen. Back then, I, an unbeliever, scoffed at these Mexican superstitions as I was taught in Anglo school.

Four years ago a red snake crossed my path as I walked through the woods. The direction of its movement, its pace, its colors, the

"The Sioux idea of living creatures is that trees, buffalo and men are temporary energy swirls, turbulence patterns . . . . You find that perception registered so many ways in archaic and primitive lore. I would say that it is probably the most basic insight into the nature of things, and that our more common, recent Occidental view of the universe as consisting of fixed things is out of the main stream, a deviation from basic human perception."
—Gary Snyder

"We say release, and radiance, and roses, and echo upon everything that's known; and yet, behind the world our names enclose is the nameless: our true archetype and home."
—Rainer Maria Rilke

"mood" of the trees and the wind and the snake—they all "spoke" to me, told me things. I look for omens everywhere, everywhere catch glimpses of the patterns and cycles of my life. Stones "speak" to Luisah Teish, a Santera; trees whisper their secrets to Chrystos, a Native American. I remember listening to the voices of the wind as a child and understanding its messages. *Los espiritus* [the spirits] that ride the back of the south wind. I remember their exhalation blowing in through the slits in the door during those hot Texas afternoons. A gust of wind raising the linoleum under my feet, buffeting the house. Everything trembling.

We're not supposed to remember such otherworldly events. We're supposed to ignore, forget, kill those fleeting images of the soul's presence and of the spirit's presence. We've been taught that the spirit is outside our bodies or above our heads somewhere up in the sky with God. We're supposed to forget that every cell in our bodies, every bone and bird and worm has spirit in it.

Like many Indians and Mexicans, I did not deem my psychic experiences real. I denied their occurrences and let my inner senses atrophy. I allowed white rationality to tell me that the existence of the "other world" was mere pagan superstition. I accepted their reality, the "official" reality of the rational, reasoning mode which is connected with external reality, the upper world, and is considered the most developed consciousness—the consciousness of duality.

The other mode of consciousness facilitates images from the soul and the unconscious through dreams and the imagination. Its work is labeled "fiction," make-believe, wish-fulfillment. White anthropologists claim that Indians have "primitive" and therefore deficient minds, that we cannot think in the higher mode of consciousness—rationality. They are fascinated by what they call the "magical" mind, the "savage" mind, the *participation mystique* of the mind that says the world of the imagination—the world of the soul—and of the spirit is just as real as physical reality. In trying to become "objective," Western culture made "objects" of things and people when it distanced itself from them, thereby losing "touch" with them. This dichotomy is the root of all violence.

Not only was the brain split into two functions but so was reality. Thus people who inhabit both realities are forced to live in the interface between the two, forced to become adept at switching modes. Such is the case with the *india* and the *mestiza*.

Institutionalized religion fears trafficking with the spirit world and stigmatizes it as witchcraft. It has strict taboos against this kind of inner knowledge. It fears what Jung calls the Shadow, the unsavory aspects of ourselves. But even more it fears the supra-human, the god in ourselves. Voodoo, Santeria, Shamanism and other native religions are called cults and their beliefs are called mythologies. In my own life, the Catholic Church fails to give meaning to my daily acts, to my continuing encounters with the "other world." It and other institutionalized religions impoverish all life, beauty, pleasure.

The Catholic and Protestant religions encourage fear and distrust of life and of the body; they encourage a split between the body and the spirit and totally ignore the soul; they encourage us to kill off parts of ourselves. We are taught that the body is an ignorant animal; intelligence dwells only in the head. But the body is smart. It does not discern between external stimuli and stimuli from the imagination. It reacts equally viscerally to events from the imagination as it does to "real" events.

So I grew up in the interface trying not to give countenance to *el mal aigre,* evil non-human, non-corporeal entities riding the wind, that could come in through the window, through my nose with my breath. I was not supposed to believe in *susto,* a sudden shock or fall that frightens the soul out of the body. And growing up between such opposing spiritualities how could I reconcile the two, the pagan and the Christian?

No matter to what use my people put the supranatural world, it is evident to me now that the spirit world, whose existence the whites are so adamant in denying, does in fact exist. This very minute I sense the presence of the spirits of my ancestors in my room. And I think *la jila* is *Cihuacoatl,* Snake Woman; she is *la Llorona,* Daughter of Night, traveling the dark terrains of the unknown searching for the lost parts of herself. I remember *la jila* following me once, remember her eerie lament. I'd like to think that she was crying for her lost children, *los* Chicanos/*mexicanos.*

Gloria Anzaldua
Borderlands/La Frontera

"It is a sorcerer's idea that the parameters of our normal perception have been imposed upon us as part of our socialization, not quite arbitrarily but laid down mandatorily nonetheless. One aspect of these obligatory parameters in an interpretation system, which processes sensory data into meaningful units and renders the social order as a structure of interpretation."
—Carlos Castenada

Nature here is sentient, quivering with meaning, ready to communicate to us through languages we have forgotten. To call this world view anthropomorphic seems not only patronizing, but a fearful effort to contain and control the enormity of communion available.

Living in Dreamtime

The Aborigines listened through all their senses to the various languages that permeate the natural world—for example, languages emitted by trees, celestial bodies, rocks, wind, water, fire, shadows, and seeds. In closely observing, imitating, or questioning a tangible phenomenon, one is able to listen to a message of the nature of reality as a whole. The Dreamtime stories arose from listening to the innate intelligence within all things. In many Aboriginal languages the word for *listen* and the word for *understand* are the same. The symbolic or poetic understanding we derive from contemplating natural form is dependent on a metaphoric model in which one thing stands for or is understood in terms of another. For example, a botanical tree, with its roots embedded in the earth and its branches reaching into the sky, may stand as the metaphysical "tree of life," the connecting link between the upper and lower worlds. We believe these metaphoric relationships are generated solely by human "intelligence" and exist only in the human language. For the Aborigines, however, the knowledge and understanding gained and reiterated as metaphor derives from an intelligible energy actually emanating from the observed form—the seed, tree, or stone—to which subtle sensory centers in our body respond.

On a day's hike into the remote wilderness of a mountainous national park, I began musing on this subject. After walking for hours, I fell and lay, as if embraced, in the thick, soft layers of red and gold leaves. I opened my eyes and met with a strange sensation that rippled through my body. My mind full of language and concepts began to dissolve into a world of twisting forms, of stretching, giant cassarina trees, sensual dancing eucalyptus trees, and the entangled, bleached bodies of those trees that had fallen. I

"This room was where people went formally to communicate directly with Oneness, in what we might call meditation. They explained to me the difference between Mutants' [white people's] prayer and the Real People's [Australian Aborigines'] form of communication is that prayer is an outward talk to the spiritual world, and what they do is just the opposite. They listen. They clear thoughts out of their mind and wait to receive."
—Marlo Morgan

had to pull out for a moment to remind myself to listen and smell. Then it began—a nearly subliminal chattering of voices that seemed to radiate from the trees themselves. Some were transformed into ideas in my mind, others reached into my heart and groin with a sort of wordless understanding. While merging into the consciousness of this wondrous forest, I also felt distinctly human and very feminine. I felt a rush of joy for having glimpsed a world in which the Aborigines must live every day and every moment.

Johanna Lambert
Wise Women of the Dreamtime

Also see Marlo Morgan's *Mutant Message: Down Under,* the story of a white woman's "walkabout," available from M.M. Company, P.O. Box 100, Lee's Summit, MO 64063, 816-246-6365.

————————————————

"What both Freud and Jung called 'the unconscious' is simply what we, in our historically conditioned estrangement, are unconscious of. It is not necessarily or essentially unconscious."
—R. D. Laing

In spontaneous mystical experiences, many people speak of an intensification of one of the senses—here and with the following selection from Kathleen Raine—it is sight. In Pati Airey's "A Certain Humming" it becomes a ringing in the ear.

Arrival

The small, pale green desk at which I'd been so thoughtlessly gazing had totally and radically changed. It appeared now with a clarity, a depth of three-dimensionality, a freshness I had never imagined possible. At the same time, in a way that is utterly indescribable, all my questions and doubts were gone as effortlessly as chaff in the wind. I knew everything and all at once, yet not in the sense that I had ever known anything before.

All things were the same in my little bedroom yet totally changed. Still sitting in wonder of the edge of my narrow bed, one of the first things I realized was that the focus of my sight seemed

"It is through conscious individual existence that the developing consciousness becomes organized and capable to awaken into its own reality."
—Sri Aurobindo

to have changed; it had sharpened to an infinitely small point which moved ceaselessly in paths totally free of the old accustomed ones, as if flowing from a new source.

What on earth had happened? So released from all tension, so ecstatically light did I feel, I seemed to float down the hall to the bathroom to look at my face in the mottled mirror over the sink. The pupils of my eyes were dark, dilated and brimming with mirth. With a wondrous relief, I began to laugh as I'd never laughed before, from the soles of my feet upward.

Within a few days I had returned to Ann Arbor, and there over a period of many months there took place a ripening, a deepening and unfolding of this experience which filled me with wonder and gratitude at every moment. The foundations had fallen from my world. I had plunged into a numinous openness which had obliterated all fixed distinctions including that of *within* and *without*. A Presence had absorbed the universe including myself, and to this I surrendered in absolute confidence. Often, without any particular direction in mind, I found myself outside running along the street in joyous abandon. Sometimes when alone I simply danced as freely as I did as a child. The whole world seemed to have reversed itself, to have turned outside in. Activity flowed simply and effortlessly, and to my amazement, seemingly without thought. Instead of following my old sequence of learning, thinking, planning, then acting, action had taken precedence and whatever was learned was surprisingly incidental. Yet nothing ever seemed to go out of bounds; there was no alteration between self-control and letting go but rather a perfect rightness and spontaneity to all this flowing activity.

This new kind of knowing was so pure and unadorned, so delicate, that nothing in the language of my past could express it. Neither sense nor feeling nor imagination contained it yet all were contained in it. In some indefinable way I knew with absolute certainty the changeless unity and harmony in charge of the universe and the inseparability of all seeming opposites.

It was as if, before all this occurred, "I" had been a fixed point inside my head looking out at a world out there, a separate and comparatively flat world. The periphery of awareness had now come to light, yet neither fixed periphery nor center existed as such. A paradoxical quality seemed to permeate all existence. Feeling myself centered as never before, at the same time I knew the whole universe to be centered at every point. Having plunged to the center of emptiness, having lost all purposefulness in the old sense, I had never felt so one-pointed, so clear and decisive. Freed from separateness, feeling one with the universe, everything including myself had become at once unique and equal. If God was the word for this Presence in which I was absorbed then everything was either holy or nothing; no distinction was possible. All was meaningful, complete as it was, each bird, bud, midge, mole, atom, crystal, of total importance in itself. As in the notes of a great symphony, nothing was large or small, nothing of more or less importance to the whole. I now saw that wholeness and holiness are one.

Passing the campus chapel, I remembered how I had been taught in church to think of myself as here on earth and of God as above and out there, to aspire to heaven as in some future time and place, to emulate the lives of others. How tragic it seemed that anyone should be distracted in this way from a firsthand knowledge of Reality. My entire education had taught me only to stand in the light. Nothing had been added, but only the delusions of this education removed. I knew now that eternity is here always, that there is no higher, no deeper, no separate past or future time or place. How could love be other than this all-encompassing Oneness to which we can do nothing but open ourselves?

I felt that I was done forever with all seeking, all philosophic and religious doctrines, all fear of dying or concern for the future, all need for authority other than this. If I could continue in this state of *Open Vision* I felt certain that whatever happened, everything would be right just as it was.

Years before I had sought a rule that would apply to everything I did, even to washing dishes. Now I simply washed the dishes. In the most simple of bodily feelings and the most ordinary of daily tasks, living was transformed. I had never felt so completely whole and in one piece or enjoyed my bodily feelings so much. Breathing had changed, had become deeper, more rhythmical. Hands, eyes, voice, all seemed quieter, more relaxed. With seemingly boundless energy every task become effortless and light. Running exuberantly home from classes or work, bounding up two flights of stairs to my third-floor rooming house room, I would fall soundly asleep for a

"It is not I who create myself, rather I happen to myself."
—Carl G. Jung

"The path of love and the path of insight lead into the same garden."
—Stephen Mitchell

quick, daytime catnap, then waken shortly feeling wonderfully refreshed. With spontaneous gusto, I found myself eating lightly whenever hungry (gaining ten much-needed pounds in a few months). Even my handwriting changed.

As for my relations with others, another person now filled my shoes. Laughter and delight seemed to fill my life. Somehow I had become more human, more ordinary, more friendly and at ease with all kinds of people. Apparently I appeared happy and smiling too, for strangers often came up and spoke to me.

I had no idea what I could have done to have deserved these miraculous changes but I felt the most inexpressible gratitude for them. They had enriched my life beyond compare. Literally everything had become interesting. As for my school work, it improved in some areas and declined in others. I was less concerned with meeting conventional demands.

But of all the changes that had occurred, the one that seemed to me in some mysterious way to be the key to everything else was the change in vision. It was as if some inner eye, some ancient center of awareness, which extended equally and at once in all directions without limit and which had been there all along had been restored. This inner vision seemed to be anchored in infinity in a way that was detached from immediate sight and yet at the same time had a profound effect on sight. Walking along the street I was aware of the street flowing past and beneath me, the trees or buildings moving past all around and the sky moving above as if I were immersed in one flowing whole. A child-like *unknowing* pervaded perception. The immediate world had acquired a new depth and clarity of color and form, an unalloyed freshness and unexpectedness. Rooted in the present, *every* moment opened to eternity. Along with this, there was a sharp single-pointedness to the focus of attention which caused me to feel that I was looking straight and deeply into whatever entered my attention. Yet paradoxically I felt blind. This is difficult to describe. It was as if my attention were now rooted in some deeper center so that my everyday sight, my eyes, released from their former tension to reach out and see the world outside, were now as free as if they had been blanked out, eliminated altogether. Another incidental change I noticed was that no matter in what direction I looked, no shadow of my nose or face ever appeared in the clear field of sight as apparently it had occasionally done before. I also found other people's eyes fascinating, as well as those of animals, looking into them as if into my own. This change of vision was so impressive that I went to the University Medical School library and searched in the card files under the headings of vision, sight, and eyes trying to find some reference to this new kind of vision. There was nothing, not a clue. Still I remained convinced that this change in vision was somehow basic to all the other transforming changes.

What I called *Open Vision* not only awakened appreciation for the inexhaustible delights of everyday living, the smell of smoking damp leaves, the taste of fresh Michigan apple, the sounds of the thrush in the early morning. It had also made me more aware of the sufferings of others, so much of it self-inflicted. . . .

Flora Courtois
An Experience of Enlightenment

"Do not despise the world, for the world too is God."
—Muhammad

Kathleen Raine, a British poet, is now in her eighties. Throughout her life she studied the poet William Blake whom she considers her teacher and guru. Here, she sees, in Blake's words, "eternity in a grain of sand/eternity in a wildflower."

Seeing Things As They Are

I kept always on the table where I wrote my poems a bowl with different kinds of moss and lycopodium and long and deeply did I gaze at these forms, and into their luminous smaragdine green. There was also a hyacinth growing in an amethyst glass; I was sitting alone, in an evening, at my table, the Aladdin lamp lit, the fire of logs burning in the hearth. All was stilled. I was looking at the hyacinth, and as I gazed at the form of its petals and the strength of their curve as they open and curl back to reveal the mysterious flower-centers with their anthers and eye-like hearts, abruptly I found that I was no longer looking at it, but was it; a distinct, indescribably, but in no way vague, still less emotional, shift of consciousness into the plant itself.

"How do you know but ev'ry Bird that cuts the airy way, Is an immense world of delight, clos'd by your senses five?"
—William Blake

Or rather I and the plant were one and indistinguishable; as if the plant were part of my consciousness. I dared scarcely to breathe, held in a kind of fine attention in which I could sense the very flow of life in the cells. I was not perceiving the flower but living it. I was aware of the life of the plant as a slow flow or circulation of a vital current of liquid light of the utmost purity. I could apprehend as a simple essence formal structure and dynamic process. This dynamic form was, as it seemed, of a spiritual not a material order; of a finer matter, or of matter itself perceived as spirit. There was nothing emotional about this experience which was, on the contrary, an almost mathematical apprehension of a complex and organized whole, apprehended *as* a whole. The whole was living; and as such inspired a sense of immaculate holiness. Living form—that is how I can best name the essence or soul of the plant. By "living" I do not mean that which distinguishes animal from plant or plant from mineral, but rather a quality possessed by all these in their different degrees. Either everything is, in this sense, living, or nothing is; this negation being the view to which materialism continually tends; for lack, as I now knew, of the immediate apprehension of life, as life. The experience lasted for some time—I have no idea how long—and I returned to dull human consciousness with a sense of diminution. I had never before experienced the like, nor have I since in the same degree; and yet is seemed at the time not strange but infinitely familiar, as if I were experiencing at last things as they are, was where I belonged, where in some sense I had always been, and would always be. That almost continuous sense of exile and incompleteness of experience which is, I suppose, the average human state, was gone like a film from sight. In these matters to know at once is to know for ever.

Kathleen Raine
Farewell Happy Fields

332

For many, a sense of cosmic consciousness begins with a connection with nature, especially trees. Trees are also often used in women's poetry and fiction to provide a link between self and nature, self and the sacred, and even as a means of communication across a planet.

The Many and the One

"the temple bell stops ringing but the sound keeps coming out of the flowers"
—Basho

Spring is in the air. The breeze is gentle with the smell of birthing, the earth radiates freshness, the birds sing with more abandon than they have for months. The first wildflowers are in bloom in the deep forest: the hardy toothwort, the delicate purple shooting star. The tender green of new growth is everywhere. Grass has even sprouted through some cracks in the concrete of my floor: what better testament to life renewed?

I cannot stay inside. I gather up my quilt, pull back the blanket door, and venture forth.

The breeze plays with my hair as I make my way after an invisible pull toward the creek. On the southern slope of the hill that falls steeply to the stream, not far from the yurt, but out of sight, there is a tiny natural shelf in the hillside. I spread my quilt on the earth, which is still damp from winter rains.

The day is cool, but the slope is sheltered from the wind, and its angle catches the full power of the sun. I lie down, arms outstretched, motionless against the earth.

The earth molds itself to my curves: we fit. The sun reaches deep, through skin to bone, through surface to center. I smell the rich damp warmth of almost spring, see through my fingers and pores, listen with my bones, forget to breathe.

My attention is drawn to a small oak tree, not far from where I lie. Outlined against the clear blue sky, little bits of newborn green are barely visible on the tips of the gray moss-covered branches. Strings of Spanish moss drip toward the earth, dancing now and then in the breeze. A jay lands on a branch near me, cocks his head, and flies away again. The wind rises slightly; the whole tree responds, limbs swaying. Though my little shelf is hidden from the wind, I seem to feel its push against me, too, as I watch the little oak.

"I slowly enter into each nature form—the earth, trees, rocks, water—letting them possess me, so that I too become the huge wave rising and falling, the redwood log whispering, the autumn tree approaching winter, the smaller rock forms as guardians of the Grand Canyon, or the birds soaring above the mountain summit."
—Betty LaDuke

I sense the branches moving, feel the creak of winter stiffness, feel new life begin to run through its body as the sun and wind pull and push. I feel the pull on kinky limbs, the sluggishness of parts still half asleep that respond only slowly to the call of the sun. I feel the breeze blow off the tree's winter coat and awaken something inside, deep within the core. And I sense the tree responding, branches swaying, bulky body moving slowly, sluggishly, as it can.

And then I *am* the tree. Another jay alights and I feel its touch as on a distant extremity. I am still here, still flat on the hillside hidden from the wind, but somehow I extend above and beyond and around myself to include the tree, the earth, the rocks, the breeze.

The earth, the rocks, the sky, and I interpenetrate. We are one. I feel a deep, beatific relaxation. The boundaries that I think of as "me" are suddenly no more than illusion. My body's limits are a product of the same surface tension that allows a water bug to skate on top of a pond. Now, as I lie here, the tension is released, the illusion suspended. The varied personalities and centers of energy that make up my place on the hillside merge, and all of life flows into and out of one another. And the many—the wonderful, entertaining, diverse manifestation of life—become gloriously One.

Barbara Dean
Wellspring: A Story from Deep Country

Just as intensified vision preceded Flora Courtois's experience, Pati Airey says that before she slips the traces of her everyday personality and enters an altered state, she feels an unusual pressure in her inner ear which sets up a humming noise.

A Certain Humming

A certain humming takes place . . . perhaps of moonbeams.
It seems they are chording, or harmonically tuning
      the earth at her inner core.

This is the desert, at the summer solstice:
sitting atop of intersecting Ley Lines,
at first alone . . . later four other women show up.

Not a word is uttered, yet simultaneously
we raise our arms and cup the moonbeams,
projecting them into the earth
in various configurations.

Later, alone again, I sit and meditate.
The rock feels electric,
with a low aural hum
that appears to come from the innermost heart of Gaia.

It seems as if the moonbeams strum the planet
      and scratch her back,
the harmonic so deep it resonates my cranial cavity.

All I knew was a familiarity that riped through and splattered
      logic and language.

I felt right at home.

Stripping down naked

*"There's a strange frenzy
in my head,
of birds flying
each particle circulating
on its own.
Is the one I love
everywhere?"*
—Rumi

"Can we listen to the breeze without calling it breeze? Talking together we have to use words so that we can listen together, but the listening is not the words. The listening is openness, to what's not knowable."
—Toni Packer

(obviously clothes are an impediment)
I go to the edge of the rock
where I lie hanging upsidedown.

The decompression of my organs seems to help.
Casting out the Book of Doubt,
I feel so much love streaming forth
it makes the atmosphere steamy.

Love flows to the stratosphere, and so do I, riding moonbeams.

I stretch through the cosmos,
love splayed open upon a starry wheel,
guided energetically,
acting as a medium
for this transpiring

which always takes place,
and triggers unspeakable memory.

All sound altered, my body-electric
an orgasm beyond form and knowing.
I lie there, humming,
insideout, spinning among the stars . . .

then suddenly swept down to earth,
with no recollection of time.

Somewhere we performed this kind of interaction
ages ago and ages to come.

Pati Airey, artist

For the German mystic Anna Katharina Emmerich visionary experience formed a constant part of life. She saw angels and demons, watched words come out of the mouths of those who were praying "like a fiery ray" and ascend to God, and observed evil thoughts that looked like "the oddest nasty beasts" run through a pilgrim's mind "as on a paved road." ("That is very true, unfortunately," the pilgrim agreed.)

Angel Flight

The angel summons me and leads me hither and thither. I travel with him very often. He takes me to persons whom I do not know or have seen once; but also to such as are otherwise quite unknown to me. He even takes me across the sea; but that is swift as a thought, and then I see so far, so far! It was he who led me to the queen of France in her prison. When he comes to me to lead me on some journey, I usually see first a brightness, and then a form suddenly emerges shining from the night, as when the light of a dark lantern is suddenly uncovered. When we travel it is night above us; but a shimmer flies over the face of the earth. We travel from here through familiar landscapes to regions farther and farther away, and I have the sensation of uncommon distance. Sometimes we travel over straight roads; sometimes we cut across fields, mountains, rivers, and seas. I have to measure the whole way with my feet, and often even climb mountains with great effort. My knees are then painfully tired; my feet are burning; I am always barefoot.

My leader floats sometimes before me, sometimes beside me. I never see his feet move. He is very silent, without much movement, except that he accompanies his brief answers with a gesture of the hand or with a nod of the head. He is so transparent and shining, often very solemn, often mixed with love. His hair is smooth, flowing, and shimmering. He is without head covering and wears a long priestly robe with a blond shimmer.

I speak with him quite boldly, only I can never quite look him in the face, I am so bowed before him. He gives me every instruction. I avoid asking him many questions; the blessed contentment when I am with him prevents me. In his words he is always so short. I also

"But once it appeared to me—if I may say it, although I dare not assert it as certain—that I had been outside the body. But how and when my soul left its body, how it threw off the body, I cannot tell. For so lightly and suddenly, in an instant, as it seemed to me, did my soul throw off the cloak of flesh, as when one clad in an open cloak is running along the road, and the cloak slips suddenly from the shoulders of the runner."
—Alpais of Cudot
(1150-1211)

see him while awake, when I pray for others, and he is not with me, I call him so that he may go to the other person's angel. And often when he is with me I say to him, "Now I'll stay here; you go there and bring consolation!" and I see him going that way. If I come to great waters and do not know how to get across, suddenly I am on the other side, gazing backward in astonishment.

Anna Katharina Emmerich
(1774-1824)

"The result is not more than these three words: I got burnt and burnt and burnt."
—Rumi, on mystical union

"For several days I have been constantly between seeing with the senses and supernatural sight. I have to compel myself forcibly; for in the midst of conversation with others I suddenly see quite different things and images before me, and then I hear my own speech like that of another and it sounds crude and muffled, as if the other were speaking through a barrel. I also feel as if I were intoxicated and might fall. My conversation with the speakers continues calmly and often in a more lively manner than usual, but afterward I do not know what I have spoken, yet I speak quite coherently. It costs me considerable effort to maintain myself in this double state. I see what is present with my eyes, dimly, like someone who is falling asleep and already starting to dream. The second sight wants to snatch me away by force and is brighter than the natural sight, but it is not through the eyes."
—Anna Katharina Emmerich

Spiritual Emergency

Christina and Stanislav Grof use the term *spiritual emergency* to describe the situation when a spiritual process turns into a crisis. Spiritual emergencies are "critical and experientially difficult stages of a profound psychological transformation that involves one's entire being." They may include nonordinary states of consciousness, intense emotions, visions, voices, strong visual images, and other physical and psychical manifestations which center around a religious or spiritual theme. Often episodes include sequences of psychological death and rebirth, memories from past lives, cosmic consciousness or feelings of oneness with the universe, and encounters with mythological or alien beings. These states—which are recorded in sacred literature throughout the ages—can be profoundly healing and may lead to opening, growth, and/or transformation. They can also be filled with pain, terror, and severe disorientation. Sometimes people land in mental institutions during the eruption of the inner forces which constitute their spiritual crisis. Often drug and alcohol dependency and other addictions are forms of spiritual emergency.

The Grofs discuss the process in detail and suggest a number of different strategies to help a person (and those around her) cope. In terms of trying to live in the everyday world while in the grip of a spiritual transformation, they advise that you:

(1) Play evocative music and express emotions though the use of sound and movement. Play music that enhances the experiences you are undergoing, then lie down and let the feelings express themselves. You may find that you cry, scream, shake, move in unexpected ways. This often brings immediate relief and release. You may also produce the same effect through dance or yoga. Keep your attention focused internally.

(2) Do dreamwork. Dreams are often continuations or completions of waking experiences during a spiritual emergency. Keep a notebook by your bed and write down your dreams when you wake. Reserve a quiet period in the day in which you can work with dream imagery, drawing or conducting a dialogue with figures in the dream. Ask yourself the meanings of the dream and investigate the origins of the feelings involved.

You might find someone sympathetic but objective to share your dreams with, or consult one of the many good books available on dream experience, such as Patricia Garfield's *Creative Dreaming*, Ballantine, 1974.

(3) Express yourself artistically. Because strong visual imagery frequently plays a large part in a spiritual emergency, painting, drawing, and sculpting help to externalize experiences and make them easier to understand and process. They also provide a channel for strong physical and emotional energies. You do not have to

"Without words, it comes. And suddenly, sharply, one is aware of being separated from every person on one's earth and every object, and from the beginning of things and from the future and even a little, from one's self."
—Lillian Smith

"We and the sun and the trees, all is perpetual flowing. It's only the kind of senses we have that do this stop-photography. In actuality, everything is moving all the time, and it can be scary as hell."
—Joanna Macy

possess artistic talent in order to profit from artistic expression--realistic representation is not the point. The images that appear may be abstract shapes, the interplay of colors, or representational figures, and they may not make sense at first.

The physical process of sculpting in clay can provide a powerful outlet for intense emotions, and the three-dimensional aspect of your sculpture can add to your knowledge of your inner images.

Some people find that it helps to keep a painting or drawing journal, starting and ending the day with an entry. You might want to have a supply of paints, brushes, markers, crayons, paper, and clay on hand.

(4) Practice focused meditation. Similar to the Jungian technique of "active imagination" (see *Encounters with the Soul* by Barbara Hannah, Sigo Press, 1981), this method allows you to use physical and mental relaxation to work with issues, images, emotions, or problems that stem from your spiritual emergency. Use soft music, lie on the floor, and relax. Let your mind roam through images or emotions that are part of your process. To clarify a particular aspect of your journey, gently guide your consciousness to that part of the experience, telling yourself to pass through it, asking yourself what you see around you, how you react physically and emotionally, and what the imagery is trying to tell you. Open yourself to the insights that this may provide.

Leave yourself plenty of time to finish the process, then guide yourself back to everyday life, sense the room around you, feel yourself in you body. Stretch. Later you might want to paint or draw what you experienced.

(5) Develop simple personal rituals. Many spiritual disciplines use rituals for purification or protection which may be adapted to help ease you through your spiritual transformation. Be creative in finding a ritual that will work for you. If you believe it will be of use, it usually will. A few suggestions: while taking a shower, imagine that the water flowing over you is washing away emotional baggage and debris; envision that the fire you are watching in the fireplace is consuming your inner obstructions; visualize giving all of your problems to the ocean, the desert, the stars. Wrap all of your troubles in a large bundle, see yourself standing on the edge of cliff as you throw it into the sea, asking that the sea take it from you.

Practice covering yourself with an imaginary deep blue or white light that shields and protects you against unwelcome energies.

If handled skillfully, a spiritual emergency can result in a newfound depth of meaning to your life, inner peace, and a sense of homecoming.

○ For those who need to ground, meditation teacher Jack Kornfield recommends eating meat and jumping up and down. Some Tibetan lamas suggest beating on the soles of your feet; others find that working with food or gardening helps.

Spiritual Emergency (Jeremy P. Tarcher, 1989), the anthology edited by Stanislav and Christina Grof, discusses a number of different manifestations of spiritual crises, suggests ways to alleviate them, and includes an excellent bibliography. Christina Grof's *The Stormy Search for the Self,* Jeremy P. Tarcher, 1990, is also helpful. The Grofs founded SEN, the Spiritual Emergency Network, which is designed to educate the public and provide resources for those in a spiritual crisis. Bernadette Roberts's *The Experience of No-Self,* Shambhala, 1982, describes her journey through uncharted territory. Roberts's experiences—like those of Courtois and others—also involved a change in vision.

"You will not grow if you sit in a beautiful flower garden, but you will grow if you are sick, if you are in pain, if you experience losses, and if you do not put your head in the sand, but take the pain and learn to accept it, not as a curse or punishment, but as a gift to you with a very, very specific purpose."
—Elisabeth Kubler-Ross

"God's grace is the beginning, the middle, and the end. When you pray for God's grace, you are like someone standing neck-deep in water and yet crying for water. It is like saying that someone neck-deep in water feels thirsty, or that a fish in water feels thirsty, or that water feels thirsty."
—Ramana Maharshi

After she had been given the last rites during a near-fatal illness, Dame Julian of Norwich had a series of sixteen revelations or "showings" in the span of two days in which she had a direct experience of God's goodness. "As truly as God is our Father, so truly is God our Mother," she reported. "I understand three ways of contemplating motherhood in God. The first is the foundation of our nature's creation; the second is his taking of our nature, where the motherhood of grace begins; the third is the motherhood at work. And in that, by the same grace, everything is penetrated, in length and in breadth, in height and in depth without end, and it is all one love."

Revelations, dated 1373

Because of the great, infinite love which God has for all humankind, he makes no distinction in love between the blessed soul of Christ and the lowliest of the souls that are to be saved . . . . We should highly rejoice that God dwells in our soul, and still more highly should we rejoice that our soul dwells in God. Our soul is made to be God's dwelling place, and the dwelling place of our soul is God who was never made. It is a high knowledge to see inwardly and to know that God, who is our creator, dwells in our soul. And it is a higher and more inner knowledge to see and to know that our soul, which is created, dwells essentially in God. From this essential dwelling in God we are what we are. And I saw no difference between God and our essence, but it was all God.

And this I saw with full certainty, that it is easier for us to acquire knowledge of God than to acquire knowledge of our own soul. For our soul is so deeply founded in God and so infinitely gathered in that we cannot acquire knowledge of it until we have knowledge of God, its creator, to whom it belongs. Yet I saw that it is needful for us to desire to know our own soul in wisdom and truth; and therefore we are instructed to seek it where it is, namely in God. And so we shall come to know them both in one through the gracious guidance of the Holy Spirit. Whether we are moved to know God or our soul, both are good and true. God is much closer to us than our own soul, for he is the ground in which our soul stands. For our soul sits in God in true rest, and our soul stands in God in sure strength, and our soul is rooted in God in endless love. Therefore if we wish to acquire knowledge of our soul and enter into fellowship and covenant with it, we must seek it in God our Lord, in whom it is enclosed.

Julian of Norwich
A Revelation of Divine Love

For more on the female imagery of God, see Caroline Walker Bynum's *Jesus as Mother,* University of California, 1982.

After Catherine of Siena prayed that God create in her "a clean heart and renew a right spirit," she had a vision that God came to her, opened her left side, and removed her heart. For many days she complained that she had no heart. Her confessor told her this was impossible, but she insisted that with God, everything is possible. During prayers one day, a light shone around her, and out of the light the Lord appeared bearing a reddish and shining object. He opened her left side once more, placed the heart inside, and said, "See, beloved daughter, just as I took your heart from you the other day, so I am now giving you my heart, with which you will live from now on."

The Confessor Confesses

Once when she [Catherine of Siena] lay upon her bed, burdened with many pains, and desired to speak with me of certain things which the Lord had revealed to her, she summoned me in secret. And when I had come to her and stood at her bedside, she began, though feverish, to speak in her usual way of God and to tell of the things that had been revealed to her that day. But when I heard such great and unheard-of things, I said in my heart, forgetful of the grace

"The manner in which one receives communication from blessed spirits in a vision is difficult to tell. Everything that is said is uncommonly brief. From one word I learn more than otherwise from thirty. One sees the idea of the speaker, but one does not see with the eyes, and yet everything is clear, more distinct than now. One receives it with pleasure, like the blowing of a cool breeze in hot summer. One can never repeat it wholly in words . . . ."
—Anna Katharina Emmerich

"Once on a fine spring day, Rabi'a's servant called to her to come out and behold the work of the Creator. 'Rather, you come in,' answered the saint, 'and view the Creator Himself. Contemplation of Him keeps me from beholding His creation.'"

previously received and ungrateful for it, "Do you suppose that all the things she says are true?" And while I thought thus and turned toward her who was speaking, her face was changed in an instant into the face of a bearded man who, gazing at me with staring eyes, gave me a great fright. And the face was rather long, of middle age, and had a beard that was not long, the color wheat, and in appearance it displayed such majesty that it thereby revealed itself as the Savior. Moreover, at that time I could not distinguish any other face than this. And when I raised my hands to my shoulders in consternation and terror, crying out, "Who is this who is gazing at me?" the virgin answered, "He who is." When this was said, this face disappeared suddenly, and I saw clearly the features of the virgin, which I had previously been unable to distinguish.

From the Notes of Raimund of Capua
Confessor of Catherine of Siena
(1347-1380)

As the mystical side of Islam developed, Rabi'a al-Adawiyya, born circa 717 A.D. in Basra—now Iraq—was the first to refer to God as the Beloved, thus expressing a personal relationship with the Divine that has come to be identified as the core of Sufism.

Who Marries?

Hasan once asked Rabi'a whether she would like to take a husband. She replied, "The marriage contract is bound to a 'being.' But here 'being' is absent. Of myself I am unaware; alone through Him I am, and under the shadow of His will I exist. My husband must be sought from Him."

"How did you attain to this station?" questioned Hasan.

"Through losing all my attainment in Him," she replied.
"How do you know Him, then?" Hasan inquired.
"You know 'how,'" she answered. "I know without 'how.'"

> Javad Nurbakhsh
> *Sufi Women*

For more on Rabi'a, see: Camille Adams Helminski, "Women and Sufism," *Gnosis Magazine*, Winter 1994, Margaret Smith, *Rabi'a the Mystic, and Her Fellow Saints in Islam*, Rainbow Bridge, 1977 and Charles Upton, *Doorkeeper of the Heart: Versions of Rabi'a*, Threshold, 1988.

_____

"If there were I-consciousness in me, I could express who I am. As it is not there, I am what you choose to say about me."
—Anandamayi Ma

Contact with the Beloved provides yet another method of attaining transpersonal experience, one very common among Sufi mystics. Here the supplicant is Christian.

Prayer of Adoration

O God, let me rise to the edges of time and
      open my life to your eternity;
let me run to the edges of space and
      gaze into your immensity;
let me climb through the barriers of sound
      and pass into your silence;
And then, in stillness and silence
      let me adore You,
Who are Life—Light—Love
without beginning and without end,
the Source—the Sustainer—the Restorer—
      the Purifier—of all that is;
      the Lover who has bound earth to heaven
      by the beams of a cross;

the Healer who has renewed a dying race
    by the blood of a chalice;
the God who has taken man into your glory
    by the wounds of sacrifice;
God . . . God . . . God . . . Blessed by God
    Let me adore you.

Sister Ruth SLG
The Oxford Book of Prayer

Patricia Robertson, a Quaker, studied Chinese medicine in England. She now lives in Santa Barbara, California. When I asked her about her church, this is what she said:

A Quaker's Stillness

Quakers believe that god dwells within every single person. But we need to be quiet to hear God. Our world is full of yang; there is too much activity, too much busyness. We have to slow down. Meditation is yin, it means sitting in stillness "to be done unto" rather than to do. That fertilizes the soul. In church last Sunday, it came to me that I needed to be so still that I could hear a bell ring on a distant planet. We need to be that still to hear God.

Patricia Robertson, acupuncturist

A book of related interest is *Slowing Down in a Speeded Up World*, by Adair Lara, Conari Press, 1994.

A Catholic nun for ten years, Bernadette Roberts has raised four children since leaving the cloister. She lives in Northern California.

Path of Silence

Through past experience I had become familiar with many different types and levels of silence. There is a silence within; a silence that descends from without; a silence that stills existence; and a silence that engulfs the entire universe. There is a silence of the self and its faculties of will, thought, memory, and emotions. There is a silence in which there is nothing, a silence in which there is something; and finally, there is the silence of the no-self and the silence of God. If there was any path on which I could chart my contemplative experiences, it would be this ever-expanding and deepening path of silence.

Bernadette Roberts
The Experience of No-Self

"The kingdom of God does not come if you watch for it. Nor will anyone be able to say, 'It is here' or 'It is there.' For the kingdom of God is within you."
—Jesus of Nazareth

Dedication of Merit

May all beings benefit from the use of this book.

Conari Press, established in 1987, publishes books for women on topics ranging from spirituality and women's history to sexuality and personal growth. Our main goal is to publish quality books that will make a difference in people's lives—both how we feel about ourselves and how we relate to one another.

Our readers are our most important resource, and we value your input, suggestions, and ideas. We'd love to hear from you—after all, we are publishing books for you!

For a complete catalog or to get on our mailing list, please contact us at:

Conari Press
1144 65th Street, Suite B
Emeryville, CA 94608
phone: (800) 685-9595
fax: (610) 654-7259